LOVING A LADY

BROTHERHOOD
OF THE
BLACK
TARTAN
BOOK 3

NICHOLE VAN

Fiorenza Publishing

Loving a Lady © 2020 by Nichole Van Valkenburgh
Cover design © Nichole Van Valkenburgh
Interior design © Nichole Van Valkenburgh

Published by Fiorenza Publishing
Print Edition v1.0

ISBN: 978-1-949863-07-9

To Judy
For your loving support and infectious enthusiasm.
You are deeply missed.

To Dave
For always encouraging me to take one more step forward.

PROLOGUE

Prizefighting should be a required part of every young lady's education. For Lady Violet Kerr, this realization was much like a thrown fist—abruptly jarring.

And yet, it made an unlikely sort of sense.

Such knowledge would enable a lady to effectively defend herself, should the need arise.

And it would certainly help a lady understand how to behave should she unexpectedly encounter a prizefighting match.

Such as the one currently facing Violet.

She leaned closer to the carriage window, steadying the spyglass she held to her right eye.

Down the hill, past the parked carriages, and over the heads of hundreds of spectators, two men threw punches at one another in the center of a roped-off rectangle of grass.

The spyglass brought small details into sharp focus—the boxers circling the ring, the white puffs of breath drifting in the autumn air, the sweat glinting on their bare fists. One deflected a particularly savage blow with his forearm. The other danced back, wiping blood from his nose. A bag of prize money tied to one corner stake swayed in the slight breeze.

Violet presumed etiquette books would insist a lady look away. That she should not be studying half-dressed men through a spyglass taken from the storage compartment beside her seat.

And she would look away. She *would*.

It was just . . .

The sight of two men in a battle for dominance, stripped to the waist—bare-chested and streaked with dirt—blood running in rivulets down their cheeks . . .

It was all alarmingly compelling. Nothing in eighteen years of life had prepared her for such graceful savagery.

Heavens! She could *hear* the sickening thud of fist on flesh even from this distance.

In short, she better understood why her cousin, Lord Smithson, had insisted upon stopping the carriage.

They had left Marton Hall after luncheon, intent on making social calls, Smitty cheery and ebullient. In hindsight, Violet should have been suspicious of his bonhomie. Smitty habitually grumbled through afternoon visiting hours.

Of course, all had become clear once the gathered curricles and coaches came into view. Belatedly, Violet recalled Smitty's enthusiasm for prizefighting. How could she have forgotten? He subscribed to *Boxiana*, for heaven's sake.

At first, Smitty pretended to be unaware of the fight—*What ho? Is there a mill about to begin?* and *I say, is that Alton's carriage? Lord Michael is here?*—but he quickly capitulated under Violet's hard stare, stammering that he had promised to join Lord Michael for the fight and surely she could be a good egg and wait in the carriage for half an hour, could she not? She was all but betrothed to Lord Michael, after all, and Smitty felt it his duty to foster the friendship.

Violet had sent her eyes skyward.

Prizefighting was technically illegal. Or, rather, the assembling of hundreds of men to *watch* a fight was illegal. The illegality, however, did not deter enthusiastic crowds. Consequently, matches were announced only days beforehand and held outside town, giving local magistrates little time to react.

Violet adjusted her hold on the spyglass, angling her body for a better view. How fortunate Smitty's coachman had parked the carriage in such a way that Violet could see the fight. Her carriage was just one of many parked upon the knoll, a veritable sea of phaetons, barouches, and traveling coaches all empty of passengers. The coachmen, grooms, and other servants had left *en masse* to join their employers in watching the mill.

She darted a glance at the Duke of Alton's crest on the carriage beside hers. Lord Michael *was* here—a dashing Corinthian with sweeping hair, a contagious smile, and soulful eyes that studied her with rapt attention. In short, Violet rather liked him. Or rather, she liked how much Lord Michael liked *her*.

Was it wrong to adore someone for the way they adored you? Was that the sort of affection which led to marriage? Violet felt far too young to be contemplating such momentous decisions.

Regardless, she had to have a care for her reputation. Her mother, Lady Kildrum, would give her a frightening set-down should she learn of this prizefighting escapade. To that end, Violet pulled the curtain tighter around the spyglass, closing off even a sliver of light.

She did *not*, however, stop watching the match. Why deprive herself of this decidedly educational opportunity? Besides, Dahlia would undoubtedly demand a minute description of it later. Her younger sister was relentless, both in her admiration of the opposite sex and her longing to see the wider world.

From the few words Smitty had uttered before he darted out of the carriage, the shorter of the two pugilists was the Hammer of the Cornwall, a boxer favored to become the next heavyweight champion of England. She recognized the Hammer's distinctive profile from an engraving in *Boxiana* which Smitty had left lying about (and Violet had taken a minute—or fifty—to peruse).

A brute of a fellow, the Hammer had dark hair and a bulbous nose that had been broken one too many times. The Hammer had arranged this bout with an unknown boxer in order to attract attention before a prominent fight at Fives Court in London next month.

Given all this, Violet was surprised to find the Hammer's untried opponent holding her attention. "The Red Renegade," Smitty had called him. "A pretty-faced newcomer with a ridiculous by-name. He's a bit of a recluse who appeared on the circuit a few months ago. The Hammer should rout him quickly."

Smitty neglected to mention that Red was a giant of a man, standing nearly a full head taller than the Hammer, his fiery hair glinting in the autumn sunlight. And, yes, he was admittedly young and handsome, with even features and a defiantly-straight nose.

But Smitty had misjudged Red's abilities.

The man's sheer size should have rendered him clumsy and slow, but Red darted in and out of the Hammer's thrown fists with startling ease. Even to Violet's untrained eye, the elegance of his form and the skill of his movements did not seem those of a newcomer.

Hammer was favored to win the bout handily. But instead, he seemed to be nearly on the ropes. Given the hoots and howls of the spectators, she was not alone in her surprise.

The Red Renegade lived up to his revolutionary moniker, throwing punch after brutal punch, each landing with a gruesome *thwack*. The Hammer was not entirely ineffectual, she supposed, as blood streamed from Red's nose and dripped down his chest from a gash along his collarbone. A faint steam rose from their heated bodies.

Hammer darted inside Red's long arms, throwing two hard punches to Red's stomach. Red barely flinched at the violent blows.

Instead, Red swayed back with Hammer's momentum and then rocked forward, using the entire force of his body to propel a harsh fist into Hammer's jaw.

Hammer crumpled into a heap, a marionette doll with its strings cut. He did not rise.

Red stood over him, chest heaving. The crowd roared. Two men rushed through the ropes to Hammer—the man's second and water boy, surely.

A frown dented Violet's brow. She spun the spyglass, scanning the bodies crowding against the ropes.

Where were Red's men? His second and water boy, the people who supported him?

No one came to his side. Was the man . . . alone? Was that why he was called a *renegade*?

Hammer remained unconscious, the faint lift of his chest the only indication he yet lived.

Silence descended.

Spectators rose on tiptoes. Would Hammer revive?

His second tried to rouse the unconscious boxer—even going so far as to toss water on his face—but the Hammer lay unmoving.

Red's hand was raised in victory.

The crowd bellowed its displeasure.

Watching as she was from a distance, Violet saw the ripples running through the gathered men, the outrage over Red's triumph. Red was more skilled than they had supposed. Most of the men had surely bet against him. The bet-takers would lose a princely sum today.

The crowd surged against the ropes, the stakes straining, the prize-money bag swaying with the motion.

Violet saw the moment Red ascertained he was no longer facing spectators, but an angry mob. With that same startling agility, he snatched the stake money—his prize for winning—and launched himself over the ropes, pushing through a thinner section of the crowd with blinding speed and tearing up the hill. Men gave startled yelps before turning to give chase.

Violet was so taken aback by the turn of events, it took her several seconds to assimilate one important fact:

Red was racing toward the gathered carriages.

Racing toward *her* carriage, in fact.

Dropping her spyglass with a gasp, Violet pulled the curtain shut with a tight snap.

She sucked in a rapid breath, pressing a hand against her sternum. Was she truly *trembling* over this turn of events?

How ridiculous. Surely Red would not invade her coach.

Hers was only one of scores of carriages. The curtains were drawn; no one could see her. She would just wait quietly in the dim interior for Smitty and the servants to return. Red and the ensuing chaos would surely pass by.

It was just . . .

The panicked desperation in Red's eyes as he ran had seared her vision. He was younger than she had supposed, not much older than her own eighteen years. His was not the face of a fraudsman.

No, his expression was more akin to how she imagined a sailor might witness his mainmast cracking in two during a violent storm . . . anguished panic and utter despair.

A single set of footsteps approached, the *thump-thump-thump* mimicking Violet's own heartbeat. A rush of harsh breathing followed. Was this Red then?

She heard a roar of voices from farther away.

Solitary footsteps and rasping breaths rounded her carriage and then paused before moving off, retreating.

Violet loosed a sigh, but it was a short-lived reprieve. A flurry of boots approached at a run.

"Where did 'e go?" a voice panted. "He wasn't billed as a champion. Blimey bastard cheated us!"

"He won the fight fair, I reckon," a second breathless voice added. "I thought he'd go down with those punches to his bread basket—"

"Bah! He shouldn't have been capable of darkening the Hammer's daylights like that. I want my money returned with interest. Coward ran like a scared dog!"

"Over there! Near the trees!" someone else shouted.

"No, mate! He's in the carriages!" another called.

Several minutes of footsteps coming and going ensued, voices retreating and shouting questions.

In other words, absolute confusion.

Violet sat quietly, that hand still pressed to her chest.

A measure of outrage slowly furrowed her brow.

Red had not *cheated*. Though others may have discounted his talent, he had won the fight fairly to her eyes.

But her compassion for Red aside, she faced a larger problem—what if someone opened the carriage door? Would the men assume her to be a lightskirt? Or would she be recognized? And, if so, how damaging would this be to her reputation?

Most importantly, how angry would her mother be?

Violet's mother was the Countess of Kildrum *suo jure*—an earl in her own right. Occasionally, titles in the Scottish peerage were created in such a manner that they could pass to the eldest daughter should she have no brothers.

Violet's mother had been an only child. And Violet herself had no brothers. Just three younger sisters—Dahlia and the twins, Aster and Rose.

As any heir to an earldom, Violet had been raised to shoulder the mantle of countess when the time came, assuming the responsibility of thousands of lives. Part of that duty was to marry well, something the gentlemen of the *ton* well-understood. Lady Violet Kerr was more than just a wealthy, titled heiress; she was a stepping stone into the Peerage itself. By marrying her, a gentleman would launch an aristocratic dynasty of his own.

Consequently, since being presented at Court six months ago, Violet had been lauded and eagerly pursued. She thought again of Alton's carriage beside hers and Lord Michael's courtship. How would Lord Michael react were he to find her here? Angry? Or would he laugh at the lark?

And how troubling to be considering *marrying* the man when she knew him so little.

This was the problem with decisions, she decided. The older one became, the more life-altering one's choices. A single poor decision could have far-reaching effects.

A voice called at a distance, startling her. Scuffling noises and voices passed by her carriage again, shouting for vengeance against Red.

What would happen if the mob caught him? Would he be able to fight his way free?

She pursed her lips, facts and conclusions flitting through her mind.

Red had fought a popular champion at great personal risk. His were the actions of a man who had little to lose and much to gain. What desperation fueled his fists?

More footsteps approached, quieter this time.

A faint skitter of sound.

Violet stilled.

Closer. Closer.

Silence.

The door handle of the carriage wiggled.

Oh!

Now someone decided to try the door?

Violet wrapped her hand around the barrel of the metal spyglass.

But . . . what good would the spyglass do? Any violence or screaming on her part would only bring more onlookers.

She sucked in a breath and shrank farther into the dim interior, all but pressing herself into the opposite corner.

The door cracked open. A giant of a man loomed, scanning his surroundings, his back to her.

His *enormous* back.

His enormous, *bare* back.

The man stepped rearward into her carriage with an astonishingly lithe grace, folding his body nearly in half to squeeze through the door, his weight so perfectly balanced that the carriage scarcely rocked. He half sat on the seat opposite Violet, beginning to close the door.

Finally, Violet exhaled.

The man's head whirled at the sound, one hand still on the door handle.

Violet stared into Red's bloodshot eyes.

She should scream.

That was the decision she should make. It was an obvious, *clear* conclusion.

Scream, summon Smitty or Lord Michael or *someone,* and deal with the consequences—

Violet *knew* this.

And yet . . .

The utter bleakness of Red's gaze pinned her in place.

The man had no hope. None. He fully expected to be torn to bits by the angry mob.

His hopelessness clutched at her heart, wrapping tightly around that impulsive part of her that did not turn away from horror.

This man was not looking for a savior.

But Violet was the product of generations of women raised to protect and care and, most significantly, *act*.

So she made her choice. A tiny one.

Violet pinched her mouth shut and gave the faintest nod.

Red needed no further encouragement. He pulled the door shut and slid fully onto the seat opposite her.

He braced his forearms on his thighs, chest heaving, attempting to catch his breath.

His labored breathing mimicked Violet's own rapidly rising panic.

Of *all* the decisions to make—!

To allow a half-naked *hulk* of a man inside her carriage?!

If anyone were to catch him with her—!

Merciful heavens, . . . whathaveIdone!

Red had been large from a distance. Up close, he was positively overwhelming. A thrumming mountain of a man.

Sweat dripped from his body, streaking through the blood and dirt on his chest, giving him the appearance of a half-melted candle. He still clenched the stake bag tightly in one giant battered fist. Blood money in truth.

Violet leaned away, pressing against the squabs at her back.

He lifted his head at the subtle movement.

"I willnae hurt ye." His voice rumbled, a low whisper of sound, Scotland thick in his accent.

Her lungs hiccupped.

A rush of voices and footfalls sounded outside, men calling and whistling.

He studied her, his own breathing slowing. For all his brawn, his eyes held a softness that even the dim light could not mask.

Red's brogue was familiar . . . and yet, not.

Though Violet would inherit a Scottish earldom, she considered herself more English than anything. After all, most of her life had been played against the background of the family townhouse in London and her English father's small estate near Marton Hall in Warwickshire. Her family only visited the ancestral estate—Kilmeny Hall, in northern Scotland—every summer into autumn.

But it was still . . . home.

So when Red said, *I willnae hurt ye* in his rolling brogue, she instinctively believed him.

He sat stiff and unmoving, his body a coiled spring, ready for action.

"I only intend tae hide here for a moment. Just tae catch my breath, and let the worst of the clamor pass." He angled his head, indicating the crunch of boots on gravel.

She nodded and then swallowed, turning away as more snippets of conversation rolled past them.

She could feel Red's eyes on her, surely cataloging the cut of her fashionable bonnet, the fur lining her cloak, the fine wool of her pelisse underneath. Her hand curled into the carriage blanket across her lap, tightening.

"I shouldnae be here, I ken that," he murmured. "It isnae proper."

Hah! A ghastly understatement.

But Red's words were soft, ringed with care. She could practically *feel* the gentleness in him.

"My cousin promised he would only be gone for a moment." She did not add that nearly an hour had since passed.

"I will leave shortly, lass."

Violet knew she could correct him to say 'my lady' instead of 'lass.' But she liked how Scotland sang in the roll of his consonants, the expansiveness of his vowels.

A scratching noise on the door caused them to jump.

"Violet?" A male voice hissed from outside. Red's eyebrows shot up at the sound of her name. "Are you still in there?"

"Smitty?" she replied.

She darted an apprehensive look at Red.

"Glad you replied." Smitty cleared his throat. "I don't want to risk opening the door. Wouldn't do for someone to see you."

"Very wise of you." Violet continued to stare at Red.

"Terribly sorry about the fracas. There was a bit of a set-to after the mill." Smitty's voice shook with excitement. "You should have seen it! The newcomer took Hammer down with a savage blow to the jaw. Darkened his daylights and dropped him like a stone—" Smitty broke off with an embarrassed cough. "Ehrm, I suppose I should not be describing such things to a lady."

Violet rolled her eyes. *Now* Smitty decided to have a care for her sensibilities?

"When will we depart, Smitty?" she asked.

"I'm off to find John Coachman. I'll send him and the grooms over to return you to Marton Hall."

"You are not accompanying me?"

A moment's hesitation. "Well, I ran into George Buckley who came with Lord Michael, and now we're all off to have a pint in the village. I'll make my way home later. It's better this way, Violet. I would never hear the end of it if someone were to catch you here. No chance anyone will see you if I don't climb into the carriage. I'll have you off in a trice."

His footsteps retreated.

Well, that was a solution, she supposed.

She turned back to Red, his eyes carefully watching her.

"Your cousin?"

"Yes, Smitty has many admirable qualities, but he *can* be a bit of a rattle." She cleared her throat. "I will have the coachman stop once we are well away from this. The servants are loyal and will say nothing."

Violet's eyes drifted down his wide chest as she spoke. Bruises bloomed alongside the rapidly-drying blood. Gooseflesh pebbled his skin. It was October, after all, and the man was scarcely dressed.

Her brow furrowed.

"You are cold," she whispered.

She lifted the wool carriage blanket from her lap, extending it out to him—a wordless offering.

He froze and stared at the blanket, eyes flaring in surprise. As if such an act of care were . . . astonishing.

He let out a slow, stuttering breath and then took the heavy wool.

"I am in your debt." His voice was rough, emotion thick at its edges. He pulled the blanket over his shoulders. "Thank ye, lass."

How could this brute fell a man like the Hammer with a single blow, yet be brought low himself by simple human kindness?

"I accept your thanks, Red."

"Red?"

"Pardon. Is that not your sobriquet? The Red Renegade?"

Silence for a beat.

He shifted. "I'm no renegade. And though my hair is red, I dinnae ken to be red in truth."

His jaw clenched, as if *red* were more of an epithet than a moniker.

"No?" She angled her head.

"Nae. I'm no' made of choler and madness." He lifted one large, battered hand. "This fist is not me, not my truest self."

Violet's breath hiccupped.

His were the words of a wounded soul.

What a conundrum he was.

Was nothing about this man to be anticipated?

"Then wha—" She flinched as another rush of voices passed the carriage. "If not red, then what?"

He paused, gaze meeting hers.

Her heart beat once . . . twice . . .

"I am a teal's wing," he finally said. "The blue-green of a feather."

Ah.

A poet, then.

"The color of freedom," she whispered. "Or perhaps . . . *hope*." She barely breathed that last word.

He continued to lock eyes.

His chest rose and fell in synchronization with her own. Up. Down.

And then he swallowed with a jerked nod.

Violet's heart raced.

How odd to be here with this unexpected man.

He claimed to be the color of hope and yet, he clearly had none. Who or what had placed such bleakness in him?

How could this be the same person she had just witnessed fight with brutal precision?

It felt unnatural. As if this man were made for joy and calm, but instead found himself caught in a fenced circle of brutality and blood. A Catherine wheel spinning round and round.

"*Why?*" Violet could hear the bafflement in her tone. "Why, then, do you fight?"

Red sat straighter and clenched his jaw, the tendons in his neck standing in sharp relief. The sheer size of him saturated the interior of the carriage.

A loud laugh sounded outside. Men shouted in reply.

Violet winced, head turning toward the sound.

The noise drifted away.

She looked back at Red, his eyes still studying her.

"Why do most men fight?" he finally said. "I need money."

"Ah." She paused, certain that his words were only a partial truth. "It seems a brutal way to earn . . . money."

"Aye, it is. But I earned more today than I would from ten years hard labor elsewhere."

"But you could have been killed."

"Aye."

Such nonchalance showed a rather alarming lack of self-preservation.

"Surely there is someone you fight for?" She spoke instinctively. Surely, he would only take such risks for a loved one. "Someone who needs the money you win?"

He flinched at that, as if her words had struck truer than the Hammer's fists. His fingers tightened around the money bag in his hand, his mouth drawing into a firm slash. A bleakness haunted his eyes.

He swallowed, his Adam's apple rolling in the dim light. "I dinnae speak of—"

Red cut off as more footsteps rushed past the carriage, men calling back and forth again. A conversation slowly surfaced out of the sound.

" . . . been a bit of a farce today. Lost a pretty penny on this," a voice said as the footsteps stopped right beside Violet's carriage. "Can you see Smitty coming yet?"

Violet hissed in a breath, recognizing Lord Michael's baritone. The carriage beside hers rattled.

"No, not yet," Lord Michael's companion replied. "He'll be along soon, I reckon. Intelligent of you to invite him. He'll help you set your finances to right."

"Pardon?"

"Smitty. He's cousin to Lady Violet, is he not?"

"Yes, but what is your point, Buckley?"

"Heard you are all but betrothed to Lady Violet, is all."

Violet gave a sharp inhalation, her eyes jerking to Red's.

He had gone exceptionally still across from her, his massive hands drawn into fists between them. He had heard Smitty call her Violet. And given her reaction, Red likely understood that the men were speaking of her.

"Yes," Lord Michael said tersely.

A brief pause.

"Yes? That's all you are going to say?" the second man scoffed, feet shuffling. "You are tantalizingly close to marrying the most sought-after heiress in the entire kingdom. You should be in alt. Are you not keen on the lady then?"

She swallowed, dropping her eyes to stare at her twined fingers. Nothing good came of eavesdropping. But what else could she do at this point? Put her hands over her ears?

"My *father* is keen on the lady," Lord Michael snorted, "so why does my own opinion matter?"

The bitterness in his voice was a near tangible thing.

Violet barely stifled a gasp.

Oh!

Lord Michael always appeared to be so charmed and delighted by her company. It was what she liked best about him. Was he truly being coerced into offering for her?

"Any man would relish being in your position, Lord Michael," the companion huffed a laugh. "Hard to believe you are that put-upon—"

"Would *you* wish to marry Lady Violet?"

A long . . . long . . . *long* pause.

Oh, gracious.

A blush scorched her cheeks.

Violet looked up into Red's eyes.

How ghastly to have a witness to this conversation.

And yet . . . Red's gaze held no judgment. If she had to label the emotion, she would say it was . . . empathy.

"Well . . ." The second man's voice drifted off.

"Precisely," Lord Michael ground out. "Yes, there are advantages to the match, but such a marriage comes with the lady herself."

"She is rather tall . . . bit of a termagant, too, I reckon."

Lord Michael snorted again. "I would have called her a headstrong Amazon who will spend her life attempting to wear her husband's breeches. She is certainly *large* enough to fit into them easily. But as I prefer marriage over an officer's commission, I have been given no other choice. My father is adamant."

His companion murmured condolences. "At the very least, you might be able to rusticate Lady Violet in the country and enjoy life in Town."

"'Tis my only consolation—"

"Ho, Michael!" Smitty's voice rang. "I managed to find our coachmen!"

The men exchanged greetings. Smitty directed his coachman and groom to return to Marton Hall.

All the while, Violet stared at her clenched hands, her heartbeat a drum in her ears.

Had she truly just heard—?

Had Lord Michael really just said—?

Sounds drifted in and out. Lord Michael and company loudly laughing as they climbed into the carriage beside hers. The clang of the horses stirring in their harness. The jolt and rocking of the carriage as her own groom and coachman alighted.

The carriage jerked into motion.

She lifted her head and locked eyes with Red. Lord Michael's words pinged between them, a pulsing condemnation.

. . . a headstrong Amazon who will spend her life attempting to wear her husband's breeches . . .

Violet could practically hear her naiveté shattering.

How could she have been so stupid? So *foolish* to believe Lord Michael's attentions to be genuine? That he viewed her as more than just the sum of title, fortune, and familial connections?

Violet bit her lip, desperate to stem the telltale sting in her eyes.

She would not weep in front of a stranger.

"Dinnae believe him, lass," Red's brogue rumbled in the dim light.

Violet nodded, biting down harder, hating the tremble in her lips.

It did no good.

A tear fell. And then another.

She would have expected Red to react as most men did when confronted with feminine emotions. They panicked or ignored or reproached.

Instead . . . he witnessed.

"Dinnae let him bank your fire, lass."

"It is not so easy," she sniffed, clutching at the seat as the driver sprung the horses, causing the carriage to lurch.

"Och, but it is." He shrugged a large shoulder. "People see me as muscle and brawn. They see a man tae beat with fists, to earn them wagered bets and provide an afternoon's entertainment. If I've learned one sad truth, 'tis this: one doesnae have tae *like* something tae be skilled at it. I *loathe* prizefighting. It appeals tae the very basest part of humanity."

Violet's tears fell harder.

"But inside, I am . . ." He drifted off, voice hesitant . . . as if the rocking of the carriage was lulling truths out of him.

"You are? Inside?" She licked a tear off her upper lip.

He shook his head, his voice a whisper. "Goose down and pattering rain."

Oh.

She snatched a pained, gasping breath.

"You are a poet." The words escaped before she could call them back.

He stilled.

"I am haunted," was his enigmatic reply. "A kissing cousin to poetry. Close . . . but not quite."

"H-haunted," she hiccupped, wiping her cheeks, her mind whirring, trying to capture Lord Michael's revelation in words. "If you are haunted . . . then I am *hunted*. A fox to ground. Silly fox to think that all that attention—the hounds giving chase, the riders pounding over fences—might mean that the pursuers *value* her. That they won't tear her apart once captured."

Red studied her, eyes glittering in the dim light. His face was more suggestion than form. The curve of a jawline. The outline of lips.

"I run from my past," he finally said, the words seemingly dragged from him. "I bruise and batter tae escape it." He lifted the money bag meaningfully. "Do ye run, as well?"

A lengthy pause.

Violet clenched her hands once more.

Do ye run, as well?

Even thirty minutes past, she would not have said *no*. But now?

"My future," she whispered. "I fear my future."

"Ah."

The carriage creaked on for a beat. The tackle clattered. A rut jostled Violet to the side. The coachman's whip cracked.

Red shifted, lifting the curtain to peer out. They both stared at the green countryside rolling by. The blanket across his chest slipped to reveal a bare shoulder, muscle rippling beneath his skin.

Violet swallowed and looked away.

He would leave soon. He must.

She would never see him again.

The thought panged and pulsed in her chest.

"How odd . . . we meet at this moment." Red let the curtain fall, head turning back to her. "Where I will take my winnings today and use them tae purchase a new future, leaving my haunted past behind. But . . . what will *ye* do?"

The care in his eyes pinned her in place.

She understood his unasked question:

Will you allow the hunter to catch you?

Would she accept the future mapped out for her? Would she walk into a marriage such as the one Lord Michael described?

Or would she fight for something else?

She swallowed against the rough ache in her throat, her eyes drifting to the money bag clenched in Red's bloodied hand. The *thud* of that same fist hitting Hammer's flesh still rang in her ears.

He claimed to be running from his past, and yet he literally fought for his future.

Could she do the same?

What will ye do?

She didn't *know.*

Lord Michael's revelations were too raw, too new.

She didn't know what she wished to do.

And this stranger before her would leave at any moment, and she feared he would take her courage with him.

Red continued to study her with intent eyes.

Could he stay? Could she see him again? He seemed strong enough to bear her concerns, wise enough to listen without judgment.

But he had to leave. He *must.*

Something of her thoughts must have shown on her face.

"Whatever ye do, let it be bold," he said, leaning toward her, as if wishing to impart what wisdom he could in the brief seconds given them. "What did that louse of a lord call ye? Termagant? Bah! I say *capable.* Headstrong? No. I prefer *determined.* An Amazon? Och! The Amazons were *warriors.*"

The carriage slowed. Red pulled back the curtain again. A tollbooth came into view. Forest stretched beyond.

He reached for the door handle.

No! He would leave? *Now?*

"Be an Amazon, lass. Be a warrior and fight for what ye want." He slid toward the door, the carriage blanket dropping away.

She stretched out her hand. "But—"

He shook his head. "I'll always remember the fine lady who helped a brute of a Scot with grace and kindness. Ye have a heart of great courage."

Red opened the door and was gone.

1

SEVEN AND A HALF YEARS LATER

ANGUS, SCOTLAND
MARCH 19, 1820

Someday, Ewan Campbell vowed he would become more comfortable having a good blether about the state of his life.

And he would.

Some day.

But not today.

"So are ye pleased with the situation then?" Dr. Alexander Whitaker asked. It was his third question in as many minutes.

"Aye," Ewan replied. It was his third monosyllabic answer.

Ewan ran a hand through his hair, the thick red thatch resisting, tugging at his scalp.

"A regular gab, ye are, when talking about yerself, Ewan," Alex chuckled, the chill March air puffing white with his words. "Ye ken more phrases than *aye?*"

Ewan made a face somewhere between a grimace and a resigned grin.

Trust Alex to never let him be. His friend was a healer to his core. Once he noticed a problem, he coaxed and cajoled until he worked out any hurt that might linger, physical or otherwise.

"Aye, Alex, I am content with the situation. Ye know me, though—"

"That I do. Ye dinnae like talking about yourself." Alex flipped up the collar of his greatcoat, tucking into the heavy fabric. "Which, given how much of your soul ye paint into your fine artwork, I'm fair surprised. Seems ye'd be less reticent with an old friend."

Ewan grimaced in truth, drawing the warmth of his great kilt tighter around his shoulders.

Yes, Ewan painted. And, as an act of creation, his artwork did contain bits and pieces of himself. But—

"There is not enough of you in this. I see line and form, but I don't see Ewan Campbell," a former teacher at the Royal Academy had once said. *"Any blushing debutante can paint something pretty. However, it takes a true artist to paint meaning, to explore soul in art. You've mastered pretty. Now . . . work on finding meaning. Mediocrity never led to greatness."*

In short, Ewan was no better at discussing himself in visual form than verbal.

Contrary to Alex's belief, he did *not* paint his soul into his artwork.

That was the problem.

A cold breeze tugged at Ewan's plaid. The lower half of his great kilt wrapped around his waist, the upper half he had unpinned and wrapped around his shoulders and head as a cloak.

The two men were braving the chill March air to stroll through the walled gardens of Muirford House. The enormous country house—the residence of Andrew Langston, Earl of Hadley—dominated the skyline behind them. Alex and Ewan had arrived from Edinburgh the afternoon before, and now they awaited the arrival of two more guests—Master Kieran MacTavish and Sir Rafe Gordon.

The men—Ewan, Alex, Andrew, Kieran, and Rafe—had formed a lifelong friendship while on a scientific voyage to the South Pacific.

Each man had played a part in the endeavor.

Andrew, a student of the natural sciences, had envisioned and financed the journey.

Rafe, Andrew's close friend and a fellow student, had joined him.

Alex had been hired as a doctor to the gentlemen.

Kieran had been the master and navigator of their ship, *The Minerva*, serving under the captain and commander, Captain Martin Cuthie.

For his part, Ewan had been plucked from a deluge of applicants to illustrate their scientific finds. It seemed an odd move for a painter—to take a position better suited to an illustrator—but coming on the heels of knowing how much soul his painting lacked, Ewan had been eager to find a less *expressive* outlet for his talents.

Today marked four years to the day since that awful night in the South Pacific. When Captain Cuthie had betrayed them, beating Rafe and Andrew nearly to death, setting a native village afire, and marooning them all on a far-away island.

Worse, the sixth member of their band, Jamie Fyffe, had died in the aftermath of the events. To honor Jamie, they called themselves the Brotherhood of the Black Tartan. In fact, Ewan's great kilt was formed from a length of the dark plaid they had created to remember Jamie— stripes of red, white, and green all set against a black ground.

Today they gathered on the fourth anniversary of Jamie's death to commemorate their fallen friend's life. And given the events of the past several months, they had much to discuss.

Now if only Kieran and Rafe would arrive.

To pass the time while they waited, Ewan had left the house, intent on the walled garden and a much-needed walk. Alex had joined him at the last second.

Ewan clasped his hands behind his back as they walked, not minding the silence. As usual, he found himself slowing his stride to match Alex's shorter legs. It wasn't that Alex was a particularly small man.

Rather, Ewan was a giant.

He dwarfed everything. Men. Chairs. Beds. He spent his life ducking through doorways and under ceiling beams and hearing phrases like, '*Cor, he's a big 'un, isn't he?!*' and '*He must be a prizefighter, I reckon.*'

Was it any wonder he had spent so many years literally fighting his way out of poverty and deprivation?

Alex chuckled. "Ye truly are not going to say anything else about the situation, then?"

The good doctor was a hound to scent, it appeared.

That old feeling rose in Ewan's chest, the one that tasted like panic and rendered his hands clammy. It was a salmon-colored emotion—cold and slimy and unpleasant.

"'Tis not much tae say." Ewan swallowed, hoping Alex would drop the topic but knowing he likely wouldn't. Why *did* talking about his inner thoughts induce such anxiety?

"Not much tae say?" Alex snorted. "Sir Joshua Kerr, one of the most famous painters in the country, hires ye to be his personal assistant, and ye shrug it off like it's any other Tuesday?"

"Well, when ye put it that way . . ." Ewan sighed. "I suppose I am . . . delighted."

"*Delighted?* Are ye the vicar's wife talking about next month's collection for the war widows?" Alex's voice went breathy and sing-song. "*I am so delighted at all we have accomplished this month . . .*"

Ewan managed a rueful grin. "Aright! I give. I'm pleased as Punch! That better?"

"A bit."

Ewan *was* thrilled at the opportunity.

Sir Joshua Kerr was indeed one of the most famous painters in all of Britain. And like most painters of his clout, he needed an assistant to help with the grunt work of painting—blending pigments, underpainting, transferring sketches, and blocking in background details.

Ewan had been hired to *be* that assistant.

"I do apologize if I have seemed flippant about the opportunity," Ewan nodded toward Alex. "The chance tae work so closely with Sir Joshua will hopefully open more doors for myself. Ye know how hard it's been tae build my commissions in Edinburgh. My work is sound, but none have heard of me. This could be a chance tae further my own name."

"That's been your ambition for as long as I've known ye. I have no doubt that ye will accomplish it."

Ewan nearly sighed. He appreciated his friends' support and yet . . .

Mediocrity never led to greatness.

Until Ewan found a way through mediocrity, he knew greatness would elude him.

"Any other news to share?" Alex asked the words simply, but Ewan mentally shied away from the question.

This was the problem when speaking with Alex. The man didn't stop prying until he had worked loose anything that ached or stung.

A moment of quiet. Birds trilled and a pheasant rustled in the underbrush.

"Have you heard from *her*?" Alex dropped the question into the silence.

His casual words landed with the force of a blunt upper-cut. Ewan barely held back a grunt.

No need to ask to *whom* Alex referred.

Ewan wanted to remain silent. He could not alter the past. She had made her own choices and betrayed his trust. Why dwell on things that could not be changed?

But Alex did not merit silence. His question came from a place of love and concern. His friend remembered the story Ewan had told him four years ago today, huddled in the dark and horror of that night. The glowing embers of the burned-out island village had been too reminiscent of another night, another similar fire . . . and Ewan had been helpless to hold the pain in, dark memories spilling out. Alex, bless him, had listened as calm and collected as ever, offering what healing he could.

And so Ewan swallowed and then shook his head. "No. Not a word in over eight years. I sent letters to the vicar in the region last summer, but I never had a reply. I cannae say, at the moment, if she is even alive or no."

"Will you visit? Try once more to see her?"

"I cannae say. Loch Carron is not an easy place to reach, even at the best of times. The journey would take weeks to complete." Ewan shied from the excusing words, from the implication that Mhairi was not worth the trouble and time it would take to find her.

She was. She infinitely was.

But the journey to Mhairi would be as much emotional as physical . . . and both were distances Ewan was unsure how to navigate.

If ye're going to be a painter, then be a painter. I tire of this game, she had hissed. *Go make a name for yourself, Ewan.*

Heaven knew, he had been trying.

He scuffed his feet, sending a pebble rolling toward the flowers lining the path. Despite the weather, daffodils had pushed aside the drooping snowdrops and reached skyward, their lemony color optimistically cheerful against the drab browns of winter.

Daffodils always signaled the beginning of 'gold season,' as Mhairi had called it. Daffodils bloomed, followed by gorse and then broom. Two months of nothing but yellow flowers along every lane and patch of uncultivated land.

Mhairi loved this time of year—

Ewan pressed a mental hand on his thoughts.

Enough. Do not dwell in the past.

He had left it long ago.

"AT LAST, YE'VE come in from the cold." Andrew Langston, Earl of Hadley, greeted Ewan and Alex as they opened the library doors from the back terrace. Andrew jerked his chin toward Kieran and Rafe sitting before a roaring fire, enjoying a spot of tea.

Stepping through the library doors after Alex, Ewan re-wrapped the upper-half of his great kilt to be a sash rather than a cloak, pinning it in place with a large brooch, before joining his friends in front of the warm fireplace. He embraced Kieran and shook Rafe's hand, asking about Lady Sophie Gordon, Rafe's new bride.

Predictably, Ewan's stomach rumbled, a loudly embarrassing sound. His large body required food in endless amounts.

Fortunately, Andrew had luncheon at hand. Two footmen carried in trays of food, setting them on an expanded gateleg table. One of the footmen could not stop staring at Ewan, his head turning over and over to take in a third and fourth look.

Ewan could practically hear the conversation once they returned to the kitchens. *Och, I dinnae ken a man could be so large. His hands were the size of platters . . .*

This had forever been Ewan's lot, had it not? His outsized body always garnered some reaction—fear, surprise, lust, shock—but *never* indifference.

Ewan would never be inconspicuous.

Just like he would never cease being hungry. The gnaw of hunger was an old friend. He had spent too many years on the brink of starvation, literally fighting to keep food in his belly.

And so he ignored the footman's gawking and proceeded to pile a plate high with roast beef sandwiches and crumbling shortbread.

Sitting back in a chair and tucking in to his feast, Ewan watched his friends exchange pleasantries. Alex congratulated Rafe on being granted a baronetcy by King George IV, hence the new title of Sir Rafe Gordon. Rafe commented on the large portrait Ewan had painted last autumn of Andrew and Jane, now hanging over the fireplace in the drawing room.

But as they spoke, Ewan's gaze was drawn back to Andrew's tight expression. It was echoed in Rafe's stiff shoulders and the tense slash of Kieran's mouth as he downed a glass of whisky.

It was a sickly-orange emotion—tense and taut—that snapped at the heels of their camaraderie and doused the room in a garish light.

Ewan swallowed a mouthful of shortbread and brushed off the lingering crumbs.

"What has happened?" he asked into the chatter.

Every head swung his way, question marks hanging in the air.

"Something has occurred," Ewan repeated. Not a question, this time.

Rafe winced, the white scar tracing his cheek tightening.

Andrew folded his arms across his chest, that same grim set to his features.

"Of course, you would notice this first, Ewan," Alex said, swinging his gaze between them all. "What happened?"

Kieran shook his head and reached to pour himself another dram. "'Tis nothing a drunken stupor cannae fix."

Ignoring Kieran's jab, Andrew reached across the desk behind him. "Apparently, this was printed in the *Aberdeen Journal* last week."

He handed a newspaper cutting to Alex. The doctor tilted it so Ewan could read as well.

NOTICE

The sinking of The Minerva is not what it seemed. Promises were broken, and the debt has not been paid. Those who survived should be held to account.

Alex let out a low whistle. "Another one?"

"Aye," Andrew nodded.

Last October, a similar notice had appeared in the *Edinburgh Advertiser*.

"There has tae be a link between the notices," Rafe said.

"Undoubtedly," Alex agreed. "But why are they appearing now— nearly four years on—and what on earth do they mean? We know of no debt."

Kieran knocked back another finger of whisky, giving every appearance of a man determined to drink himself insensible as quickly as possible.

He reached for the whisky bottle again.

Alex scooted it out of Kieran's reach.

"Perhaps ye should switch to tea," Alex said. "Consider it some doctorly advice."

"Nae." Kieran shook his head. "This is definitely a problem for alcohol."

"Alcohol is never the answer, Kieran."

"O'course it is." Kieran leaned forward and grabbed the bottle. "It helps me forget the question."

He poured himself another finger of whisky.

Ewan frowned, exchanging a concerned look with Alex.

Of them all, Jamie's death had hit Kieran the hardest. Though none of his friends understood exactly *how* hard. That information was Ewan's alone.

Up until six months ago, they had assumed that they were the only survivors of the wreck of *The Minerva* four years earlier.

Then the notice had appeared in the *Edinburgh Advertiser.* Threatening letters had followed soon after.

Rafe had discovered in November that somehow Captain Martin Cuthie had survived the sinking of *The Minerva.*

How the man had survived . . . none of them could say. And since that time, Cuthie had utterly disappeared.

But Cuthie's survival had torn open the barely-healed wounds of Jamie's death. Kieran had been slowly unraveling over the winter. Every time Ewan saw his friend, he had a glass of whisky in his hand and a bleak deadness in his eyes. Kieran was far too young to have such a world-weary expression.

"What else?" Ewan asked.

Tension still hung in the room. That bitter orange color clinging to furniture and dripping down the walls.

With a hefty sigh, Andrew reached for a piece of foolscap on the desk behind him, snapping the paper.

"This arrived with the evening post. It's a notice from a magistrate in Aberdeen. After a blethering introduction, he eventually says, 'I know that a formal inquest was held three years ago pertaining to the sinking of *The Minerva.* However, new evidence has come to light. Given that nearly eighty of His Majesty's citizens lost their lives when *The Minerva* sank, we feel we cannot allow this new claim in the *Aberdeen Journal* to go un-investigated. Would your lordship be at leisure in two weeks' time to answer a few questions?'" Andrew handed the letter to Alex. Ewan read over the doctor's shoulder.

Mmmm.

"The tone of the letter certainly isnae brusque or threatening," Ewan said, looking back up at Andrew. "I would guess that the magistrates simply want to do what they do best—make some noise and assure the public that there is nothing amiss."

"Aye," Alex agreed. "But what 'new evidence' does the magistrate have? Cuthie is alive somewhere. And that complicates this."

Andrew grimaced. "I am well-aware of that fact." He ran a tired hand over his face. "If only we could *find* the blasted man. My Runner from Bow Street keeps turning up empty-handed."

"Cuthie has gone to ground like the true rat that he is," Rafe snorted. "Probably skulking around the Caribbean or some such, waiting for this to die down."

"He can't hide forever. Someday, he will resurface—"

"Ye should just say it." Kieran shifted forward in his seat, reaching again for the whisky bottle. Alex snatched it away this time, placing it on another table out of reach. Kieran scowled. "I am the most at risk here."

"Pardon?" Rafe asked.

Kieran continued to stare at the whisky bottle, as if contemplating wrestling Alex for it, the muscles in his jaw clenching over and over.

Ewan nudged Kieran's boot with his own, drawing his friend's gaze, hoping to communicate empathy through his expression.

Kieran raised his head, a dreadful bleakness in his pale eyes.

"Youse all were guests aboard the ship," Kieran said. "I am the only one who was a crew member. If the government decides tae officially open an investigation, my actions that night could be viewed as mutinous. We've always known this. It's why we stay mum about the voyage. We dinnae want anyone asking too many questions."

Silence greeted his words.

Kieran, Ewan noted, did not seem particularly concerned about his own well-being. Often Ewan felt as if he were watching the life slowly drain out of his friend. But then, Ewan knew the true depths of Kieran's suffering, the painful secret he harbored.

Ewan could not blame the man.

The fire popped in the hearth, the coals settling.

The dancing flames tossed Ewan back to that night in the South Pacific.

Their journey had been an adventure up to that point. At least for Ewan. He had never left Britain before the trip, so every port, every new plant and animal, was utterly fascinating. Four years ago, they had dropped anchor in the harbor of a native village in the New Hebrides.

The locals had been friendly, immediately collecting plants and animals for Ewan to draw. Their time there had been idyllic.

Until the day that Cuthie had ordered the villagers to be taken as slaves and sold for profit on their way back to Britain.

Of course, the Brotherhood absolutely refused to go along with Cuthie's plan. The subsequent fight had turned bloody, but as far as Ewan knew, no one had been killed. The violence had ended when Cuthie torched the village and then sailed *The Minerva* out of the harbor under moonlight, marooning the rest of them. Only Jamie had remained aboard *The Minerva*, held captive by Cuthie.

They did not know the specifics of what transpired after that.

The Brotherhood had been rescued weeks later by a passing Portuguese whaler. The crew of that ship had told tale of sailing through the wreckage of *The Minerva*. All evidence pointed toward the ship having been sunk by a hidden reef. The crew were presumed lost at sea, including Jamie.

But then Cuthie had appeared on the docks in Aberdeen last autumn. And now there were more mysterious announcements being posted in the broadsheets.

What had truly happened to *The Minerva*?

And Kieran *was* at risk if the magistrate moved to open a full inquiry.

Ewan watched emotions flicker across his friend's face, world-weary sorrow mixing with somber desperation.

"I will not allow them to prosecute ye, Kieran." Andrew's voice was a low, tense hum. "As an Earl of the Realm, I have considerable power."

"Aye," Rafe agreed. "And Sophie's father and other friends in Parliament will also side with us, should the case come to light. We will fight for ye."

Kieran shook his head. "Ye think I care about myself at this point?"

"Kieran—" Ewan began, reaching out a hand toward him.

"Nae, if youse lot are going tae do anything, *find* Cuthie." Kieran sucked in a steadying breath, fire flashing in his eyes. "I have tae know what happened to Jamie, how it ended in truth—" His voice broke.

Ewan's heart panged.

Andrew and Rafe exchanged glances. Alex placed his palm on Kieran's arm.

They had all mourned Jamie's death.

Before he died, Kieran's former mentor, Charles Fyffe, had asked Kieran to watch over his son, James. And so when Jamie came onto *The Minerva*, Kieran had forged an almost instant bond with the youth, taking on the role of protector.

Ewan knew only too well how close Jamie's death had come to nearly breaking Kieran four years ago.

Finding out that Cuthie had lived, that perhaps *others* had lived, had been an agony, tearing open the wound of his friend's sorrow.

"Aye," Ewan agreed. "We all need to know what happened to Jamie."

Kieran nodded, gaze far too glassy. He turned to look into the fire, wiping his eyes with a thumb.

Cuthie's appearance had shattered whatever calm and acceptance Kieran had achieved. The threat of a government investigation and being charged with mutiny would only exacerbate Kieran's precarious mental state.

Logically, Kieran knew that it was nearly impossible for Jamie to have survived. He had said as much to Ewan the last time they spoke of it.

But his friend's pain remained a palpable thing. Ewan knew only too well the depths of such grief—the aching gash left by someone vital being torn away to an unknown fate.

Andrew, Rafe, and Alex thought they understood the nature of Kieran's grief. But privately Ewan had heard them wonder why Kieran's pain was so acute four years on.

But Kieran's wound cut far deeper than the others in the room understood. Only Ewan knew that Kieran's grief was doubly-horrific and truly well-founded.

More than once, he had pressured Kieran to speak with the others. If they all knew the truth of the situation, they might be able to offer support.

But Kieran refused.

And it was not Ewan's secret to tell.

Instead, Ewan would leave for Aberdeen and his new position as a painter's assistant, hoping the others found answers before Kieran unraveled entirely.

2

Violet Kerr, Lady Kildrum, was attempting to solve her third catastrophic problem of the day.

And, as usual, she struggled to know what decision to make.

The first catastrophe had been the abrupt departure of her sisters' governess *cum* lady's companion, Miss Compton. Miss Compton's mother had taken deathly ill, so Violet did not begrudge the woman requesting a leave of absence.

But Miss Compton's loss had led to the second catastrophe—a lack of a proper chaperone for Violet's twin sisters, Aster and Rose. Over breakfast, Rose had bemoaned the worn ribbon on her green silk gown. Granted, shabby ribbons were hardly a true emergency, but Rose insisted that the problem be solved *rightthisinstant.* New ribbons were needed for

Lord Graham's dinner party, and with Miss Compton gone, who would escort Aster and herself to the haberdashers today? Their father had been unmoved by her plight, indicating his displeasure with his daughters' chatter by snapping his newspaper more than usual.

The third catastrophe, and legitimately the most worrisome, had occurred after breakfast with the arrival of Violet's solicitor and steward. She surveyed the gentlemen seated in her study, her polished oak desk stretching between them.

"Your financial situation, my lady, is not quite as robust as it could be," her solicitor, the aptly-named Mr. Lawyerly, was informing her in his dry voice. "The debt your late mother incurred in order to alleviate the famine of '16 comes due in October—"

"The Manna Loan," Violet said, using the name her father had given it—money that had been used to feed the hungry, just like manna fed the Israelites in the wilderness.

"Aye," Mr. Lawyerly nodded. "The very same. Your late mother is to be commended for her generosity. The former Lady Kildrum made a tremendous personal sacrifice that year to ensure all her tenants were fed and housed."

Violet nodded. All of them remembered 1816, the catastrophic Year without a Summer. The skies had remained gloomy and cloudy year-round. It had *snowed* in July, for goodness' sake, the never-ending frosts destroying crops. Violet's family had retreated from their townhouse in London, her parents wary of the hunger riots in Town. But upon returning to Scotland, they realized their thousands of tenants faced similar food shortages.

Violet's mother simply could not allow her people to starve. And so she had taken out a loan to purchase grain from Italy to supplement her people's meager rations.

Mr. Lawyerly continued, "I am certain your late mother anticipated being alive to deal with the repercussions of the loan. But alas, that is not the case. At present, the earldom does not have the liquid capital needed to repay it. Therefore, my lady, it would be prudent to make . . . *decisions.*"

Her steward, the *inaccurately*-named Mr. Shambles, nodded in agreement.

"I understand your mother intended to sell on the management of the southern tack, my lady," he said. "The grassum paid to lease the land would bring a substantial sum, more than enough to settle the Manna Loan."

"Yes." Violet nodded, drumming her desktop, mind sorting through options but not seeing an obvious answer, as usual. "As you had said, the grassum for leasing the tack would allow me to pay off the Manna Loan. But leasing the tack would result in a decrease in income in subsequent years."

"This is true, my lady." Mr. Lawyerly leaned forward in his chair. His gray hair poked out in back, giving him a habitually flustered look. "The only other way to raise the capital needed would be for you to sell the London townhouse, which I know was your childhood home. Or . . ." He smiled wanly. ". . . consider marriage to a wealthy gentleman."

Violet's face froze into her 'polite mask.'

Marriage? For money? Was that her answer?

Whichever decision she made—sell the tack, sell the townhouse, or marry into money—would have long consequences . . . consequences she could not entirely foresee from the beginning.

What was she to do?

And when, when, *when* would she stop asking that question?

For nearly the thousandth time, she wished Dahlia were here to give her advice. Her younger sister would break the choices down for Violet with uncanny clarity—pointing out the happy memories the townhouse represented, or outlining creative ways they could economize after selling on the southern tack.

How could Violet be five and twenty and *still* unable to trust her own mind and act? Wasn't age supposed to confer confidence at some point?

She caught a glimpse of herself in the mirror hanging on the opposite wall. Did she truly appear so maniacal? Blue eyes too wide, color high on her cheeks, an extra set of wrinkles at the corners of her eyes. As usual, the brown ringlets framing her face were already unraveling. Her hair had a singular lifelong goal—to militantly resist curl, no matter how small. How was Violet to lead an earldom when she couldn't even convince her *hair* to behave?

It had been two years since Violet had inherited the coronet of Countess of Kildrum, *suo jure*—in her own right.

As in, no one else would solve these problems for her.

As in, all decisions stopped at her desk.

A fact that others found equally surprising.

"But how was your mother a countess and your father not an earl?" a baffled young lord had once asked at a London ball.

"The title comes from my mother, not my father. My father is the Honorable Mr. David Kerr, a younger son of Viscount Trimbull, but he is married to my mother, Lady Kildrum."

"Pardon?"

"There have been no male heirs in my mother's family for four generations. The first Earl of Kildrum had no sons, so his Writ of Summons included a clause that the earldom could pass through the female line."

"No sons at all?! For four generations?" The poor man sounded properly horrified. "B-but, why?"

"I suppose because God did not wish my maternal ancestors to have sons," Violet replied, *tone ever so dry.*

The man blinked. "So you will inherit the title, just as your mother did, even though you have younger sisters?"

"Yes. In the Scottish peerage, when there is no male heir in the direct line, the title can pass to the eldest daughter. I understand matters are handled somewhat differently in England."

The conversation had not improved from that point. The lordling had struggled to understand how a *woman* could manage an earldom. To be fair, he had a valid point.

How *was* Violet to manage it?

Some days she awoke panicked to feel the title's leaden weight on her shoulders.

Yes, she had been groomed for the position of Lady Kildrum from birth, but that had simply involved endless instruction on etiquette and precedence. Her mother had assumed Violet would live as she had— bouncing between their London townhouse and small English estate. Management of their extensive Scottish holdings would be left mostly in others' hands.

At the moment, Violet knew only enough to comprehend how little she actually knew.

For generations, the Countesses of Kildrum had divided their land into tacks which were then managed by tacksmen. Unlike England, where nobles usually managed their lands directly, nobles in the Highlands relied on tacksmen. These tacksmen would pay a fee—a grassum—to lease tacks of land for a specified period of time (usually nineteen years). The tacksmen would oversee the lands and pay a portion of the rents they collected back to the landowner, the annual tack-duty.

For the Countesses of Kildrum, the tack grassums provided a jolt of income immediately and a residual trickle from tack-duties. The tacksmen also removed the countesses from managing the day-to-day affairs of their lands.

However, in recent years, Scottish nobles had come around to the point-of-view of their English neighbors and had begun re-consolidating their lands from the tacksmen. After all, the tacksmen were middlemen, skimming profits off tenant rents.

Violet had seen this firsthand just ten months prior when one of her tacksmen had passed away, releasing a small tack back to the earldom. Instead of selling the tack on, Violet had listened to her uncle, Sir Joshua Kerr, and hired Mr. Shambles to administer to it. It was a wee tack, after all, and manageable enough for one man to oversee without hiring additional staff.

The result had been a decided uptick in her monthly income. Violet clearly saw that, over time, retaining control of the land directly would prove significantly more profitable.

But now a second tack had come to the end of its term. An enormous tack. A *fiefdom* of a tack. Land that would require an entire office of stewards to manage. Stewards that Violet would then have to oversee herself.

Her father, along with Mr. Lawyerly, wanted Violet to sell the management of the tack to a tacksman, allowing her to pay off the looming Manna Loan and, in the process, shield herself from the unladylike ugliness of tending to estate matters.

Violet was not sure. The long-term dividends of keeping the tack for herself were compelling. It was, after all, fiefdom-sized. Loads of tenants equaled loads of rents to be paid.

The problem, of course, was that Violet had no idea how to go about administering to the colossal tack. The mere thought paralyzed her. Like the title itself, it was too much too soon.

As if hearing her thoughts, Mr. Lawyerly sat forward. "You know your late mother, may she rest in peace, wished for you to leave the management of your lands to others. She never dreamed you would shoulder the burden yourself. She would expect you to sell the southern tack and use the grassum to pay off the Manna Loan."

He was not wrong.

But Mr. Lawyerly—of Lawyerly, Hammer, and Shaw—had been a solicitor to the Earldom of Kildrum for the past twenty-five years. The man remembered Violet's days in leading strings, and because of this, his advice tended to be more avuncular than professional.

This was *usually* a positive thing.

Today, Violet was not so sure.

"Forgive me for saying this," he continued, "but if you do not sell on the tack, you *must* consider marriage, my lady." Mr. Lawyerly swallowed, his expression hesitant. "I understand that Lord Graham has been courting you, as of late."

Right. Yet *another* decision that Violet had to make.

This one, at least, she could dodge for now without incurring consequences.

"Lord Graham has not made an official offer for my hand, Mr. Lawyerly." Violet held up a silencing palm when her solicitor would speak. "So until he does, the point is moot—"

Snick.

The door to her study opened, and Violet's father, Mr. David Kerr, walked in with purposeful strides.

No knock. No polite inquiry.

But then her father considered Violet's desire to run the earldom to be a passing fancy.

Mr. Kerr spared a glance for the two men seated before her desk before turning to her.

"How may I help you, Father?" she asked before he could speak.

Given how quickly his eyes drew into veiled slits, he did not appreciate her dry tone. "Violet, as we have discussed at length in the past, I do not consider it appropriate for you to be closeted with not one, but *two*, men."

"Yes, Father," Violet replied with equal restraint, "and as we have also discussed, such closeting is necessary to the wellbeing of the estate, which, in turn, touches upon the health of our finances. These meetings are essential. We agreed that a proper chaperone would be sufficient to protect my reputation."

"I see," her father said, voice tight. "Given that Miss Compton left the premises this morning, I am curious as to how you are managing to be properly chaperoned at the present."

Violet blinked slowly and then pointed at the maid quietly darning socks behind Mr. Lawyerly and Mr. Shambles.

Mr. Kerr followed the direction of her finger, noted the maid, *finally* nodded a greeting to her solicitor and steward, and then turned back to Violet.

A long breath of silence ensued.

A muscle in her father's cheek twitched. Though he had recently passed his fiftieth birthday, her father was still a dominating physical presence. Tall and lean with receding pepper-gray hair, his blue eyes snapped with sharp intelligence.

Violet held her father's steely gaze.

She sympathized with her father. She truly did.

The early death of his wife had thrown him into a bizarre limbo.

As *husband* to a countess, her father had retained legal rights over Lady Kildrum's actions and money.

However, as *father* to a countess who had reached her majority, Mr. Kerr had no claim on the earldom or its finances. Unlike his wife, he no longer had a legal relationship with his grown daughter.

An emotional connection, surely. But not a legal one.

Yet he was still the legal guardian of Violet's twin sisters—Aster and Rose, aged seventeen—and as such, had much to say about their upbringing, but sparse financial resources to make his opinions a reality.

In short, her father was no longer truly master of the house. And when he felt Violet was making choices contrary to her mother's wishes—which was often—he could do nothing about it except rage at her in his impotence.

Therefore, before he began another tirade, Violet launched a counter-attack. "I do appreciate you bringing up the subject of Miss Compton's absence, Father. Aster and Rose have set their sights on visiting the haberdasher this afternoon, and without Miss Compton, they will have no proper chaperone—"

"Bah!" Her father waved a hand, dismissing the idea. "I do not have time for such frivolity. I have far too much writing to accomplish today. I am not some minion to do my daughters' bidding. Surely a footman or groom could escort them."

Violet finally gave into the urge and rubbed her temples, closing her eyes.

The younger son of an English viscount, her father had been destined for the church, a vocation that he had eagerly embraced. Over the years, he had channeled this devotion into writing religious treatises and arguing obscure doctrinal points with his colleagues from Oxford. Things he claimed left him little time for his daughters.

This was always the conflict, was it not? Her father was quick to disagree with Violet's choices but rarely offered support.

Moreover, how could her father so blithely ignore *this* issue? Had Dahlia's predilections taught him *nothing*?

With a hefty breath, Violet raised her head and met her father's gaze. "And which footman or groom would that be, Father? Tom, the handsome footman that Aster flirts with incessantly? Or would you prefer Angus, the burly groom that she makes eyes at every time she visits the stables? Or perhaps you would prefer my sisters spend the afternoon discussing ribbons with Mr. McKay in his shop? You recall Mr. McKay, do you not? I believe Aster eloquently described him last week as the man who puts 'the *dashing* into haberdashery.'"

Her father's expression became stonier and stonier as she spoke. Dimly, she noted the stray wisps of gray around his ears, the deep lines of his forehead. Signs of age that tugged at her.

"I hardly need to remind you, young lady, to cease employing such a tone with me." Granted, there was nothing elderly about his voice.

Violet clenched her teeth so hard, she quite feared she heard something crack. "Not five minutes past, you yourself rightly pointed out the importance of having a chaperone at all times. I am concerned for my sisters' reputations—as I am sure you can imagine, based on past *situations*—particularly as Aster continually displays more enthusiasm than sense. Heavens, sir, Aster is my heir—"

"The girls need to be married, Violet, not off gallivanting around the countryside."

Ah, yes. That other sore spot in the family—the fact that Mr. Kerr had *three* unmarried daughters.

"Father, I must take issue with your characterization of a trip to the haberdasher as *gallivanting around the countryside*. Besides, you literally just said you wished them to marry. Presenting themselves favorably at a dinner party will surely assist in that, making the visit to the haberdasher essential."

Mr. Kerr's nostrils flared, but as he could find no fault with her words—or perhaps not trusting himself to reply without shouting (truthfully, the dice could land either way)—he merely nodded his head in one brief jerk, pivoted, and left the room. The harsh *clack* of the door resounded with his annoyance.

Violet swallowed and shot the two men still seated before her a smile that the mirror informed her was more maniacal than calm.

"Where were we, Mr. Lawyerly?"

"Lord Graham." Her solicitor cleared his throat. "His lordship has hinted that he might be interested in leasing the southern tack himself."

That furrowed Violet's forehead. "Why would Lord Graham wish to lease a tack, particularly such a large one? He has his own lands to manage."

Mr. Lawyerly glanced at his papers, studiously avoiding Violet's gaze. "I believe his lordship sees it as a stepping stone closer to yourself, my lady. Perhaps a way to further intertwine his life with yours."

Ah.

Reginald Graham, Lord Graham. The wealthy, English nobleman who had purchased an estate near Kilmeny Hall about five years ago. Her late mother had been vocal in her wishes for Violet to marry Lord Graham.

"If you are of a mind to consider a suit from Lord Graham, that would likely affect our current decisions." Mr. Lawyerly continued, shuffling some papers.

Violet nodded, resisting the urge to bite her lip and fidget.

This was the problem with decisions. They were never done and dusted. They had consequences that lingered . . . like shame and guilt and regret.

What *did* she, Violet Kerr, wish?

She wished her mother were still alive.

She wished Dahlia had not made the decisions she had.

She wished her father were an ally rather than an adversary.

She wished she did not have to shoulder the weight of the earldom and its thousands of dependent lives at such a young age.

She wished that her smallest decisions did not have such far-reaching effects—

Angry, bickering voices sounded from the hallway outside.

"I did not!" Rose screeched.

"You most certainly did!" Aster returned.

Violet sighed. She *wished* that her younger sisters would magically become paragons of decorum and propriety.

The door flung open. Two young women burst into the room. One tall and curved, like Violet. The other of average height and dainty, like their mother.

Violet liked to think of her sisters as identical twins inside, not out. Being nearly seven years Violet's junior, the girls had received haphazard attention. The years preceding their mother's death, they had been virtually ignored, as Dahlia and her problems had greatly distracted their parents. Since their mother's death, the twins had been coddled, empathy for their grief outweighing discipline.

The result was a pair of independent, out-spoken young ladies.

Mr. Lawyerly and Mr. Shambles shot to their feet.

"Violet! Aster stole Darcy again!" Lady Rose, the taller of the two, pointed a shaking finger at her sister.

Lady Aster tossed her dark curls. "I most certainly did not. You got Darcy yesterday. You may have Bingley or Willoughby today. Heavens, you may have the whole lot for all I care. But Darcy is mine!"

"Girls!" Violet tried to get through to them without shouting . . . with absolutely no success.

"Willoughby?!" Rose gave a pretend shudder. "Why should any lady want Willoughby as a suitor, even a pretend one?! The man is a cruel scoundrel!"

Aster paused, frowning. "Willoughby is not your preferred book beau?"

"Of course not. The man is an utter scapegrace. I think you are confusing him with Captain Wentworth."

"How could one possibly confuse Willoughby with Wentworth?" Aster frowned deeper. "The letter 'W' is the only similarity between the two—"

"Girls!" Violet tried again, slapping a hand against her desktop.

Her sisters jumped at the sound, turning to look at Violet.

"First," Violet strove to keep her voice calm, "have either of you considered moving beyond Jane Austen to other authors? Perhaps some Ann Radcliffe?"

"Ann Radcliffe?" Rose looked aghast. "Her heroes are such drivel—"

"Hardly *drivel*," Aster interrupted, placing a hand on her hip and turning back to Rose. "Do you not remember Hippolitus who climbed the castle wall—"

"Oh! He was quite dashing."

"Yes, particularly when he cuts the heroine free—"

"Enough," Violet said. "As much as I adore arbitrating who gets which book beau, I am afraid I have other matters to attend to today."

She looked pointedly at the solicitor and steward who followed their banter like a game of lawn tennis, eyes bouncing to and fro.

"We are terribly sorry to have interrupted." Aster dropped her gaze, shooting the men a demure look, no matter that they were both married and twice her age. "Father is refusing to escort us into town."

Violet closed her eyes.

She loved her sisters, she did. Just as she loved her father. But their strong personalities often led to conflict. Though Violet supposed Dahlia had been cut from the same cloth.

Only their mother had been able to hold them all together, her silken threads of love and words creating a net of security around them all . . . a net Violet had not fully appreciated until it was forever severed.

"Where is my bouquet of beauties?!" A loud voice boomed from the hallway.

Violet nearly sighed with relief.

Sir Joshua Kerr, their father's youngest brother, strode into the study.

At last! The only other sane member of the family.

Uncle Joshua made an exaggerated study of the room with his quizzing glass before startling when seeing Aster and Rose before him.

"Hah! Here they are!" he exclaimed. "My beloved bouquet, as beautiful as ever!"

Violet couldn't help but smile. Their mother had named her girls after flowers—*as they are a garden of beauty to me*, she had often said—and so Uncle Joshua always referred to them as his bouquet.

Violet often thought of Sir Joshua as the father she wished she had. Joshua was nearly his brother's opposite in every way.

Where David was stern and religious, Joshua was unfettered by the concerns of society.

Where David was vain and self-righteous, Joshua was self-deprecating and full of *joie de vivre*.

Uncle Joshua had come to live with them after her mother's death, moving his artist's studio from London. He had stayed because he insisted that the 'light in the white guest room made for the finest paintings in Britain.'

Violet privately believed he remained to look after her and her sisters. Regardless, she was forever grateful for Uncle Joshua's calming presence, particularly on days like this one.

"Uncle," Violet smiled and came around the desk, pressing a warm kiss to his cheek. "I am so glad that you have ventured out of your studio. Aster and Rose were just expressing a wish to visit the village."

"Ho, ho!" Sir Joshua wagged his eyebrows at Aster. "You wish to go dashing after the haberdasher, is that it?"

Aster flushed bright red.

Not a good sign.

No slow top, Uncle Joshua winked at Violet before extending his elbows to his two nieces.

"I shall be delighted to escort you both, but be warned, there will be excessive teasing. We shall leave Violet to her . . . business." Sir Joshua nodded agreeably to the other two men in the room before whispering loudly to Violet's sisters. "I understand they are discussing Lord G today."

The mischievous look her uncle shot her said Violet would be included in said teasing. She closed her eyes, biting her tongue in a bid to stay silent.

"Lord G? Is that true, Violet?" Aster swiveled to look at her.

Everyone in the room knew how much Violet detested hearing Lord Graham referred to as Lord G.

So, naturally, her sisters and uncle called him nothing else. It was beyond maddening.

"Lord *Graham* is a minor player in our conversations," Violet said. "Now, Uncle, please escort my sisters into town before I lose my patience altogether and decide to remove the ribbon stipend from their pin money."

Hah!

It appeared Violet *could* make a decision when driven to the end of her tether.

Sir Joshua shot her another wink as he led the girls out of the room.

Violet gratefully sank back into hammering out solutions to various problems with her solicitor and her steward.

She hoped her immediate troubles had been tamped down.

A hope she was allowed to keep . . .

. . . for approximately two hours.

3

There is a . . . man at the door, my lady."

Violet looked up from her current problem—should they plant oats or potatoes in the west field?—to see her butler, Irvine, standing in the doorway to her study.

Her steward and solicitor had departed an hour ago. Of course, no significant decisions had been made. She had asked for more time to ponder her options.

Debating what to do about the Manna Loan felt insurmountable. The consequences of the decision were so far-reaching. How could she account for them all? Sell the tack and potentially endanger their future finances? Or sell the London townhouse and, with it, the thousands of happy memories of her mother and Dahlia?

So, Violet had descended to lesser matters. In other words . . . oats or potatoes? *That* decision was possibly . . . surmountable.

"Pardon?" she asked Irvine.

"There is a . . . *man* at the door, my lady." The slight hesitation in Irvine's voice was the only sign of his agitation.

Violet set down her pen.

"I . . . see," she said, though her tone implied that she did not, in fact, *see*.

Why would Irvine bring this to her attention? As a butler, it was his duty to scrutinize all visitors and deal with them accordingly.

Violet supposed he was to be forgiven as Irvine was new to the position of butler—he had been promoted from head footman only six months prior—and had yet to acquire the unflappable aplomb and discernment of a more seasoned veteran.

Her stare must have been more menacing than bewildered as Irvine wilted under it. He cleared his throat. The sound echoed in the room, causing the house maid, still mending garments in the corner, to jump.

"He is a rather *large* man, my lady." Irvine lifted his hands upward and then apart, tracing the shape of a giant in the air.

Violet continued to stare, again unsure what to do with this information.

Irvine swallowed. "He wishes to speak with Sir Joshua. He says he has been summoned to 'work' with him on an art project."

"Is he to be a model for my uncle then?" Uncle Joshua often hired local laborers to pose as muscled figures for his paintings.

Not that Violet would ever admit to peeking, but the men were, indeed, . . . muscular.

Aster and Rose weren't the only Kerr women who appreciated a well-formed man. Violet was simply better at hiding her fascination.

"I believe so, my lady. But Sir Joshua is still in the village with Lady Rose and Lady Aster. I told the man to return tomorrow morning when Sir Joshua will be in his studio, but the man insists that lodging was part of the contract. He wishes to wait for Sir Joshua to return. Normally, I would have a pair of footmen escort the man from the premises for such cheek, but he is a bit too *large* for threats of physical violence to be effective."

Ah. "I see," she repeated yet again, this time actually meaning the words. At last! A decision that she could make. "Please show the man in. Perhaps authority and reason will work where brute strength will not."

She stared Irvine down for a moment, hopefully giving him another stern, authoritarian look.

It must have been effective because Irvine's shoulders sagged as he bowed and left.

Hah! She was not entirely ineffectual.

Of course, her uncle would hire a giant to model for him. Uncle Joshua was desperate to finish his *magnum opus*, a work he described as 'the Battle of Waterloo depicted as an allegory of Alexander the Great and the Battle of Granicus.'

The monumental work would definitely require multiple, beefy models to accurately capture the brawny grandeur of Alexander's Greek army.

Her uncle intended to submit the painting to the Royal Academy's Summer Exhibition. The Exhibition was the most prestigious art competition in Britain and could ensure—or, in the case of Uncle Joshua, *solidify*—an artist's reputation and career.

A few minutes later, Irvine walked back through her study door.

"Mr. Campbell to see you, Lady Kildrum," he bowed.

Violet rose to her feet, expecting to see a rough laborer stroll in on Irvine's heels.

Instead, a well-dressed gentleman stepped into the room. He was not kitted out in the first-stare of fashion, but the cut of his dark-green swallowtail coat and the brass buttons on his silk waistcoat exuded the skill of a fine tailor from a larger city such as Edinburgh.

She was going to have to speak with Irvine about classifying their callers more clearly. This man was decidedly *not* a day laborer.

Though Irvine had not exaggerated his size.

Violet was not a small woman, a fact that others brought up, over and over. An Amazon, as Lord Michael had described her years ago. She was used to being the tallest woman, often even the tallest *person*, in a room. Her height would have been more tolerable had she been svelte. But even there she was thwarted. Instead of inheriting her mother's more boyish physique, Violet had a woman's curves.

But she felt positively dainty beside this man. She had to look up, up, up to meet his eyes.

More to the point, Violet recognized him immediately.

The shock of red hair, the sharp lines of his face, the intensity of his gaze.

The sheer presence of his formidable body.

Memories assailed her.

The blood streaming down his bare chest . . .

The loud *thwack* of fist on flesh . . .

The humiliation of Lord Michael's dismissal in his hearing . . .

The gentleness of the man's final words to her:

Ye have a heart of great courage.

Red.

Red was in her study.

He was every whit as potent as her memory painted him.

"Thank you, Irvine," she managed to murmur. "That will be all."

THE BUTLER COULD have left the room trumpeting like an elephant for all Ewan knew.

His attention was consumed by the woman standing behind the desk.

Her.

Even nearly eight years on, he recalled the timbre of her husky voice and the striking color of her eyes.

Vividly the interior of that carriage rose in his mind's eye. Her face moving in and out of shadow, those incredible, eggshell-blue eyes—not quite true green, not quite true blue—catching the dim light over and over.

The color had come to represent compassion in his paintings—a bowl holding much-needed bread, the dress on a child's doll, the stone in a mother's earring. A symbol of her kindness.

Ewan had never told anyone about the lady in the carriage. Not even Alex.

How could he capture the quiet touch of her on his life? The warmth of her humanity had countered his icy despair, giving him the strength to rise out of the ashes of Mhairi's betrayal.

He had genuinely never thought to see her again, particularly not here, in northern Scotland. They were worlds away from that cold field in England.

Lady Violet, they had called her then, meaning she was the daughter of an earl or a duke.

But now . . . she was Lady Kildrum, as the butler had said.

In the end, had she married that lord who had said such cruel things? Ewan desperately hoped she had not. The Lady Violet who had showed such care to a stranger deserved better than that.

Belatedly, Ewan remembered the gentlemanly manners hammered into him through years of association with Andrew and Rafe.

"Lady Kildrum." He bowed, precise and deep.

"Mr. Campbell." She nodded her head in greeting. No curtsy. But then a lady would never curtsy to a painter's assistant.

They were not equals, not by any measure.

"Will you please be seated?" Lady Kildrum motioned to a leather chair in front of her desk.

Ewan nodded, darting a glance at the maid sewing in the corner. Her eyes flicked up and down his body, gaze flaring wide. He offered her a wan smile before turning to the chair.

He sat. The armchair heaved a sigh of protest. Ewan could not blame the poor thing. He was quite sure he looked ridiculous seated thus, like a normal-sized man sitting in a nursery chair, knees tucking toward his chest. Thank goodness he was wearing trews today and not his habitual great kilt.

He managed a tight grin at Lady Kildrum, as she took a seat behind the desk. She shot him a glance, expression unreadable.

She moved a stack of papers to the left, placing a pencil atop them, before lacing her hands together on the desktop.

She had lovely hands, long fingers with narrow, elegant fingernails, neatly trimmed and manicured. His fingers itched to draw them.

But as he imagined drawing the lines of her fingers, he noted another interesting fact—

Lady Kildrum did not wear a wedding ring.

Which was . . . odd. Surely there was a Lord Kildrum, was there not? Ewan was not fluent on forms of address, but he knew that you could not have a Lady Kildrum without there being a Lord Kildrum, too. Lords and ladies who bore a title were almost always a matched set.

He tore his gaze from her hands, bringing his eyes back to her face.

Should he speak first? And if so, what should he say? Surely she had utterly forgotten about their prior meeting, so mentioning those moments in her carriage would be absurd.

The silence stretched. Lady Kildrum was cataloging him as thoroughly as he had cataloged her. He sensed that her intelligent gaze missed nothing, from the tailoring and cut of his clothing to the wary hesitance in his voice.

Why was the room suddenly so warm?

He hated his fair skin. Sometimes it seemed as if the slightest errant thought would cause him to blush. Even now, he could feel the scalding heat threatening to climb over the edges of his jaw.

Finally, he cleared his throat. "Thank ye for speaking with me, Lady Kildrum."

She nodded her head. "I suppose I could pretend that I do not recognize you." She dropped her eyes to the desk and then raised them back to his. "But given how you froze upon entering the room, that would only force both of us to lie. And I am an acolyte of truth-telling whenever possible."

She *did* remember him.

The sharp candor of her words nearly stopped his breath.

Ah, yes. *This* was another reason why she had stuck so in his memory. The refreshing openness of conversation with her.

"Aye." He shot her a small grin. "I remember ye well, my lady. I dinnae think I can ever truly express my thanks for your kindness that day."

"I was glad to be of assistance." She paused before continuing, "You informed Irvine that you are here to work with my uncle, Sir Joshua Kerr?"

"Your uncle? I dinnae ken that he was your uncle. But aye, I'm here to work with Sir Joshua. I dinnae realize that this wasnae his own house."

"No, my uncle came to live here after the passing of my mother two years ago." Her expression softened, as if their past acquaintance had knocked loose some of her reserve. "He keeps insisting that he will leave and return to his studio in London, but that has yet to happen."

Ewan wondered if Lord Kildrum was an indulgent husband to tolerate his pretty wife's relatives running amok in his household.

Though, Ewan supposed, if he himself had such a pretty wife, he would struggle to deny her anything.

"I shall try tae stay out of the way of the household as much as possible, then," he said. "I dinnae want my presence tae be a bother."

"Pardon? Why do you say that?" Her brow dented. "How long do you anticipate staying?"

Had Sir Joshua not informed her of any part of Ewan's visit? Worry crept into his thoughts.

"Sir Joshua didnae specify a term" he hedged, "but I reckon we should be through the projects he described afore Christmastide."

"Christmastide?!"

Her outrage was disconcerting. Ewan's own alarm grew.

Was his employment not a foregone conclusion? Sir Joshua's letters had certainly made it seem so, but Kilmeny Hall was not the older painter's own home. Did Lord and Lady Kildrum need to sanction Ewan's stay here?

Ewan had only met Sir Joshua a handful of times, but the man's bonhomie had been palpable. He struck Ewan as the type to make decisions without fully consulting others.

So if this were the first Lady Kildrum had heard of Ewan joining her household, she was understandably dismayed. He winced, images of dealing with a haughty Lord Kildrum blowing through his head.

Blast Sir Joshua for landing him in this predicament! How could Ewan stay on, knowing that his presence was unwelcome?

But how could he bow out? Working with Sir Joshua was vital to Ewan's career.

Something in his expression cut through Lady Kildrum's own concern.

"Forgive my outburst," she said. "It is only, I am puzzled why my uncle will need you as a model for so many months?"

Now it was Ewan's turn to sit back, nonplussed.

"Model?" he asked.

"Yes." She cocked her head. "Are you not here to model for uncle's Greek battle painting? I know he prefers to use prizefighters whenever possible."

Ah.

Something acidic and hot swelled in Ewan's stomach . . . more than just his habitual hunger.

Something that dripped a caustic green and tasted suspiciously like *shame.*

"Such excellent musculature. Do you see that, the line there?" The icy-cold end of a paint brush trailed over his bare ribs. "Remember, he is a brute, not a man. His body is merely a series of lines and shapes. It is not an actual whole—"

Ewan shook off the memory.

Given how he and Lady Kildrum had first met, her assumption was logical.

But that was his past. He would never return to that place.

As if on cue, his stomach growled. Not a wee, polite sound that one could dismiss as the distant lowing of cattle.

No, it was a mortifying rumble, reverberating round and round. A gremlin lodged within.

Lady Kildrum's eyebrows flew to her hairline. Ewan pressed a hand to his stomach—which affected the sound not at all and only highlighted his predicament—and willed the blush climbing his face to subside. The dry bread and cheese he had hours ago at an inn had been inadequate.

"Sally." Lady Kildrum looked past him to the maid in the corner. "Will you order up some tea and a tray of sandwiches for Mr. Campbell?"

Ewan closed his eyes, his cheeks flaming.

But he had perceived this about Lady Violet . . . ehr, Lady Kildrum . . . all those years ago, had he not? She noticed and acted. And again, as like before, admiration for the lady rose in his chest.

The maid bobbed a curtsy and popped her head out the door, speaking to a footman outside before returning to her seat in the corner.

The entire episode only served to deepen Ewan's blush.

"Thank ye, my lady," he finally managed to say. "That is most kind. As ye can see, I am not a wee man. My body burns through food at an alarming rate."

She gave a small smile.

"As to my time here," he continued and then took in a steadying breath, "I must correct your assumptions. I am not come to model for Sir Joshua. I have been hired as his assistant."

Ewan was not sure how he expected her to react to this information, but stunned silence was *not* it.

Though perhaps he should have anticipated it. After all, he had been half-dressed, battered, and dripping blood when last they met. Her lady-ship naturally assumed that such brutality was still part of his life. How was she to know that he had left it behind the moment he stepped out of her carriage?

No one in his career as an artist knew of his prior existence as a prizefighter, and vice versa.

His past was best left as precisely that—passed.

"You—" Lady Kildrum paused, a V forming between her eyes. "You . . . are an artist?"

"Aye," he nodded. "That I am."

That furrow deepened. "An artist of such skill that my uncle, Sir Joshua Kerr, hired you to assist him?"

Ewan considered himself to be a man not given to masculine dis-plays of prowess, his physique and past career choices notwithstanding.

He loathed his skills as a prizefighter. He took no pride in them.

But he admitted to some vanity when it came to his talent as a painter. He had suffered and sacrificed greatly for his art. After all, a man did not become a professional painter without believing passionately in his own skill.

Ewan vowed that someday *everyone* in Britain would know his work. Employ with Sir Joshua was just one of the many steps toward that goal.

Assuming Lord and Lady Kildrum didn't sack him beforehand.

"I studied under Sir Joshua at the Royal Academy of Arts, and I do believe your uncle saw merit in my work, which is why I am here."

"You went from prizefighting to . . . painting?" That sharp V remained between Lady Kildrum's eyes, as if the dichotomy of him were too great.

"Aye. I was fighting my way tae London and the Royal Academy when we met that day in your carriage," he answered steadily. "Ye might say I choose beauty over brutality."

He met her gaze evenly, his jaw surely sticking out in stubborn tenacity.

Her expression was best described as . . . highly skeptical.

His pride could not allow that to remain.

"If ye would be so kind as tae hand me that pencil and a sheet of foolscap"—he motioned toward her desk—"I would be happy tae confirm my skill for your ladyship's approval."

If she found his words forward or improper, she did not show it.

"Merely a quick sketch of your ladyship's face," he assured her.

Lady Kildrum nodded. She slid the requested paper and pencil across the desk to him and then handed him a hard-sided ledger to use as a desk.

Ewan placed the foolscap atop the ledger, balancing the lot on his knees, and began to draw.

Lady Kildrum sat with one elbow on her desk, hand propped under her chin. Her expression was likely irritation, but Ewan chose to see it as bemusement. The weak afternoon light filtered in from the window behind her, rimming her head in a celestial halo.

Abruptly, in his mind's eye, she was no longer Lady Kildrum, but Athena in her bower. The goddess of wisdom.

The pencil lacked the fluidity of the Italian charcoal he preferred when sketching, but it was tolerable. Lady Kildrum's eyes appeared first, then her finely arched eyebrows, her pert nose.

Ewan recognized that by Society's standards, Lady Kildrum was likely not counted a traditional beauty. But he had long felt that precise beauty was tedious.

Lady Kildrum was *interesting*, her eyes a little too widespread, her chin a smidge too long, her forehead a bit too wide. And yet, all together, her features created a compelling woman.

As he was wont to do when drawing, he lost track of time. He lingered on the lines of her tapered fingers, the tactile drape of her hair slipping from its curl. It was not quite ashy blond nor rich brown nor reddish umber, but some shade in-between them all. And more to the point, it resisted being curled—stubborn in its determination to remain straight.

He found it utterly charming.

Ewan filled in the background with quick pencil marks, using the white paper to convey the suggestion of the light streaming behind her, the rim of gold circling her head.

Part of him longed to transfer the sketch to canvas. How would it be to linger on her face, to spend hours leisurely brushing paint in layer after layer?

He could already see it in his mind's eye. He would begin with a ground of soft blue to act as an undertone for the yellow and orange paint atop it, giving the image luminosity and depth—

A throat clearing finally brought him back to himself. He looked up and blinked, seeing the butler standing in the doorway.

Lady Kildrum remained behind her desk, that inscrutable expression on her face.

"A repast has been laid in the breakfast room for Mr. Campbell, my lady," the butler said, his tone loudly communicating his disapproval of Ewan's presence in the household.

"Thank you, Irvine." Her ladyship nodded her elegant head. "Mr. Campbell can await my uncle's return there."

"Very well, my lady," Irvine replied.

Ewan smiled tightly and rose to his feet. He set the ledger and pencil back on the desktop but retained the foolscap in his hand.

Lady Kildrum stood as well, the scent of lavender wafting across to him. He noted that she was tall . . . remarkably tall, in fact, and curved in ways that a man appreciated. He kept his eyes firmly on her face.

She truly was unaccountably lovely. Briefly, he wondered if her husband treasured her as thoroughly as he should.

Such thoughts, of course, were utterly unhelpful. And, to be blunt, improper. He excised them from his brain with a surgical exactness that would do Alex proud.

Ewan bowed.

"Thank you for our conversation, my lady." He took a step forward and extended the sketch.

She took it, eyes darting down to the paper.

Silence descended.

Lady Kildrum remained riveted on his sketch, pressing fingers to her sternum, a hard swallow moving up and down the elegant column of her throat. Her eyes darted back and forth over the paper.

He could paint her like this, too . . . the swooping line of her profile bent to look at the foolscap. Faint blue light casting purple shadows along her jawline, luminous golden sun behind, all representing the fascination that—

He turned from her with a jerk, swallowing hard. He nodded at the butler before following the man out of the room.

But damn if he didn't almost look back.

4

Violet stared at the drawing long after the door closed behind Red . . . ehr, Mr. Campbell.

She was accustomed to seeing beautiful art quickly rendered. Her uncle, after all, was Sir Joshua Kerr, a leading member of the Royal Academy of Arts. Heavens, her uncle had been *knighted* five years previously for his contributions to the artistic merit of Britain as a whole.

In short, Violet was not easily impressed by displays of artistic greatness.

But this . . .

In the space of a few short minutes, Red had created such . . . beauty. The drawing *breathed* with life.

Violet stared down at her own face, drawn with life-like accuracy and yet brimming with that intangible something that stamped it as *Art*.

He had sketched her as Athena—the ghostly form of an owl on her shoulder pronouncing her identity—a goddess in her heaven, looking down on mere mortals below. She appeared radiant, the secrets of nations hidden in her eyes, the glory of her power streaming in the light from behind.

Was this how Red saw her? The goddess of wisdom? *Her?!*

The very idea was so far off the mark she nearly laughed. She was still struggling to determine the wisdom of oats versus potatoes.

Hardly a goddess-level problem.

Moreover, the entire experience brought home *why* she remembered Red so many years on. Partially, it was his size and rather unique coloring, the sense of such battered desperation . . .

But it had been the *dichotomy* of him that lingered. How mismatched the man was. A poet's soul in a prizefighter's body. But even in that, she had not grasped the magnitude of what hid beneath his exterior. The sheer vibrance and beauty of it.

Watching him sketch had been . . . fascinating. His enormous hand gripping the pencil, the other hand bracing the ledger and paper upon his knees. The pencil was absurdly tiny in his hand, a child's plaything. And yet he had moved it across the paper with fluid ease, his brows drawn down in concentration. The tightly leashed control of his towering body focused down, down, down to such a small point.

Her brain, most unhelpfully, paired that memory with another—Red seated across from her in that carriage, bare-chested and endless rippling muscle—

Heat scorched Violet, a dowsing flood of longing.

She braced her hands on her desk, eyes closed, willing her wayward imagination to behave.

She might share much of her sisters' endless interest in the opposite sex, but Violet could not allow baser instincts to rule her head. She must keep her reputation spotless. She could not entertain thoughts of this wholly unsuitable Highlander vastly below her station, no matter how compelling his art or how alluring his broad shoulders—

Enough.

Violet took another steadying breath.

Red—*grrr,* Mr. Campbell!—was simply no one to her. And must always remain no one.

You hear that, body?! No one!

Violet set Mr. Campbell's sketch aside, intent on continuing her assessment of the estate's current planting schedule, but the drawing hovered at the edge of her vision, nearly humming with vitality.

The problem, of course, was that even though Violet knew she must resist the lure of attraction to someone so unsuitable, the *reality* of that attraction remained.

Mr. Campbell was alarmingly magnetic, a potent mixture of raw masculinity and captivating artistry.

Seeing him had thrown her back to overhearing Lord Michael that afternoon. Even nearly eight years on, she could still feel the burn of humiliation, listening to Lord Michael's words outside the carriage while staring into Mr. Campbell's eyes.

Violet was not so naive as to assume that she would marry for overwhelming love. But she expected that her husband would genuinely *like* her. Being a countess should at least afford her that low bar.

And so, she had roundly rejected Lord Michael's offer of marriage when it came, much to his lordship's shocked dismay. In the aftermath, Lord Michael had spent months attempting to convince Violet of the sincerity of his affections. Even Smitty had tried to change her mind. To no avail, of course.

And now the lot had come full circle, with Lord Graham hovering as a suitor and Violet staring once more into Mr. Campbell's eyes.

Yes, she wanted a husband and children. In her more truthful moments, Violet acknowledged that she longed for the physical intimacy of marriage. But along with that, she wished for a husband who put her first and foremost. Someone she could always rely upon to guard her interests.

Mr. Campbell's drawing hummed at the edges of her vision, sending her thoughts pinging round and round. How could she concentrate on planting schedules now? Slamming her ledger shut, she excused the upstairs maid.

Violet crossed through the music room and was halfway across the central great hall when murmured voices and a low giggle drew her attention.

Had her sisters returned from town then?

Frowning, Violet followed the sound around the corner, pausing beside an enormous potted fern.

The door to the morning room stood ajar. Mr. Campbell appeared to be finishing his repast and was quietly reading . . . something. Was it a letter?

But that was not the problem, per se.

Aster and Rose were positioned across the wide hall and to the left of the door, allowing themselves a fine view of Mr. Campbell's back and partial profile.

" . . . sure he's not a new gentleman in the neighborhood?" Rose was saying.

"I am certain," Aster replied. "Were such a man to have appeared, the village would be abuzz with the news. Is it too much to hope that perhaps Violet decided to hire us a dashing tutor?"

"That man is *far* too large to be a tutor."

"You are quite right. He likely isn't a dancing instructor either, more's the pity."

Violet's jaw dropped at Aster's words. How could her sister say such a thing! After everything that had happened *last* time—

"Shhh, Aster!" Rose swatted her sister's arm. "You mustn't say such things, even in jest. Violet would have our hides—"

"Oh, tush!" Aster interrupted. Mr. Campbell angled his head toward the sound, causing Aster to drop her voice further. "Surely you have already imagined how it would feel to dance a waltz with one such as him." She rocked a thumb toward Mr. Campbell. "I certainly have."

Aster's words sent a tumble of images through Violet's mind. Red smiling down at her before wrapping one of his enormous hands around her waist and pulling her toward him, encircling her in the security of his arms, the heat of his palm a brand against her spine—

Aster's giggle stopped the daydream in its tracks—*thank goodness.*

Violet shook her head.

How was she to guide her sisters through the London Marriage Mart and everything that moving into true adulthood required? She could barely manage her own life.

This situation spelled disaster.

It appeared all three of the Kerr sisters were at risk of developing a tendre for this man.

Mr. Campbell might be in her uncle's employ, but unless Violet acted *now*, the situation could rapidly devolve into an absolute catastrophe.

And the Earldom of Kildrum could ill-afford another calamity.

Dahlia's disastrous behavior and tragic death stood as a warning for them all.

The gossips were possibly right—there was perhaps a baseness in Kerr women that needed to be stamped out.

Mr. Campbell could not be allowed to stay.

Violet pivoted round and went hunting for her uncle.

Though . . . silver lining—

If presented with a dire enough consequence, it appeared Violet *could* make a bigger decision after all.

EWAN SHIFTED IN his chair in the breakfast room, attempting to ignore the murmur of female voices outside the door. He reached for another roast beef sandwich, washing it down with a swallow of excellent tea.

Despite the lukewarm welcome from Lady Kildrum's staff, they had not skimped in their hospitality.

A sibilant, feminine *hush* sounded from the hallway. The back of Ewan's neck pricked. Were the maidservants ogling him? He had found that women generally had one of two reactions to his size—fear or an almost unhealthy fascination.

In this case, either reaction would certainly validate Lord and Lady Kildrum's concerns about his presence at Kilmeny Hall. It was one thing to welcome a stranger into one's home. It was something else entirely when said stranger was a looming giant of a man.

Ewan disliked that his physical size could never be a neutral thing.

His eyes drifted to the sheet of foolscap beside his plate—a letter from Alex that had arrived at Kilmeny Hall. The butler had been irked to find it in the morning's post, likely because it presaged Ewan's lingering on in the household. Again, he felt that stab of unease, that his presence here might prove a problem for Lady Kildrum.

Take it one crisis at a time.

With a deep breath, he lifted Alex's letter, rereading the pertinent bits.

> *I have been kept awake these past several nights, concerned about Kieran. A mutual friend mentioned that Kieran has been unraveling, taking more and more to the bottle. There is even a rumor circling that his preference for whisky caused him to be dismissed from his current ship.*
>
> *I must be honest with you, Ewan. I find Kieran's conduct to be some-what baffling. We all know that he felt Jamie's loss most keenly. 'Twas only to be expected. But Cuthie's survival appears to have shattered Kieran's peace in ways I do not understand. Do you ken there might be something else influencing his behavior?*
>
> *I know you and Kieran have always been close. Perhaps you could send him a few words of encouragement. Anything to stem the tide of this destructive behavior . . .*

Ewan set the foolscap down, scrubbing a hand over his face.

Ah, Kieran.

Things must be bad indeed for Alex to lose sleep over Kieran's behavior. Alex was basically unflappable.

Ewan did not pretend to fully grasp the emotions assailing Kieran. But he could empathize with his friend's wounds.

They had all loved Jamie. Vividly, he remembered that afternoon on Vanuatu, charcoal pencil in hand, sketching Jamie from life. His friend had laughed at the antics of the village children, head back, eyes glowing with that *joie de vivre* that was so distinctly Jamie. The carpenter's mate had been like a sibling to Ewan.

But Kieran's bond with Jamie was unique, moving toward family in truth. Ewan could only think that Kieran's burden would be lightened if he shared the full extent of it with the rest of the Brotherhood.

"You should tell them your secret, about the future ye planned, what it meant for ye and Jamie," Ewan had urged him before leaving Muirford House a few weeks ago. *"It would help. I know it."*

"Nae, I dinnae want their sad looks. Yer pitying mug is bad enough—"

"Kieran, ye ken there is a difference between compassion and pity. I feel compassion *for ye, ye know that."*

Kieran nodded and looked away, his eyes glassy. He blinked twice, swallowing over and over.

"Jamie would not like to see ye destroying yourself like this," Ewan pressed his point.

Kieran nodded again, jaw clenched, hands fisted at his side.

"It's just—" His voice broke and he swallowed. *"It's just that . . . with Jamie's death, I feel like I possibly lost a son."*

Another giggle from the hallway had Ewan shifting in his seat.

He would write Kieran and Alex as soon as he was shown to his room.

Assuming Lord and Lady Kildrum allowed him to stay.

The former prizefighter in him knew not to count his punches. But right now, they seemed to be coming one after the other.

"UNCLE, MR. CAMPBELL simply cannot stay." Violet had cornered Sir Joshua in the entrance hall and ushered him into the large drawing room so they could converse without being overheard.

"Pardon, child?" Her uncle looked at her with fond amusement. Violet often thought of Sir Joshua as her father's alter ego. The men looked alike—both tall with salt-and-pepper hair and bright blue eyes.

But whereas the whole came off as moralistic religiosity on her father, it hummed with bohemian vitality on her uncle.

Of course, that could also be due to her uncle's love of brightly-colored waistcoats. Today's choice was orange silk embroidered with purple filigree.

"I know you heard me the first time, Uncle. Mr. Campbell cannot stay here."

"Of course, the man can stay. I hired him, did I not? I'm fair desperate for the help."

"Uncle—"

"Now, now, Violet, Ewan is a remarkable talent—"

"Ewan?"

"Mr. Ewan Campbell." Sir Joshua rolled his hand—*please keep up.*

Ah. Red's Christian name was Ewan.

Violet batted it around in her head—*Ewan, Ewan, Ewan.*

She was terrified to examine why she liked it so much.

Her uncle continued on, "They say he is the next Ingres. His talent is boundless, and the lad is only at the beginning of his career. He simply requires someone to push him into greatness."

Violet closed her eyes, seeing the quick sketch now resting in her box of treasures in the bottom drawer of her desk. No doubt her uncle was correct about Mr. Campbell's skill.

Unfortunately, Uncle Joshua was missing the finer point of the conversation. But then, her uncle held unconventionally egalitarian views on class and the interaction between the sexes.

In short, the societal implications of the situation did not occur to him.

Her mother had insisted it all began with Joshua's own past. At twenty, her uncle had fallen deeply in love with a farmer's daughter. Naturally, Violet's aristocratic grandfather refused to allow his son to marry so far beneath himself. Joshua and his lady love had stolen away, intending to elope to Scotland. But her grandfather had interrupted their plan, dragging his son away from the ruinous influence of such a 'lower-class hoyden,' as he referred to her. Months later, Joshua had discovered that his father had all but forced the girl to wed another man.

Uncle Joshua had never married, whether from a broken-heart or disillusionment, Violet could not say. But her uncle had a strong dislike for 'aristocratic narrow-mindedness,' as he called it.

Violet stifled a sigh. "I am not doubting Mr. Campbell's innate talent, Uncle. I am merely pointing out that the man's presence is a problem."

Sir Joshua reared back his head. "How so? I fail to understand your logic, child. I am desperate for help. He will assist me with my *magnum opus* and earn a nominal wage. In return, I will continue to act as Mentor to his raw talent, leaving my stamp on the next generation. Ewan will be part of my legacy. It all makes perfect sense—"

"He is an artist, Uncle. He will live here and eat here and be among us every day—"

"That gives me an idea." Joshua snapped his fingers. "We must inveigle him to paint a portrait of you. Mr. Campbell is a talented portraitist."

"A portrait?"

"Of course." He nodded, his eyes developing that gleam of inspiration she knew all too well. "Every previous title holder has had their portrait done. Why not you?"

He waved a hand, indicating the enormous portraits lining the wall opposite them.

The first earl, Violet's great-great grandfather, in his armor from the Nine Year's War, a sword in his hand.

His daughter, Violet's great-grandmother, in an ermine-lined cape and gold-shot brocade, a tiara on her head.

Her daughter, Violet's grandmother, in a pink powdered wig and wide rectangular skirt, a scepter of justice in her hand.

Her daughter, Violet's mother, in the loose fashions of the French Revolution, a ledger on the desk beside her and children's toys at her feet.

All the subtle trappings of authority and domesticity. The power and prestige Violet needed to pass along to the next generation, unblemished by her own actions.

"The tradition must carry on," Uncle Joshua continued. "It is about time we celebrated your investiture as the new countess. A formal portrait is an excellent place to start. I have heard Mr. Campbell painted a remarkable work for Lord and Lady Hadley—"

"Uncle, this is ridiculous. I am not going to sit for Mr. Campbell. Should I require a portrait, I would have no one but yourself paint it." Violet glanced pointedly at the life-size painting behind her, the last one Uncle Joshua had painted of the Kerr women—Violet's mother with her four daughters.

She generally avoided looking at the painting.

Uncle had captured them all so well, particularly the former Lady Kildrum's maternal gaze. What Violet wouldn't give to have her mother here? To solicit her advice?

And then there was Dahlia with that mischievous fire in her eyes, almost taunting the viewer. The very spark that had been Dahlia's downfall. Though Violet had played her own part there, had she not? The guilt of her own behavior forever lingered—

Violet swallowed back the lump in her throat, turning away.

She was a barely healed wound, and as usual, the painting was a painful reminder of what it had felt like to be whole.

"You are very kind, my dear," Uncle Joshua was saying, "but it is good to have another artist's vision. Besides, I haven't the time at the moment. Why are you so set against the idea? Mr. Campbell is here. I am certain he would welcome the prestige of the commission. Do you doubt Mr. Campbell's skill?"

"Uncle, Mr. Campbell's abilities as an artist are not my concern here. As I keep saying, I am troubled by his presence in this house."

"His presence? How so? Your father and myself are also in residence, so propriety is being met."

"Yes, perhaps in the strictest sense of the word. However, my sisters living in proximity to Mr. Campbell is an entirely different matter. The man has *Peril!* scribbled across his broad chest." She swiped a hand in a broad arc. "He is an unequivocally handsome artist who gives every appearance of being kind-hearted and well-spoken."

"Broad chest. Unequivocally handsome," her uncle nearly crowed, slapping his knee in delight. "Has the Highland laddie caught your eye, lass?"

"No, he has not," she lied, willing away her telling blush. "Rather Mr. Campbell is practically catnip for a young lady—"

"Catnip?" Uncle Joshua laughed harder. "Perhaps we should say *lady-nip*, eh?"

"Enough, Uncle! Have you forgotten what happened the *last* time an engaging man resided under the same roof as a Kerr daughter? Has memory failed you so thoroughly?" Violet snapped and then winced at the echo of her father's tone in her voice. Though she very much related to his frustration in this moment. "There are currently two other young women in my care. *They* have certainly noticed your new assistant and are eager to claim Mr. Campbell's attention."

She waved a hand at the portrait behind her, the motion invoking the specter of Dahlia's decisions.

That seemed to finally sink in.

Her uncle's brows pulled down.

Violet softened her tone. "Uncle, I know you snap your fingers at most societal conventions, but dismissing them does not remove the very real consequences for breaking them. Indiscreet behavior on the part of a young lady is seen as evidence of a wanton baseness of character. This baseness is assumed to be the result of poor breeding. No one wishes to marry into such a family, as others fear this baseness will taint their own bloodline." How had Violet become this person? Rattling off societal conventions as if she were a stuffy dowager? And yet . . . the stakes were too high to do otherwise. "Because of Dahlia's scandalous actions, we Kerr sisters are already viewed as potentially damaged goods. We court disaster to have Mr. Campbell housed in the same building ourselves. You must see this, Uncle?"

Sir Joshua sighed. "Dahlia's so-called 'scandalous' actions are not those of yourself or your sisters. People who will judge you are not worthy of your attention—"

"Uncle, regardless of how unjust the judgment, I must still live with the very-real consequences of it. Dahlia's decisions still affect us and how we are perceived. If we wish to marry well and still be received in society, my sisters and I must hold ourselves to a higher standard."

Silence hung for a moment.

"I see." Uncle Joshua pursed his lips for a moment and then clapped his hands. "Well, Mr. Campbell and I will have to remove ourselves to Old Kilmeny Castle, then."

Violet paused, rebuke on her tongue.

But . . .

Uncle Joshua had suggested a rather sensible solution.

Old Kilmeny Castle was the original seat of the Earls of Kildrum, perched atop a bluff overlooking the ocean, a perfect vantage point to spot would-be invaders.

Family lore had it that the first earl's wife had detested the cold, damp medieval castle and convinced her husband to build Kilmeny Hall, a more modern building with enormous windows, symmetrical architecture, and light-filled rooms.

But Old Kilmeny Castle still stood proudly on the estate, a quarter-mile away. Though ancient, Violet's mother had ensured that the castle remained ready for guests. *If I am paying the window tax on the structure, I will ensure that the property is, indeed, worthy of habitation,* she was wont to say.

"That is . . . acceptable." Violet conceded defeat.

"Wonderful. Glad to have solved the problem. Though I will continue to insist that Mr. Campbell be commissioned to paint your portrait." Uncle Joshua smiled, that teasing gleam back in his eyes. "I'll see to removing the imminent *Peril!* from your house immediately."

He winked at her before walking away.

5

"I anticipate we will set up our respective studios tomorrow," Sir Joshua said, sitting forward and extending a poker with a slice of bread on the end over the crackling fire.

"That seems an excellent idea." Ewan cut a strip of cheddar cheese onto a plate that rested on the small table between their chairs.

He and Sir Joshua were seated before the enormous fireplace in the great hall of Old Kilmeny Castle. Light flickered out from the fire, casting long shadows across the room. The faint sound of waves crashing on the cliffs below the castle filtered through the thick walls, as did an errant draft or two, fluttering the candles.

Fortunately, Ewan and Sir Joshua were tucked into a pair of hooded chairs or, as Ewan would have called them, *heided-stuls*. The tall-backed chairs wrapped over their heads and captured the heat from the fire, turning their small section of the cavernous room rather cozy.

Sir Joshua had arrived as Ewan finished up the repast Lady Kildrum had ordered for him. The painter had pumped Ewan's hand enthusiastically, apologizing for his tardiness.

As ever, Ewan was struck by the older man's endless affability. Sir Joshua had taught several of Ewan's classes at the Royal Academy, but Ewan had not formed a close relationship with the man. That said, he had recently learned that Sir Joshua had advocated for Ewan to receive a much-needed scholarship to fund his studies at the time.

Sir Joshua utterly dispelled the myth of artists being tortured, vain souls. He laughed at himself and complimented others with ease. How could a talent of such impressive genius be housed in this good-natured man?

Ewan often wondered if the older painter's amiability was borne of pain. The kind of hurt that scrubbed a man raw and reduced life to its most essential components, bringing fundamental truths of love and kindness into sharp focus. It seemed the only explanation for the depth of feeling in Sir Joshua's art and the affability of his personality.

In short, Sir Joshua was a conundrum.

So it was with good humor that Sir Joshua explained that the chaperone to Lady Kildrum's sisters had taken a leave of absence, resulting in Ewan and himself being banished to the ancient castle to "give the lasses the run of the great house."

Ewan was quite sure it was a polite way of saying that *Lord* Kildrum did not particularly appreciate having a brute of a fellow thrust into his household at a moment's notice.

Ewan could hardly blame his lordship. Had he a wife as lovely and caring as Lady Kildrum, Ewan would certainly want her to himself. They would nestle together before the fire on a chilly evening, her snugged into the curve of his chest, pressed against him from thigh to shoulder—

Ewan stopped the thought right there.

Enough. The lady is married. You are a better man than this.

Ewan clenched his hands into fists and, once more, forcibly cut Lady Kildrum from his mind.

After greeting him, Sir Joshua had dispatched a harried pair of maidservants to air rooms and make up beds for them in the old castle. His employer promised that there would be more permanent staff arriving tomorrow, as if Ewan were a gentleman like Sir Joshua and required tending to.

Now, hours after sundown, the few servants had departed, and Ewan and Sir Joshua huddled in front of a fire in the great hall, eating a late supper of toasted cheese and bread, all washed down with some excellent whisky from the earldom's distillery. Sir Joshua had swapped his clawhammer coat for a ruby-red banyan, the color clashing with the older painter's orange waistcoat.

Sir Joshua was nothing if not colorful, Ewan was coming to realize.

The painter checked the state of his toast and, ascertaining it to be adequately hot, he layered a slice of cheese atop before extending the whole back over the fire again.

"This castle may be old, but it certainly doesn't lack for atmospheric charm, does it now lad?" the older man said, shooting Ewan a wry grin.

"Nae, sir." Ewan craned his head around the high back of his chair, surveying the deep shadows dancing in the dim firelight. Shields and the occasional claymore glinted from the walls. The furniture was sparse and most still covered in ghostly-looking Holland cloth. "Ye willnae need to look far tae find swords and such as props for painting."

Sir Joshua chuckled. "Right you are, my boy. I've been sketching ideas for months, but now I am fair itching to get paint on canvas."

Sir Joshua went on to describe how he intended to place the modern Battle of Waterloo into the larger context of traditional allegorical painting. He conceptualized the battle between Alexander the Great and the Persian army at Granicus to be a mythological metaphor for the conflict between Wellington and Napoleon on the fields outside Waterloo.

Ewan listened attentively, devouring a thick slice of toast and cheese. He reached for the loaf and cut off another slice, slid it onto a poker, and extended it over the fire.

"Of course, such a grand scope cannot be done on a small scale. The piece will be monumental in size, nearly twelve feet across." Sir Joshua smiled, ruefully. "When subsequent generations hear the name 'Sir Joshua,' it is my intent that this painting will leap instantly into their minds."

Knowing the older painter's style as he did, Ewan could almost envision the image—writhing, half-clothed muscular figures alongside horses, the whole lot twisting in motion and delineated in bold color.

"Ye'll be the toast of the Academy's Summer Exhibition," Ewan nodded.

"That is my wish; I shan't deny it." Sir Joshua grinned. "I aim for the king to purchase the painting for the Royal Collection."

Every year, the Royal Academy of Arts solicited artists to submit works to be included in their prestigious annual exhibition. Anyone could submit, but only a handful of the best works were chosen for the Exhibition. To have your work singled out and honored by the Royal Academy was the pinnacle of an artist's career.

The selected pieces covered the walls from floor to ceiling in Somerset House for several months, making those hung "on the line" or at eye level the most esteemed. Thousands of Londoners from all walks of life paid a shilling to tour the exhibit, marveling at the talent and skill displayed.

Sir Joshua darted a side-glance at Ewan in the dim light. "What will you be submitting to the Exhibition this year?"

Ewan froze, toast held over the fire. "Pardon?"

"The Exhibition, lad. What will you be submitting to it?" Sir Joshua cut another slice of bread off the crusty loaf between them and patiently wiggled it onto the poker for toasting. Ewan forced his breathing to remain even, acting for all the world like the older man's question hadn't detonated like cannon fire in Ewan's brain.

"I . . . I cannae say that I've given the matter any thought," Ewan replied, pulling his bread back and making a show of inspecting it before returning it to the fire.

That was a bald lie.

He thought of little else, sometimes. How he would make his name. How he would achieve the fame and success of a painter such as Sir Joshua.

But Ewan knew his own limitations. His skill and technique were excellent. But great art was not borne of technique alone. It required unique pieces of self. What part of Ewan would be grand enough for the Royal Exhibition?

"Your silence reeks of self-doubt, lad," Sir Joshua continued, plucking Ewan's very thoughts from his skull. "But I know you have the potential to create something powerful. The scene doesn't need to be grand, per se. It simply needs to be innovative in some way. Did you attend the Exhibition last summer?"

Ewan nodded, the remarkable images shuttling through his brain.

"Do you remember Mr. Constable's painting? *The Haywain?*"

Again, Ewan nodded. The image tumbled through his memory—a pastoral countryside with a cottage along a river, a large hay wagon resting in the middle of the water. The subject was banal . . . commonplace. Simply a farmer allowing his animals to cool off in the stream on a hot summer's day.

However, the image had been celebrated both for its simplicity and its use of modern art techniques, rejecting the almost clinically clean lines of paintings by Monsieur David or Monsieur Boilly, and opting instead for a sketch-like suggestion of form and light.

"Mr. Constable has been following the lead of other artists, like Mr. Goya in Spain. There is even talk that their suggestive use of light and shadow—you recall how it is? More a fleeting impression of shape and form than actuality?—well, some say that will be the future of art. You simply need a unique eye. And *that*, based on your time at the Royal Academy, you have got in spades." Sir Joshua paused. "Don't let the compliment go to your head."

Sir Joshua brought his toast closer, examining the bread for readiness, before placing it back into the fire.

Ewan pulled his own slice out of the fire and placed a thick slab of cheddar cheese on it.

"Here is the thing," the older man continued. "We're living in progressive times. Generations past, artists relied solely on patrons. The patron would tell us what to paint and how to paint it. And in some ways, that hasn't changed. We *all* paint portraits of dowdy ladies and prized hunters when called upon."

"I've heard discussion of how the Royal Academy, along with the *Salon de Paris*, are changing this." Ewan took a bite of his toast.

"Hah! Precisely!" Sir Joshua nodded his head toward Ewan in acknowledgment. "The exhibitions are public spectacles of art. Thousands attend and form opinions. Works can gain a popular following and, from there, progress to sale. For us artists, this is a boon. We can create whatever sings to our soul and allow the buyer to find the painting, not the other way around."

Sir Joshua took his toast out of the fire, gingerly sliding it off the poker and onto a plate sitting beside him.

"The problem, of course, is creating works that speak to others."

"Ah." Ewan barely suppressed a grimace. "Easy to say . . ."

"Harder to do . . . yes, you have the right of it." The older man placed a thick slice of cheddar cheese on the hot bread before continuing on, "Like a doctor, we artists must open veins and bleed before seeing results. If your art is not making you uncomfortable as you create it, it will never have the power to touch another."

Sir Joshua paused, fixing Ewan with a serious, intent gaze. Ewan saw a flash of something behind the older man's eyes. A hint of buried pain, a sense that Sir Joshua's geniality *was* hard won on the back of misery.

When the man continued, his voice betrayed that rasp of pain:

"We bleed every time we paint, lad. Never forget it."

The words hit Ewan with visceral force.

A bite of bread stuck in his abruptly dry mouth.

We bleed every time we paint. Never forget it.

He mentally cringed, Sir Joshua's words blending with those of other teachers over the years.

I need to see more of you *in this, not just pretty lines.*

Somehow Mhairi's voice leapt into the mix.

I want ye painting somewheres far away from here, Ewan. Dinnae come back until ye've made a name for yourself.

That familiar salmon-colored emotion rose, the one that choked his throat and stifled his ability to speak of himself.

As if sensing Ewan's turmoil, Sir Joshua swallowed a bite of toast before saying, "The world is littered with men who neglected to fulfill the measure of their promise. I see your paintings, but I will be honest—" The man paused and shook his head. "—I have yet to see you *bleed*. As artists, we can have no secrets. Our inner turmoil is fodder for public consumption. If you wish to be great, find the courage to paint your demons."

Sir Joshua took another large bite of bread as if his words had not landed like a fist to Ewan's jaw, setting his head to buzzing.

Find the courage to paint your demons.

The very words implied that Sir Joshua had faced his own demons, conquered them in his art.

However, they also summed up the difficulty of Ewan's situation with brutal efficiency—

In order to paint your demons, you had to face them first.

The salmon color flooded his vision, a cold and clammy thing that seized his chest in a vise.

Ewan brushed crumbs from his fingers, wondering if the hammering of his heart was as audible as it seemed.

"You look like a kicked dog," Sir Joshua snorted.

"That bad?" Ewan managed a wan smile.

The older man shrugged. "You'll get used to the idea. If nothing else, facing your personal demons spurs important emotional growth. Think upon it tomorrow as we set up our studios."

Mmmmm, about that . . .

Ewan swiveled to look at the large windows against the wall opposite the fireplace.

"That seems exceptionally large for a castle window." He pointed to the shutters.

Sir Joshua looked over his shoulder. "Yes, it is quite large. I seem to remember some tale of Lady Kildrum's grandmother enlarging the windows in order to use the castle as a summer house. And if my sense of direction and orientation serves me right, the window should face south, which will help with the light."

Ewan nodded, his brow furrowing. There was an implication in Sir Joshua's comment that jarred Ewan, but he couldn't put his finger on what precisely it was.

Likely just the combination of a long day's travel, an even longer afternoon spent under microscopic inspection, and now late-evening advice and soul-searching in an admittedly eerie place.

"If so, the great hall should make an excellent studio," Ewan said.

"Agreed. I may have to thank Lady Kildrum for casting us out of Kilmeny Hall." Sir Joshua winked at Ewan and then took a large bite of his cheese and toast.

For his part, Ewan had barely suppressed a grimace at Sir Joshua's words . . . *casting us out.*

So Ewan's arrival *had* been a source of contention. He greatly disliked the thought of being a burden, that his presence caused ill-will.

He reached for the loaf of bread and sawed off a yet another thick slice for himself. Sliding the bread onto the poker, he stretched it over the hot coals, taking a moment to gather his thoughts.

Ewan sighed inwardly. There was no help for it. He *had* to make what amends he could.

"My arrival seemed tae upset Lady Kildrum." He laid the words gently. "I wouldnae want to be a source of contention, so I hope that Lord Kildrum wasnae too indisposed with my arrival."

There. He had expressed his concern. Clear. Straight-forward.

"Pardon?" Sir Joshua paused mid-bite. "Lord Kildrum?"

"Aye." Ewan lifted his toast out of the fire, making a show of inspecting it in order to keep his tone light and seemingly unaffected.

He finally dared a glance at Sir Joshua.

The older man was eating his toast, staring at Ewan with a positively *bemused* expression on his face.

"When you speak of Lord Kildrum, lad, are you referring to my elder brother?"

Ewan paused. "Nae, I thought to refer to Lady Kildrum's husband."

"I thought as much," Sir Joshua chuckled. "Lady Kildrum does not *have* a husband. At least, not yet. She's a countess *suo jure*. In her own right."

"In her own right?" Ewan echoed.

"Yes, indeed. Our Lady Violet inherited the earldom from her mother, who had it from her mother. It is the oddest twist of fate, I tell you, with these Kildrum women."

Sir Joshua's words from earlier flooded back . . . *Lady Kildrum's grandmother enlarged the window in order to use the castle as a summer house.*

If Lady Kildrum were married to Lord Kildrum, why would her grandmother have lived here, too? It would have been Lord Kildrum's grandmother, no?

That was why the sentence had bothered him.

But . . . there was *no* Lord Kildrum.

All the pieces slotted together.

With no Lord Kildrum, Ewan and Sir Joshua had needed to quit Kilmeny Hall for reasons of propriety. No one had been offended.

More to the point . . . Lady Kildrum was *not* married.

The force of Ewan's relief was . . . telling.

Attraction and infatuation roared in, a lion cut loose from its chains.

The memory of Lady Kildrum from that afternoon swamped his vision and this time he did not force it out.

Instead, . . . he lingered, mentally tracing over the image.

The way the glowing light had caught in the irises of her eyes, deepening their color and turning them into the teal-blue of Loch Carron on a sunny day in July. The fragile gentleness of her long fingers. The sinuous curve of her waist as she stood to bid him farewell.

Reality, unfortunately, was not far behind, eager to come crashing down on his fanciful thoughts.

Lady Kildrum was a *countess,* an earl in her own right. She was of the same rank as Andrew Langston, Lord Hadley. Ewan loved his friend dearly, and Andrew had never once made Ewan feel less-than due to the enormous difference in their stations in life . . .

But the gulf between himself and Andrew was prodigious and deep. And though Andrew probably didn't tally the differences, for Ewan, they were seemingly numberless.

Case in point—Ewan hadn't immediately picked up on all the clues as to Lady Kildrum's exact circumstance. Though Andrew and Rafe had acquainted Ewan with many of the rules of etiquette and decorum over the years, much still escaped his grasp. He merely knew enough to thoroughly understand how little he actually knew.

Ewan often felt like a monkey, dancing to an organ-grinder's tune—a trained animal aping the manners of his betters, having the general form, but lacking innate grace.

In short, he may admire Lady Kildrum and find her beautiful and fascinating, but such attraction would only lead to heartache on his part. Moreover, his smallest inadvertent action might sully her reputation. Ewan could not bear it if his presence caused her harm.

And any of it could jeopardize his employment. Ewan had worked too hard and too long to do anything to endanger his career as a painter.

So to that end . . . no matter how alluring her appeal . . . he would be avoiding Lady Kildrum for the duration of his stay at Kilmeny.

That decided, Ewan pulled his dinner from the fire and slid his toast and cheese onto a plate, allowing it to cool for a moment. Sir Joshua was nearly done with his toast. Ewan reached for his tumbler of whisky, sipping appreciatively.

"Though on the topic of Lady Kildrum," Sir Joshua said, "I told her earlier today that you would be painting her portrait."

Ewan choked, coughing loudly for several seconds.

Sir Joshua finally had to resort to thumping his back.

"P-pardon?" Ewan gasped, wiping tears from his eyes.

Sir Joshua chuckled, as if something in Ewan's reaction had greatly delighted him.

"Portraits, lad. I'm officially asking you to paint a portrait of my niece."

Ewan blinked, trying to absorb this news. A portrait? *Him?*

Yet . . . hadn't he already envisioned himself painting her?

That being said, three issues presented themselves in quick succession.

One, why was one of the most celebrated painters in all of Britain asking *him* to paint a portrait of his niece?

Two, portraiture wasn't his personal strength. He preferred portraits that also doubled as something more monumental and allegorical in scope.

And three, painting a portrait was often an intimate experience, a time of lingering and looking deep into someone's soul.

Things this situation decidedly did *not* need.

Ewan feared for the state of his own heart were he to spend too much time in Lady Kildrum's presence.

Sir Joshua laughed again. "You look as if someone stepped on your grave, lad. I promise painting her will not be so bad."

Ewan managed to collect a few of his wits. "You are too kind, sir, to think to trust me with this. But I must ask, why are you yourself not painting her portrait?"

"Bah! I've painted Lady Kildrum at least half a dozen times. She needs something new, a different eye, as it were. And after everything she has suffered these past two years . . . well, a clean portrait and a fresh start is not a bad thing, now is it? And it will be good for you, too."

Ewan paused on Sir Joshua's words.

. . . after everything she has suffered these past two years . . .

He disliked the thought that someone as kind and effervescent as Lady Kildrum had suffered.

"I thank ye, sir," Ewan said, "but will this not encroach on the time I have to help yourself?"

"Nay, lad, I think we will be able to find a compromise. I already have plans for the ground and background figures that I'd like you to sketch in for me. And then I was planning on asking you to model for General Parmenion, as your physique will be well-matched to the composition I have in mind. But all this will leave you with time to work on your own projects. Doing a portrait of my niece will give you a chance to enhance your standing among the aristocracy and earn you a tidy sum, as well. If you are to succeed as a painter, you must learn to think in term of finances, not just your artistic heart."

Ewan swallowed.

Sir Joshua's reasoning was sound.

Ewan would be a fool to pass up an opportunity such as this.

He would just need to find a way to paint Lady Kildrum's soul on a canvas without losing his own heart in the process.

6

The weather has been *Excessively Fine*, as of late, has it not?" Lady Graham nodded her head, taking the cup of tea Violet offered.

"Indeed, it has, Mother." Lord Graham smiled before resting an elbow on the fireplace mantel.

Violet managed an echoing smile of her own.

Aster and Rose surreptitiously nudged one another, Aster rolling her eyes skyward out of Lady Graham's sight. Mr. Kerr scowled at his daughters, clearly biting back a reprimand.

Violet's smile turned strained. "Yes, my lady, the weather has been decidedly lovely. Hopefully, it will hold for your dinner party next week."

Violet's father sent his younger daughters one last stern look before turning back to Lady Graham. "We are looking forward to it, my lady."

Violet poured tea for Lord Graham, adding a dollop of milk and two sugars.

"Precisely as a I prefer my tea, Lady Kildrum." He accepted the proffered cup with a small bow. "Thank you."

The warmth in Lord Graham's eyes caused Rose to titter.

Their father cleared his throat.

Heavens.

Lord Graham and his mother had come calling this afternoon, which was in itself not exceptional.

However, this *was* their third such visit in the last ten days. Violet was not confused as to why they were calling more frequently. Lord Graham's interest in her was well known. Aster was of the opinion that Lord Graham, a baron with his own holdings in England, had relocated to their corner of Scotland for the express purpose of courting Violet.

"After all, with you as his wife, Lord G's son will become an earl," she had said earlier that week. "It's all rather calculating."

Violet, of course, was undecided as to what she should do. Even if Lord Graham *had* purchased the estate next door in an attempt to ingratiate himself, it did not therefore follow that such an action was reprehensible. It showed a certain sense of determination and perseverance.

Additionally, Violet admitted she found Lord Graham handsome, with his even features and strong jawline. Even the threads of early gray at his temples, despite the man being only thirty-two years of age, enhanced the soberness of his address.

And, to put the matter rather crassly, Lord Graham had the financial resources to pay off the Manna Loan. The cynical part of her worried that his wealth contributed to his apparent handsomeness. Were he poor, would she find him as attractive? Though, heaven knew, marrying for money was a time-honored tradition amongst the aristocracy.

Moreover, his mother would be helpful in sponsoring Aster and Rose through their presentation at Court next year.

All excellent reasons to consider Lord Graham as a suitor.

Decisions. Decisions.

Across from Violet, Aster stirred her tea, shooting wide-eyed looks, as if to say, *I cannot believe you are considering marrying this man.*

Rose nibbled on a biscuit.

Violet handed a cup to her father as silence descended on the drawing room. Her father's stern look was the opposite of her sisters'. His blue eyes said, *Encourage Lord Graham's attentions. He is the match your mother and I wished you to make.*

She knew that her father wished to see Violet comfortably settled, just as he and her mother had been comfortably settled. The problem, of course, was that her father equated 'comfortably settled' with 'happy.'

Violet was not sure the two were so closely allied.

Though, she supposed her parent's marriage *had* been a happy one, as far as aristocratic marriages went.

But it did not follow that Violet was guaranteed such felicity with Lord Graham.

As if reading her thoughts, Lord Graham snared her gaze, giving her a warm smile.

Lady Graham sat primly on the sofa, her black skirts pooling on the carpet. King George III had finally passed away in January, and as such, the kingdom was to observe six months of mourning for the monarch. In other words, black and gray clothing for all.

However, the new king—George IV, the former Prince Regent—had run out of patience with the never-ending bleak attire. After two months of mourning, he had proclaimed an end to it. Violet had happily shed her black garments for jewel colors.

Lady Graham, however, felt that the new king had acted in poor taste.

"A *Monarch* should be honored to the *Fullest Extent*," she had said more than once. Lady Graham had an excellent knack for capitalizing words as she spoke. For example, she was '*Excessively Fond* of teacakes,' and found the vicar's sermons to be '*Delightfully Instructional*.'

They all sipped their tea in quiet, a hush settling over the drawing room. Her sisters continued to make small facial expressions, silently voicing their opinions. Lady Graham was no favorite of theirs, which was unfortunate, as her ladyship could be helpful in sponsoring her sisters' debut at Court. Naturally, the twins were ecstatic over the idea of finally having a London Season. But a Season necessitated being presented at Court first.

The problem, of course, was that as an unmarried lady, Violet could not sponsor her sisters herself. And even if Violet *were* to marry and sponsor her sisters' presentation at Court, she did not understand the minutiae of London Society well enough to navigate the Season without the assistance of someone like Lady Graham. One wrong move on Violet's part could negatively impact her sisters' future.

This was why decisions were endlessly difficult, why she stalled again and again. Her choices always begat consequences, and how was she to consider and comprehend all the possibilities?

Lady Graham broke the silence first. "I understand you have a *Guest* in your home, Lady Kildrum."

"I gather you are referring to Mr. Campbell, my lady?" Violet replied.

"Is that the *Man's* name?"

No, his name is Ewan.

Thankfully, Violet managed to keep that bit to herself.

"I have found Mr. Campbell to be an agreeable addition," Aster said, her smile one step shy of combative.

Violet barely squelched a sigh.

"*Agreeable?*" Lady Graham's eyebrows shot to her hairline. "I hear the man is a giant. Mrs. Brown said he is a *Violent Highlander,* a veritable *Porphyrion.*"

Aster's jaw dropped. "I beg your pardon, my lady, but I cannot think that Mr. Campbell deliberately *chose* to become so large—"

"Aster!" Mr. Kerr reprimanded, silencing her.

Aster sat back with a huff.

Their father cleared his throat. "I am sure that Lady Aster merely wished to express her belief that Mr. Campbell, like us all, is one of God's sheep."

Violet was quite sure Aster had *not* meant that.

She sent her sister a quelling look. *Please behave.*

Lady Graham sniffed, taking a healthy swallow of tea.

As her mourning attire attested, Lady Graham considered herself the self-appointed adjudicator of societal propriety for the entire county.

So, naturally, her ladyship would not let the matter drop until she had said her piece.

"Harrumph," Lady Graham gave Aster a disapproving look, "Regardless, I assured Mrs. Brown that this *Highlander* could not be staying at Kilmeny Hall, as such behavior would not be *Suitable* for *Young Ladies.* 'Lady Kildrum would *Never* countenance such a *Man* in her household,'

I told her, 'Not after what happened the *Last Time*.' The *Outcome* of that debacle was only to be *Expected*."

Oh!

Violet managed to stifle her own pained inhalation. But it was a close thing.

Rose looked at her teacup.

Aster stiffened and looked away, jaw clenched in silent mutiny.

Even their father looked on in stony silence.

"Mother," Lord Graham said softly, reprimand in his voice. He shot Violet an apologetic look.

Lady Graham sipped her tea, confident in the righteous indignation of her words.

Violet stirred her tea. It was as useful as any activity when one's insides were roiling. She bit her inner cheek, fighting to keep her emotions in check.

In a sense, Lady Graham was correct. Dahlia's actions *had* tainted them all. Violet and her sisters had to be ever vigilant and guard against even a whiff of impropriety.

But the *outcome* Lady Graham referred to was Dahlia's death.

It was an appallingly cruel thing to say to her family. To view Dahlia's demise—the death of a fellow human being—as proper recompense for ignoring society's strictures.

Worse, Violet could not scream the defense of Dahlia currently clogging her throat. She could not jab a finger at Lady Graham and shout her furious outrage over the woman's vicious tongue. She could not recount the thousand ways she had loved her sister, the never-ending pain of losing her far too soon, the guilt that still rode Violet hard . . .

Mr. Kerr met Violet's roiling gaze, accurately reading her chaotic thoughts.

"As I said, Lady Graham," he said, shifting his gaze to her ladyship, "we are all God's sheep and should be afforded His Grace, whenever possible."

It was as close as her father would ever come to defending Dahlia, Violet supposed.

Lady Graham raised an eyebrow.

Violet took in a fortifying breath, though her tone remained slightly more acerbic than her late mother would approve. "I cannot speak to Mr. Campbell's origins, Lady Graham, aside from the fact that he hails from the western Highlands. Sir Joshua hired Mr. Campbell to assist him in finishing several canvases."

"Precisely," Lady Graham replied, "aside from being *Ludicrously Large*, Mr. Campbell is an *Artist*."

Her ladyship spat the word *artist* much as one might say *criminal* or *prostitute*—with suitable horror and moral outrage.

Aster opened her mouth.

Violet shot her a warning glance. *Don't you dare say a word. You've already done enough harm.*

The last thing the Kerr ladies needed was to give the local gossips more rope with which to hang them.

Violet turned back to their guest with a tight smile.

"Yes, Mr. Campbell is indeed an artist, my lady. I cannot think that his physical size is of import when discussing his artistic merit." Violet was proud she managed to keep her tone steady.

Something in her had risen to Mr. Campbell's aid.

Or perhaps it was more that she could not vocally defend Dahlia, and so she settled her energy on advocating for Mr. Campbell instead. It wasn't that she believed Mr. Campbell needed defending, per se. The man struck her as more than capable of protecting himself.

It was rather she *felt* his misalignment. That he was constantly judged for an exterior appearance that did not match his internal life. Others looked at his size and appearance and assumed him to be a threat. Had the man been diminutive and feminine in appearance, her neighbors' comments would likely be less caustic.

Mr. Campbell deserved to be judged on his actions and words, not simply his appearance. Those who took the time to speak with him would quickly learn that he was a kind and soft-hearted man.

Something of Violet's frustrated thoughts must have shown on her face, as Lord Graham jumped into the fray.

"Mother, Mr. Campbell is Lady Kildrum's guest and, as Lady Aster pointed out, can hardly be faulted for his size alone. I am sure she and Sir Joshua would not invite a Philistine into their home."

He shot Violet an apologetic smile, as if to say, *Please forgive my mother. You know she means well.*

Violet managed a wan smile in return.

This was why she considered a suit from Lord Graham.

He had always struck her as the quintessential English gentleman: pleasant, gracious, polite, and secure in his place in society. He was the sort of man who would appear a gentleman no matter how he was dressed.

Of course, Violet acknowledged that part of his appeal stemmed from his physical height. Lord Graham was at least three inches taller than herself. Violet had spent her life looking down on potential suitors. It was pleasant to have to look up, if only slightly, for a change.

She ignored the insidious voice that pointed out how much larger Red—Mr. Campbell!—was than Lord Graham, how small and safe she would feel beside him—

"I, for one, rather like Mr. Campbell," Aster said, unable to hold her tongue a second longer. "Uncle says he is one of the most talented young artists in the country at the moment." She lifted her chin, as if daring Lady Graham to nay-say her.

"Yes, it is a privilege to have him here," Rose continued, mouth prim. *Oh, dear.*

Lady Graham would surely read her sisters' defense of Mr. Campbell as being more evidence of the wayward temperament of all the Kerrs— the taint of baseness that had begun with Dahlia and had now spread to her sisters.

Violet could feel a further tirade brewing.

Lord Graham correctly read Violet's slightly panicked expression.

"We mustn't pester Lady Kildrum over her guests, Mother," he said, trying to steer the conversation away from less treacherous waters. "This Mr. Campbell is of little import."

"Harrumph," Lady Graham said again. "I suppose this Highlander's *Actual Appearance* is beside the point. Surely he is not *Lodged* under the same *Roof* as your sisters, Lady Kildrum?"

"In that, you are absolutely correct, Lady Graham," Mr. Kerr said, answering the question, though it had been aimed at Violet. "My brother and Mr. Campbell instantly recognized the impropriety of Mr. Campbell's presence and decamped to Old Kilmeny Castle two days ago. We have not seen them since."

"How sensible," Lord Graham looked at Violet again. "I am sure it was Lady Kildrum's virtuous example that led them to make the correct choice."

Lady Graham sniffed again. "Well, I suppose that is for the best. With such *Impressionable Young Ladies* in the house—" She shot Aster and Rose a repressive look. "—one cannot be too careful. Once *Scandal* has become attached to a family, it can be *Difficult to Root Out*. Therefore, greater *Precautions* must be taken, as I am sure you are aware, Lady Kildrum."

Lord Graham shot Violet another apologetic look. But he did not contradict his mother's words.

Violet smiled tightly and stirred her tea again.

This also illustrated why she was, as of yet, unsure about Lord Graham.

Despite mild protestations, his opinions gave every appearance of aligning with his mother's.

Yes, Dahlia's behavior had violated norms that Society held dear. And yes, the remaining Kerr sisters had paid—and were *still* paying—a price for them. But it did not follow that Dahlia's actions were entirely wrong or reprehensible. She had simply made a choice that had led to catastrophic consequences.

And yet, Violet was quite sure Lord Graham did not see the situation this way. Sometimes, he displayed a small-mindedness that belied the elegance of his appearance. A hint that though he was handsome on the exterior and kind when it was convenient, Lord Graham's interior thinking was not quite so comely.

Lord Graham assumed that Violet would follow in her own mother's footsteps, becoming the perfectly proper lady—relinquishing the management of her estates to tacksmen and stewards, and retreating to the seclusion of child bearing and running her household.

And even to *that*, on principle, Violet was not necessarily opposed.

It was just . . . every time she attempted to envision such a life . . . . Lord Graham smiling at Violet from the opposite end of the dining room table, Lord Graham lifting one of their children onto his knee, Lord Graham reading to her on a cold winter's evening as she stitched a pillow cover—

Ugh.

That was the problem.

She simply could *not* imagine it. She longed for a husband and family, and yet with Lord Graham . . . her brain sputtered and churned and offered up hazy scenes at best.

And how could she contemplate marrying a man without being able to foresee a future with him?

7

Violet was still pondering the conundrum of Lord Graham a day later as she pored over a letter from Mr. Lawyerly, urging her to address the looming issue of the Manna Loan. The debt was due in October, and "it behooves us to make decisions now, while we still have multiple options."

To paraphrase Mr. Lawyerly's words: *Please make a decision before the choice is made for you in the form of a debt collector appearing on the stoop of Kilmeny Hall.*

Violet sighed. *That* would certainly give Lady Graham something delicious to gossip over.

Did you hear the Scandalous News, *Mrs. Brown* . . .

Granted, Violet had finally resorted to flipping a coin to decide whether to plant oats or potatoes—potatoes had won.

That strategy seemed less useful when addressing the Manna Loan. After all, it was a multi-faceted problem that could not be reduced to a simple heads-or-tails binary.

What to do?

The sound of raised voices drifted through the closed door of her study.

The twins were arguing yet again, this time debating the more terrifying fiend—Dr. Frankenstein's monster or Lord Ruthven from *The Vampyre*. Initially, they both agreed that Lord Ruthven was the more chilling villain.

But then Aster had postulated that perhaps such delicious foreboding could turn Lord Ruthven into a potential book beau.

Rose, of course, countered that no one would want a vampire for a lover. The very idea was absurd.

Given how their voices carried throughout the house, Aster was not relenting her point of view.

Their father periodically emerged from his study to order the twins to *cease this racket!* Mr. Kerr was deep into writing a new treatise on the importance of showing patience and long-suffering in trials. His daughters' inability to be silent was an impediment to this.

Violet had yet to point out the hypocrisy to him.

The entire scene continued to play beyond her study door—

"Aster, there is *nothing* romantic about a lover drinking blood from your vein. It's vilely horrific!"

"You are fixating on the wrong point, Rose. Giving your very life's blood to sustain an admirer is the ultimate act of love—"

"Girls! *Silence!*" Their father roared. "Such talk is vulgar in the extreme! I cannot concentrate!"

Violet realized she simply could not be in the house another moment. She had to seek some fresh air.

Or at a minimum, air that was less . . . shouty.

And less . . . vampirey.

Fifteen minutes later, Violet slipped out the library door and down the steps to the rear terrace.

Her feet took her across the flagstones, through the walled garden, out a door in the garden wall, and up the rise that protected Kilmeny Hall from the endless ocean winds.

As she crested the top of the knoll, the North Sea appeared.

She paused, savoring the panorama, the brisk wind tugging at her bonnet and cloak.

From her earliest memories, she had adored this view. The vastness of the ocean. The red sandstone cliffs extending up and down the coast. The green sweep of fields and gorse. This landscape was a soothing calm on a sunny summer's day and a glorious terror in the throes of a January storm.

Today was somewhere between those two extremes.

Clouds raced across the sky, painting the world in dappled light. Wind rippled the wide expanse of the North Sea and pelted her skin, billowing her cloak behind her.

The endless blue horizon was broken only by the crenelated tower of Old Kilmeny Castle, perched atop the cliff's edge. The castle was a lonesome sight, a solitary, boxy tower within a curtain wall that had disintegrated to dirt in more than one place. Only the central keep remained tall and stalwart. Surely there had been a time, perhaps five hundred years ago, when the castle had been a thriving beacon of civilization and culture.

Now, it was a plaintive reminder of a long-forgotten past.

Violet started down the path toward the castle, clutching her cloak, keeping the wool closed around her, the cool wind racing over her bare hands. Much to her mother's despair, Violet had never really taken to gloves. Something about the leather on her skin always rendered her antsy. Consequently, she only wore gloves when propriety absolutely insisted upon it.

Or, in other words, when she might encounter someone gossipy.

Fortunately, windswept coastlines were usually gossipmonger-free. The wind sucked the air from her lungs, but it offered privacy.

As a child, Old Kilmeny had been her escape when they visited Scotland each autumn. The romantic ancient castle where she and Dahlia would play knights and ladies. She could still see Dahlia racing through the ancient keep in one of the crumpled, old-fashioned gowns they found in a trunk in the attic, her younger sister pointing and ordering Violet about.

Dahlia insisted on being the princess, the lady of the keep, the one to be protected and adored by the gallant knight.

Violet was always the knight.

In retrospect, Violet wasn't sure why she had agreed to be the knight every time.

Perhaps that was simply the power of Dahlia's charisma. Her sister's effortless ability to love people and cause others to love her wholly in return.

Violet bit her lip, shaking her head and forcing back the sudden emotion clogging her throat.

Even two years on, thoughts of Dahlia were an endless wound, never healed and easily disturbed. The effects of Dahlia's choices—of Violet's guilt and involvement in those choices—reverberated in a seemingly endless loop, echoing through daily life at Kilmeny Hall.

The vicious sting of Lady Graham's words from the afternoon before reared up.

The outcome of that debacle was only to be expected.

Violet clenched her teeth.

Enough!

Surely there were much safer mental paths for her to trod.

Such as . . . why hadn't *she* ever been the lady of the castle? Why had the role always gone to Dahlia?

Violet was destined for the part from birth. And yet, she had always been the guardian.

The Knight Protector.

It was odd, now that she pondered it.

Was this why she struggled to sell on the tack to pay off the Manna Loan? The Knight Protector in her felt the need to personally oversee the tenants—all those hundreds of people—who lived within the enormous tack? To watch over them and ensure that they were treated with fairness?

Granted, she had no idea *how* to go about managing the vast lands. The very thought threatened to overwhelm her. Surely she could hire stewards, but that meant even more meetings and further decisions about oats versus potatoes. And certainly at some point, a coin toss would reveal its weaknesses as a decision strategy.

Perhaps it *would* be kinder to sell the tack to a tacksman more capable and experienced than herself.

The castle loomed as she drew closer. Gorse grew tall and dense nearer the ocean, going from manageable shrub-size to towering tree-like thickets. Its golden-yellow flowers sent a shock of color through the landscape. It was as if the harsher the conditions, the more the bush thrived.

Violet was sure there was a profound life's lesson in this. Her brain was simply too frayed to process it at the moment.

The castle wasn't her destination today. She didn't wish to intrude on her uncle and Mr. Campbell.

Besides, her wayward thoughts about the Highlander were better contained if she starved them of fresh nourishment.

Instead, she skirted the castle and followed a well-worn path that wound near the cliff's edge. Here, the cliffs zigzagged along the coast, a dizzying blend of exuberant green grass and reddish stone, all dotted with white seabirds. The cacophony of their calls blended into the roar of waves crashing below.

Violet picked her way along the trail, stepping over stones and hopping the occasional boggy patch. The sun peeked out from the racing clouds, skittering light and shadow across the ocean.

Tilting her head upwards, she let the sun wash her face.

She breathed deeply, the fresh air and soothing sounds cleansing the cobwebs in her lungs and mind.

This was what her day had lacked. This freedom, the fresh air, sunlight upon her cheeks—

Ahhhhhhhck!

Violet tripped over something on the path.

The next few moments moved through time like a spoon through honey—slow, sticky, and glossed with a bizarre sort of golden haze.

Her arms flailed, akimbo, skirts tangling her legs. Her weight pitched forward, and she fell, hand smacking against something solid before diving head first toward a large boulder.

But a screech of alarm had barely passed her lips when a steely arm wrapped around her waist, pulling her upright as easily as one might snatch a rag doll.

The world abruptly straightened.

Violet's heart beat a frantic tempo in her chest, her hands pressed to her sternum, as if to verify that she was, indeed, still whole.

She was unharmed.

She had not dashed her brains upon the rock, after all.

Her mind raced, frantic to puzzle out the last few seconds.

Before falling, she had caught a flash of something beside her feet.

The image came back to her now—Mr. Campbell seated on the leeward side of the large stone outcropping, his body in partial shadow, the man's hulking form merging with that of the rock.

His foot, unfortunately, jutted out, partially blocking the path.

Violet, with her head upward, soaking in the fleeting sun, had tripped over his boot.

Mr. Campbell had somehow caught her before she hit the ground.

Worse, had she struck him as she fell? The sting of her hand insisted she had.

She swallowed, her relief rapidly morphing into awareness. All five of her senses flared to life at once.

The harsh tang of her breathing.

The flush of blood in her veins.

The scent of soap and wool.

The sight of a strong hand pressing against her stomach, a muscled arm wrapped around her waist.

The murmur of Mr. Campbell's voice near her ear.

"Are ye hurt, lass?"

Violet gasped at the sound.

It was partially the fizz of his western isles' accent—that trace of Gaelic in his vowels, the lingering hiss at the end of *lass*.

But it was more than that.

She *felt* his words, a puff against the shell of her ear, a rumble of sensation chasing up her spine.

Heavens, she was practically enveloped by him, held against his chest. He was so *deliciously* large. The heat of his body surrounded her, scalding from hip bone to shoulder blade.

How had he managed this?!

He had been sitting on the *ground*, of that her flash of memory was sure.

In the breath of time after she tripped, the man had somehow leapt to his feet, absorbed a blow from her own hand, and caught her—with one arm, no less!—before she cracked her head.

It was an astonishing feat of reflexes and strength.

But that had been his *forte*, had it not? As the Red Renegade, the prizefighter in a ring . . . an enormous brute of a man with cat-like quickness.

Such astonishing strength lay coiled in his body. A promise of the immense damage he could inflict should he choose.

I willnae hurt ye.

His words from long ago fluttered through her mind. A reminder of the dichotomy of him.

"Are ye hurt?" he repeated, some urgency in his voice. "Ye took quite the tumble."

"I am whole, thanks you." She stepped forward. He instantly released her.

The entire event had only taken seconds to occur, and yet, Violet's skin burned where he had touched her. She was quite sure she would feel the imprint of his hands for days.

She turned to face him.

That might have been a mistake.

Violet feared she had avoided tumbling head first into one peril, a boulder, only to be faced with a greater one—*him*.

He loomed over her.

The sensation was still novel.

Given her own height, Violet had rarely, if ever, experienced *looming*.

She found she rather liked the feeling. The act of having to look up, up, up to a man's face.

He was in a great kilt and appeared for all the world like a medieval laird, an ancient inhabitant of the castle itself. The earthy russet-and-gray tartan cloth wrapped around his hips and upper body, emphasizing the breadth and depth of his enormous chest. A shorter dark gray coat sat underneath the kilt, a white neckcloth quickly tied at his throat.

All he needed was a broad sword and a gigantic horse.

She swallowed and lifted her head a fraction higher, meeting his eyes. *Oh!*

She had not noticed his eye color before now. They were an astonishing hazel—the colors of autumn . . . amber and green and brown.

Her heart continued to thump like a mad beast in her chest. This time, she was quite sure it was *not* from startled fright.

He was simply so . . . *big.* It was ludicrous to even think it, as of course the man was a giant. Surely he tired of people harping upon his size, as if that were the only dimension of his existence worth comment.

But he *was* a mammoth of a man.

More to the point, at this very moment, head tilted back to look him in the eye, she marveled at feeling small and dainty for once. He could engulf her in that chest of his, wrap his arms around her and cocoon her against him, nearly surrounding her.

Her blood fizzed and popped at the thought. How marvelous would that be—

Violet forced herself to take in a slow breath.

Do not fantasize about the attractive painter.

You are a countess. Countesses do not moon over low-born artists.

No matter how tempting.

"Are you all right, Mr. Campbell?" she asked. "I fear I struck you on my way down—"

"Me?!" Mr. Campbell's autumnal eyes widened as if astounded. "Hurt by a blow from a wee thing like yourself?"

Violet was also quite sure this would mark the first and *last* time anyone referred to her as *wee.*

"Well, my hand continues to smart," she said, shaking said hand, "and so I can only assume it incurred a similar damage to yourself—"

"Dash it, lass! My muckle foot nearly sent ye tumbling to your death, and ye're asking after *my* health? I'm only grateful I was able tae catch ye in time—"

"Oh, heavens!" Violet looked around them, *finally* noticing the painting accoutrements and small canvas tossed aside as he had lurched to save her. "Not only did I strike you, I fear I have ruined your work."

She bent to pick up the scattered paintbrush and painter's palette, now resting in the grass, handing them to him.

"It was only a trifle, my lady. No harm done." He lifted up the canvas, tilting it face down and away from her view. Violet only caught the briefest glimpse of it.

She rather desperately wanted to see more.

Which, in all truth, was a problem. Because part of her feared that she wanted far more than to casually view the man's painting.

She wanted to study every canvas he painted, ask questions about line and color, and see if that connection she had felt all those years ago was real.

Such thoughts will only lead to heartache.

Remember you have two younger sisters who are currently relying on you maintaining an impeccable reputation.

And yet, she could not help asking, "May I see it?" She motioned toward the canvas in his hand.

He stilled, as if her question gave him pause. "I . . . uh . . ."

Was he . . . bashful?

And why did she find that fact adorable?

"I promise to be kind," she said.

"Kind?" He squinted at her. "Och, I dinnae doubt that your ladyship will be kind." He paused. "But will ye be *honest?*"

"Honest? About the painting?"

"Aye." He shifted the canvas. "I've been exploring an idea your uncle had suggested, and I wouldnae mind an opinion. But it must be an honest one."

"I can *try* to be honest."

He tapped his chin, as if thinking. "I seem tae recall a woman—suspiciously like yourself, I must say—not three days ago declaring she was an acolyte of truth-telling."

Violet paused, shading her eyes to look up at the man.

Was he . . . ?

Was he subtly . . . *teasing* her?

His face remained inscrutable as he continued, "I quite liked that statement, I must say . . . the truth-telling. As an artist, I only improve my craft when others provide criticism. I dinnae ken to being offered platitudes like a fruit-trimmed Easter bonnet."

"Fruit-trimmed Easter bonnet?!" she laughed.

"Well, aye!" He straightened to his full height. "Ye ken what I mean. Some lass arrives at Easter Sunday services in the most ridiculous bonnet imaginable—lemons and . . . whatever citrus—around the brim of her bonnet." He made a circling motion with his hand around his head, as if to illustrate his point. "She looks absurd, but no kind soul takes pity and tells her this. Instead, her friends compliment her *stunning* bonnet, while whispering behind her back that it is a travesty of fashion—"

"Something tells me there is a story here."

"Ye dinnae wish tae hear it, lass." He shook his head.

"No, you are convincing me that I need to hear the tale in its entirety."

"Nae, 'tis not a tale for the faint of heart. Ye heard me mention the citrus, did ye not?" He held up his hand and shuddered, eyes shutting as if in pain of the memory.

Violet giggled.

Giggled?!

When was the last time she had giggled about . . . *anything*?

Countesses *suo jure* did not giggle. They were to look bemused, tolerant, and provide fond condescension when called upon.

And so, right now, giggling felt . . . glorious. An effervescent lightness in her blood that made her want to spread her arms wide and twirl.

She settled for glancing down at the painting still in his hand. "Have you painted lemons and oranges then? A cathartic purging of events that haunt your nightmares?"

Now *she* was teasing.

His answering grin said he did not mind.

He hesitated before saying, "Ye'll have tae decide that for yerself, I suppose."

He handed her the painting with a shrug, as if it were a mere trifle.

But the paint leaping off the canvas was anything but that.

No citrus or bonnets.

Instead, the coastline continued on the canvas, the same mix of green and white weaving amongst the reddish cliffs. But the scene was slightly different than the one before her eyes, a dream-like sketching of form and light.

In his image, the cliffs descended to a golden beach. A small crofter's cottage nestled into the security of the green hills at the opposite end of the beach. Not a more modern, white-washed house with twin chimneys on each end.

No, the building in the painting was a blackhouse, the bare stone medieval houses she knew to be plentiful in the western isles. The building's low stone walls rose to a thatched roof with no chimney, despite the haze of smoke coming from the roof line.

A young woman in traditional Highland dress—an earasaid of earth-toned tartan wrapped around her shoulders and head—walked toward the house, basket balanced on her hip.

Blackhouses were said to be primitive places. Dwellings where live-stock lived alongside their masters, and the fire place was merely a ring of stones in the center of the room, no chimney to draw the smoke. Those unfortunates who yet lived in such homes were said to be at the very edge of existence.

But something in the blue-green of the ocean, in how the curve of the woman's body mimicked the curve of the hill surrounding the cot-tage—the light raking from left to right—spoke of comfort.

Violet had lived with Sir Joshua long enough to recognize how art could take a preconceived notion and turn it topsy-turvy. That in such hands, even the most unsophisticated of dwellings could speak of home.

Worse, she found herself craving to understand everything about the painting. What had he been thinking as he painted it? Why had he chosen these colors? This scene?

"Ye're taking a wee while to formulate an opinion, my lady." Mr. Campbell stared down at her, expression still unreadable. "Should I have painted citrus in the end?"

"Quite the contrary." She handed the canvas back to him, steadying her breathing. "I was merely surprised at how much you have managed to convey with a few brush strokes defining a house and a woman."

He stilled, as if unsure how to take her words. "You're going tae have to explain yourself a wee bit more."

She paused, gathering her scattered thoughts. "The forms feel almost . . . *liquid*, I guess is how Uncle would describe it. As if I am seeing more than is actually there."

"Aye." His expression relaxed, excitement seeping in. "I have been trying out a different technique, painting outdoors tae better capture the landscape. Most painters work indoors and that has its merits, tae be certain. But there is something about the ephemera of color and the play of light that is more immediate when painted directly from nature. I've been speaking with Sir Joshua about it, how to incorporate it more."

Oh.

As he spoke, Mr. Campbell's eyes lit with fire and a humming enthusiasm filled his tone.

It was not unlike watching gaslights flare to life, dark one moment, and then brimming with dancing energy the next.

Or, perhaps a more apt analogy, akin to how pigment and brush strokes took raw material and created image and emotion and meaning.

It was now painted across Mr. Campbell's handsome face.

"It is remarkable." The truth slipped from her lips without her consciously thinking it.

She wasn't sure if the descriptor referred to him or to his work. Perhaps a bit of both.

Fortunately, Mr. Campbell lacked artifice or vanity and took her words at face value.

"I am right pleased to hear it, Lady Kildrum. The paint has been fighting me a wee bit this afternoon." He pointed to an area where the yellow gorse met the edge of the sandstone cliffs. "When I work outdoors, I paint *alla prima*—"

"*Alla prima?*"

"Aye, 'tis a painterly technique. Typically, ye layer in the paint a wee bit at a time. But when working *alla prima*, ye do it all at once, not waiting for paint to dry properly between layers. If you're no' careful, the colors can get a wee bitty garbled, not to mention that the wind and fresh air causes the paint to dry unevenly. So it can be a challenge."

"Your technique is astonishing . . ." Violet paused, questioning the wisdom of voicing her thoughts. But they had begun by telling truths all those years before in her carriage. It seemed a shame to stop now. "But that isn't what I was referring to earlier. I was pondering how your light and form create meaning. How you construct the soul of the painting, as it were. Everything tells me that this place, this house. . ." She pointed to the canvas. "This *woman* . . . they are important to you somehow."

She lifted her gaze to his at her last words.

The sun blazed through the racing clouds right at that moment, bathing him in sunlight. And so she clearly saw the way he froze, an almost panicked sort of look flashing across his face before he ruthlessly suppressed it.

The entire event should *not* have been fascinating.

It should *not* have sent Violet's mind to puzzling.

And yet . . .

What happened to you? Who is the mysterious woman? she wondered. *What is your story?*

"How do ye reckon that, my lady?" he finally asked. "Why do you think there is hidden meaning here?"

Mmmm.

Why *did* she think it to be so?

She pondered, tucking a wayward strand of hair behind her ear. Birds called over the ocean, flying upward toward the cheery sun now dancing across the ocean.

Her words had been more feeling than conscious thought. And wasn't that nearly the very definition of art?

But as she looked at it more closely, she realized that it wasn't entirely true.

"All the lines lead to the house and the woman." She pointed at the canvas. "The horizon of the ocean, the break of the cliffs, the row of gorse just there . . . it's as if everything in the painting is pointing inward, a large arrow saying, 'Here! Pay attention to this place.'"

Silence greeted her words. Mr. Campbell stared at the painting for a moment before raising his eyes back to hers.

"That is . . . observant of you, my lady. I do not suppose I set out to find meaning when I began this. I merely wished to capture the silver-gold of the sun on the ocean and the play of light across the cliffs."

She nodded. "Sometimes meaning happens anyway. Even when we least expect it."

His eyes locked with hers for a heartbeat. And then two.

Violet felt spellbound, tangled in the web of their words, in the breadth of what was left unsaid.

Much to her horror, she realized she had been drawn into the conversation, bit by tiny bit. But then, this was how things had happened all those years ago when they first met.

Mr. Ewan Campbell with his calming deep voice and measured replies was effortless to converse with. The man had made her *giggle*, for heaven's sake!

How simple it would be to remain here. To continue their discussion, to plumb his thoughts and find that aching similarity of thought she suspected they shared—

No.

She could not permit it.

Was this the curse of the Kerr women? To continually want that which was, for lack of a better word, forbidden? Her fascination with the man *had* to end now, before her emotions traveled any further down destructive paths.

Too much rode on Violet's behavior. No whiff of scandal could be attached to her name. Dahlia's actions had already caused so much damage. Anything more, and Aster and Rose would have no chance at marrying within their own class.

Much as it pained Violet to agree with Lady Graham, the lady had a point. She did need to take greater precautions to protect her reputation.

To that end, Violet took two steps back, placing much needed distance between them.

"I thank you for letting me interrupt your painting."

"'Twas nothing, my lady. Thank ye for your kind words."

Their gazes tangled, his eyes holding a soft sadness, a sort of ache . . . as if he had heard her thoughts and understood her reasons for leaving so quickly, but like her, regretted what could never be.

She nodded her head and turned to leave.

Just walk away, Violet. Do not say anything more.

But her mouth refused to listen. She took only three steps forward before turning around again. He had not moved from his position. Had he been watching her leave?

"Have you considered using the greenhouse?" she asked.

"Pardon? Greenhouse?"

"There is a greenhouse on the leeward side of the castle tucked into the gorse. You have to walk around the castle to see it." She pointed back toward Old Kilmeny. "My late mother had it built as she enjoyed cultivating camellia flowers, and the greenhouse receives excellent light. But the building hasn't been used in several years."

A long pause. "Are ye encouraging me to cultivate citrus in earnest, my lady? Face my traumatic memories head on?"

Another giggle threatened to break through.

"Only if the fancy strikes you, Mr. Campbell." Violet was unable to stop a smile. "The greenhouse has beautiful views over the ocean and receives ample daylight. But the building is also quite damp, which might prevent the elements from drying your paint so quickly." Violet could feel the heat rising in her cheeks under his intense scrutiny. "You may wish to attempt painting there."

"No citrus, then?"

"No citrus."

He heaved a put-upon sigh. "I suppose I shall simply have to make do without." He grinned abruptly, confirming his teasing tone.

Drat the man! He was entirely too likable for her peace of mind.

He bowed, a small, precise motion. "Thank ye, my lady."

She nodded her head once more and turned on her heel.

Though her pace was measured and calm, most of her felt as if she were fleeing temptation as fast as her feet could carry her.

8

For Ewan, the next few days flew past in a blur of creative activity.

He began by helping Sir Joshua set up his studio in the great hall of the castle. Lady Kildrum's grandmother had indeed enlarged the windows, letting in an astounding amount of sunlight. Sir Joshua had beamed for days after observing the beautiful lighting conditions.

A small army of servants descended, moving furniture and carting stacks of canvases from Sir Joshua's studio in Kilmeny Hall. Now all the paintings—in various stages of completion—rested in the great hall, leaning against the old stone walls. A sheer drapery had been hung over the south-facing window, allowing Sir Joshua to diffuse the light, if necessary.

Each morning, Ewan would assist Sir Joshua in whatever needed doing on the man's large canvas, whether that was mixing pigments, filling in background elements, or modeling for various figures as the older painter sketched.

Though the great hall was large enough to accommodate both men, Ewan preferred to have his own studio. His enormous body took up more than its fair share of space, and he loathed feeling like an imposition. Moreover, he needed the freedom to experiment without eyes peering over his shoulder.

The greenhouse, Ewan discovered, was simply . . . brilliant. Despite Lady Kildrum's words, he had been expecting a rather ancient building with inadequate panes of glass.

Instead, he found a beautiful, modern structure with wide, arched windows on two sides and a bank of skylights. Not only was it light-filled and secluded, the air inside was somewhat damp. This humidity would slow the drying of his oil paints, allowing him to work the paint *alla prima* even longer.

It only took him a couple hours to move his canvases to the greenhouse and hang panels of gauze over the windows to diffuse the light, as needed. From there, he was free to paint in well-lit solitude.

Over the next few days, Ewan managed to avoid thinking overly much about Lady Kildrum.

Well . . . more or less.

Every time the sun glowed over the ocean, the green-blue of her eyes popped into his mind.

And each time he walked into his glasshouse studio, he mentally thanked her for the perceptive suggestion. It had been kind and thoughtful.

But then . . . didn't those two words sum up Lady Kildrum?

He had accidentally tripped her, nearly sending her tumbling headlong into a stone outcropping. Given this, he would have expected her to lash out in fright and anger, berating him for his clumsiness.

But not Lady Kildrum. Instead, she had shown concern for *him*. Concern that she—a countess, no less!—might have inadvertently hurt him as she fell.

Was that why he had shown her the painting of Mhairi and the blackhouse? It was unlike him to share something so intensely private.

Yet, Lady Kildrum made him feel safe. Because he recognized the compassion within her. That she would be gentle with what the painting revealed.

And she *had* been thoughtful, taking time to formulate her clever observations, laying her words with kindness.

Though, he supposed, the word *kind* was rather inadequate. Kindness wove through Lady Kildrum's actions the way the sun warmed the earth—effortless and yet vital to those who received it.

In his mind, she moved through the air in glittering strands of red and gold, gilding everything she touched.

He didn't *want* to admire her more and more. Admiration and infatuation were useless emotions in this situation and would only lead to heartache for himself.

And yet . . .

Just the memory of catching her atop the cliff, of pulling her against him, sent a wash of awareness through his blood and settled a yearning tightness in his chest.

She had been a lush armful—tall and curved and molding into his arms as if she belonged. Days on, his body still burned from the touch of her waist, the soft give of her hips branded into his hands.

She was the sort of woman he would never worry about breaking. A lady who would always meet him head on.

He longed to know her better. To have the right to query her opinion whenever he wished, to gather all the sweet goodness of her into his arms—

He took in a long, stuttering breath.

So . . . perhaps he wasn't doing as well as he supposed.

Nothing would come of his thoughts of her.

Nothing.

He *knew* this.

He had to quash every ounce of attraction he felt for her.

How piteous would it be to allow this fascination to deepen?

He was the son of a Highland crofter. A nobody. So monumentally below Lady Kildrum's station in life as to be a nonentity . . . a grain of sand to her palace.

At best, such infatuation would render him miserable and ridiculous, pathetically longing after a woman so monumentally above him socially.

At worst, his attention could taint Lady Kildrum's reputation and, in turn, destroy his prospects as a painter.

They were star-crossed lovers, in truth. Any association between them could only end in embarrassment, scandal, or ruin. Likely a toxic mix of all three.

He ignored the voice that whispered he was a painter, and a damn fine one at that.

That his star was rising.

That he fully intended to become a Somebody.

There were precious few professions in Britain that could elevate a man's status from lowly provincial to dinner guest of the King.

One was being a celebrated artist.

The other?

Prizefighting.

The irony was not lost on Ewan.

Champion boxers were feted in the broadsheets and extolled in *Boxiana*. But Ewan had never been interested in acquiring fame through his fists. The celebrity of prizefighting was a hollow thing, unable to mitigate the ugliness of the sport.

In the end, Ewan had been glad to eschew his Red Renegade moniker and lose himself in painting. The beauty of art justified the commitment and struggle it commanded.

His overarching goal remained the same—to become a man like Sir Joshua, knighted for his substantial contribution to art. An artist who would be remembered long after his death for the beauty and meaning he had given to the world.

But Ewan recognized *that* eventuality was decades off. And even then, such men did not court and marry women from the highest reaches of the *ton*. They were merely allowed to mingle with them.

He would not make a fool of himself, haring after Lady Kildrum like some gauche, *glaikit* oaf.

His solution, therefore, was to avoid her ladyship as much as possible. He would only see her during their portrait sessions together which were set to begin next week. Eventually his fascination would die, and she would fade into the background of his thoughts.

Eight days after Ewan's arrival, a small stack of letters was waiting for him in the great hall, having been brought down from Kilmeny Hall. Several were from clients and fellow artists.

But three stood out.

There was a letter from Alex, responding to concerns over Kieran. Kieran had been dismissed from his post. Fortunately, Alex had convinced Kieran to stay with him for the time being, if only to monitor his whisky consumption.

Alex wrote:

> *Kieran refuses to talk with me about Jamie. I still sense that there is something more to this story that I don't understand. It has all set me to wondering if someone else might know the particulars. And if so, would they tell me in order that I might help our friend?*

Ewan winced at the question. Alex, being the good doctor, was clearly probing for information.

Ewan *did* know, of course. He knew the source, the reason for the depth of Kieran's pain.

But Ewan had to ask his own question—if Alex *did* know, could he assist Kieran?

Ewan pondered it for a moment and then rejected the idea.

There was nothing positive to be gained by spilling Kieran's secrets.

The damage to Kieran's psyche if Ewan betrayed his trust would be far worse than any additional help the information would lend Alex.

More to the point, in the end, it wasn't Ewan's secret to tell.

He would say nothing to Alex.

Even so, Ewan suffered in his silence. He *hated* being so far from Kieran and unable to do anything to help.

A quick glance through the remaining letters confirmed that Kieran had not written.

Ewan would write both Alex and Kieran immediately.

In other developments, Andrew had met with the magistrate in Aberdeen.

He wrote:

The magistrate was excessively polite and conciliatory. His questions were direct and straight-forward. Clearly, the government does not wish to blow this entire affair out of proportion. They are merely acting rationally upon information they have received. I answered all his questions to the best of my knowledge, making it clear that we had assumed everyone aboard ship was lost based on our experiences. I also noted that Rafe had seen Captain Cuthie last autumn in Aberdeen.

During our discussion, the magistrate let slip a vital piece of information. He mentioned that he had been able to independently confirm that at least one other member of The Minerva (aside from ourselves and Cuthie) had survived. When I pressed him to know who, the magistrate insisted the information is confidential, as he is still gathering testimony.

Obviously, this bit of news troubles me greatly. I immediately notified my Runner in Aberdeen. He thinks he might be able to unearth an address for this survivor from the magistrate's office. If he does so, Rafe and myself are planning to call upon this other survivor and knock loose what information we can. Specifically, I want to know who is posting these notices in the newspapers and why. It might be a foolish hope to think we could learn more about Jamie's death, as well, but it's hard to dismiss the idea either.

We were hoping we could persuade you to join us, if and when we have an address for this other survivor, as you are always a help in such situations. I pray Sir Joshua will be willing to spare you. Also, I've been in contact with Alex regarding Kieran, and we've decided not to tell him about this development, for obvious reasons . . .

Ewan nodded. Of course, he would accompany his friends. He would speak with Sir Joshua about it over dinner.

And, yes, they were wise to keep the information from Kieran. Their friend did not need more hope and worry poured onto the smoldering fire of his grief.

Ewan set Andrew's letter aside and picked up the final letter.

It was . . . unexpected.

I must apologize for my tardy reply. I found your inquiry buried in my predecessor's correspondence. Unfortunately, I do not have favorable news to impart. I do not, currently, have a parishioner by the name of Mhairi McDoughal. There was a family by the name of McDoughal in the area years ago, I am told. I do not know if this is the same family to which you refer. That said, I will pass along this request to others in the diocese, as I am a relative newcomer here . . .

Ewan took in a deep, slow breath.

And then he reread the words, more slowly this time.

It confirmed nothing. Mhairi was simply no longer living in that parish. She had likely moved away.

She could still be alive.

Of course, even if she lived . . . what did it signify? She had made her position agonizingly clear all those years ago—

He was not wanted.

Ye need to stay gone, Ewan. I dinnae ken tae see ye again.

What did he hope to gain by trying to contact her? Anger her further? Add more disruption and tension to her already difficult life?

He snapped the letter, clenching his jaw, swallowing back the emotion thick in his throat.

Because he knew the answer:

Nothing.

Even if she yet lived, it would gain him *nothing*.

"WE HAVE BOTH been invited to dine with Lord Graham and his mother, Lady Graham, tomorrow evening," Sir Joshua announced over dinner.

They were dining alone in the great hall, as usual. Sir Joshua had not employed a cook. Dinner often was whatever Ewan and Sir Joshua could warm over a fire (usually cheddar and toast). Occasionally, the cook in Kilmeny Hall sent down some braised lamb or roasted beef. Thankfully, tonight was one of those evenings.

Ewan chewed his roast beef. Sir Joshua fixed him with his blue gaze . . . the same aqua-blue as Lady Kildrum's eyes, Ewan noted. Which also happened, at the moment, to match the vivid blue silk of Sir Joshua's waistcoat.

"Lord Graham?" Ewan asked.

"Yes, he is the nearest neighbor to Kilmeny Hall—an English lord who purchased the adjoining estate a few years ago." Sir Joshua cut into his slice of beef with a decisive motion. "Lord Graham thinks to make himself cozy with our Violet."

Our Violet.

Heaven help him. Ewan liked the sound of that.

"Violet hasn't shown excessive interest, but it was her mother's wish that she and Lord Graham marry," Sir Joshua continued with a shrug. "My niece will turn twenty and six in October. My brother feels it is high-time she chose a husband. The trick, of course, is finding the proper gentleman."

Ewan nodded, the roast beef sticking in his abruptly dry throat.

Of course.

This was the state of her life.

He was an *eejit* to be astonished that Lady Kildrum had suitors. She must be one of the most sought-after ladies in all of Britain. It therefore followed that men courted her.

Ewan felt, yet again, the embarrassment of his unwelcome attachment to Lady Kildrum.

Yes, she had taken pity on him nearly eight years before and shown him remarkable kindness when he needed it most.

Yes, he admired her intensely and sensed that they viewed the world through a similar lens.

Yes, she was clever and kind and stunningly beautiful, and a man would have to be dead to not wish to hold her in his arms.

But it was all entirely one-sided.

She would marry elsewhere. Someone of her class, as well she should.

He would not allow his wayward emotions to paint him a fool. Or worse, impede him from achieving his goals.

Ewan mentally took her glittering strands of red and gold and forcibly cast them from his mind.

Sir Joshua continued on, "Between you and me, Violet needs to look farther afield than Lord Graham. The man is a bit arse-headed. Violet could do better."

"Ah." Ewan dabbed at his mouth with his napkin. "And why should an English lord, even an arse-headed one, invite a man such as myself to dine with him?"

"Never doubt yourself, my boy." Sir Joshua pointed his fork at Ewan. "You are here as my assistant and a skilled painter in your own right. 'Tis only natural that you should be invited."

Ewan raised a skeptical eyebrow.

Sir Joshua met his gaze and then shrugged.

"It could also reflect the fact that another family who was to attend had to cancel due to poor health. I imagine Lady Graham is keen to even numbers at her dinner table and satisfy her ladyship's curiosity regarding yourself," he acknowledged. "Still . . . do not doubt yourself or your right to dine with the greatest of the greats. That's the secret to long-lasting success. Act like you belong, and soon, you shall."

Ewan nodded his head, chewing on a bite of meat.

Act like you belong and soon, you shall.

It was actually sound advice.

Ewan had attended formal dinner parties before. Andrew would never allow Ewan to sit out of such events, no matter how Ewan pleaded. Instead, his friend had (rightly) pointed out that Ewan needed to feel at ease mingling with those of all walks of life. And Andrew's wife, Lady Hadley, had been kind enough to tutor Ewan further on social niceties last summer.

Sir Joshua echoed the thought. "It will be a good opportunity for you to mingle in Polite Society, such as it is around here. Moreover, you are to start Lady Kildrum's portrait the day after next, so this will also be a chance to witness my niece in her typical *milieu* and develop ideas for your session. I trust you have been making some preliminary sketches?"

Ewan froze, a forkful of beef roast halfway to his mouth.

Preliminary sketches? Of Lady Kildrum?

Hardly. How was Ewan to dwell upon her portrait when he had been forcibly forbidding himself to even think the lady's name?

But what else could he say?

Painting Lady Kildrum's portrait was an important commission for him. He could not afford to make a muck of it.

And so, he swallowed his bite of beef, smiled at Sir Joshua, and said, "Of course. I cannae wait to begin. Dinner will be an excellent opportunity, as ye say."

Now, he simply had to make it true.

9

I say, Sir Joshua, how long will Mr. Campbell be assisting you?" Lord Graham asked from the top of the table, fixing a polite smile on Sir Joshua.

Ewan suspected the question was meant to be small talk between the two men, but Lord Graham had spoken loud enough for the entire room to hear, his voice carrying to Ewan himself at nearly the opposite end of the table. Lord Graham's behavior had to be deliberate.

They were few in numbers this evening, as Sir Joshua had said.

Lord Graham and his mother.

Ewan and Sir Joshua.

Lady Kildrum, her father, and her sisters.

The local vicar and his wife.

As such, table manners were more informal. Or, at least, that is what Sir Joshua had stated in the carriage earlier. People talked across and even down the table to one another.

Ewan sat beside the vicar's wife, who kept nodding her head as Lady Graham deplored the paucity of decent lace. According to Lady Graham,

Venetian lace was of such *Poor Quality* this year that her ladyship simply *Could Not Countenance* it. Lady Rose sat on Ewan's right, speaking about a novel with Lady Aster across the table.

Was it any wonder, then, that Ewan's attention had drifted toward Lord Graham seated at the opposite end of the table with Lady Kildrum at his right and Sir Joshua at his left?

Ewan took a small bite of loch trout, trying to decide how he felt about Lord Graham. The man was different than Ewan supposed—younger, handsomer, taller. But it was more than just his lordship's appearance.

On the one hand, Lord Graham had been welcoming to Ewan, shaking his hand and saying all the customary polite phrases.

On the other, his lordship kept asking these loud, prodding questions that felt *weighted*. As if he were determined to underscore, time and again, that Ewan's presence here was temporary, that Ewan was not one of them and never would be.

"I cannot rightly say how long Mr. Campbell will be with us, my lord," Sir Joshua replied cheerily. "I do not wish him gone anytime soon. Mr. Campbell is an extraordinary talent."

Lady Kildrum smiled across from Sir Joshua. "You speak truth, Uncle. I believe we have all been impressed with Mr. Campbell's skill as an artist."

Something in Ewan's chest loosened at the praise.

But her words morphed Lord Graham's smile from polite to a strained slash. His lordship did not appreciate losing any part of Lady Kildrum's attention. Ewan had already noted the rather covetous way his lordship looked at Lady Kildrum.

Granted, Lady Kildrum *was* astonishingly lovely this evening. The yellow satin of her dress glittered in the candlelight, casting gold reflections onto the pearls around her neck. Though as was their wont, the curls framing her face had begun to slip their shape. Did Lord Graham find that fact as charming as Ewan did?

"I predict Mr. Campbell will be the talk of London after the Royal Academy Summer Exhibition is through." Sir Joshua pointed his fork at his niece. "Mark my words."

"Will Mr. Campbell be submitting then?" Lord Graham asked.

"Absolutely!" Sir Joshua beamed. "It would be a travesty for him to keep such talent hidden under a bushel, as it were."

Lord Graham shifted his gaze to Ewan down the table—not surprised to find Ewan listening in on their conversation—maintaining that same tight smile that did not quite reach his eyes.

Clearly, his lordship was not enthusiastic about Ewan's presence in the neighborhood. Knowing this, why his lordship had decided to include Ewan in the invitation to dinner remained a mystery.

Lady Kildrum followed Lord Graham's gaze, locking eyes with Ewan, expression unreadable. Granted, they had hardly exchanged a word beyond pleasantries.

But as they had sat down to dinner, Ewan had noticed the lemons and limes artfully displayed in the center of the table. He snagged Lady Kildrum's gaze and darted his eyes to the citrus, subtly pointing them out to her. She shot him a small, amused grin in return, silent awareness humming between them.

Given how Lord Graham's gaze had bounced quickly between Lady Kildrum and Ewan, his lordship was not blind to that awareness. Was that the source of his lordship's animosity?

"A talent, you say? How interesting," Lord Graham replied to Sir Joshua, his tone light but belied by the tense set of his jaw. "And here I was, unaware that behemoths could specialize in painting."

Ewan's expression froze, mimicking the sinking feeling in his stomach.

This was Lord Graham's third jab at Ewan's size. As if that solitary note were the only one worth playing where Ewan was concerned. As if his out-sized body were a problem that needed to be solved.

Ewan imagined swirling bands of a dark yellow-green around Lord Graham. It wasn't the bright green of jealousy, but rather the corrosive color of bile.

Or perhaps the hue was more a reflection of Ewan's own resentment. That this man would likely win Lady Kildrum's hand for himself. That Lord Graham would spend the rest of his life basking in the glory of her red-gold light.

"I cannot say that physical size has ever been a factor in determining one's artistic talent, my lord." Sir Joshua's words were mild but sheathed in steel.

"Excellent point, Sir Joshua," the vicar joined in with a gruff laugh. "The Good Lord reveals our talents irrespective of our physical features."

"Be that as it may, certain professions are dependent upon size." Lord Graham reached for his wine glass and looked down the table, fixing Ewan with a steely stare. "Would you not agree, Mr. Campbell?"

It was a rather absurd question, Ewan supposed. But he could hardly say as much.

"In some cases, my lord," he said instead.

There. A nice, diplomatic reply.

Ewan caught Lady Kildrum's gaze. A wee dent had appeared between her fine eyes. But she averted her face before he could examine it further.

"Perhaps," Lord Graham said, his tone indicating that he was not ready to drop the topic, "some would say that a man of Mr. Campbell's stature should pursue a different career, one more commensurate with his size. Seems a shame for so much brawn to be wasted on daubs of paint. Why Mr. Campbell would be well-suited as a soldier or bodyguard. Or with the proper training, a career in pugilism. Have you ever considered doing such a thing, Mr. Campbell?"

The blunt directness of the question was not unlike a sharp jab to the *solar plexus*. Ewan barely held back a gasp.

Every eye swung his way.

Only one person in this room knew of his past as a prizefighter. Ewan forcibly avoided meeting Lady Kildrum's gaze.

The burn of a tell-tale blush climbed his cheeks.

What was the good of being six and a half feet tall if he blushed like a school girl at every turn? Particularly in a setting such as this?

Worse, how to answer without telling an outright lie? Or giving further offense to Lord Graham?

Or allowing his eyes to drift to Lady Kildrum and reveal more than he should?

VIOLET WATCHED THE blush climb Mr. Campbell's face, the painter clearly discomfited by Lord Graham's pointed questions.

She understood what Lord Graham was doing. She had witnessed the scene countless times over and over from others of her class. The 'polite' questions that emphasized the hierarchy of society and cemented everyone's 'proper' place.

All with the intent of relaying a decidedly-pointed message—

You do not belong here. You are not one of us.

Mr. Campbell, like most, had received the message loud and clear. And now was in the awkward position of having to reply without offending his host.

Worse, Violet knew how much the painter detested prizefighting.

Swallowing, Mr. Campbell replied, "I cannae say my temperament is suited tae prizefighting, my lord. I dinnae ken tae the sport myself."

"Pardon? What isn't there to admire about prizefighting?" Lord Graham sat back with an affronted huff. "When removed from the rookeries, 'tis a noble sport. Even the king himself is a devotee. Many a lesser man has raised his name and prospects through appearances in the ring. Were I to have been born without privilege, I would have sought skills as a prizefighter post-haste." Lord Graham smiled widely, as if to say, *Such a concept is absurd as, of course, I would have been born to privilege.* "As is, I spar at Gentleman Jack's when I am in Town and with my valet when I am not. One never knows when such skills will be necessary. If you find your interest in painting waning, Mr. Campbell, say the word. My valet could provide you with a list of pugilists who could assist you in establishing a *true* career."

Mr. Campbell's face grew more and more remote as Lord Graham spoke. The man was fully aware that Lord Graham was insulting his intelligence, his craft as a painter, as well as attempting to squelch any thoughts that Mr. Campbell had of rising above his station in life.

Violet felt Mr. Campbell's anger and embarrassment keenly.

It was bullying, pure and simple, and Violet always found it distasteful.

Moreover, Lord Graham's pettiness did not recommend him to her. It was an ugly side of his lordship that she had never seen on full display.

She knew of only one infallible way to stem Lord Graham's words.

Violet loudly cleared her throat and pressed a hand to her chest. "Heavens, Lord Graham, all this talk of prizefighting has quite overset my nerves. I cannot imagine what my poor sisters must think of such conversation. Prizefighting, indeed!"

Though she despised pretending to be a hapless female, her words were not wrong. Prizefighting was not an appropriate dinner conversation, particularly with Aster and Rose present.

Lord Graham jerked, as if coming back to himself, gaze swiveling to hers.

"I most sincerely apologize, Lady Kildrum." He shook his head. "I clearly got carried away with my enthusiasm for the sport. You are correct, such a topic should be dropped."

He smiled then, remorseful, eyes contrite.

Violet believed him to be sincere.

But remorse and apology did not excuse the underlying belief system that had led to his behavior in the first place.

She dared a glance down the table to Mr. Campbell. The man was back to eating his fish, ears still crimson at the tips.

Her pulse was a lump in her throat.

Violet wrestled with her warring impulses. As a lady, she needed to meet the traditional expectations heaped upon her. And yet, she recognized that the culture which dictated those expectations was inherently unfair.

Her attraction to Mr. Campbell was not the *reason* Lord Graham's arrogance offended her . . . well, at least, not entirely.

It was just . . . Mr. Campbell did not deserve to be made to feel less than. No one did.

Movement at the far end of the table caught Violet's eye.

Lady Graham was staring at her, the black satin of her ladyship's gown glinting in the flickering candlelight.

Oh, dear. Had too many of Violet's thoughts been painted across her face?

"Harrumph. Thank you for the reminder, Lady Kildrum," her lady-ship said, flicking her gaze to her son. "I must say, you posed a *Good Question*, Graham. Asking about Mr. Campbell's tenure here is wise, I daresay. One can never be too *Careful* when it comes to protecting the reputation of those who might be prone to *Foolish Choices* and *Scandalous Behavior*. Disaster inevitably follows. The *Judgment of God*, if you will. Heaven knows I have witnessed the *Horror* of younger siblings haring after the *Mistakes* of their elders, always with similar results."

Violet nearly gasped at the sheer audacity of Lady Graham's words. It was one thing to have implied, as she had a week before, that Dahlia's death was the inevitable result of her behavior.

But then to boldly state that Violet's other sisters would likely meet—and deserve!—a similar fate . . .

Given how quickly Uncle Joshua's head snapped upright and Aster's eyes widened, others' shared Violet's shock.

Only her father nodded his head, as if in wise agreement. "Indeed, Lady Graham, you speak from a well of wisdom. We must all play the part the Lord has assigned us. Those who choose to stray from that path must often pay the ultimate price."

Father spoke the words with a pious solemnity, as if they were mere trifles and not a cruel condemnation of Dahlia.

How could he! His own daughter! And in such a callous tone! But then . . . Father had never shown much compassion for Dahlia, had he?

Violet set down her fork to hide her shaking hands and bit her lip, willing back the angry tears that threatened.

Thankfully, Uncle Joshua came to the rescue.

"Indeed, brother," he said. "Have I told you all the tale of the time I was called upon to paint the Duke of Marlborough's prized hunting dog?"

She appreciated Uncle Joshua's quick actions. His words staved off another painful barrage of sanctimony and allowed Violet time to regroup. She stabbed at her food throughout her uncle's story, smiling in the appropriate places.

However, the pain of her father's dismissal of Dahlia continued to ache, leaving Violet repeatedly blinking back the sting in her eyes.

How could he act as if Dahlia's memory had to be scrubbed of all its beauty and light, condemned to darkness because of her one ill-advised choice? How could his heart be so untouched by the painful sorrow of Dahlia's loss?

Worse, Violet could do *nothing*. Lady Graham's reminder was true. Dahlia's decisions had tainted them all, and the slightest deviation from decorum on the part of herself or her sisters would be met with instant reprisals.

And still . . . Violet dared another glance down the table to Mr. Campbell.

As if helpless against the pull, his head lifted, eyes meeting hers.

His gaze told her that he had not missed a single nuance of what had been said.

One heartbeat.

Two.

He gave her the faintest glimmer of a smile.

And then looked away, Adam's apple bobbing as he swallowed.

Violet felt abruptly bereft.

Like that moment atop the cliff when she had stepped out of his embrace, the shocking loss of his warmth, of the cocoon of his comfort.

And just like then, they were now turning away, taking separate paths.

Paths that could not include one another.

10

D o you require anything else, Mr. Campbell?" Irvine asked.
Ewan surveyed the drawing room. The drapes had been situated to let just the right amount of sunlight in, furniture moved and repositioned to provide a proper backdrop.

"Everything is as it should be," Ewan said. "Thank ye."

He likely should not be thanking servants—he inhabited some limbo between the servants and their mistress—but it went against his very nature to not acknowledge thanks where it was warranted.

"Very well, Mr. Campbell. I will inform Lady Kildrum that all is prepared for her." Irvine bowed a small, stiff movement before leaving the room.

The clack of the door resounded in the silence.

Lady Kildrum's portrait sitting would begin shortly.

Ewan swallowed, taking in a fortifying breath.

Ye can do this.

She is but a lass like any other.

Yet in that, Ewan knew he deluded himself.

Lady Kildrum was *nothing* like other lasses.

Vividly, the image of her seated beside Lord Graham at dinner came to mind. She had glowed like a diamond apart, eyes snapping in outrage for the subtle wee abuses Lord and Lady Graham sent his way.

And what did Lady Graham's comment about 'scandalous behavior' and 'foolish choices' have to do with the Kerr family? Her ladyship's words had clearly strung another thread of tension through the room.

Ewan sometimes felt as if he had arrived in the middle of the third act of a play and was now trying to piece together the plot.

Only time would tell if the story was a tragedy or a comedy.

He wandered the drawing room as he waited for Lady Kildrum to arrive. The portraits of previous countesses lined the walls. Large, monumental paintings of women in clothing of the past century. He noted the subtle nods to title and station—a coronet, a scepter, a diamond necklace, the yards of expensive lace and satin. What items would he include for Lady Kildrum?

But it was the painting hanging opposite the fireplace that held his attention—a monumental piece, extending from floor to ceiling, and done in Sir Joshua's unmistakable hand.

In the middle of the painting sat a beautiful lady of middling years. The style of her brown hair and the cut of her gauzy, flowing gown proclaimed the scene to have been completed around a decade past. Four girls surrounded the lady, each of varying ages, from school girls to late teens.

The former Lady Kildrum and her daughters.

The older woman gazed straight at the viewer, her expression exuding a calm competence, as if to say, *I am the lady of the manor, and my daughters are my heritage.* In the background, Ewan could make out the shape of Kilmeny Hall and its grounds.

Ewan noted the familiar form of the current Lady Kildrum linking elbows with her mother.

Lady Violet as she had been known then.

Sir Joshua had captured the spark in her green-blue eyes, a sense of adventure and life. She rested against her mother's arm with a carefree smile, as if she had no worries or fears.

Lady Violet's smile no longer held that lighthearted ease.

Ewan recognized the younger figures of Lady Aster and Lady Rose. But there was another young woman between Lady Kildrum and Lady Aster in age.

A fourth daughter. Another flower.

Dahlia, he kenned she was called. He had heard servants murmur the name here and there.

The minutes dragged by and Lady Kildrum did not appear.

Ewan paced the room, his gaze returning again and again to the painting.

Why did the family not speak of Dahlia? She was a pretty thing— petite and delicate like her mother—looking out at the viewer with mischief in her eyes.

Was she simply married and no longer in residence?

But, if so, why did no one mention her—

Crack.

The door opened.

Ewan whirled to see Lady Kildrum enter in a flutter of skirts.

Lady Kildrum was a vision.

Her dress was cinched just under her bustline, allowing layers of gauze and silk to cascade around her, all in shades of green-blue that perfectly matched her eyes. A stiffened lace collar stood upright around her neckline and ropes of expensive pearls looped her throat and winked from her coiffure. Her hair had been coaxed into ringlets at her temples, although the droop in the curls hinted that they rebelled at the treatment.

The observation nearly made him smile.

But, given the impact of her on his senses, Ewan feared he was going to need a moment or two to gather his scattered wits.

Fortunately, habit kicked in and he remembered to bow.

"Lady Kildrum."

"Mr. Campbell," she replied, turning her head as a maid entered behind her and took up residence in a corner.

Ah. A chaperone. That was wise.

Taking a deep breath, Ewan forced himself to operate in a professional manner.

"If ye please, Lady Kildrum." He motioned toward the chair he had placed in the middle of the room, draperies hanging behind it. "My intention today is simply tae become familiar with your likes and dislikes. I intend tae do some preliminary sketches that I will then compile together into a plan for the final painting."

Nodding her head, Lady Kildrum passed by him, her movement sending a wave of fresh lavender rushing over him. Ewan gave a few instructions for her to stand beside the chair, leaning her hip against it and resting her hand along the chair back.

Smiling tightly, Ewan picked up his large sketchbook and a piece of his preferred charcoal.

He began to sketch.

But it only took a few seconds for him to realize that they were both far too stiff.

She stood rigidly, as if afraid to relax in his presence.

Ewan was tense and nervous, his lines jittery and awkward.

She is only a client. Nothing more.

His emotional attachment to Lady Kildrum was surely bleeding into the room, a sort of dingy gray miasma that coated the walls and clung to her, an unwanted guest. Understandably, Lady Kildrum reacted to the tension by stiffening her muscles.

Ewan hated that his own inability to control his infatuation made her feel so uncomfortable. He had to cease this. It served no purpose.

Mentally stretching, he slipped further into his professional demeanor.

"If ye would be so kind, my lady, please describe the elements that ye like in other portraits," he said. "This will help me ken how tae go about painting your likeness."

If Lady Kildrum found his question off-putting, it did not show. She did, however, relax a wee bit, the line of her shoulders becoming less rigid.

"I cannot say for sure," she began.

"What do you *dislike* then?" he asked. "I know citrus tae be right out."

A soft snort of laughter. "You will not paint lemons into the scene?"

"Nae, but sometimes 'tis easier tae understand what ye dinnae want."

A dent appeared between her eyes.

"Understanding is to be found in opposition, not similarity," she nodded, rephrasing his words.

Clever, lass. "Aye."

She pursed her lips. "Well . . . I dislike artifice in a painting. I am biased, of course, but I've always felt as if Uncle Joshua is excellent at capturing not only his clients' likenesses but also their spirit. It's as if he paints a bit of someone's soul into every work."

Ah. Ewan's heart swelled in his chest.

"Insightful," he murmured.

He found himself leaning into the timbre of her voice as she spoke. He imagined the sound to be lines upon his page, a nearly physical impression that he could outline with his charcoal. His hand moved, sketching the sound into form.

He could feel himself sinking further into that creative languor, where time and space stretched and twisted and all that existed was the *scritch-scritch* of his pencil on paper.

Mhairi had always referred to it as his *'painterly state.'*

But thoughts of his past were not welcome at the moment, and so Ewan pushed them aside.

His mind was so focused on drawing the shapes and lines of Lady Kildrum, so caught up in his act of creation, that words tumbled out of his mouth before he was able to carefully ponder them beforehand.

"Do ye like the painting Sir Joshua did there?" He nodded toward the enormous canvas to his right.

She followed his motion, pausing.

"My uncle is a remarkably talented painter," she finally replied, "and the canvas reflects that."

Ewan froze, his charcoal stilling in his fingers. Her words were polite and yet . . . essentially empty.

He lifted his eyes from his sketchbook. "Aye. I dinnae disagree with ye on that score. But how do ye *feel* about the painting?"

She met his gaze for a second before breaking the contact and turning back to look at the canvas beside them.

Was it just his imagination that her eyes lingered on the fourth sister?

Ewan knew he should likely drop the subject. Change the topic and move on to safer waters.

But something in her eyes as she gazed tugged at him. There was pain there.

The painting *hurt* Lady Kildrum. The glittering shades of red and gold that tangled around her dimmed as she looked at the canvas.

Empathy ballooned in his chest, sending words tumbling from his mouth—

"I cannae help but notice there are four lasses in the painting, yet I've only met three sisters currently residing in Kilmeny Hall. Does that influence how ye view the painting?"

Lady Kildrum sucked in a sharp breath, as if his question were a blow.

Ewan instantly wanted his words back. He had hoped to help.

Instead, he greatly feared he had abruptly made everything that much worse.

11

Mr. Campbell's words jolted down Violet's spine, sending a startled blast of discomfort through her body.

. . . there are four lasses in the painting, yet I've only met three sisters currently residing in Kilmeny Hall . . .

Violet swallowed.

The question was inevitable, she supposed, particularly after the disastrous dinner party the other evening.

Her eyes drifted over the canvas. Memories of the hours spent posing for Uncle Joshua assailed her. Aster and Rose had been barely nine years of age and had found the experience a trial. Aster had kept up a non-stop stream of questions. Rose had squirmed and shifted, unable to sit still for even a minute at a time. Dahlia, at a more mature sixteen, had sighed and rolled her eyes at her younger sisters.

Mother had been stoic, admonishing the twins over and over.

Violet had been seventeen, just a few months before embarking on her first London Season. She had stood motionless, following uncle's orders, keeping her arm looped through her mother's. How excited she had been. Her whole life before her, on the cusp of womanhood and so much possibility.

How do ye feel about the painting?

The truth?

Violet hated it.

Not for how it portrayed them all, per se.

But for the happiness it represented.

The paradise lost.

For the bittersweet memory of the time when the two people Violet loved more than anything—her mother and Dahlia—were yet living.

Before she had been left so very alone.

She felt Mr. Campbell's eyes on her, her skin tingling from the weight, but when she turned back to him, his head was bent over his drawing.

Had he been sketching her as she tumbled into memory? And, if so, what stories did her expression tell?

He was dressed in a great kilt again—this time a blue-and-green tartan—a slightly crisper version of the kilt he had worn when she encountered him atop the cliffs. A lock of his ginger hair tumbled across his forehead. Her fingers itched to push it back.

He flipped over the page and then continued sketching, hazel eyes occasionally raising to skim her.

The sheer intensity of his focus was . . . disarming. Riveting.

Though, he had sketched her once already. And in that moment, he had drawn her as a goddess. But she had goaded—no, dared!—him to capture her. Depicting her as a goddess could have been a gentle jest.

How did his artist's eye truthfully see her? And why did she fear his answer?

Would he see the teetering imbalance of her? The fractured sense of self and rampant vacillation?

Would he see the jagged wounds of Dahlia's decisions—

No . . . that wasn't quite it. Guilt forced her to acknowledge the full truth.

Would Mr. Campbell see the jagged wounds left by the decisions Violet had *encouraged* Dahlia to make?

There. She could admit as much.

The steady calm of Mr. Campbell's presence loosened her tongue.

"The fourth figure is my younger sister, Dahlia," Violet answered after a moment. "I imagine you have heard of her by now."

"I have heard the name, yes. But little else." His head remained bent over his sketchbook. "She is the sister just younger than yourself?"

A long pause and then Violet replied:

"Yes. She was. Dahlia *was* the sister just younger than myself."

Mr. Campbell's head snapped upright, as if her words were a physical thing traveling with enough force to push his chin upwards.

Dahlia *was*. Past tense.

The pain of it surged in Violet's chest. How could it be over two years on and Dahlia's loss still feel so very *present*?

Violet's eyes drifted again to her sister.

Uncle Joshua had captured Dahlia's unquenchable spirit so thoroughly. Her sister had a charming smirk that won her many friends and admirers. She had been the prettiest of them all with dark-brown hair, delicate features, and ice-blue eyes. Some had called her a fey creature, so magical was her allure.

But to Violet, Dahlia was more than just a lively companion.

Dahlia had been her closest friend, her favorite confident.

No matter what happens, we will always have one another, Violet had always said.

No matter what, Dahlia would reply.

But death had broken that promise.

"Dahlia was . . . fire," Violet said, her words dropping into the hush of the room. "She could illuminate any room with her presence, always ready for a laugh or a lark. I loved her dearly."

Mr. Campbell paused his sketching, as if the weight of her pain affected him. The hold on his sketchbook relaxed slightly.

"I am sorry tae have never known her. She sounds remarkable."

Violet's eyes pricked and stung at the empathy thrumming through his simple words.

Was this why she had felt compelled to defend Mr. Campbell at dinner? To force others to see the gentle soul within?

"She was," she whispered, turning her head and biting the inside of her cheek, desperate to swallow back the surge of emotion.

Silence hung.

Violet's lip quivered, forcing her to close her eyes.

Mr. Campbell's voice carried to her, drifting softly. "Didnae St. Paul taunt death in the New Testament? *O, Death, where is thy sting?* I've often pondered that. Perhaps death has no sting tae those that die. But it is a thousand small cuts tae those who remain. Endless wee wounds reminding us of what we have lost."

His words hummed, vibrating strings of meaning.

Violet found herself helplessly lifting her eyes to his.

He had stopped sketching, as if the weight of her loss sat heavy upon him.

Their eyes held . . . and held.

She saw it in the quiet compassion of his expression—he *knew*.

He understood the endless sting of death come too soon. The kind of sorrow that never fully heals.

One simply learns to live with the pain.

His chest rose and fell in perfect synchronization with hers.

Abruptly, Violet saw that she hovered at the precipice of a very great fall. Of giving more of herself than she should to this man. She could feel it creeping closer and closer.

And yet, she could not help the words that spilled out of her.

"Dahlia was a true free spirit." Violet smiled, tremulous and quivering. "But it was that very free-spiritedness that caused her downfall, in the end. I am confident you did not miss the undercurrent running through dinner the other evening."

Mr. Campbell snorted, a soft puff of sound. "Lady Graham's words were clearly pointing toward a specific incident."

"Yes, well, it is a cautionary tale, as they say."

He paused and then said, "I would hear the tale, if ye will tell it."

She swallowed, her eyes drifting to his long fingers holding the charcoal pencil. The same long fingers that had effortlessly spanned her waist, snatching her out of harm's way with astonishing, tensile strength. Her breath hitched at the remembered press of those fingers into her skin.

A cautionary tale, indeed.

Violet feared for her own emotional safety.

If nothing else, perhaps explaining Dahlia's shame would insert a much-needed wedge between herself and Mr. Campbell. Remind them both of the folly of their current course.

She nodded. "I suppose you will inevitably learn of Dahlia's sad story from a servant or neighbor, so you might as well hear it from me now."

Violet took in a deep breath, eyes staring into the distance, and resisting the urge to brace her hands on her knees.

Mr. Campbell, as if wishing to give her the illusion of privacy, returned to his sketchbook, head bent over his work, allowing her to speak without the added discomfort of meeting his gaze.

Yet another example of the deep well of consideration and compassion within him.

She ran her hands down her skirts. "I'm sure you remember the Year without a Summer."

"Aye," he said, not lifting his head, hand sketching. "The cold felt endless. There was famine that autumn and the year that followed."

"Yes. My family quit our townhouse in London and returned here to help the tenants. It felt like the end of days, at times. Heavens, there was even a strong earthquake felt from Aberdeen to Inverness—"

"Och, I had nearly forgot about that." He shot her a wry look before returning to his drawing. "The earthquake twisted the spire of the Old Kirk along the River Ness, if I recall."

"We certainly felt it here. It rang the church bells and toppled chimney pots. But the earthquake was just one in a string of calamities that autumn. As you said, summer crops failed and disease set in. My mother was beside herself with worry over our tenants."

Violet could still see her mother bent over her desk, hand to her forehead as she tried to find the funds to buy grain for her people. When so many landlords were abandoning their tenants to their fate—whether through famine or clearances—her mother had not. She had instead extended compassion and charity. In the end, Violet's mother had borrowed the money—the Manna Loan—and sent for grain from Italy.

"Naturally, in the midst of this crisis, my mother was concerned for our education, wanting us girls to retain our 'London polish,' as she called it. Consequently, she engaged the services of a certain Mr. Martinelli to tutor myself and my sisters in dancing and music. As you might imagine, Mr. Martinelli was witty and handsome and prone to longing gazes while pushing back his mass of windswept hair. It was all rather Byronic."

Mr. Campbell flashed her a rueful smile. "I've heard tales of the perils of dashing hair."

"Well . . . Dahlia was certainly enraptured. My parents were too caught up in the struggles of the estate to see how deeply and quickly Dahlia fell in love. And to be fair, Mr. Martinelli was more than the sum of his alluring coiffure. Dahlia insisted there was a tender goodness in him that she adored."

Violet did not add the most critical piece of the story.

She had *encouraged* Dahlia's affections and attachment to Mr. Martinelli.

"You are free to choose, you see," Violet had said. "You aren't saddled with the earldom. You can marry whomever you would like—"

"Well, yes, but you shouldn't give up hope, either. Lord Michael was simply one bad egg, Violet. I have faith you will find your own love in time."

"Perhaps . . . but you? You can live now! You can find happiness with your Mr. Martinelli. You have the option to live the life that I cannot. I envy you for that."

"But my behavior will reflect on you all. I cannot cause Mother such pain—"

"We shall find a way, Dahlia. Mother and Father will relent. They love you. Perhaps Father can find some way of furthering Mr. Martinelli's career, particularly if it means your happiness—"

Violet clenched her jaw against the familiar flood of guilt. The horror that one small decision had wrought. If only Violet hadn't urged her on. Would Dahlia have acted so rashly—

She pushed back the tide of memory, the endless *what ifs*. That way lay madness.

"The rest, as I am sure you can surmise," she continued, "is a story as old as time itself. Mr. Martinelli and my sister began a passionate love affair. When our parents *finally* wised to the situation, Mr. Martinelli was sacked. My sister was forbidden to speak with him. As a deeply religious man, my father was beside himself with righteous fury over her behavior. But, of course, by then the damage had been done."

Mr. Campbell lifted his head from his sketching. "Was Dahlia harmed?"

"Harmed? No. But she *was* increasing." Violet mimed a hand rubbing a rounded belly. "She and Mr. Martinelli were very much in love and wished to marry. My parents absolutely refused their permission, but we live in Scotland. Dahlia did not need their permission to marry here."

"Of course. A handfasting before witnesses is as legal as a church and a priest."

"Precisely. You can guess the rest, I suppose. Dahlia slipped out of the house one night and eloped with her Mr. Martinelli. The scandal was immense. My parents cut Dahlia off entirely," she said. "My father was nearly apoplectic, insisting Mr. Martinelli was not to receive a single shilling of Dahlia's dowry. He stormed about, proclaiming that Dahlia was doomed to a life of misery and unhappiness. My mother took to her bed for several weeks, weeping incessantly. Dahlia had always been her favorite, you see—"

"Favorite? But how—"

"No, I can see that you wish to dissemble," Violet held out a staying hand, "but you do not know my late mother. She loved me, of that I am certain. And I loved her and deeply miss her guiding influence. But our love was often a fractious thing, full of stubborn silences and disappointed hopes. I often wonder if my mother and I were too alike, in the end.

"But Dahlia was my mother's opposite. Their love was complementary, and my mother doted upon her. And so when Dahlia eloped with a lowly dancing master, forcing my mother to cut her off in order to salvage the reputations and prospects of her other three daughters . . ." Violet drifted off.

"Dahlia broke your mother's heart," Mr. Campbell supplied.

Not just Dahlia, Violet thought. *I broke my mother's heart by encouraging and supporting Dahlia in her rebellion. By not informing them of what she intended to do.*

Violet did not add that bit.

If Violet had not been such a staunch ally, would Dahlia have acted as she had?

Violet would never know.

Instead, she nodded, taking a moment before continuing. "We did not return to London and our life there. My mother and father felt the storm of scandal was better weathered far away from the *ton*. Initially, my parents forbade me from writing Dahlia, but I disobeyed them at every turn. I would not cease contact with my beloved sister. I *could* not. I sent her my pin money . . . anything to help her know that I still loved and supported her." Violet was compelled to take responsibility for her part in Dahlia's behavior. "Given the infamy of her elopement in this corner of the world, Dahlia and Mr. Martinelli relocated to Edinburgh. He took on students there to provide for them. My sister's letters gave every appearance of being cheerful and happy, but who knows . . ."

"Aye. Was she truly happy, your Dahlia? Or did she merely put on a good face tae justify her choices?"

"Precisely my own questions." Violet let out a slow breath. That was almost the worst part. That Violet had fostered Dahlia's decisions, and her sister had ended up miserable in the end. "Regardless, Dahlia was delivered of a baby boy six months after her marriage. I was overjoyed for her. Her letters continued to be joyful and cheery, though she did occasionally request funds of me. Their finances were quite a tangle."

"As are most of the newly married, I would hazard," Mr. Campbell said, his hand ceasing sketching.

"Yes, I suppose you are correct. All seemed well enough, but then, when the baby was eight months old, he was taken ill. A putrid sore throat, the doctor said. He died within a fortnight." Violet paused and then forced out the next words. "Dahlia soon followed."

Mr. Campbell's shoulders slumped at her words, as if the death of Dahlia and her son were an abrupt weight on his shoulders.

"Both of them? So quickly?" He shook his head. "And yourself, so far away."

"Their deaths came as a terrible shock to us all. My father retrieved their bodies—Dahlia and her son—from Edinburgh to have them buried in the family plot here in Kilmeny."

Violet did not add that her father was kinder to Dahlia in death than he had been in life. Aster insisted that their father's anger and grief over Dahlia was indicative of the depth of his love. Violet wanted to believe her.

"The loss of Dahlia and her baby sent my mother into a steep decline of spirits." Violet swallowed. "She passed away eight months after Dahlia."

Violet finished by spreading her arms wide, as if to say, *And here we are now.*

"So many shocks, piled one atop the other." Mr. Campbell braced his forearms on his sketchbook, wrists dangling loose over the edge. "Ye scarcely had time tae catch your breath before another was upon ye."

She nodded. So much calamity and scandal and death packed into too little time.

As with his words earlier, he did not flinch from the emotion swirling in the room. Instead, he faced it, joining her in bearing the stinging cuts of grief. A sailor braced into the wind, allowing it to buffet and assail him.

Only someone who had faced a similar storm would behave so.

She hadn't realized how much she needed a witness to her pain and guilt until this moment. Someone to look into her soul and say, *I understand. I have stood in this place, too.*

Violet turned back at the large painting hanging beside her, noting the twinkle in Dahlia's eye, captured just as it had sparkled in life. Her mother's gaze looked out at her, soft yet stern . . . also accurate.

"You asked me earlier how I feel about this painting?" She nodded toward it. "I find it painful . . . bittersweet. A melancholy reminder of a happier time, when cares and life were simpler and those I loved best were yet living."

His shoulders sagged. "It is an echo then, the painting. A reverberating reminder of what was lost."

Violet nodded, but did not add other truths.

That the weight of her own guilt was often crushing.

That the aftermath of Dahlia's ruination and elopement had shattered their former way of life. London was forgotten. Illustrious neighbors had shunned their company. Violet's suitors had abruptly evaporated.

Her father had retreated into his writings, thinking excessive piety would absolve them. Her mother had slumped into melancholy and eventually faded altogether. Aster and Rose had been left to fend for themselves, rebelling against the tighter strictures placed upon them.

For her part, Violet had been the one to pick up the pieces, to shoulder the burden of the estate and move forward.

Even before Dahlia's death, the family had endured the snide remarks, the hushed whispers, the achingly-polite-but-pointedly-refused invitations. They mourned the abrupt change to their status, the sudden concerns for Violet's prospects, the genuine fears for Aster and Rose's. Dahlia's eventual death had done nothing to stem the tide of criticism.

Violet had never realized how ephemeral their position was until one scandalous decision—a decision she encouraged!—nearly obliterated it.

She and Mr. Campbell stared at one another for a long moment.

What sting of death do you bear? she wondered. *What pain has carved such empathy?*

Violet swallowed and looked away.

You must let go of this fascination. It can only lead to regret.

Several years ago, Uncle Joshua had taken herself and Dahlia up the coast to visit the Bullers o' Buchan, a churning cauldron cut by the ocean. Waves would wash through a sea arch and crash into the towering cliffs with devastating force.

Violet had known she needed to step away, to witness the awestruck scene from a safer distance.

And yet, she had not been able to stop her feet from traveling closer and closer to the crumbling cliff's edge, transfixed as she was by Mother Nature's fury.

The sight had been too compelling and Violet heedlessly naive to the dangers.

The red sandstone had rung with the call of wild birds and shrieked with the wind that whipped Violet's pelisse around her and tugged at her skirts. Waves crashed and rumbled the ground beneath her feet.

Looking at Mr. Campbell now, Violet felt the same powerful pull, the urge to creep closer and closer to the edge, to risk a catastrophic fall.

The view was too breathtaking to turn away.

That said . . . Lady Graham had not been entirely wrong with her words the other evening:

Disaster *did* often follow foolish choices and scandalous behavior.

Violet swallowed hard.

She could not—she *would* not—repeat Dahlia's mistakes. She would not choose heart over duty. Aster and Rose deserved better. Her mother's memory deserved better.

Unfortunately, Violet feared her attempts to put distance between herself and Mr. Campbell had just misfired spectacularly.

Sharing threads of one's soul had a tendency to do that.

She had wished to step back from the cliff's edge, to run far and fast from these errant feelings.

He and she had been here before, had they not?

When she had tumbled on that clifftop and Mr. Campbell had clutched her to him, one large hand branding her hip, the opposite palm sprawled across her stomach.

That day, she had managed to physically step away from him.

But today, instead of pushing out of his arms once again, she had metaphorically clasped his hand and invited him to enjoy the view with her—him watching her with those understanding eyes, feeling the strength of his support—each taking a step closer to the cliff's edge and the perilous consequences of tumbling over.

This hazardous dance *had* to stop.

Because if not, Violet feared she would one day cease caring to push him away.

12

The weight of Lady Kildrum's sorrow stayed with Ewan. The bleakness in her eyes, the flatness of her tone. All masks hiding a chasm of grief and pain.

The very gravity of it seemed emblematic of the lady herself.

Violet.

Her name evoked the color ultramarine, a blue-purple paint made from crushed *lapis lazuli*. The pigment was outrageously expensive, so artists used it sparingly. In the Middle Ages, ultramarine was the color of the robes of the Virgin Mary—the extravagant cost of the paint being an outward symbol of the devotion of the artist and his patron. And so now, in art, whenever the color ultramarine was used, it inevitably invoked the Madonna.

While sitting for her portrait, Lady Kildrum had become Violet for him—a rare treasure of a woman with the cares of the world on her shoulders.

He was helpless to think of her any other way.

Two days after that portrait session, Ewan stood in the damp coolness of his glasshouse studio. The sun had cleared the horizon only an hour previous, and its warmth had not yet evaporated the condensation trickling down the inside of the windows. Ewan's breath left him in white puffs.

He would be helping Sir Joshua after luncheon, but this morning was for him alone.

He tapped his fingers against his kilt, surveying the canvases leaning against the stone wall opposite the bank of windows.

Ideas and thoughts pounded him, creative bursts of scenes and compositions.

His eyes dipped to the clifftop painting . . . the blackhouse with its amorphous smoke, the golden sand of the beach echoed in the silver-gold crest of the ocean waves.

How had Violet understood the profound depth of this scene? The gaping hole it left in his heart?

He lifted the painting up, tracing a finger along the figure walking toward the house.

Mhairi . . . a basket braced on her hip with an earasaid wrapped around her head, the wool woven in the brown and russet tartan of their village. He could nearly hear her singing *Fear a' Bhàta* as she walked, the Gaelic lyrics mingling with the hiss of the waves—*Mo shoraidh slàn leat 's gach àit' an téid thu.*

My farewell to ye where'er ye go.

Ewan's throat closed, and he abruptly found himself blinking.

This was why he did not linger on such memories. They rendered him weepy and suffering and filled with such helpless *anger* . . .

Hurt from the wounds of Mhairi's betrayal.

Fury over his powerlessness to help her.

Eight years. Eight years of living his life without her. Of being unable to reach her in any way. Eight years since he had broken that promise made long before—

Care for Mhairi. Keep her safe.

He had done a piss-poor job of both.

The guilt of it would forever be his burden, like Atlas, doomed to carry its weight.

Ewan scrubbed a hand through his hair, shaking away the morose thoughts.

He had begun the painting as an exercise based on Sir Joshua's words from that first night in the castle:

We bleed every time we paint. Never forget it.

The problem, of course, was that such metaphorical bloodletting was agonizingly painful. Was it *truly* necessary to create great art?

If you wish to be great, find the courage to paint your demons.

Ewan sighed again.

He wanted that greatness. He ached for it.

He had sacrificed *everything* for it.

Mhairi had as well, in her way.

He had to honor that sacrifice, to give this everything he had.

But thoughts of Mhairi sent him winging through the past, landing on the one memory he wished most to avoid—the leaping flames, the ghastly screams echoing through the night—

No!

He shuddered, running a shaking palm over his face. He braced his hands on the work table near his easel, chest heaving, that salmon-colored emotion swamping him. He could feel the tense quivering in his muscles, the same bloody reaction.

Would that night never cease to haunt him? Was the trauma of it embedded in the very sinews of his body?

He swallowed, over and over.

Violet's voice rose in his mind, her bravery in telling him about Dahlia. The quiver in her words as she faced the pain.

He may not be ready to face the memory of *that* night, but he could still be brave and examine other painful memories.

As if the dam had been burst, image after image assailed him.

He snatched up his sketchpad and began drawing.

It felt as if the ghosts of women he had lost were looking over his shoulder.

VIOLET TRIED TO avoid Mr. Campbell.

Well . . . she *thought* about trying, at least.

Or rather . . . she felt guilty for *not* thinking upon trying.

She genuinely did. Honest truth.

She was hand-caught-in-Cook's-biscuit-tin guilty over her lack of concern.

The problem, of course, was that even as a child, such guilt had not stopped Dahlia and herself from raiding the kitchen every time Cook's back was turned.

Guilt, as it turned out, was a terrible motivator.

Worse, Aster and Rose had taken to calling Mr. Campbell by his Christian name—Ewan.

Not to his face, of course. But Violet overheard their comments:

"Ewan was looking terribly fine this morning. Did you not see?" and "Did you hear Ewan and Uncle are coming for dinner tonight? You mustn't monopolize him this time."

Naturally, Violet corrected her sisters every time—*He is to be referred to as Mr. Campbell or sir, nothing else!*—for all the good it did.

Their father was nearly apoplectic.

"Have you no sense at all, daughters?!" he railed against the twins one morning after breakfast. "Are you deaf to Lady Graham's censure? To the very real consequences that this nonsense leads to? You were old enough when Dahlia ran off to comprehend the repercussions of her actions."

Violet bent her head over her egg cup, not wishing to be drawn into the argument.

"We are not planning on running away with Mr. Campbell, Father," Rose attempted to reassure him. "It is merely talk that Aster and myself consider humorous."

"Humorous? I fail to find anything jovial about it, young lady. Behavior leads to habit. And I cannot imagine the scandal should you behave like this in front of a gentleman."

"Well, Father," Aster joined in, "it is fortunate that there are no other gentleman about besides Mr. Campbell—"

"I would scarcely categorize Mr. Campbell as a gentleman." Their father's fork clattered to his plate. "He was certainly not born to it."

Violet longed to roll her eyes. Instead, she stabbed a toast soldier into her egg yolk.

Rose reached for a warm potato scone. "Perhaps not, but his manners and demeanor are certainly more agreeable than those of many other gentlemen—"

"Then I daresay you have not met enough proper gentlemen, daughter," Mr. Kerr replied.

"I could not agree more, Father," Aster said, voice treacly sweet. "Our lack of interaction with gentlemen is truly appalling. Perhaps we could visit the London townhouse this autumn."

Aster looked at her fingernails as if her suggestion was of no import. But the sheer nonchalance of it made Violet wonder if her sisters had staged this entire scene simply to manipulate their father into taking them to London.

Gracious. The twins were a handful.

"I am not going to London," their father shuddered. "The very thought is anathema. Young ladies should be able to reside in the country without falling into folly! You will cease flirting with the man—"

"We do not *flirt* with Ewan—"

"Mr. Campbell! The man is to remain *Mr. Campbell* to you all. I will hear no more on this subject!"

Of course, Aster and Rose did not change their behavior.

They simply stopped talking about Mr. Campbell in front of their father.

It only took two days before Violet was mentally referring to him as Ewan herself.

Heavens, but it was all such a slippery slope.

It didn't help that Uncle Joshua and Ewan had begun trekking up to Kilmeny Hall to dine each evening.

"I am weary of eating cheese and toast with cold ham," Uncle had said, running a hand down his lemony-yellow waistcoat. "And why go to the expense of employing two cooks?"

Uncle was his usual gregarious self during these dinners. But Ewan proved himself an amiable dinner companion. Though not as theatrical as her uncle, he possessed wry wit and a clever mind. Moreover, he was exquisitely mannered and comfortable dining *en famille.*

Given what Violet knew of Ewan's past—which was, admittedly, not much—she found this a puzzle.

Her sisters were not wrong: Ewan appeared the consummate gentleman. And yet, as her father had noted, he had not been born into the gentry class.

His speech marked him as coming from the western isles, and as such, she assumed his upbringing to be humble. The kilts he typically wore testified of this.

That said, there was significant refinement to him. Ewan owned fine clothing and wore it like a gentleman when the need arose. And he knew how to behave in polite society.

Even more puzzling were the letters that kept arriving for Mr. Campbell.

In all truth, the letters themselves were nothing extraordinary. Everyone received post.

It was just . . . his letters were franked by some rather illustrious persons.

Two came with the Earl of Mainfeld's signature scrawled across the bottom, supplying the postage. Another arrived with the Marquess of Wanleigh's name signed.

Violet knew it could simply be a coincidence. Peers often left franked envelopes for guests. It was one of the advantages of having friends with connections to the peerage—postage supplied *gratis.* So perhaps the letters were from clients with connections to the Peers franking the post.

But there were so *many* noblemen.

Lord Hadley appeared to be the most prolific. Violet had counted no fewer than five letters franked with the man's name.

She knew it was none of her business. But still she mused over the puzzle of it.

Ewan could easily be conducting business with connections to these nobles. Heavens, the lords themselves could *be* his clients.

But Ewan spoke only of clients in Edinburgh. The letters were franked by noblemen living primarily in England. So why would English clients be soliciting a painter living in Edinburgh instead of London?

Ugh.

Ewan's correspondence was his own affair.

She should feel *guilty* for prying.

But, again, guilt was a poor motivator.

She *should* be spending her time trying to make a firm decision about what to do with the Manna Loan coming due.

Meetings with her solicitor were inconclusive.

"The loan is a pressing concern, my lady," Mr. Lawyerly said on a dreich Monday morning. "Have you pondered selling on the large, southern tack?"

No. She hadn't. Not to the degree required.

How did she wish to repay the loan?

Sell the fiefdom-sized tack and use the grassum to pay it off, which is what her mother had wished her to do?

Violet could, but doing so left the tenants in another's hands, not to mention incurred a loss of future revenue.

So . . . perhaps she should retain the southern tack and sell the London town house instead?

But Violet shied away from selling the townhouse in Mayfair. The building embodied her childhood, from the wisteria her mother treasured creeping over the front portico to the scuffed armoire in the study where she and Dahlia would hide from their nurse. The house was a vivid reminder of her mother and Dahlia and the thousands of memories they had made there together.

And, of course, if she sold the townhouse in order to retain the large tack, then she would have to hire stewards and staff and oversee the lot herself. She envisioned endless choices between oats and potatoes.

The thought could give her nightmares.

But it could come out all right, too. She didn't *dislike* working with Mr. Shambles to manage the much smaller tack.

Staring at the problem was a bit like looking into the black depths of a sea cave. She could only suppose what lay beyond. It could be just more wet stone and dank air. Or it could be Aladdin's Cave of Wonders, full of crystal stalactites and wondrous shapes.

But in order to know which it would be, one had to enter the cave.

Violet rubbed her forehead.

"Are there any other solutions to consider, Mr. Lawyerly?" she asked. "Anything at all?"

He pursed his lips. "I suppose, if your ladyship is truly opposed to selling the tack or the townhouse, we could consider mortgaging the townhouse to pay the Manna Loan. Of course, such a mortgage would negate any increased revenue from retaining the tack, so in the end, it feels rather pointless." He cleared his throat. "It is why I have not suggested it as a solution up to this point, my lady."

Mmmm. Yes, incurring another loan to pay the first would be . . . unhelpful.

Mr. Lawyerly laid his next words carefully, "I must be honest with you, my lady. If you wish to retain both the tack and the townhouse, you will likely need to marry."

Violet barely managed a nod.

That was the third solution, was it not? Marry someone wealthy. Someone who would manage the tack for her and pay off the Manna Loan without anything having to be sold.

Someone meaning Lord Graham.

Not that the man had officially offered for her.

Not that she necessarily wished to marry him.

"It would be wise to begin making decisions, your ladyship," Mr. Lawyerly continued.

Ah, yes . . . decisions!

Her nemesis.

In the end, she begged a few more weeks to ponder the problem.

Of course, the only questions she *wanted* answered were those pertaining to a certain Highland painter who sent her thoughts down forbidden paths.

And so, when yet *another* letter arrived from Lord Hadley for Ewan, Violet called for her bonnet.

She needed some exercise, after all, and the weather was lovely. A short walk down to Old Kilmeny Castle would allow her to stretch her legs and perhaps clear her mind.

Even better, it meant she could deliver the letter herself.

13

Violet found Ewan in his greenhouse-turned-studio.

The large, glass door was ajar, likely to let out heat as the day had warmed considerably.

Sunlight filtered down through gauze-draped skylights and bounced from the wall of windows facing the ocean, creating a symphony of glowing light in the space.

Ewan stood with his back to her, concentrating on the canvas in front of him.

That same russet-and-gray great kilt wrapped around his hips, but he had loosened the upper half that normally swathed his chest, causing it to drape behind, the weight of the plaid hanging nearly to the heel of his scuffed leather boots. He had shed his coat, too, and therefore painted in his shirt sleeves. No cravat or waistcoat. Just a shirt and kilt.

It was a state of dishabille that should have had Violet retreating back up the path—or, at the very least, blushing cherry red—but instead, she stared from the greenhouse doorway, drinking in the sight.

Her greedy eyes skimmed the flex of muscle underneath the shirt linen—the faint color of his skin, the ripple of his shoulder blade as he brushed paint onto the canvas.

He held a palette in his left hand. The few times a governess had forced a palette into Violet's palm, it had felt enormous. A giant, unwieldy fan of a device.

However, like everything else about him, Ewan's hands were mammoth-sized. And so his palette became a child's plaything in his palm. His brush strokes were similarly incongruous, dainty and delicate.

She remembered Lord Graham's words from the dinner party a week past.

Seems a shame for so much brawn to be wasted on daubs of paint.

And as it had then, indignation rose in her chest.

From the bit of the painting she could see peeking out, *nothing* about the man's talent was squandered effort.

As if feeling the weight of her scrutiny, Ewan turned.

Something flashed across his face—surprise? dismay?—and then vanished behind a polite mask.

"Lady Kildrum." He set down his palette and dropped his brush in a cup of turpentine before snagging a rag and wiping his hands. He gave a small bow. "Tae what do I owe the pleasure?"

"A letter came for you." Violet stepped fully into the greenhouse and extended the letter in her hand, abruptly aware of how flimsy her reasoning sounded. "I was walking this way and thought to deliver it."

She might as well have said, *I was desperate to see you, and so I snagged on this paltry excuse.*

If he agreed with her thoughts, he didn't show it.

"Thank ye." He took the letter from her, glanced at the front, and then merely held it at his side.

Violet chewed on her cheek.

Drat.

What was she hoping he would do? Read it to her aloud? Confide all his secrets?

Ugh.

Worse, her eyes snagged on the neckline of his linen shirt, the V of the open collar acting like an anchor to her gaze, dragging it down to the exposed skin there. The feeling of being tucked against that very chest flooded her, sending heat chasing along her skin.

She nearly swayed toward him, so strong was the pull.

Before she could make an even greater fool of herself, she spun in a circle, as if taking in the greenhouse.

Paintings leaned against the walls. The canvas she had seen him painting atop the cliff was placed in front. But there were snippets of others. A hawk-nosed profile here. The glimmer of pink satin and a frilled bonnet there.

Soon she found herself lost in russet horizons and green trees and boundless oceans.

Eventually, she circled back around.

Ewan had opened the letter, reading it with furrowed brow.

Violet seized the opening. "All good news, I hope?"

He lifted his head, eyes a question mark.

She motioned toward the letter.

"Aye," he nodded. "It seems I must away to Aberdeen tomorrow."

"Aberdeen?"

"I've some business to attend to. It willnae take long."

He turned from her and tossed the letter onto his work desk as if it were of no consequence.

Mmmm, business with Lord Hadley? What could that be?

Violet swallowed, pushing the thought away.

Stop this.

Let it be.

Her eyes drifted back to that tantalizing V of skin, the hollow at the base of his throat.

She really should leave. What was she accomplishing by being here anyway? Other than distracting the rugged Highlander from his work while ogling him like a lovesick school girl?

But Ewan shifted sideways, finally giving her a clear view of the painting on his easel.

Violet froze.

It was a woman.

A *beautiful* woman with a heart-shaped face—broad forehead and pointed chin. Her dark hair was unbound and fell in tight ringlets around her face, the curls painted in shades of black with shimmery blue-black highlights. Eyes of nearly colorless silver peeked out. The woman had a mischievous look to her, as if all the world were a lark, and she simply could not wait to embark upon it.

Dahlia had displayed such a spirit.

Violet noted the tartan draped around the woman's shoulders and found herself looking between the woman on the easel and the clifftop canvas with the female figure carrying the basket.

Were the tartans similar? Was this the same person? The woman who put shadows in Ewan's eyes when he spoke of loss?

And if so, who was she to him?

It took several more minutes of quiet observation before Violet realized that Ewan watched her watching.

Violet stepped back, startled.

To her disappointment, he had pulled the length of his great kilt back across his chest, pinning it with an enormous brooch at his shoulder. The mass of plaid effectively covered that distracting V of skin.

"Pardon my intrusiveness," she said. "I became a little lost there."

"Nae bother."

"She is beautiful, so full of life." Violet motioned toward the painting. "Is it an accurate likeness?"

He shrugged, the mass of his shoulder momentarily outlined under his shirt linen. "I like tae think so."

Violet *had* to ask further. Her curiosity was too strong. "Is she a client of yours?"

"No. She was . . ." A long pause. ". . . someone I used tae know."

"A lost love?"

He gave a faint smile. "Something of the like."

Ah.

"She *was* . . ." Violet lingered on the word. "She was lost to you in the same way Dahlia was lost to me?"

Wordlessly, Ewan looked at the painting and then nodded. "Aye. She is gone. I paint her from memory."

Heavens. "Your recall must be formidable."

"Perhaps." He shrugged, eyes still on the canvas. "Or maybe it is simply the power of her memory."

Well.

That was . . . illuminating.

And perhaps somewhat humbling.

It underscored, yet again, how little she knew about this man.

Heaven help her, though . . . she wanted to know more and more.

So instead of taking her leave—like good sense and propriety insisted she should, like Lady Graham and other sticklers would require—she continued to ask questions.

"How did you know this—" She waved a hand to indicate the canvases stacked around the greenhouse. "—was what you wanted to do?"

Perhaps his answer could help guide her own decisions.

Or, at least, that was the excuse she told herself.

"Painting?" He raised his eyebrows. "I cannae say that I knew. It was . . . simply impossible tae do anything else."

Violet frowned. It sounded too simplistic. "Yes . . . but certainly there was a point at which you had to make a choice, correct?"

"How so?"

"Well," she floundered for a moment and then settled on bare truth. "When we first met, all those years ago, you claimed to be running from your past."

Was she a fool to be revealing how precisely she remembered that conversation? His panicked desperation? Her curiosity to know what had driven him to such extremes?

She looked away, taking a few steps toward the bank of glass windows and the endless ocean beyond, willing her blush to *Cease!* with only minimal success.

She could *feel* him behind her. The sibilant *shush* of wool rustling. The slight hitch of his breath.

Gooseflesh flared to life across her shoulder-blades, as if her very skin itched for him.

"Aye." His voice rumbled, hesitant. "And you said you were running from your future."

Oh!

She turned back to him in a whirl.

How could she have forgotten that bit?

She so clearly remembered him stating he was running from his past. But she had neglected her own response—

She ran from her future. Or rather she *wished* to run from it.

She had not, of course. Yet another thing she could not decide upon.

He met her gaze, eyes saying what his words had not.

I remember you. That meeting lingered with me, as well.

He had his hands clasped behind his back. Light from the skylights washed down from overhead, raking his shoulders and hair, casting the rest of him in shadow.

"Were you a painter then?" she nearly whispered.

He nodded slowly, eyes never leaving hers. He shifted, hands still behind his back, the motion pressing one massive shoulder into the fabric of his shirt.

"*Why?*" Her voice came out on a broken breath, shocking even her with its baffled confusion.

"Why fight when I could paint?"

Now it was her turn to nod.

"What was it Lord Graham called me at dinner last week?" He glanced upward, as if trying to recall exactly, but they both knew the gesture was merely for show. The words still rang in Violet's ears. "Something about brawn being wasted on daubs of paint, I believe. Lord Graham isnae the first man tae voice such an opinion of what I should or shouldnae be doing with my own body."

He leaned back against the stone wall opposite the windows, moving entirely into shadow, though his autumnal eyes continued to glitter in the low light. He folded his arms across his chest, his body appearing relaxed. Only the flex-and-release of his right fist testified of inner turmoil.

"I wanted tae stop fighting. I dreamed of it," he continued, swallowing. "But this may come as shock tae ye, I didnae grow up in the lap of luxury. Becoming a painter, as it turns out, isnae something a poor lad can easily aspire to."

His tone had a hint of steel in it. As if he dared her to acknowledge the lowliness of his upbringing, the giant gulf between them socially.

She lifted her chin, meeting his challenge.

I would never think less of you, she willed her eyes to say.

"How then?" she asked. *How did you become a painter? What was your path?*

A cloud flitted across his face and then he relaxed, scrubbing a hand over his jaw.

"Prizefighting led me tae painting."

"Pardon?"

"'Tis true." He shot her a rather grim excuse for a smile. "I have a natural ability tae fight. It isnae anything I ever wished for, but it simply happened. You were born a countess. I was born a prizefighter. As a youth I quickly learned I could earn more in an hour with my fists than a month's work in a field. At the time, prizefighting seemed a preferable way tae provide a living.

"I also discovered it wasnae the only way for my body tae earn me money. As you know, artists constantly need models from which tae draw. Prizefighters are ideal subjects. A local vicar, who fancied himself something of a painter, asked if I would model for him. That first afternoon, watching him sketch . . ."

Ewan paused and looked beyond Violet, eyes gazing out over the endless blue of the sea beyond her shoulders.

He shook his head. "It was as if someone had struck a match in a dark room. The world flared tae life. Line. Shadow. Light. And *color*. So much color."

He waved a hand, as if the sheer astonishment of it were too breathtaking, too miraculous to explain in mere words.

"I was . . . overcome. I begged the vicar tae repay my modeling efforts through lessons and supplies. He agreed." Ewan took in a shuddering breath. "Picking up charcoal for the first time . . . putting it tae paper and breathing form tae life . . . I realized that, up until that moment,

I had been merely existing. Drawing and sketching and creating . . . *that* was living.

"I was voracious. I took on more fights so's I could earn more coin tae purchase art supplies. I paid for lessons by modeling for more skilled painters, tolerating being viewed as more animal than man. It all culminated in the fight that day outside Warwick." He pinned her with his golden hazel eyes, reminding her of those minutes so long ago. "I used the money I won that afternoon to travel to London, as I've mentioned before. I bought myself as fine a set of clothing as I could and begged my way into the Royal Academy."

He spread his arms wide.

And here I am.

So few words for such a monumental journey. Surely there was much he omitted.

Violet dared a glance at the dark-haired woman resting on his easel. How did she fit into his story? Why was that blackhouse on the ocean meaningful?

"I've outpaced my past, for better or worse," he said, drawing her attention back to him. "But if I may be so bold, my lady, ye have the look of a woman who is still running from her future."

Violet barely stopped a sharp inhalation.

They stared at one another for a long moment.

Thoughts warred in her head.

Denial? *Hah! What nonsense. I have embraced my future.*

Distraction? *So . . . when will you leave for Aberdeen?*

But . . .

The man was practically a prophet.

She looked away, reaching to run her index finger along the row of paintbrushes neatly laid on the work table. The bristles were soft overall but prone to prick if turned just the right way.

Very much like this moment in their conversation.

She *was* running from her future, was she not? Or rather, running from what society and her parents expected her future to be. Was it not the source of all her indecision?

"I was a born a countess, as you said. A countess!" She gave a disbelieving laugh. "My path has been laid for me from the cradle. Privilege. Wealth. And yet . . ." She swallowed and then uttered the words she had never dared say aloud. "And yet, I am so desperately lost. I am not running from my future, per se . . ." She paused, thinking for a moment. "It's rather . . . that I cannot envision my future. And because I cannot envision it, I cannot make decisions. And, as a countess, that *is* a problem."

Violet was mortified to feel tears pricking her eyes.

Ugh.

She turned away, giving him her back, staring out of the bank of windows. The ocean was calm today, a sea of white-speckled blue.

Silence hung. The call of seabirds drifted in. The soft crash of waves on the cliffs below the greenhouse sounded.

"How can I be nearly six and twenty and still not know the shape of my own life?" She meant the words to be calm, but they spooled out in an agonized breath.

"What is it Polonius says tae his son in *Hamlet?* . . . *To thine own self be true.*" A beat. "What is your truest self, my lady?"

"My truest self?" Her reply was swift. Immediate. "I am simply Violet Kerr. Nothing more. Nothing less. Not Lady Violet. Not Lady Kildrum. All the rest of it . . ." She waved a hand over her head. "All the rest feels like so much window dressing—frills and bows and faradiddle that has very little to do with reality. So . . . perhaps that is why, no matter how hard I try, I cannot force my mind to accept the decoration as my own."

A pause.

She did not say her other truths.

That in her naive thinking as Violet Kerr, she had encouraged Dahlia to follow her heart. That she had made decisions based on desire when she should have been thinking of the dedication to duty her station required.

Violet swiped at an errant tear that escaped.

Enough.

"You must think me the veriest ninnyhammer," she huffed a laugh, turning to face him. "Weeping over my life as if it were some dreary thing."

But saying the words did not banish her tears.

"Dinnae discount your tears, my lady." Ewan took three steps to his work table and retrieved a white handkerchief, extending it toward her. "Sometimes a good *greit* is necessary."

Violet shot him a watery smile and reached for the handkerchief, but in her bleary-eyed state, she reached too far, and ended up wrapping her palm around his fingers.

She nearly flinched at the shocking heat of the unexpected contact. The rough smoothness of his skin scalded her fingertips. Worse, she lingered in that moment, palm resting atop his, gazing at their hands like some crazed ninny. As if she could somehow store the scalding heat of him in her bones.

He moved his hand, and she all but snatched the handkerchief and turned aside to dab at her cheeks.

The handkerchief smelled of heather and called to mind a barren moor after rain.

Mortification scalded her lungs. What he must think of her?

"I am such an ungrateful fool," she sniffled. "I, at least, *have* choices. So many women do not. 'Tis absurd to cry over my poor decision-making abilities—"

"No. I cannae leave ye to believe such a thing," he said. "I've watched ye make plenty of wee decisions. But I can well understand how large choices would feel overwhelming given the stakes involved."

She paused and looked back to meet his eyes. And then swallowed over the intensity she saw there.

He continued, gaze softening. "Ye lost your mother and sister in back-to-back blows . . . the kind of battering hits that take a fighter down and out." He would know. Hadn't she witnessed him doing that exact thing to the Hammer all those years ago? "Ye've been *grieving*, lass. Of course it's difficult tae understand what your path should be, particularly when so many are relying on ye. Ye've been living crisis to crisis for years, wandering in the dark for so long, you've lost sight of the path. Have some care for yourself."

"Were it possible, I would have walked away years ago, I think." She hiccupped. "But my sisters . . . despite my father being their guardian, they do require a woman's care. And I cannot abandon the tenants and tradesmen who depend upon the earldom. I may have not wanted to be a countess any more than you wanted to be a prizefighter, but in my case, I cannot give it up."

"Ah, lass." His voice thrummed with feeling. "Your sense of duty is tae be commended. I admire ye for it. But perhaps ye've been Lady Kildrum for so long, ye've lost a bit of yourself in the duty of the title. That isnae a bad thing. But ye've forgotten to consider the wishes of your own heart."

She stilled, pondering the truth of his words.

Was this true?

Had the guilt and grief over encouraging Dahlia to follow her heart actually had the opposite effect of stifling Violet's own?

And if so . . . what was she to do about it?

"Perhaps." She wiped her cheeks again. "I just wish I knew how to proceed forward."

"If ye were lost in a wood and couldnae find the path, ye would not assume that the path existed, but ye were simply too blind tae see it. No, that would be madness. Instead, ye would assume that if ye could not see it yet, then ye had not found the path. Ye would keep looking." He pondered her for a moment and then swept a hand toward the open door. "I often find a walk helps me sort through problems. Would ye care tae join me? I would gladly listen, if ye'd like to talk it out."

Violet looked out the open door. The coastal path snaked along the clifftops, wind rippling the grasses into waves mimicked by the ocean beyond.

To walk and talk with him. To step into the wild sea air and divulge the more intimate thoughts of her heart.

Duty insisted that she leave *righthisinstant*.

That was the correct course. The Lady-Graham-approved course.

But . . .

Her *heart* wanted the wind in her hair and the fresh scent of ocean and gorse buffeting her skin. She ached for his voice in her ear. To confide in him. To leave another piece of herself in his gentle care.

The choice stretched before her . . . two paths from which to choose—duty or desire?

These were not metaphorical routes she contemplated.

No.

The paths literally forked right outside the greenhouse door—

One path retreated back over the hill to Kilmeny Hall. The other ran straight ahead, winding its way along the cliffs.

Go straight on, she could practically hear Dahlia urge her. *Spend time with the delicious Highlander.*

The wind and waves drowned out any other thought.

And so . . . Violet Kerr made a decision.

She smiled, nodding.

Ewan motioned for her to pass through the doorway first before falling into step beside her.

Violet took in a deep breath, letting the ocean air chase the cobwebs from her lungs.

"Now, my lady, tell me what troubles ye," he said, clasping his hands behind his back.

And so, Violet did.

As the fresh ocean air tugged at her bonnet and the *shush-shush* of waves blended with the call of gulls, she told him about the looming Manna Loan and the possible solutions. Though she may have left off the bit about marrying Lord Graham.

And as they jumped across a small burn running down to the sea and waded through sea grass that clutched at her skirts, she discussed her worries about managing her own lands . . . should she choose to keep the large southern tack.

When they paused to study a particularly picturesque view of waves crashing against sea stacks lining the cliffs, she mentioned the tension with her father and her concerns for her younger sisters, their need to have a London Season and be properly married off.

Ewan listened attentively, the weight of his attention fully upon her.

He asked questions and prodded her to open up more.

By the end, when they stopped to watch a group of puffins squabble over a choice cliff ledge, Violet was nearly hoarse from speaking.

But her burdens felt lighter somehow . . . more surmountable.

"So you're trying to decide whether tae manage the lands yourself, is that right?" he asked, turning his attention away from the quarreling puffins.

"Precisely."

"So . . . do ye like managing lands? Do ye ken to agriculture?"

Violet blinked. And then blinked again.

Honestly, no one had ever asked her that.

"I don't . . ." She paused and then shook her head, neck craning back to meet his eyes. "I don't know."

"Well, there ye are. I would think that should be your first goal. Discover if ye even *like* managing crop rotations and researching farm techniques. That's what I would do."

He had leaned closer as he spoke, the heat of his body looming larger and larger.

The attraction that had been simmering between them flared, like a spark to dry tinder.

His eyes drifted down her face, as if painting her to memory.

Violet certainly felt touched. Everywhere his gaze landed burned as if scorched. Forehead. Cheeks. Lips.

He might as well have dragged a fingertip across her skin for how it tingled and goosebumped to attention.

Her chest heaved, her heart lurching to a gallop.

"Ye may have been born a countess," he continued, voice barely carrying to her ears, "but it is a testament tae your sense of self that ye can still feel apart from it. As ye said, ye are Violet Kerr . . . no more, no less. A whole world encompassed in that. Duty and concerns of the estate aside, why not discover what Violet Kerr likes and dislikes? What is it ye *desire* tae do? From there, ye might be able to suss out the shape of your future."

Longing clenched Violet's chest in a vise.

He was right, of course.

It was brilliant advice.

Unbidden, her eyes drifted to the cliffs behind him. To thoughts of falling and chasing what was forbidden.

Because . . . what if, after all that soul-searching, she decided she wanted *him* to be her future?

And what happened when she longed for a future that could never be?

14

"So this is the address ye were given?" Rafe asked, peering out of the carriage window.

"Aye," Andrew said, brow furrowing as he followed Rafe's gaze.

Ewan couldn't blame his friends for being hesitant.

The carriage had come to a stop before a stone cottage on the outskirts of Old Aberdeen, the original medieval town just north of Aberdeen proper. The noon-day sun peeked through the clouds, trying to banish the gloom with only marginal success.

The cottage was a ragged sort of place from the worn thatch of the roof to the oilskin nailed over the small windows. Every line of the structure proclaimed the poverty and pain of those who lived inside.

All in all, not unlike a typical blackhouse on the western isles.

Not that Ewan said as much.

"Perhaps I should have had my Runner actually visit first," Andrew continued.

Rafe grunted.

The plan had been simple. Andrew's Runner from Bow Street acquired the address of the witness the magistrate had interviewed—the unknown second crewman who had survived the wreck of *The Minerva*. The Brotherhood had wished to visit first, fearing too much attention might send their prey scurrying to ground, as Captain Cuthie had done.

Though his friends had not directly said as much, Ewan knew he was along to act as hired muscle. Not that Andrew or Rafe viewed him that way exclusively, but there was no need to shrink away from a bald reality.

Cuthie was a violent, cruel man. His crew had not been much better, particularly the men most loyal to him. If one of those men lived in this cottage, trouble would not be far behind.

And now, staring at the cottage through the carriage window, Ewan could not dismiss the idea that this place was one of violence and hardship. It practically oozed from the dank gray stones, a dark, red-tinged miasma.

But they needed answers. Who was placing the notices in newspapers? How had Cuthie, and potentially others, survived? And, most critically, might Jamie have lived?

Everything pointed to their friend being dead. Jamie's silence alone confirmed it. But the murkier the situation became, the harder it was to believe that fully.

"I'll go knock first." Ewan nodded at Rafe and Andrew seated across from him. "Be the burly manservant."

Andrew and Rafe frowned, their expressions nearly synchronized.

Ewan leaned away. "What did I say?"

"We did not invite you along to be our bodyguard, Ewan," Andrew said, voice flat. "Rafe and I are fully capable of defending ourselves."

"Aye. We asked ye tae come because we value your input," Rafe seconded.

Ewan raised his eyebrows. His friend's comments were . . . unexpected.

"I . . . thank ye," he said after a moment's hesitation. "But truthfully, youse both realize that it makes sense tae send the Highlander tae the door first, right?" He motioned to his great kilt, the plaid a length of Jamie's tartan today. "They willnae be suspicious of me."

Rafe shook his head and sent his eyes skyward. "Such lack of suspicion comes from your uncanny ability tae put others at ease."

"Aye," Andrew agreed before waving him on. "Out with ye. Go be your gentle Highlander self."

Ewan huffed a laugh and saluted them before stepping out of the carriage. The cottage was only one of several houses down this wee lane. He could feel cautious eyes peering out of doors and windows. Fortunately, Andrew had the good sense to bring a plain black carriage instead of a gilded one decorated with his coat of arms. But still, a private coach of any sort was certainly unusual in these quarters.

Ewan knocked on the cottage door. He could hear the wail of a babe and the scuffling noise of children beyond.

No male voices, at the moment. Thank goodness.

Just because Ewan *could* fight, it did not therefore follow that he relished the prospect.

The door creaked open.

Two wee brown eyes set in a wee dirty face stared at the bottom of his kilt and then traveled up, up, up to finally lock eyes with him.

Ewan smiled.

The eyes widened and the door slammed shut.

"Ma, there's a giant on the stoop!" a child's voice rang out.

Mmmm, perhaps he should have allowed Rafe to come, after all.

Frowning, he leaned forward and called through the door, roughening his accent. "I'm no' a cruel giant. More of a friendly one, if ye must know."

That may or may not be true, Ewan supposed, depending on who else was behind the door. He wasn't always gentle, no matter what his friends said.

"I simply wanted tae ask youse a question if ye wouldnae mind opening the door," he continued.

Another scuffle. The hiss of voices back and forth.

The door creaked open.

This time a woman's wary eyes met his. She was thin and haggard, a child on her hip.

"How may I help ye?" she asked, licking her lips nervously.

He recognized the expression in her face. He had seen it countless times growing up.

Despair. Desperation. Defeat.

Mhairi would look like this. If she yet lives, that is.

The thought flitted through before he could bat it away. And on its heels that salmon-colored feeling scoured him . . . the lingering anguish and anger, all laced with his own impotence and cowardice—

Ewan swallowed.

"Ewan Campbell, at yer service." He nodded at the woman, pasting a placating smile on his face. He spared a glance at the children behind her, their eyes wide as they scanned his bulk.

"Ye said ye have a question for me," the woman replied.

"Aye. I ken that ye have some connection tae the men on *The Minerva*."

Ewan may as well have slapped her. The woman's head went back and her nostrils flared.

Her wary expression increased a hundred-fold.

"Did the magistrate send ye?" she hissed, leaning forward. "I already told 'em all I know."

Ewan held up his hands. "I'm no' from the magistrate. In fact, I was on the ship, too." There was no reason to hide the information. "I lost a good friend when *The Minerva* sank. I just wanted tae know who else had survived and how."

Her expression relaxed slightly. She glanced behind him. Ewan followed her gaze and noted that Rafe and Andrew had stepped out of the carriage.

"They were on the ship, as well," he said, turning back to the woman.

She hesitated, obviously wary of inviting three large men into her house.

Ewan pulled a half-crown from his pocket and extended it to her. "For your time."

She looked at the coin. Ewan knew full well it was probably more than she saw in an entire month.

Finally, she nodded and snatched the coin. "Very well." She opened the door wider.

Ewan stooped down and entered the cottage.

The interior was just as mean as the exterior. Bare, unplastered walls. Sparse furniture. The stench of unwashed bodies and rotting straw on the floor. His head brushed the low wooden ceiling.

Nothing about this scene was new for him. It was as if he had stepped into his own childhood.

He counted three other children, all several years older than the babe. Two sat on the solitary bed in one corner. The other stood against the opposite wall. A weak fire flickered in a fireplace at one end of the single room.

At least the house *had* a fireplace. The house he had grown up in only had a fire-ring in the middle of a hard-packed dirt floor.

Rafe and Andrew stepped in behind him, nodding at the woman in greeting.

The woman darted a glance at them, surely noting the fine cut of Rafe's coat and the winking silver of Andrew's buttons.

She turned back to Ewan in his humbler great kilt and simple coat. Just as he would have, in her place. Talk with the man who was someone more like herself.

"I suppose ye be wanting tae know what I told the magistrate," the woman began, licking her lips. "It isnae much, unfortunately. My husband is Robert Massey."

Ewan sucked in a breath.

Massey.

Captain Cuthie's first mate. A brute of a man. Whereas Cuthie had an almost preternatural ability to inspire loyalty in his men, Massey's only talent was sowing fear and administering pain.

Mrs. Massey shifted the baby to her other hip, bouncing him as he fussed.

One of the children grabbed a polished stick and handed it to the bairn. He snatched it and began to gnaw, drool dribbling down his chin. Likely teething, the poor thing.

Mrs. Massey shot them a nervous look. "We was told Robert had died, ye see . . . drowned in the wreck. But then he showed up last summer. Just walked through the door, as if he had only been out for a pint at the pub." She darted a glance at the other children and then back at the babe in her arms. "But . . . Robert had been gone for nigh upon four years by that point. I thought he was dead. We didnae have any way tae care for ourselves with Robert gone, as he was. And so I had tae find a way tae . . . provide for my bairns."

Ewan looked again at the baby.

Ah. Yes, that math wasn't hard to do.

Mrs. Massey met his eyes, intuitively seeing him as someone who had to make similar choices.

Ewan nodded. He well understood the desperation of impending starvation.

"Ye can imagine how Robert took tae finding wee Samuel here. He was only a month old at the time. Robert wasnae understanding of the . . . decisions I had made, thinking he was dead. He had a lot tae say about it."

Ewan mentally winced. He was quite sure he understood exactly how Robert had expressed his anger over being cuckolded. He had seen too many bruises on women growing up.

What compromises had *this* woman had to make over the years? Could this be Mhairi's lot, as well?

A sick sensation coiled in Ewan's stomach, cold and clammy and pink.

Why hadn't he tried harder to reach her? Why?

Though . . . he *had* returned, just once, had he not?

But to no avail.

I've already cast ye out once. Ye need to stay gone, *Ewan. I dinnae ever want tae see ye again.*

Was he right to not have pushed harder? To have resorted to a letter to the vicar instead of traveling back to Loch Carron himself?

Or were these just excuses he told himself, to justify running from the pain of his past like a coward?

Mrs. Massey swallowed. "Finally, after he had said his piece, Robert calmed down and told us the tale of his shipwreck. He claimed that only he and Captain Cuthie had survived. The ship had been nearly obliterated in the explosion—"

"Explosion?!" Andrew said, his voice a little too loud.

Mrs. Massey flinched, raising her arm up to shield her baby.

The motion broke Ewan's heart.

Andrew stared at the woman, eyes wide with horror, reading her reaction just as Ewan had.

"No one will hurt ye," Ewan held out a calming hand.

"Aye," Andrew said, tone much quieter. "My sincerest apologies. I didn't mean to startle ye."

Mrs. Massey relaxed her arm and nodded, cuddling her babe tighter.

"Please continue, Mrs. Massey," Ewan said. "We hadnae heard anything about an explosion. We thought the ship dashed upon a hidden reef."

She shook her head. "The magistrate asked me the same question. *What did Robert mean by an explosion?* But Robert didnae say anything else beyond that. Just that he and Cuthie were thrown clear of the boat in the explosion, as they were standing on the quarterdeck at the time. Them's were his exact words. I suppose it could just mean that the ship hit the reef with an explosion or somesuch. I dinnae ken what he meant exactly by an explosion.

"The crew were killed, Robert said. Every last one of them. Robert and Cuthie managed tae gather together enough boards from the wreckage tae fashion a wee raft. They sailed for two days, following the currents, until they reached an island. There was a small village on the island, and they lived there for two years until an American ship visited. It took them a good while tae work up the money for passage back home. That's alls I know."

She turned to the babe again, bouncing him.

Andrew cleared his throat. "There have been notices published in papers in Aberdeen and Edinburgh. Do ye happen tae know anything about them?"

She shook her head. "No. Robert certainly isnae behind them. He isnae the sort to waste coin on such a thing."

TWO HOURS LATER, Ewan sat across from Rafe and Andrew in the private dining room of an inn in Old Aberdeen. The remains of haggis with mashed neeps-n-tatties sprawled across the table. Ewan relaxed back, relishing the feeling of a full stomach. It never lasted long, unfortunately.

"I'm going tae send my steward to Mrs. Massey," Andrew said, drumming his fingers on the tabletop. "I reckon there is a wee cottage on my land that could benefit from a tenant to tend the garden there."

"That's right kind of ye," Ewan replied. "She shouldnae be left tae pay for the sins of her husband."

The fire popped in the grate.

Rafe took a sip of his whisky. "What do we do with her information?"

"We've been saying for months now that Jamie's silence is the only proof we need. That Jamie has tae be dead." Ewan reached for his own glass. "But Massey and Cuthie took over *three* years tae return to Scotland—"

"—so possibly, Jamie is alive and has simply taken longer to return to us," Rafe finished the thought.

"Precisely."

None of them wanted to maintain false hope. *Nothing* led them to believe that Jamie yet lived.

And yet . . .

"Will ye still count me a friend when we're old and gray, Ewan?" Jamie laughed, leaning against the railing of the ship.

"Aye, Jamie," Ewan smiled. "That I will."

"How do we tell Kieran about this?" Andrew let out a heavy sigh. He raised his eyes to meet Ewan's.

Ewan shrugged. "In his last letter, Alex said Kieran was somewhat improved—or, rather, had at least stemmed the tide of his drinking."

"Do we have tae tell him?" Rafe countered.

"Aye." Ewan said. "I think we do."

"It won't go well." Andrew scrubbed a hand over his face.

Rafe nodded in agreement. "Kieran seems to be . . ."

"On a razor's edge?" Andrew offered, reaching for the whisky bottle.

"Aye," Rafe said. "I sometimes think that his grief feels . . . disproportionate."

Ewan squirmed, the secret he held pulsing in his chest.

Kieran's grief is well-founded, he longed to say. *Any of us would behave similarly, given the same situation.*

Instead, he bit his tongue to keep from spilling secrets that weren't his own.

Andrew stared glumly into the fire before swallowing back the remainder of his whisky.

"How go things with Sir Joshua?" Rafe asked.

"Excellent." Ewan eagerly embraced the change of topic. "The painting is going well."

His friends stared at him.

Rafe cocked an eyebrow. Andrew sighed and made a beckoning motion.

Right. They wanted more.

Ewan rubbed the back of his neck. "Sir Joshua has been encouraging me to submit to the Royal Academy Exhibition."

"Hah! We've been saying the same for years now." Andrew slapped his hand on the table. "Have ye begun the painting ye will submit?"

"I cannae say for sure," Ewan replied.

Andrew and Rafe poked and prodded until Ewan told them all about Sir Joshua's comments, his own sense of indecision, and the challenges facing him as he worked—namely assisting Sir Joshua and painting the portrait of Lady Kildrum.

"Lady Kildrum, eh?" Rafe tapped his chin. "Seems like I have an acquaintance with her. Tall? Brownish hair?"

"Aye, that would be her. Painting her portrait has been an honor. Her ladyship has become something of a . . ." Ewan drifted off, trying to think of the right word. Confidant? Pal? He finally settled on, ". . . friend."

Friend.

The simple word felt too small and yet, somehow, too intimate. Who was he to claim a friendship with the Countess of Kildrum?

He thought back to that last conversation in his greenhouse studio. Lady Violet facing him, washed in light pouring through the skylights overhead, the vivid blue-green of her eyes mimicked in the ocean behind her.

He had adored the throaty timbre of her voice as she spoke about her life. Her care for her tenants had been a pulsing force in the air. So many landowners never bothered to see their tenants as actual people. And yet, Violet did.

She refused to simply make the easiest decision and instead sought to make the *best* one.

He had thought her utterly remarkable. And so he had urged her to act.

Had he pushed too hard? Had he, in his wish to help, been too adamant?

But . . . she clearly did not dislike him. Why she had *dragged* her palm over his hand, reaching for that handkerchief—

Unfortunately, just the thought of it was enough to tighten Ewan's breathing and render him light-headed, a blush climbing his neck.

Dammit.

"Ahhh," Andrew sat back.

Rafe's eyes flared wide.

Neither of his friends misunderstood Ewan's hesitation.

Their somewhat stunned silence only caused his cheeks to burn brighter. He could nearly *feel* the mortification oozing from his pores, emotion painting his skin.

He might as well have trumpeted his infatuation from a rooftop.

"I can understand the appeal, Ewan." Rafe reached for more whisky. "Ye have good taste in women."

"Aye." Andrew nodded. "About time ye showed some interest in a fair lassie—"

"Please, say no more, the boths of ye." Ewan scrubbed a hand over his face. Why did blushing have to be so damn uncomfortable? "Ye needn't bother to castigate me for my stupidity. I ken well that I am an eejit tae even look at such a high-born lady."

Silence hung for a moment.

Andrew spoke first, laying his words ever-so-carefully. "As a titled peer in her own right, Lady Kildrum can marry where she chooses. I would applaud the lady for having the good taste tae regard ye as a potential suitor."

"Aye," Rafe agreed. "I would, as well. But in my experience, high-ranking ladies often feel the pressure of society even *more* keenly. So in this case . . ." His voice drifted off.

They said nothing more.

Not quite a *condemning* silence, Ewan acknowledged. But definitely a pause ringed round with all the societal impediments and impossibility of Ewan contemplating anything more than casual friendship with a lady like Violet.

"Let us drop the topic." Ewan eagerly reached for the whisky. Could he get drunk enough to forget the scalding embarrassment of this conversation? "I ken what I am and what I am not. I know that I will never be a gentleman."

"Don't dismiss yourself so quickly." Andrew waved a hand. "Being thought a gentleman is merely so much physical trapping. A well-cut coat. An elegant bow. Now being a gentleman in truth—a man who is truly *noble* of heart like yourself—that is much rarer."

"Aye," Rafe agreed. "The best of humanity runs in your veins, Ewan."

Now Ewan was blushing due to his friend's kindness.

But their pause around Violet had been telling. Their hesitance more than anything underscored the futility of his admiration.

"Though I appreciate your kind words, youse and I both know that it takes more than a noble heart to be considered a gentleman." Ewan paused. "At least, as society sees it."

"Ye always seem tae be operating under the assumption that your upbringing somehow lessens ye." Rafe folded his arms. "I ken that there are segments of our society that try to convince ye of it. But in reality . . . it simply isn't true."

"Aye. The belief in yourself starts here." Andrew tapped his temple. "We cannot let ye believe ye are less than any of the rest of us."

Ewan darted a glance back and forth between his friends. "Be that as it may, I have to *live* within this society."

"True," Andrew agreed. "And ye are wise tae be careful with Lady Kildrum. I dislike the thought that a high-born lady might be trifling with ye."

Rafe took a healthy swallow of whisky. "I don't recall Lady Kildrum being the sort to play games."

"Regardless," Andrew added, expression serious. "Lady Kildrum is fortunate tae have your regard."

"Amen." Rafe lifted his glass in a salute.

"Do ye want us tae put in a good word for ye?" Andrew tossed his head toward Rafe with a sly grin.

"That's an excellent idea," Rafe grinned. "Explain the advantages tae her ladyship—"

"Please, no!" Ewan all but shuddered, holding out a staying hand, that blush roaring back. "Her ladyship can make her own decisions. And we all know that she would be wise to not choose me."

After all, hadn't he told her about his history with prizefighting in an attempt to send her scurrying back to her gilded mansion, happily rid of him?

And yet, Violet had absorbed his story as if he were discussing Eton and attending balls in London, not his own hard-scrabble existence.

Talking with her was like hearing his own heart vocalized. And given the furtive glances he caught from her, he couldn't stem the thought that perhaps Violet might feel the same way.

Of course, at the end of the day, she would still be a countess, and he would still be . . . what? A former crofter and prizefighter with a penchant for painting?

"In the meantime—" Andrew clinked his glass with Rafe's. "—I am looking forward to seeing your work not only accepted to the Royal Academy but hung 'on the line' this year."

Ewan managed a weak smile of his own in return.

He understood his friends' twofold message loud and clear:

One, do not give too much of your heart to Lady Kildrum. She is a countess and will not stoop to return your affection.

Two, focus on your art and the things you can control, like submitting a painting to the Royal Academy Exhibition.

On that point, Ewan wasn't nearly so confident of his abilities. Anyone with a dab hand could recreate a scene. True art took much more.

If you wish to be great, find the courage to paint your demons.

Was Ewan ready to allow the pyre of his past to consume him?

Death wasn't the only way someone was lost.

The belief in yourself starts here.

But . . . witnessing Mrs. Massey's struggles had shone a light into that period of his past.

Ideas and images raked him. Scenes that were not quite so painful, more like flotsam and jetsam torn from the ragged bits of his trauma.

Perhaps he didn't have to drag his psyche through the painful inferno of his memories.

Perhaps something smaller would suffice.

He spent the rest of the night attempting to convince himself.

15

Violet sat in her study, a pile of books before her, listening to the new lambs *baa* in the west pasture and wind rustle through the enormous pines lining the front drive.

This was good. Quiet. Bucolic.

No distractions.

She pulled a book toward her.

A General View of the Agriculture of the County of Berwick, with observations from a Distinguished Lord advocating improvement.

That didn't sound . . . too terrible, right?

She could do this.

Even though Ewan had left for Aberdeen two days before, his charge lingered with her—

Discover what Violet Kerr likes and dislikes. Other answers will likely follow.

Those words on Ewan's (admittedly fine) lips had been a call to action. A challenge to explore.

As had his description of drawing for the first time—

I realized that up until that moment I had been merely existing.

Nothing could have described her more fully.

Since Dahlia's death, Violet had existed. She breathed and moved through her day.

But she had ceased feeling truly alive.

Ewan had found his Muse . . . the thing that illuminated his world. He knew what he desired.

What is it ye desire tae do?

His words rang in her ears.

Violet didn't know. She didn't know what she desired.

She had lain awake in bed the night before, pondering the conundrum. And somewhere between moonrise and the clock striking three in the morning, she had an epiphany.

Her guilt and regret over Dahlia had caused her to shy away from the wishes of her heart. After all, her foolish, romantic heart had led Dahlia to disaster.

But . . . Violet had finally understood a critical fact: Her fear of making another disastrous decision and the lack of knowing her own heart had combined to create a sort of paralysis.

If she was pondering managing the vast tack, she needed to know if she *liked* such a thing. Surely, her stewards would help her, as Mr. Shambles currently did, but a responsible landowner would be knowledgeable and resourceful. She did not want to shirk that duty. So if she assumed the tack, she had to be ready to act.

But . . . did she wish to do that? Was that what she *desired* her future to be? She knew it would involve more than just choosing between oats and potatoes. She would be called upon to make all sorts of choices.

How hard can it be? All I have to do is decide if I like agriculture.

She opened the book and began to read.

Or rather, she *tried* to read.

But her thoughts were pesky marauders, leaping from place to place, running between the words on the page and causing the whole to blur into one dark mass.

It was just . . .

Who *was* that dark-haired, gray-eyed woman in the painting in Ewan's studio? Who was she to Ewan? Clearly someone important, as hadn't he said something about being drawn to the power of her memory?

Did Ewan have a tragic love story in his background? A childhood sweetheart who had died of consumption, perhaps?

Violet could see it now. The once vibrant girl slowly wasting into a waif and Ewan bringing paintings to her bedside to cheer her up, wiping away tears of sadness when he left, his heart breaking—

Gracious! Violet shook her head.

She had likely been spending too much time with her sisters as of late.

She looked back down at the agricultural text before her.

Focus, Violet. You can master this.

Right. She forcibly cast all thoughts of handsome painters out of her mind and concentrated on her reading.

Ten minutes later, she thoroughly understood why so many gentlemen commented on the tedium of estate management.

Five minutes after that, she was convinced her shepherds had attached some sort of noise amplifier to the lambs. How could creatures so small make such an out-sized racket? She could scarcely hear her own thoughts.

Twenty minutes later, she jerked awake with a start, her cheek resting on the cool desktop.

Ugh.

This was not going to plan.

Massaging her temples, she took in a deep breath, attempting to recenter her focus.

I can do this.

She pushed the first book away and reached for another one.

An Inquiry into the Causes that have hitherto retarded the advancement of Agriculture in Europe, with particular emphasis on farming outwith landed estates.

Her eyes crossed before she even reached the end of the title.

Worse? It was Volume XII.

How could there possibly be *twelve volumes* worth of information to discuss?

She sighed and reached for another one.

A Country-man's Rudiments; or advice to the gentleman farmer of East Lothian.

Mmmm.

Maybe this one would be better?

She read for a bit. It wasn't *entirely* terrible. Like this chapter here:

"On the best Method of raising Elms; manuring Fallows for Wheat; and preventing the ravages of the Fly on young Turnips."

It *should* have been ghastly boring, but the method of raising elms was actually quite brilliant.

What would Mr. Shambles think of it? Did they need elms? Could they be used as a wind break for tender crops, as the author asserted?

She had no idea.

Heavens, there was so *much* to learn.

Maybe she *should* just lease the tack, pay off the Manna Loan, and give over her lands to tacksmen. After all, it had been the way of the Countesses of Kildrum for nigh upon a century, had it not?

And she could do that.

She likely *should* do that.

But . . . it felt like giving up. And just because that was how things had always been done, didn't make it the best path going forward. When faced with a choice between potatoes or oats, she would like to make an informed decision, not simply rely on tossing a shilling.

She flipped to the next chapter and continued reading about elms.

She was researching the best way to sow new trees when a knock sounded on her study door.

"Lord Graham to see you, my lady," Irvine announced.

"LORD GRAHAM, TO what do I owe this honor?" Violet asked, walking into the drawing room.

Lord Graham turned toward her, a welcoming smile on his lips.

"Lady Kildrum." He bowed, courtly and elegant. "How could I stay away from your charming presence?"

She motioned for him to be seated, and they conversed about pleasantries for a moment.

Yes, the weather had been quite nice as of late.

Yes, his mother was in good health.

Yes, her father and sisters were well, too.

Lord Graham sat back, crossing one elegant leg over another. "And what of your uncle and his . . ." He waved a hand in the air, as if searching for the words. ". . . pet, artistic pugilist? Are they yet in residence in Old Kilmeny?"

Violet's jaw dropped.

Pet. Artistic. *Pugilist.*

Lord Graham at least had the decency to look marginally regretful over his tactless description.

"If you are referring to Mr. Campbell, then yes, he is still assisting Sir Joshua." Violet kept her tone even but her eyes surely snapped with censure.

The very nerve!

She declined to add that Mr. Campbell was in Aberdeen at the moment but expected home later this evening.

What drove the pettiness of Lord Graham's words? How ungentlemanly of him to make such a remark about her uncle's guest, particularly to one so beneath Lord Graham's own station in life. It spoke of a meanness of spirit that Violet did not like.

Silence descended.

Lord Graham shifted in his chair, an agitated sort of motion that was unlike him.

Good. He *should* squirm.

A footman brought in a tea tray with some sandwiches and biscuits. Violet poured for both of them, her temper cooling along with the tea. Perhaps her own personal feelings for Ewan were bleeding over into her reaction to Lord Graham's words.

"Lady Kildrum," he said, reaching for a triangle of shortbread, "I must offer my apologies—"

"There is no need, Lord Graham," Violet sighed, sliding a cucumber sandwich on her own plate, feeling somewhat mollified at his attempt to apologize. He did possess admirable qualities. "We are friends, are we not?"

"Yes, but I fear I have given offense. I had not realized you had a specific friendship with Mr. Campbell."

Lord Graham laid his words carefully, but Violet heard echoes of his mother's censure in them.

Violet forced herself to *think* before speaking next. She had to tread carefully.

If Lady Graham discovered that Violet had been speaking with Ewan alone and unchaperoned the repercussions would be swift and severe. Her reputation would be in tatters and her sisters' prospects significantly damaged.

"Mr. Campbell is a guest of Sir Joshua, and I therefore feel it is my duty, as a lady of this estate, to ensure that all who abide here are treated with kindness."

Lord Graham smiled. "Such consideration toward those of the lesser classes is a credit to you, Lady Kildrum."

Lesser classes?!

"Indeed. Well . . ." Violet floundered, her ire rising once more. She swallowed the insults stinging the tip of her tongue and managed a tight breath. "Let us speak no more of it. Here, I will introduce a new topic: Do you have an opinion as to the best way to sow elms?"

Lord Graham startled, swallowing a bite of biscuit abruptly, sending him into a coughing fit.

"P-pardon?" he said once he had recovered. "Sowing elms?"

"Yes. I have questions about the process." Violet explained what she had been reading. "Why must the trunk knots be placed in furrows four feet apart—"

"Lady Kildrum," Lord Graham interrupted, his expression both baffled and amused. "Why should the topic of sowing elms *ever* be something to which you would subject your beautiful head?"

Violet froze. As in, actually froze—hand mid-wave, mouth open, eyes wide.

She snapped them all shut.

When she re-opened her eyes, Lord Graham had the same bemused expression on his face.

"I spoke with your father earlier this week," he said. "He has given me his blessing."

Shock jolted Violet's spine at the abrupt change in topic.

Of course, she *knew* this was where their friendship, such as it was, had been heading.

Lord Graham took her silence to be encouragement. He set down his teacup and leaned forward in his chair.

"You must know how much I ardently admire you, Lady Kildrum. You have been the object of my affection for many months." He slid off the sofa, dropping to his knees, his eyes sincere. "Would you make me the happiest of men and agree to be my wife?"

Violet found herself unequal to meeting his gaze.

I thought I had more time, a panicked part of her whispered. *I cannot make this decision quite yet.*

She lurched to her feet and crossed to one of the enormous paned windows overlooking the back terrace. She folded her arms across her chest, staring sightlessly at the gardeners trimming hedges in the Italianate garden.

She sensed more than heard Lord Graham approaching behind her.

"I know you well enough to understand that you would not play ridiculous games with my affections. Any hesitation you show will be real and true." He gave a mildly self-deprecating laugh. "As such, I cannot say that your current reaction encourages me."

Violet felt the tension in her shoulders relax.

See?! This was why she hadn't dismissed the man entirely.

He had moments of charm and self-awareness.

"I am sure I do not need to recount all the advantages to us marrying," he continued. "Our lands are adjacent, so neither of us will have to move far. I am . . . *familiar* . . . with the current financial crisis you are facing and wish you to have the full power of my coffers to address it. My mother wishes to assist you in launching your sisters into Society next year." He came to stand beside her, staring out over the garden, as well. "I care for you and consider you the finest woman of my acquaintance. Is the very thought of marriage to me so repugnant?"

"No. It is not." Not *repugnant*, at least.

But not exciting either.

She declined to add that last bit.

"But . . ." he prompted, perhaps having heard what she did not say.

Violet took in a deep breath.

How to reply?

Well . . . if she was considering marrying this man, perhaps she should start with honesty.

"I agree with all your arguments, my lord. I simply cannot decide." She gave him her truth. "I cannot decide if a life with you is what I want."

She did not, however, turn to look at him.

He stared out the window with her and then cleared his throat.

"At the risk of sounding pompous, may I offer my thoughts?"

Violet shot him a side-eye. And then nodded.

"I think that you are overwhelmed, my dearest lady. You have a woman's tender sensibilities. I admire your large heart and your wish to perform well in your responsibilities. But your position as countess must be a crushing burden. Imagine! You have been called upon to do the work of an earl! 'Tis no wonder you are overwhelmed. So it is only natural that you would struggle to understand what you want."

Violet frowned. She was quite sure that her 'tender sensibilities' were not the issue here, but she held her tongue. For the now.

"You need someone to rescue you," Lord Graham continued. "Someone who will take up his sword and battle your dragons. A valiant gentleman who will treasure you and keep you safe behind the walls of his golden castle."

Mmmm.

Lord Graham probably meant his words to be romantic and consoling.

Violet wasn't so sure.

Did she *want* to be kept as a treasure? The thought felt dull and constricting.

Besides . . . *golden castle?!*

It sounded like a euphemism her mother would have used to describe something unpleasant.

The maid has yet to empty the golden castle in your bed chamber.

Maybe the reason Violet had always been the lord when playing with her sisters had less to do with Dahlia's pushiness and more to do with Violet's own sense of self.

She *liked* being lord of manor.

She paused, letting the idea settle into her skin.

Hmmmm.

It was true.

She *did* like being lord of the manor.

It was something her heart genuinely desired.

Violet did not bemoan the weight of being the countess, per se—the long hours with her steward and solicitor, the endless tasks to discuss.

It was simply the *decisions* that did her in.

No . . . that wasn't right either.

It wasn't the decision-making itself.

It was the *knowing*.

Which direction did she wish to go? And until she knew that, how could she determine where to place her feet?

Of course, she said none of this to Lord Graham.

The silence lingered and stretched.

Finally, Lord Graham exhaled beside her. "Should I be heartened that you have not rejected me outright?"

She smiled wanly. "Perhaps."

"I am for London tomorrow and will not return until mid-July. I would kindly ask you to please ponder my proposal. Perhaps this time apart will clear your mind and allow you to understand the path you wish to take."

LORD GRAHAM TOOK his leave not long after.

Violet agreed with his suggestion. She would take these next months to ponder his proposal. Too much was riding on her decision to reject Lord Graham outright.

Her father appeared as soon as Lord Graham stepped out of the drawing room. Mr. Kerr's smiles indicated that he expected 'joyous' news.

One look at Lord Graham's tight expression told him that a marriage was not imminent.

"Why have you not accepted Lord Graham's suit?!" her father demanded, following Violet into her study after his lordship had departed. "How could you be so blind as to what is required of your station in life?"

"I am not blind to my duty, Father." Violet swept a hand to indicate her desk, piled with ledgers and those dratted agriculture books she was supposed to be reading. "I simply asked Lord Graham for some time to ponder the matter. Marriage is a large step, and I do not wish to enter matrimony without thoroughly pondering the ramifications—"

"Ramifications?! What is there to ponder further?" Her father pressed three fingertips to his forehead. "You have known Lord Graham in some capacity or another for nigh upon five years!"

"Be that as it may, Father, I have only recently begun to consider Lord Graham in a matrimonial light." Violet sat behind her desk, hands reaching for a ledger or something to mask the roil of emotions in her chest.

"You know that to be false, Daughter." Her father began pacing before her desk, his tall body filling the room. Despite his age, her father still had an out-sized physical presence. "This was your mother's *dying* wish, Violet. That you would marry Lord Graham. How can you be so insensible to what is owed your family?"

"I am hardly insensible—"

"I am severely disappointed in you." He paused his pacing, his blue eyes snapping with anger. "Do you think to receive a better offer than Lord Graham? Or perhaps, like Dahlia, you seek to lower the status of our family by pursuing those far beneath you—"

"Father!" Violet interjected, slamming her ledger shut. "I am simply trying to find a solution that will render me happy—"

"Happy?! What does happiness have to do with any of it? Marriage is less about happiness and more about compatibility. It starts with a man like Lord Graham. A kind gentleman. From there, love can grow and, God willing, will eventually result in a sense of contentment." He spread his hands wide. Violet knew that he was describing his own marriage, and he was not wrong. She supposed her parents' marriage had been a contented one. "You begin to sound like Dahlia. She supposedly married for immediate love and happiness, did she not? Much to all our horror and disgrace—"

"Yes, but at least she was happy!" Violet pressed her shaking hands together, willing herself to believe her own words. That Dahlia *had* been happy.

"How can you truly believe that? Dahlia traded a life of security for lust!" her father roared. "How could such a thing have a positive outcome? Dahlia was miserable once she had exhausted her pent-up carnal desires, bitterly regretting all her choices—"

"Enough!" Violet longed to clamp her hands over her ears and storm from the room, much as she had as a child.

"Violet, you must cease this romantic nonsense!" Her father slapped a hand atop her desk. A lock of his pepper-gray hair tumbled across his brow. "If nothing else, spare a thought for your younger sisters. They require someone to sponsor them in London. They need to marry and marry well. Even if you are willing to treat your own future so cavalierly, do not cast aside theirs, as well. Though you have ascended to the title, I am still guardian for Aster and Rose. Their care is my priority. Do not make me rethink their residence here with you!"

Violet swallowed back the angry words that crowded her tongue and allowed her father to storm from the room.

But the walls of her study felt too oppressive, too vivid a reminder of the war waging in her breast.

Snatching her bonnet and cloak, Violet left the house, stomping down the hill toward Old Kilmeny Castle.

Clouds gathered on the horizon, promising rain before evening. But the buffeting before the storm felt wild and free and utterly glorious, tugging at her bonnet and whipping her cloak into a frenzy.

Her father's words would not let her be.

Dahlia was miserable once she had exhausted her carnal desires, bitterly regretting all her choices.

Was that true? And if so, how did her father know? He had severed all contact with Dahlia. He *had* to simply be projecting his own moral assumptions onto Dahlia's situation.

And yet . . .

What if he were correct? Then what?

Guilt swamped Violet.

Guilt for encouraging Dahlia.

Guilt for considering her own happiness over the well-being of her family.

The enormity of the North Sea stretched before her, the white-capped waves and battering wind tasting of freedom. Of a wild existence waiting beyond the confines of her 'golden castle.'

A world where anything was possible.

As she stomped through the heather and gorse, she even felt a little like a warrior of old, beginning a quest.

Mmmm, perhaps *that* was how she should frame her indecisiveness—a *desire* to search out her *duty*.

She was as Ewan had said . . . lost in a wood, struggling to find the path. She simply needed to look harder, to explore further.

Regardless of her father's opinion, taking a bit more time was wise. It was prudent.

Of course, such thoughts did not stop her from roundly castigating her father, Lord Graham, and all other vexing men in her mind as she tromped down the path. Perhaps talking this over with Sir Joshua—a *non*-vexing male—would help her see matters more clearly.

Upon reaching the castle, she opted to take the long way around to the front, a path that conveniently circled Ewan's greenhouse studio.

Not that she expected to find him there. He hadn't said when he would arrive back from Aberdeen precisely, but she reasoned that it was unlikely to happen before the evening.

Regardless, when she rounded the corner and did not see his large body standing before a canvas, she experienced a sinking sensation. An emotion that felt suspiciously like disappointment.

Frowning at the waywardness of her own thoughts, she continued onward to the main door of the castle. Uncle Joshua had never been one for formalities, so Violet let herself into the small entrance foyer before climbing the stairs to the great hall.

The smell of turpentine hit her first, as it always did. The great hall had a wooden partition between the door and the hall itself, a partial wall of carved wood that, in times past, had hidden servants from view while lords and ladies banqueted in the main hall beyond.

She peeked her head through the doorway, her uncle's name on her lips.

The sound died.

Violet froze, mouth in a pursed 'O' of surprise.

Ewan *had* returned.

The scene sprawled before her like something from Scheherazade's tales . . . a fraught moment of peril in a faraway romantic place.

Ewan lay half-reclining on the floor, a stack of pillows behind his back, another underneath one knee, likely representing rocks in the land-scape. Scattered bits of armor rested around him, as if some attacker had just rent it from his body.

He clutched a flag in one hand and a sword in the other, head turned in profile, gaze fixed on the large window above Sir Joshua's head.

The image was . . . astonishing.

Her uncle was sketching like a madman.

For her part, Violet could not stop staring at Ewan.

Was he clothed? At *all*?!

A length of red silk wound around one arm and draped from hips to mid-thigh.

But every other inch of him was bare.

Legs. Chest. Feet. Arms.

So. Much. Skin.

Like that prizefight so long ago, she knew she should look away and step back.

But evidently Violet had not changed much over the intervening years. Not even her father's recent admonishment could penetrate.

She drank in the sight of Ewan with almost gleeful abandon.

Her poor eyes didn't know where to look first.

Heavens, were the muscles in his thighs truly that large?

And his chest?! It was a rippling expanse of skin, punctuated by dips and valleys.

What about that tendon in his throat? Was it as taut as it appeared? How would it feel to drag her lips across it?

Violet swayed, light-headed from sheer greedy delight.

The diffused window light bathed him in sunshine, burnishing his ginger hair to red-gold.

He rested like some defeated Greek god cast to earth, a hero fighting alongside mere mortals.

Which given Uncle Joshua's aims with this portrait, Violet supposed that the scene certainly communicated the correct message.

But . . .

Violet swallowed, dragged her eyes up and down Ewan's body one more time, and then stepped back.

A few small steps found her on the landing outside the door to the great hall. She rested her back against the wall, allowing the chill stone to cool her overheated blood.

Ugh.

This was the problem with quests.

Were they exhilarating? Yes.

But the peril?

The peril was *very* real.

She pressed her palms to her eyes, trying to quiet her mind.

Unfortunately, the exercise only succeeded in searing the scene—Ewan decadently sprawled across pillows in utter dishabille—onto the backs of her eyelids.

Thoughts tumbled through. Treacherous, dangerous wee thugs that aimed to assassinate all her good intentions.

Why was she so set on considering Lord Graham when a man like Ewan Campbell was about?

Yes, she found Ewan overwhelmingly alluring . . . but it was more than mere lust. Violet had met many a handsome man throughout the years—gentlemen concerned more with their looking-glass than any meaningful internal beauty.

But Ewan's attractiveness sprang from within. It was the beauty of his heart that rendered his exterior just that much more compelling.

Was this how Dahlia had felt? That her connection with Mr. Martinelli had been both emotional and physical? That her affections for him led to the commitment of marriage and a life together, not just the release of pent-up lust, as their father claimed?

And why was Violet denying her attraction to Ewan? Both physical *and* emotional? Why was she considering marriage to Lord Graham without equally recognizing the suitability of Ewan Campbell as a partner, no matter what society said?

And *that* was the most treacherous thought of all.

Because as much as Violet appreciated Ewan's considerable physical charms—and she appreciated them *So. Very. Much.*—they paled when compared to the power of the man's soul to utterly claim her own.

Worse, given how the memory of his bare chest lingered, how was she to be unaffected when next she saw him?

16

After his return from Aberdeen, Ewan did not see Violet for three days.

She had a megrim and did not join them the one evening Ewan and Sir Joshua ventured up to Kilmeny Hall for dinner.

She did not accompany her father and sisters to pester Sir Joshua over his progress on the *Battle of Gracchus*. The older painter refused to let them see it until it was farther along. A matter of principle, he said.

She certainly did not magically appear as Ewan worked hour upon hour in his studio.

Granted, the weather was dreich—day after day of misting rain and dark clouds.

Even so, Ewan feared she was avoiding him.

Had their shared confidences that day in his studio chased her away? Had the realization of his decidedly lowly origins finally sent her packing? Or had he overstepped the bounds of propriety in encouraging her to seek out her own desires?

Clearly, *something* had occurred to cause her to avoid his company. Would she cancel their upcoming portrait session, as well?

The thought depressed his spirits.

But a pragmatic part of him whispered it was likely for the best, was it not? It wasn't as if their acquaintance could ever be more than cordial friendship. Rafe and Andrew had all but told him to back away.

Countesses did not marry lowly crofters. Just as princes did not marry scullery maids, no matter how many fairy tales one read.

Along with his gloomy musings and the dreich weather, Ewan discovered that several of the skylights in his greenhouse were not watertight. They dripped incessantly. And given the nonstop rain, the clerk of works for the estate wouldn't be able to repair the leaks until the sun returned.

And so Ewan had gathered up his canvases and moved his studio into the great hall alongside Sir Joshua. His employer was a talkative fellow, joking and discussing techniques as they painted side-by-side, both utilizing the pale light that filtered through the large south window.

Additionally, Ewan received a brief note from Andrew, stating that he and Rafe had a tip that Massey had landed at the port in Fraserburgh, a town farther north up the coast. They were off to investigate.

On the fourth day after his return, Ewan wrapped his supplies in oiled, waterproof canvas, tugged his great kilt into a cloak, and trekked through the rain to Kilmeny Hall. He set up his easel and directed footmen to arrange the drawing room for his second portrait sitting with Lady Kildrum. She had not canceled it. Not yet.

His pulse hummed as he waited for her to arrive. How would she behave with him today? And what did it say about the true state of his heart that he was so nervous to see her?

Violet arrived punctually. A maid followed on her heels, settling into a chair in the corner to act as chaperone. Her ladyship was dressed in that same blue gown of flowing gauze and silk, its stiffened lace collar standing upright, strands of pearls looped around her neck and dangling from her ears. Of course, her brown hair still stubbornly resisted the curls coaxed into it.

She was a vision of loveliness, a welcome foil to the continued dreary weather outside.

Ewan's heart set up a steady drumbeat in his chest, a chanting rhythm he was helpless to stem.

"Lady Kildrum." He bowed.

"Mr. Campbell." She nodded, ever so politely.

And then she turned her head, a flustered blush climbing her cheeks, as if she found his presence distressing.

She said nothing more, holding her spine with rigid precision.

Ah.

So she *had* been deliberately avoiding him.

Ewan had overstepped the bounds of gentlemanly behavior with their last interaction, and she was now understandably concerned that he might assume liberties.

Every taut line of her body proclaimed her to be the Countess of Kildrum, reaffirming their respective places in Society.

It was for the best.

He chanted this over and over as he directed her to resume the position he had formulated during their previous sitting: Violet standing with one hand on the back of a gilded chair, her hip sinking into the embroidered upholstery.

He took his seat behind his canvas and picked up his charcoal. He had transferred his sketches loosely to the larger format.

He sketched.

Violet watched.

The ease that had existed between them in his studio had vanished. In its place, a coiled beast crouched. The lurking strain of their past confidences hiding in the shadows, waiting to pounce.

Violet held herself stiffly, her limbs utterly lacking the relaxed fluidity of their previous session.

The silence stretched and pulled until Ewan was sweating from the tension of it, his palms damp.

Every tick of the clock on the mantel testified to the heavy weight of the words unspoken between them.

The problem, of course, was that he still had to draw her.

Portrait painting was agonizingly intimate . . . staring for hours into another's eyes, asking questions of their soul.

In this case, every brush of his charcoal traced another part of Violet that he admired. The elegant bent of her jaw. The gentle swell of her bosom. The nip and curve of her hip as she leaned her weight into the chair.

Each line flowed as surely as if he were touching her. A hand wrapping around her waist. A finger trailing up the soft skin of her arm. A thumb following the curve of the pearls lying against her neck before rising to brush across her lush lips.

Every mark was unbearably intimate.

Worse, it was as if she could *sense* the wayward nature of his thoughts.

Her gaze skittered across his skin, generating wee shocks of electricity where they landed: chest, throat, mouth.

If she were to touch him, would it give them both a jolt? Like the friction of a wool blanket on a winter's day?

A sleepy snore sounded.

The noise ricocheted through the room. Violet startled, her hand raising to her bosom in alarm. Ewan barely stopped himself from flinching and making an errant mark with his charcoal.

He twisted to see the maid asleep in the corner, her head leaning against the wall, her mending sprawling onto the floor.

He turned back to Violet's blue gaze, expecting her to say something to awaken their sleeping chaperone.

Instead, he found her blue-green eyes brimming with laughter, her lips tightly pinched.

The maid snored again, the noise even louder.

Violet giggled, lifting a hand to her mouth to stifle her mirth.

Ewan smiled, rolling his eyes as if to say, *This is ludicrous.*

Violet giggled harder, tucking her head against her shoulder.

Ewan chuckled, waiting for Violet to raise her head and meet his eyes again.

Instead, she remained with her head bowed, her chin turning to the left, her nose practically buried in her clavicle.

Violet twitched her shoulders.

Why was she—

Oh!

The twist of her head suddenly registered the problem.

"Are ye stuck, my lady?" he whispered, walking to her.

"Yes." She lifted a hand to her ear, tugging.

He quickly saw the problem. When Violet had ducked her head to stifle her giggle, the movement had tangled a pearl earbob in the stiffened lace collar, somehow pulling the strand of pearls into the mix.

In short, she was thoroughly entangled.

She shot him a sideways glance, a blush climbing her cheeks.

"I cannot seem to free myself," she said with a rueful chuckle, motioning helplessly toward her ear. "The maid falls asleep, startles me half to death, sets me to giggling, and then I manage to snarl my jewels into a Gordian knot."

She rolled her eyes at the absurdity of her predicament, her shoulders sagging and expression becoming one of self-deprecating humor.

Abruptly, she morphed into Violet Kerr. *His* Violet. The woman who delighted and fascinated and made him wish for things that Could. Never. Be.

"It does appear tae be a bit of a mess." Smiling, he stooped over her. "Here. Allow me."

The instinct to help her felt as natural as breathing, and so he reached for the earbob without thinking through the ramifications.

It was only as the backs of his fingers accidentally skimmed her impossibly-soft cheek that he realized—

He was touching her.

And . . . he would have to *continue* to touch her if he wished to help.

Violet had gone preternaturally still.

He would have thought her afraid or wary but a quick meeting of her gaze told him otherwise. She was anything but wary.

Her vivid blue eyes had bled nearly to black. Her tongue peaked out, wetting her bottom lip.

Like himself, she was breathing in short rasps.

It was all the permission he needed to continue.

Swallowing, Ewan nodded and moved closer, his fingers continuing their slide along her jaw. Perhaps more deliberately now.

The curls at her temples threaded through his fingers, soft brushes of sensation.

He could feel her breath on his cheek as he worked. Or had she leaned closer to him, inhaling deeply?

He gently worked the earbob free from the lace collar, tugging lightly, the motion causing the back of his hand to brush against her neck over and over.

His skin thrummed from the contact.

"How . . . ," she began, her voice a puff of air against his chin.

He fully freed the earring before glancing at her.

She licked that bottom lip again. Did her eyes drop to his throat?

Heat scoured him.

Dinnae ponder the charms of the lovely lass.

Ewan sucked in a deep breath. It was supposed to be bracing, but instead sent a blast of her lavender scent straight to his head.

He was nearly dizzy from the sensory glory of her.

He swallowed and focused his work, extricating a section of the pearl necklace from the netting of the lace. In the process, his fingertips skimmed the bare skin where her neck met her shoulder. The touch scalded him.

"How was your trip to Aberdeen?" she murmured.

Concentrate on the necklace, ye glaikit oaf.

"It was excellent," he replied, proud his voice emerged steady and not brokenly hoarse.

A moment of silence.

He finished untangling the final pearl from the lace, laying it gently against her neck.

"There. All done," he whispered.

"Thank you." Her words were a puff against his cheek.

He stepped back, closing his fists to trap the lingering memory of her skin on his fingertips.

Their eyes met.

She stared up at him, mouth slightly parted, her heartbeat a fluttering pulse in her lovely throat.

Energy hummed, a bouncing zig-zag of brilliant gold.

What he wouldn't give to be welcome to take a step forward, cup her face between his palms, and bend to touch her lips. Would she gasp at the contact? Would her body rise to meet his? Would her mouth be as warm and soft as he suspected—

He turned away and returned to his easel, putting ten feet of space and a wide canvas between them.

"How have ye fared?" he asked a wee bit too loudly, causing the maid to snort in her sleep. He lifted his charcoal. "Are decisions still weighing on ye?"

"I have made no decisions, as of yet." She sighed, shooting him another rueful grin, relaxing and leaning more naturally into the back of the chair. "No, that is not true. I did read a bit about agriculture."

"Aye? Ye did?"

"Yes. And I decided that the state of farming in rural Berwick is appallingly boring."

"Berwick?! Well, of course it is." Ewan gave a bark of laughter. "Does anything interesting ever happen in Berwick?"

She laughed, a lovely throaty sound. "I suppose not. But I did read a fascinating discussion about elms."

"Elms?"

"Yes!" Her eyes lit with interest. "They are most effective as wind breaks for new plants. Did you know that there are at least four different ways to sow them?"

Ewan felt his grin stretch wider and wider as Violet waxed philosophical upon the virtues of elm farming.

All awkwardness vanished, as if mist evaporating in warm sun.

As he sketched, Ewan told her humorous stories about his time as a student at the Royal Academy.

Violet regaled him with the escapades she and Dahlia used to get in to, particularly running amok in Old Kilmeny Castle, playing lords and ladies with Aster and Rose.

"Of course, I was always the lord, defending the ladies. And the twins were young, as you can imagine, but they still joined in," she said on a sigh. "Aster, in particular, has a decidedly piercing scream. And Rose was insistent she was helpless, needing a knight to save her."

Ewan chuckled, tracing the outline of her shoulder on his canvas. "'Tis always good to take up arms in defense of a lady, I suppose."

"Yes." Violet paused, her lips quirking to the side. "Would *you* take up arms to defend a lady?"

"Of course," Ewan shrugged, thinking back to Mrs. Massey and the Brotherhood's commitment to helping her. "I would defend any person—man, woman, or child—who needed it."

"Mmmm. But what about more . . . figurative dangers?"

Something in her tone had shifted. He lifted his head.

Her expression was abruptly serious.

He set down his charcoal. "Well, figurative dangers are perhaps different. I suppose it would depend if the woman in question needed assistance in defending herself." He paused, gathering his thoughts. "I see it like this. If a woman asked for my help, I would offer it, as far as was proper. That said, as a former prizefighter, I recognize the value in knowing how to defend one's self from attack. I would want any woman in my life to have the skills necessary to choose her own destiny, as it were. There is power in knowing ye can fight your own battles, if ye ken what I mean."

She studied him for a long moment. And then smiled.

He picked up his charcoal and continued to sketch. Their conversation moved on from that point, ebbing and flowing, but never ceasing.

Ewan floated between emotions he found, quite bluntly, terrifying.

He could not afford to develop a strong attachment to Violet Kerr, Lady Kildrum.

That path led only to heartache . . . a path he feared he was already treading.

Because as Violet shot him a grin and exited the room, it felt like watching his own heart walk out the door.

17

There is power in knowing ye can fight your own battles.

Ewan's words would not let Violet be.

She liked the idea of being thought strong enough to accomplish difficult tasks on her own.

How different from Lord Graham's insistence that he would protect her at all costs.

Ewan's phrase rang in her ears over the next couple days: as rain battered the windows, as she refereed vampire arguments between her sisters, as she met with Mr. Lawyerly and Mr. Shambles to decide what to do with her lands, as she listened to her father's increasingly loud insistence that she accept Lord Graham's offer.

Of course, the painter's words weren't the only Ewan-related thing distracting her.

Flotsam bits of memory had this unnerving habit of swirling through her brain at the most inopportune times, rendering her light-headed.

Ewan lounging like a wealthy pasha, half clothed, draped in red silks.

The touch of his eyes moving over her as he sketched, setting goose-flesh skittering . . .

The feel of his knuckles dragging down her jaw . . .

She was teetering far too close to the precipice.

The view from the cliff kept becoming more and more spectacu-lar—adding a vibrant sunset and companionable birdsong, all beckoning her to linger and rest awhile—ignoring the very real peril of tumbling over the edge.

A week after Ewan's return from Aberdeen, Violet found herself again in her study, facing a stack of agricultural texts. The endless dreich days had given way to a hesitant, wary sunshine.

Her father and sisters had been invited to attend a house party in Aberdeen. Normally, her father would decline such an invitation, but he was currently attempting to garner opinions on his recent religious tract—a (tedious) dissection of the moral purpose in Paul's journeys around the Mediterranean Sea. And Aster had been vocal in her wish to meet more 'suitable' gentlemen.

Thus, a rural house party provided fodder for both their aims. Rose, it should be noted, had simply been pleased to leave Kilmeny Hall.

Fortunately, Violet had been able to formulate excuses to not accom-pany them.

Soon after their carriage rolled down the gravel drive, Violet bar-ricaded herself in her study, determined to use the abnormal quiet to balance some ledgers and study her agricultural texts.

She was interrupted two hours later.

"Lord Hadley and Sir Rafe Gordon are here to see you, my lady," Irvine announced.

"Pardon?" Violet's head snapped upward from the book she had been reading . . . ehr, *attempting* to read.

"Lord Hadley and Sir Rafe Gordon to see you, my lady." Irvine said the words with stately aplomb, but the excitement in his eyes betrayed his delight at having such august visitors. "They have asked specifically to speak with your ladyship. Will you receive them?"

Heavens! Lord Hadley? Sir Rafe?

Here?!

"Thank you, Irvine," she said, managing to contain her own shock. "Please show the gentlemen into the drawing room and instruct Cook to send up a tea tray with refreshments."

She tapped a finger on her desktop for a moment after Irvine left.

She was . . . astounded.

Sir Rafe Gordon? Did Irvine refer to the former Lord Rafe Gilbert, son of the Duke of Kendall? The broadsheets had been full of that shocking affair last autumn. She had heard that the king had granted Lord Rafe a baronetcy in January, hence his name changing to Sir Rafe.

She recalled dancing with Sir Rafe once or twice during her two Seasons in London. She vaguely remembered a dark-haired man with a roguish smile and quicksilver tongue.

As for Lord Hadley . . . Violet had not met him.

The bigger question—why were the gentlemen here? It was highly unusual for two such illustrious persons to just happen into the neighborhood for an unannounced social call.

She could only assume this was related to Ewan somehow. After all, he received letters from Hadley with some regularity.

But if they were here for Ewan, why were the gentlemen asking after her?

TEN MINUTES LATER, Violet walked into the drawing room. She had sent a footman to fetch Ewan from the castle. But first, she would ascertain the purpose behind the gentlemen's visit.

Two men instantly sprang to their feet.

"Lady Kildrum." The taller of the two bowed in greeting. "Lord Hadley, at your service."

Though *Debrett's* had informed her that Hadley was an English earl, the man in front of her was decidedly a Scot. From the dark tartan of his great kilt to the lilting roll of his speech, Lord Hadley took his heritage seriously.

"My lord." Violet curtsied.

"Permit me to introduce Sir Rafe Gordon." Lord Hadley motioned to his companion.

"Sir Rafe." Violet curtsied again. "It is a pleasure. I do believe we have a prior acquaintance?"

"Aye," he grinned, as affable as she remembered. "I recall dancing a country dance or two many years ago."

Though not as overtly Scottish as his friend, Sir Rafe still sported a sash of the same dark tartan, brighter bands of white, red, and green standing out against the black fabric.

Both men were aristocrats to their bones. The superfine coat underneath Lord Hadley's great kilt bore the stamp of the finest tailor. Sir Rafe's waistcoat appeared to be gold-shot Venetian silk.

Of course, none of this explained why the men were here. Why they had asked to speak with her.

"Forgive this intrusion, my lady," Lord Hadley said, "but we were passing through the area, returning south from Fraserburgh, and wished tae call and pay our respects."

"That is very kind of you both," Violet said as they took their seats. *Abnormally* kind, she did not add.

Sir Rafe and Lord Hadley exchanged a look, sinking into chairs opposite her.

"We recognize, my lady," Sir Rafe said, "that our presence here must appear somewhat unusual."

Violet's eyebrows shot skyward. The man was forthright, she would give him that.

"I admit to being surprised to finding you both on my doorstep," she carefully hedged.

"We shan't take too much of your time, my lady." Lord Hadley sat forward, expression somber. "To get straight to the point, we are concerned about our friend, Mr. Ewan Campbell."

"Mr. Campbell?" Violet parroted back, though *why* she could not say.

She had surmised this to be the true purpose behind their calling, had she not? "You are . . . concerned?"

"Aye." Sir Rafe nodded his head. "Ewan is quite dear tae us both."

"A friend of the heart." Lord Hadley tapped his chest.

"But, ye see, Lady Kildrum, he's a sensitive soul, our wee Ewan." Sir Rafe said the words in deadly earnest, not a trace of sarcasm.

Surprise tangled Violet's tongue. "Your . . . *wee* . . . Ewan?"

"Aye," Lord Hadley agreed, expression solemn. "We are very worried about his safety."

Were they—

Were these two gentlemen . . . serious?

Wee Ewan?!

Safety?!

They had to be bamming her.

She searched their faces for any hint of laughter.

Had they come all this way to have a good laugh at her expense? Worse, were they going to subtly mock Ewan, as well?

Indignation gathered in her chest, which had the unfortunate side-effect of sharpening her tongue.

"I must meet your honesty with some of my own," she replied, hands fisting in her lap. "I struggle to formulate a reply to your statements, gentlemen. You claim to be Mr. Campbell's friends, and yet you insist that he is *wee* and in need of care. Have either of you actually *met* Mr. Campbell?"

"Pardon?" Lord Hadley sat up straighter.

"Mr. Campbell," she continued, "is fully capable of defending himself."

"Yes," Sir Rafe nodded, "we are well aware of Ewan's *physical* size. In a bout of fisticuffs, he has no equal."

"Precisely. He is most capable and does not require hovering caretakers," Violet said.

"Mmmm. *Hovering caretakers*," Lord Hadley repeated.

Sir Rafe leaned toward his friend, murmuring *sotto voce*, but Violet heard nonetheless. "I like her."

"She certainly has fire," Lord Hadley returned, equally quiet. "That's a start, I suppose."

Sir Rafe lifted his eyes back to her. "Aside from his obvious size, what have been your impressions of Mr. Campbell thus far, Lady Kildrum?"

"Pardon? Impressions?"

"Of the more metaphorical variety."

Violet felt as if the conversation were careening rather drunkenly around the room. "Mr. Campbell is . . . as you said . . . a sensitive soul."

"And that is your only opinion of him?"

Violet sat back, nonplussed. How was she to reply to that?

Actually, your lordship, I find your friend rather delectable and have been having fantasies which would set a debutante's cheeks aflame . . .

She went with, "Mr. Campbell is one of the more remarkable gentlemen of my acquaintance."

True, but perhaps less ardently confessional.

"A *gentleman*, you say," Lord Hadley narrowed in on that one word. "You consider Mr. Campbell to be a gentleman, then?"

"Birth alone does not render one a gentleman, in my opinion. Mr. Campbell is a *gentle man* in every sense." Violet narrowed her eyes at Lord Hadley. "Furthermore, I must say I dislike the sense that you are simultaneously toying with me and insulting Mr. Campbell in the process."

A bemused sort of expression flitted across Lord Hadley's face. He sat back in his chair.

"Very well, my lady, permit us tae be a bit more blunt." Lord Hadley laced his fingers across his stomach. "Our Ewan is a man of deep feeling. He would cut off his arm tae help someone else in need."

"Aye, he will not look after his own heart," Sir Rafe chimed in. "That's why we're here, looking after it for him. As his dear friends, we dislike the thought that our Ewan is being manipulated or misused in some way."

"Aye," Lord Hadley agreed. "We need tae ensure he is being cherished and appreciated properly."

Violet frowned. "This is somewhat absurd. Of course, we have treated Mr. Campbell with respect. We have been kind and accommodating to him—"

"Yes, but what about *yourself*, in particular?" Sir Rafe interrupted.

"Me?"

"Aye. Despite not being born to it, Ewan is a gentleman, as you said. It says much about your ladyship that you would recognize that fact. Have you found the differences between your station and Mr. Campbell's to be an impediment?"

Violet reeled back, trying desperately to grasp the undercurrents of the conversation.

"An impediment? An impediment to what?"

Lord Hadley and Sir Rafe exchanged a long glance.

Finally, Sir Rafe gave the smallest nod and turned back to her.

"We fear we shall simply have to state the matter baldly." He fixed her with a stern stare. "We are acquainted with the state of affairs between yourself and Mr. Ewan Campbell."

"In other words, Lady Kildrum," Lord Hadley looked at his fingernails and then back up to Violet. "We wish to ensure that your intentions toward our Ewan are honorable."

His gaze was steady but intent. Sir Rafe, as well.

The look of men who knew full well *why* she had jumped to Ewan's defense.

Oh!

Have you found the differences between your station and Mr. Campbell's to be an impediment . . . ?

Wish to ensure your intentions are honorable . . .

Were they saying—?!

But . . . how would they know—?

Yet if they *were* intimate friends with Ewan, then they might—?

Oh, heavens!

Violet felt the blush start at the back of her neck, creeping across her chest before scouring her cheeks. She was sure her entire face was impossibly strawberry red.

Both Lord Hadley and Sir Rafe lounged comfortably in their chairs, looking on with a sort of hearty fascination.

Sir Rafe turned to his friend.

"She genuinely cares for him. I'm sure of it," he whispered cheerfully, slapping his hands on his knees. "I'm giving them my blessing."

"I'm no' so sure," Lord Hadley replied. He spoke to Sir Rafe, but his eyes remained on her. It was clear his words were intended to reach her ears. A sort of oblique warning, as it were. "And even if she does care for him, it doesnae follow that she will be willing to buck all of society for him. I dinnae like the thought of a lady toying with Ewan's tender heart. He deserves gentleness and honesty."

"Ohhhhhh!" Violet resorted to fanning her cheeks. Surely the heat of her blush threatened to catch her fichu on fire.

"I like her," Sir Rafe repeated, leaning toward Lord Hadley. "I kept telling ye the entire ride here, 'Lady Kildrum is a decent lass. She wouldn't deliberately trifle with a man.' But no, ye kept insisting that wee Ewan was in some sort of mortal peril—"

"She's a countess, Rafe." Lord Hadley waved a hand toward her, turning to speak with his friend as if Violet weren't in the room. "Ewan deserves a woman who sees him for the remarkable human that he is, not merely a noblewoman who has a fancy for strapping lads."

"Yes, but she appears to have a rather forward-thinking view of our Ewan."

"That doesnae mean she sees him as marriage material."

Violet briefly wondered if a hell dimension had just opened and slipped her into some bizarre reality. The heat practically steaming from her skin supported this conclusion.

Several facts presented themselves:

One, Sir Rafe and Lord Hadley did indeed care deeply for Ewan.

Two, neither gentleman seemed to take exception to Ewan and herself courting. In fact, they gave every appearance of welcoming such a match. (Not, of course, that she and *wee* Ewan were courting, per se, but the possibility of it . . .) Astonishingly, they appeared to be deciding if she were worthy of their friend, not the other way around.

Three, what possible answer could she give?!

I say, my lords, I give you my word as a gentlewoman that I shall not ravish your friend . . . no matter how thoroughly I am tempted.

She pressed one final distressed hand to her cheeks and then gave a shaky laugh.

"I assure you, gentleman, that any . . ." Violet floundered for the right word. ". . . *intentions* . . . I may harbor toward Mr. Campbell are entirely honorable."

"Well, that's good enough for me." Sir Rafe pressed his hands to his knees, as if he meant to rise.

Lord Hadley placed a staying hand on his friend's arm, holding him in place. The earl leaned forward, gaze intent.

"Since we're being honest here, Lady Kildrum, I need to say my piece." Lord Hadley fixed her with an icy stare. "Ewan Campbell is the *best* of men. I count him a very dear friend. I will not see him trifled with or his affections abused. If I find out that ye have dealt falsely with him, there will be words between us . . . earl to earl, as it were—"

Crack!

The door to the drawing room crashed open, saving Violet from having to respond to Lord Hadley's not-so-veiled threat.

Ewan all but ran into the room, chest heaving, hair windswept, great kilt askew on his chest.

Violet and her guests lurched to their feet.

"Came as soon as I heard . . . footman . . . brought word," Ewan gasped, panting to regain his breath. "What's happened . . ."

"Hallo there, Ewan." Sir Rafe rocked back on his heels, voice aggravatingly cheerful. "Lovely of ye to join us—"

"Aye," Lord Hadley agreed, waving an arm far too expansively to be guiltless. "Nothing amiss here. Been having a wee chat with Lady Kildrum is all."

Sir Rafe and Lord Hadley were terrible liars.

Ewan froze, lungs still working like a bellows, gaze darting between his friends and Violet. His eyes lingered on her, tracing her cheeks and collarbone, surely noting the telltale traces of her blush.

Violet could practically see the cogs turning in his brain, connecting his friends' overly-expressive bonhomie with the true intent of their visit.

"Please tell me this isnae what it looks like," Ewan ground out.

Lord Hadley pasted on an innocent expression. "I cannot say what this looks like tae ye."

"I *specifically* asked youse not to meddle in my life," Ewan replied.

"Are we meddling?"

Ewan groaned and rubbed a hand over his face.

"Out!" he commanded, pointing toward the door.

"Now, Ewan," Lord Hadley began, walking toward his friend, "we were just on our way back from Fraserburgh and wanted to have a wee chat with her ladyship."

Seeing the two men side-by-side was telling, Violet decided. Lord Hadley was not a small man at over six-feet tall. But Ewan still had several inches on him.

"Out!" Ewan repeated, jabbing his finger toward the door. "Rafe and yourself! Out!"

Sir Rafe, at least, had the decency to appear ashamed, though the grin on his lips was a little telling.

"Lady Kildrum." He sketched a bow in her direction before heading for the door.

"Ewan," Lord Hadley began again, "ye know how deeply we care about ye—"

"Out!" Ewan repeated. "Ye've overset her ladyship, Andrew. And I certainly dinnae need ye both clucking over me like a pair of mother hens—"

Violet was torn between melting into an embarrassed puddle or laughing at their lordships' sheepish expressions, hanging their heads like recalcitrant school boys.

Though it was not lost on her that Ewan and Lord Hadley were on a first-name basis, indicating a very close friendship indeed.

"Ewan—"

"Nae, Andrew, I'm no' hearing it!"

Ewan actually moved behind Lord Hadley and pushed him toward the door where Sir Rafe already stood, laughing.

Violet had to blink just to ensure she had not mistaken the absurdity of it all.

Ewan behind Lord Hadley, pushing the man much as one might propel a wheelbarrow up a steep hill.

Lord Hadley protesting his friend's hold, to little avail.

Ewan was an unstoppable force pressing his lordship closer and closer to the exit.

"Ewan, we're here because we care about ye!"

"I dinnae need such caring. Ye should be at home, caring for yer Jane."

"Who do ye think sent me here?!"

"Jane knows I can manage myself just fine!"

Finally accepting he would lose this battle, Lord Hadley twisted in Ewan's hold and fixed Violet with a steely gaze over Ewan's massive shoulder. A look indicating that even though Ewan was tossing him out, Lord Hadley would still hold Violet to her word.

Earl to earl, as it were.

Ewan slammed the door behind his friends.

He whirled to face her, hands on his hips, chest heaving once more. He scraped a shaking hand through his red hair in a futile attempt to tame the unruly mass.

To Violet's purview, he was almost unbearably attractive. This adorable hulk of a man who blushed at the slightest provocation and tossed earls out of her drawing room with outraged aplomb.

That blush of his made a grand appearance, spreading across his cheeks. Rather belatedly, Violet noted that Ewan was wearing the same dark tartan that his friends had sported.

He cleared his throat, his face growing redder by the second.

"I sincerely apologize for my friends, my lady." He waved a hand toward the door. "They mean well, but——"

"I will not have you apologize for them," Violet interrupted, taking a step closer to him. "It is clear they care deeply for you."

Ewan nodded glumly, his blush surely scorching. He refused to meet her gaze, instead staring at a point near her toes, as if the mortification of the moment were too great to actually process all at once and one had to do it in stages.

But, a quiet part of her pointed out, he had only apologized for his friends' behavior . . .

He had *not* refuted the substance of their discussion or the reason for their visit.

Ewan . . . admired her.

She knew this, of course. But it was only now truly sinking in.

He held her in regard and perhaps wished to court her.

As for her . . .

. . . she admired him, too.

So. Much.

But . . . a vast ocean of expectations and responsibilities threatened to drown her. And, as ever, the specter of reputation and her sisters' future loomed.

She should not even contemplate selfishly tossing such concerns aside, no matter how attractive and kind the man was. Such an idea was madness, was it not?

What was she to do?

And why, why, *why* was she doomed to spend her life never *knowing* what to do?!

The silence between them grew, each tick of the clock only furthering to deepen the fierceness of Ewan's blush.

18

E wan was quite sure he was going to kill his friends.

A nice slow death, of course. One that probably involved thumb screws and dangling over pits of hungry alligators.

No, not alligators. That was too kind. Sharks, perhaps?

Or perhaps he should employ wee, carnivorous hamsters who used their tiny prehensile hands to feed on the flesh of high-handed lords?

Merely tossing Andrew and Rafe out of the drawing room had not been nearly satisfying enough.

Ewan held himself at rigid attention in the center of the room, agonizingly aware of the loud gusts of air in and out of his lungs, the uncomfortable heat of the blush scouring his skin . . .

. . . the quiet, heavy weight of Violet's gaze.

He could not bear to look at her. To see the pity and discomfort in her lovely aquamarine eyes.

Yes, she likely considered Ewan a friend of sorts. But friendship did not immediately lead to a more romantic attachment.

He waited for the painful words that would come. Something achingly polite but firm, explaining that his friends were mistaken as to the state of her affections and so forth.

But she said nothing.

Finally, he broke under the weight of the ponderous silence.

"Well," he said, voice nearly hoarse, "if you will not allow me to apologize for my *glaikit* friends, then please allow me to apologize if my *own* behavior has been untoward in any way—"

"Ewan . . ."

He gasped.

Had she—?

His *Christian* name—?

His eyes snapped to hers.

There was not a trace of pity in her gaze.

Wariness? Yes.

Hesitance? Decidedly.

But pity? No.

"Violet . . ." he breathed in reply.

It seemed the only thing he *could* say. As if an entire world were hidden in her name.

"I like your friends." She smiled faintly. "They worry over you, and I am grateful that you have people in your life who care. You . . . *merit* . . . such care." A pause. "Ewan."

His blood was a stampede of hoof beats in his chest. He reminded his wayward heart that such words were not a declaration of love. Or even a statement of intent.

Violet had merely been expressing her opinion.

And yet . . . the way his name lingered on her lips . . . the whole *felt* like a caress.

Hope exploded in his chest, a dragon wrenching free from its chains and soaring into the dazzling sunlit sky.

Dimly, he tried to remind himself that poor crofters did *not* marry countesses.

That the chasm between them was too great to span.

That the fall from this height would be soul-crushingly brutal.

But in the moment, with Violet right in front of him, staring at him with such *emotion* in her beautiful eyes—

He failed to keep any thought other than *she is so glorious* in his brain.

His hands ached to hold her, to sweep her against him, to beg her to truly consider him.

She appeared equally frozen, as if fighting the same hundred warring thoughts.

Finally, she moved, stepping forward.

He watched her draw closer and closer. His mouth went dry; his breathing hitched.

She stopped toe-to-toe. Her skirts brushed his kilt, the scent of lavender engulfing him. She popped upward, pressing a hand to his chest for balance, her mouth close to his ear.

"Furthermore . . . I have greatly enjoyed every minute of our acquaintance . . . Ewan." She whispered the words into his ear, warm air blowing across his skin, sending gooseflesh flaring to attention down his spine. She sucked in a deep breath, her nose skimming the column of his throat—the barest feather-soft touch—as she stepped back.

Her eyes met his.

She gave him that same faint smile.

And then she left the room.

I HAVE GREATLY *enjoyed every minute of our acquaintance . . . Ewan.*

Violet's words were a glove slap to his senses.

Ewan was still light-headed from it thirty minutes later.

How was he to behave around her *now*? How was he to keep his adoration from shining through every look, every word?

Worse, was he going to have to *thank* Andrew and Rafe for their high-handed interference? What had they said to convince Violet to encourage his affections?

The four of them sat around the breakfast room table in Kilmeny Hall. A quick query from Violet had uncovered that neither Andrew or Rafe had eaten since breakfast. Ewan, as ever, was more than ready to eat yet another meal. Violet had ordered a cold luncheon to be sent up from the kitchen.

So now they were helping themselves to generous slices of cured ham and beef, salty cheese, and fresh bread. Ewan piled his plate high and listened as his friends and Violet chatted.

Ewan adored her like this, eyes bright with interest. He also appreciated how charming she was to his friends, despite the fact that they had surely quizzed her about him.

"I admit to being decidedly curious as to how you three formed a friendship." Violet pointed at the sash around Andrew's chest. "Does it have something to do with this same dark tartan you are each wearing? Is it a secret sign of your brotherhood?"

Andrew shot Ewan a look.

Ewan shrugged, as if to say: *My lass is a clever one.*

"Something of the like, my lady." Andrew replied.

"We all met on a voyage of scientific discovery," Rafe explained.

Andrew tossed his thumb in Ewan's direction. "We were extremely fortunate to convince Ewan to join us."

"Aye," Rafe agreed, reaching for some crumbly, aged cheddar. "Cataloging botanical finds requires a dab hand at drawing. Had such a thing been left tae me, the voyage would have been doomed from the outset."

"Scientific discovery?" Violet sat back, eyes darting to Ewan's. "Why have you said nothing of this? That sounds . . . remarkable. Where did you go?"

Ewan shrugged. "Where didnae we go? Sydney, Australia, the New Hebrides—"

"Santiago in Chile, Rio de Janeiro in Brazil," Rafe chimed in.

"Why that is . . ." Violet paused and then shook her head. "Truthfully, why have I not read of your exploits. That sounds . . . phenomenal."

Andrew sighed and sat back in his chair.

"We were on *The Minerva*," he said.

Violet lifted her chin, as if absorbing the information.

"Ah. The ship that wrecked in the South Pacific?" she frowned. "I read something in the broadsheets about it just yesterday. A description of what transpired. Though it seemed . . . fanciful."

Rafe winced.

Andrew groaned.

Ewan paused, a piece of ham halfway to his mouth.

"There was *another* notice in the papers?" he asked, looking between his friends. "But I thought ye said nothing happened?"

"It isn't much, tae be honest." Andrew drummed his fingers on the table. "Some journalist caught wind of the magistrate's interest in *The Minerva* and published a rather lurid account of the whole affair."

"A truthful account?" Ewan set down his ham.

"Nae." Rafe pushed back his plate and folded his arms, leaning on the table. "It had only the barest traces of fact. This version had a lot more blood, mayhem, and even the advent of some scurvy pirates."

"I managed to keep our names out of it, for now. We were simply referred to as a 'group of gentlemen,' but . . ." Andrew trailed off.

It was only a matter of time.

"So . . . what happened?" Violet canted forward, eyes lit with curiosity. "You do realize that you cannot entice me with a story such as this and not relate the whole of it, correct?"

Between the three of them, they outlined the details of their voyage for her, from the formation of their brotherhood, through all their trials aboard ship and Jamie's death, the plaid they had adopted to honor Jamie's life, ending with their recent trip to Aberdeen and interview with Mrs. Massey about her husband.

"What will you do if the magistrate moves to reopen a formal inquisition into the ship's sinking?" she asked.

"We cannot rightly say," Andrew replied. "We will simply continue tae look for answers and hope that the full truth will come to light."

"But . . ." Violet paused. "What about . . . Jamie? Could he have lived?"

Ewan met Andrew's gaze, their thoughts clearly on the same page.

"We reckon it unlikely," Ewan answered her question. "Jamie was a rather . . . fierce sort of person. A strong personality."

Rafe snorted. "That's putting it mildly."

"Aye," Andrew nodded, gaze withdrawn. "Jamie would have found a way tae contact us."

"Kieran, in particular, as they were the best of friends," Rafe said. "He is still taking Jamie's death to be hard."

Ewan resisted the urge to fidget, the discomfort of the secret he held weighing on his chest.

"That is the problem, is it not?" Andrew agreed. "There is no possible chance that Jamie would be alive somewhere and choose not tae contact Kieran. And yet, Kieran clings tae hope."

"Aye," Ewan said, seizing the reins of the conversation, desperate to change the subject. Keeping Kieran's secrets was already hard enough with his friends. But if Violet turned her keen mind to the problem, it would likely not take much for Ewan to spill what he knew.

And it truthfully was not his secret to tell.

Besides, discussions of Jamie were always painful, and sometimes in the face of tragedy, there was nothing to do but press onward.

Ewan should know.

The conversation wandered from there.

Andrew and Ewan devolved into talking about Jane, Andrew's wife, and the prospect of Ewan completing another portrait for them later in the year.

Occasionally, Ewan caught snippets of Violet's conversation with Rafe. They had begun by speaking of common acquaintances, but they soon diverged onto Rafe's love of his estate west of Perth.

"Half of the land is excellent for oats and potatoes, but I've begun to explore putting cattle on the northern fields. There's an MP in South Aberdeenshire who is experimenting with breeding the Angus doddy into a more hearty, usable cow—"

"Och! You're not on about the coos again, are ye, Rafe?" Andrew groaned. "Don't listen tae him, my lady. He has been talking about nothing but cows these past two weeks, and it's liable tae drive a man mad."

"Ye said ye were interested in the coos yerself!" Rafe spread his arms wide.

"Lady Kildrum isn't going tae be fascinated by your sorry bovine—"

"Actually, I am very interested in the cows," Violet interjected.

That had the effect of silencing the men.

They all turned to stare at her.

"And elms," she continued.

"Elms?" Rafe asked, brow furrowed.

"Why, yes. I manage some of my own lands, you see. And I was reading in *A Country-man's Rudiments*—"

"The chapter about sowing elms?!" Rafe snapped his fingers. "That was fascinating reading—"

"Elms? *Fascinating?*" Andrew scoffed and sent his eyes ceiling-ward.

Ewan snagged Violet's gaze, grinning over his friends' banter. She pressed her lips together, stifling a returning smile.

"Elms are no laughing matter, your lofty lordship," Rafe said. "We don't all have armies of stewards tae oversee our lands—"

"Och! Ye have got to cease with this 'lofty lordship' nonsense. 'Tis bad enough when Kieran does it—"

"When Kieran does what now?" a new voice said from the open doorway.

They all turned toward the sound.

"Kieran!" Ewan broke into a smile.

Kieran stood in the door, a rather harried-looking Irvine at his heels.

Ewan leaped from his chair, crossing to their friend.

His artist's eye instantly noted the slightly askew nature of Kieran's appearance. His kilt pinned a wee bit sloppily. His sporran not quite level. The wrinkles in his coat beneath the great kilt.

Ewan enveloped Kieran, surprised as usual at how much smaller the ship's master was than himself. Kieran's out-sized personality always made him seem larger-than-life, so it was disorienting to remember that Kieran was actually average in something.

Kieran thumped Ewan on the back and then turned to give Rafe and Andrew similarly bracing hugs. He greeted Violet, bowing prettily over her hand. Violet motioned for a footman to bring another plate for their guest.

Kieran did seem a bit better, as Alex said. He seemed his normal, ebullient self in manner, at least at first. But there was a strain to him—as evidenced by his clothing—a sense that he was pulled taut and the slightest jolt could shatter him completely.

Kieran's eyes appeared nearly feverishly bright and his face was thinner. Had he been eating enough while staying with Alex?

And why was Kieran here now? What had prompted him to travel to Kilmeny Hall?

"Are ye well, Kieran?" Ewan asked as they all retook their seats. "Alex had said ye were feeling a wee bit poorly."

"Well enough, I suppose," he said, reaching for some roast beef and cheese.

But Kieran avoided Ewan's gaze. And his hands shook as he filled his plate.

Ewan's heart clenched.

The depth of Kieran's grief felt simply . . . insurmountable.

Ewan swallowed and turned back to his own plate, his eye catching Violet's in the process.

Her lovely eyes held concern. Clever lass that she was, she had not missed the undercurrents here.

"So what brings you to Kilmeny Hall, Master MacTavish?" Violet asked.

"Well," Kieran said slowly, piling his meat atop a slice of crusty bread, "I heard word that three of my closest friends decided tae investigate something in Aberdeen that they know matters more than anything else tae me." He paused to fix them all with a hard look. "And I tracked them down tae demand why they would betray our friendship in such a manner."

19

Violet barely avoided flinching at Master MacTavish's bristling words. To Ewan's credit, he didn't react defensively to the accusation.

"I reckon I owe ye an apology," he said, tone sincere. "We should have sent word to Edinburgh and let ye know."

"Aye, Kieran," Lord Hadley chimed in. "We made a mistake."

Violet continued to listen in surprise as Ewan, Lord Hadley, and Sir Rafe apologized. They acknowledged that they had been wrong to keep their trip from their friend.

It was astonishing to witness three grown gentlemen behave, well, like . . . *gentle* men.

It rather illuminated the sad lack of such humility in other men of Violet's acquaintance.

They did not, however, tell Master MacTavish the information they had found in Aberdeen. And because they did not, Master MacTavish seemed to assume they had not found anything of merit and let the matter go.

But his pale eyes held a deadness, a clinging sense of despair.

Was this the grief the others had mentioned? The pain over Jamie's death that the discovery of survivors had reopened?

Violet's curiosity ran rampant. She longed to understand the undercurrents in the room.

Given that Violet's father and sisters were away, asking the gentlemen to spend the night at Kilmeny Hall was not possible.

But Violet insisted that they could stay with Sir Joshua in Old Kilmeny Castle. Ewan immediately seconded the idea.

This naturally led to them fetching Sir Joshua, who heartily agreed to the scheme as the castle had ample bedrooms and, as Sir Joshua put it, "The local inn is scarcely fit for human habitation."

The gentlemen *did* accept an invitation to dine at Kilmeny Hall.

After a lively dinner—well, more a dinner where everyone attempted to pull Master MacTavish from his doldrums—Violet donned her cloak and joined the men on their walk back down to Old Kilmeny Castle.

The rain and clouds of the past week had given way to warm sun, and as they were into May, daylight lingered well into the evening hours. Moreover, as cheery days were rare in Scotland, it felt criminal to let sunshine go begging.

Once they arrived at the castle, Lord Hadley made the surprising announcement that he and his wife were expecting a child sometime in the late autumn. So, of course, Sir Joshua ordered up bottles of whisky and French wine to celebrate.

Which is how Violet found herself with a glass of French wine, sitting before a roaring fire in the great hall of Old Kilmeny Castle, toasting to the health of Lord Hadley's wife and child. After a hearty round of congratulations, they all settled in for a long blether.

The evening sky had sunk through a pink sunset and settled into an inky-blue dusk. The fire kept away the slight chill and three candelabra ensured the room felt cheery, despite the clutter of the artists' studio around them.

Faces and scenes peeked out from Uncle's paintings leaning against the wall, but Ewan's distinctive style appeared as well. She had heard Ewan's tale of the leak in the greenhouse which had forced him to move his studio indoors.

Two easels with canvases on them faced the wall to the right of the fireplace. Ewan and Uncle's current work in progress, she supposed.

Her fingers itched to turn around Ewan's easel and see the work upon it. Was he still painting that mysterious dark-haired woman? Or the blackhouse on the cliff? Or had he begun her portrait in earnest?

The gentlemen drank whisky and spoke of this and that. Lord Hadley was regaling her uncle with a summary of their travels aboard *The Minerva*. Ewan and Master MacTavish were exchanging quiet words, though it appeared to Violet that Master MacTavish was sipping his whisky more quickly than the others, his joy over Lord Hadley's impending fatherhood decidedly strained.

Violet and Sir Rafe, seated beside one another, continued their earlier discussion of agriculture. They had moved from elms to cattle breeds to drainage issues. She found it rather endearing to see the formerly rakish Lord Rafe expounding upon the merits of potash versus coprolite for soil fertilizer while extolling the intelligence of his wife, Lady Sophronia Gordon, at the same time.

"Sophie has had brilliant suggestions for ways to utilize barn cats to control gopher populations, as well."

"Gophers?"

"Aye. She is convinced that some drainage issues relate to the damage gophers do as they burrow through fields."

Sir Rafe continued on, describing the problem in detail.

His ideas were fascinating. But just as interesting was the way he interjected his wife's opinion at regular intervals.

Sophie was brilliant in her understanding of animal behavior.

Sophie had the cleverest suggestion for planting rotations.

With each mention, his eyes would light with pride.

This, Violet thought. *I want this.*

A husband who will talk to a stranger about me with pride and adoration in his eyes.

The sheer force of the longing shocked her.

Partly because she seemed incapable of deciding anything, and yet this was crystalline in her mind.

Partly because she had never conceived of a marriage where husband and wife worked closely together toward a common goal.

Marriages, in her experience, were more an uneasy alliance where husbands and wives lived separate lives that only periodically connected. A marriage like the one Lord Graham offered, she supposed.

But listening to Sir Rafe was a bit akin to stepping out of a shadowy cave to find an entirely different landscape of possibility before her.

A breathtaking view of what marriage *could* be.

"Ye're keeping information from me, Ewan. I can sense it." Master MacTavish's raised voice broke through the chatter of the room.

All heads turned in his direction.

"Youse all found something in Aberdeen," he continued, downing the last of his whisky in one bracing bolt. "I know it. It's why ye deliberately went without me. It's why you're still dodging the question."

Master MacTavish looked worse for wear, Violet realized. His eyes were becoming more and more bloodshot, the gaunt hollows in his cheeks more pronounced.

Even *Violet* knew what the gentlemen had found in Aberdeen. So why keep the information from Master MacTavish? Did it have to do with what they had said about Jamie? That Master MacTavish and Jamie were close friends? But if so, how deep was Master MacTavish's grief that he would be so upset over a friend's death several years on? Or was it merely the thought that perhaps Jamie might still live?

"Now, Kieran," Lord Hadley held out a placating hand, "I fear you're getting a wee bit into your cups. We'll tell ye in the morning after ye've slept this off—"

"Who did ye find? Ye found something because you're avoiding the question."

"We didnae *see* anyone, Kieran," Ewan said, shooting a side-eye at Lord Hadley, "and we havenae lied tae ye."

"Let it be for tonight, Kieran," Sir Rafe pleaded.

"Aye," Lord Hadley agreed. "There will be enough time on the morrow to discuss it. Then we won't be bothering Lady Kildrum with our wee problems."

Violet smiled. She did not find their discussion onerous in the slightest, but she recognized an excuse when she saw one.

"Yes," she said brightly, jumping on the chance to divert the conversation as a good hostess should. "I, for one, would be delighted to hear what Mr. Campbell and Uncle Joshua are working on at the moment." She darted her eyes toward the canvases on the easels.

Uncle Joshua laughed. "Now, now, Violet, you know only too well that I will not show a work while it is in its initial stages."

"Yes, to the public at large, perhaps, but what about me?" Violet teased. "Why won't you show your favorite niece?"

She shot a quick glance at Ewan, hoping to draw him into the conversation, as well. He met her gaze but said nothing.

"Your father and sister were down here earlier in the week trying to cajole me into showing them." Sir Joshua wagged his finger at her. "But you, of all people, know perfectly well why I am reticent, you minx."

She did indeed. In his heart of hearts, Uncle Joshua was a showman. He lived for the *oohs* and *aahs* that accompanied a well-planned reveal.

Sir Joshua motioned toward Ewan. "But Ewan should show you what he has been working on. It is quite brilliant."

Ewan managed a smile, but it appeared strained at the edges. "Ye flatter me, Sir Joshua, but I rather like the idea of being more like yourself. Keep the mystery until the painting is nearly finished."

"Nonsense! The painting I saw yesterday was nearly complete."

Ewan squirmed. "Perhaps I feel a wee bit bashful about it, sir."

Violet was torn between empathy for his shyness and a small sense of frustration that Ewan Campbell would wish to downplay his talent in front of his friends.

His work was brilliant and his friends would surely wish to celebrate that fact with him.

"Was it the painting of his mysterious woman, Uncle?" Violet asked. "The very one."

Ewan's head snapped to attention, eyes flaring in alarm.

"Which mysterious woman is this?" Sir Rafe asked, obviously curious.

"Mr. Campbell is not saying," Violet said, "though she is extremely pretty."

"Aye?" Sir Rafe's smile was all mischief.

"Aye," Violet replied, joining him in mischievousness. "Dark curly hair, pale silvery eyes, and a smirking mouth. She appears to almost jump off the canvas at you, so forceful is the sense of her personality."

She had described the painting in an attempt to divert everyone from Master MacTavish's persistent questions. Given the teasing banter back and forth between Ewan's friends, she expected that they would move to ribbing him good-naturedly about the woman and the story of her would come out.

But Violet's words had a decidedly sobering effect upon the gentleman. The more she described the woman, the quieter and more somber they became until the room bounced with strained tension.

Oh, no. Violet's stomach plunged. What had she done?

"What . . ." Master MacTavish licked his lips. He turned to Ewan. "What did she just say? Is she describing—"

Ewan's expression was stone. A granite slab of reticence.

His silence was apparently all the answer Master MacTavish needed.

"I want tae see this painting." Master MacTavish rose from his chair.

Ewan leaped to his feet, intercepting him. "Kieran—"

"No!" Master MacTavish's voice reverberated through the room, a gunshot of sound. "If ye willnae tell me what has happened, ye will no' deny me this, too."

He and Ewan exchanged a long, tense look. Master MacTavish glared up at his larger friend, the size difference between the two nearly comical.

Finally, Ewan's shoulders sank.

"Very well," he whispered.

Ewan walked over to the easel against the wall. With a sigh, he turned the entire thing around, revealing the portrait that Violet had seen that day in his studio several weeks ago.

He had continued to work on the painting. The woman's hair now billowed as if buffeted in the wind, and she looked out at the viewer with coy mischief. Violet could almost hear the woman's magical laughter.

Violet had been so caught up in the painting that it took her a moment to register Master MacTavish's reaction.

Or, rather, his inaction.

He stood, staring at the painting, transfixed. His body was held at rigid attention, but his eyes danced over the image, not unlike a thirsty man guzzling water from a fountain.

He blinked.

Once.

Twice.

And then Master MacTavish collapsed. A marionette doll with its strings abruptly cut.

Ewan lunged, his preternaturally fast reflexes catching the man before he hit the floor.

Instead of releasing his friend, Ewan gathered him into a hard embrace.

A low keening filled the room.

Master MacTavish was . . . weeping.

A desolate, anguished sound. A soul broken and pained beyond sense.

The rest of them had come to their feet. Violet bounced her gaze between Lord Hadley and Sir Rafe, noting the somberness of their expressions.

What had just happened?

What had Violet unleashed?

Master MacTavish screamed. Primal. Feral in its anguish.

Violet pressed a hand to her sternum.

Oh, heavens!

Her careless words had somehow lanced the festering wound of Master MacTavish's grief.

Master MacTavish pushed to his feet, his hands threading into his hair, pulling on the strands.

Ewan rose with him, hands out-stretched, as if in supplication.

But Master MacTavish was paying him no heed. He paced the room in agitated steps, eyes darting again and again to the painting, tears streaming down his cheeks.

"Kieran . . ." Ewan continued to hold his hand out.

Master MacTavish shook his head not stopping pacing. "No!"

"Kieran, this is *destroying* ye," Ewan's voice turned pleading, pained. "We *all* miss her—"

"NO!" Master MacTavish whirled to face Ewan. "Dinnae talk like our pain is the same!"

He began pacing again, hand in his hair. Ewan stepped in front of him, placing two hands on his friend's shoulders—

"She's dead, Kieran. Ye have tae let her go—"

Master MacTavish pushed his hands away and when Ewan didn't give way, he placed both hands on Ewan's chest and shoved.

Ewan, of course, did not move. He merely looked at his friend, unshed tears in his eyes.

"Jamie is dead, Kieran—" Ewan's voice cracked. "She's *dead*. She's no' coming back—"

Violet gasped.

Jamie was the woman in the portraits?

Jamie was a . . . *she*?

She locked eyes with Uncle Joshua across the room. He shook his head in astonishment.

"How do ye know that for sure?!" Master MacTavish beat a fist against Ewan's chest. "We thought Cuthie was gone, too, but here he is! She *could* be alive."

"Kieran," Lord Hadley said, tone somber. "Ye know that is unlikely—"

"But it is possible! What God would allow a bastard like Cuthie tae live but send *my* Jamie tae her grave?"

"She would have contacted us by now. Ye know that," Sir Rafe joined in. "We've said this again and again—"

"But what if—" Master MacTavish's voice broke once more. He continued on, his tone hoarse. "But what if she *lived*? Anything could have happened to her. She would have been this wee, fiery woman tossed onto the mercy of the world! There are caliphates in the Dutch East Indies, only a week's journey from Vanuatu . . . do ye not see? She could have ended up captured and sold into slavery there. She could have been forced into a caliph's harem, or be chained in a prison somewhere. And the thought that she might be alive and hurting somewhere, pleading for me tae find her—"

"Kieran," Sir Rafe said, "we understand this. We do. But you're grasping at straws. This is destroying ye, and ye know it."

"No!" Master MacTavish swiped a sleeve over his eyes, as if the motion could banish his tears. "Ye say that from the safety of your marriage, Rafe! Ye have your Sophie. Andrew has his Jane. Your loves live and breathe! Ye will both go home tae them in a day or two and hold them in your arms and thank the heavens that your lot is not mine."

He paused, gasping, chest heaving, eyes bloodshot and pleading. "But Jamie . . . *my* Jamie . . . is *gone*. And I cannae piece my heart back together without her."

Lord Hadley bit his lip and swiped a thumb underneath one eye.

Sir Rafe folded his arms, looking up at the ceiling.

Uncle Joshua sat stone still.

Master MacTavish turned to Ewan. "Ye know how it all happened, Ewan. She was alone on that ship. Cuthie *knew* she was a woman. He knew at the end. He kept her aboard for that very reason, trapped her and sailed away like the rat he is. When I think what might have happened tae her—"

Master MacTavish broke off, his harsh breaths filling the room.

Ewan stood with his hands on his hips, head shaking back and forth.

Violet longed to wrap her arms around him.

Silence hung.

"They deserve tae know," Ewan finally said, voice like gravel.

Master MacTavish pressed his fingertips to his eyes, his chest heaving, gusting breaths wracking him.

"Kieran . . ." Tears filled Ewan's eyes. "Please. *Tell* them. Let us all share the depth your grief."

Lord Hadley and Sir Rafe looked back and forth between their friends.

Violet wiped her cheeks, not surprised to find them wet. Uncle Joshua passed her a handkerchief.

"What is it, Kieran?" Lord Hadley asked, tone soft. "We would grieve with you."

"Aye," Sir Rafe agreed.

Master MacTavish gasped, grabbing for air, as if the pain of the words choked him.

He swallowed convulsively.

"Jamie . . . when we were in Sydney . . . we were handfasted," Master MacTavish hiccupped. "Ewan . . . Ewan stood as witness."

Oh! Violet pressed a hand to her throat. They were married?!

Jamie had been his *wife*?

Handfasting was a traditional form of irregular marriage still common in the deep Highlands. When witnessed, it was considered as legal as a church marriage.

Master MacTavish dropped his hands, looking at his friends, that terrible deadness returning to his eyes.

"Jamie was . . . *expecting*," he continued. "I lost two loves that day."

Violet closed her eyes, the agonizing loss a weight on her chest.

This poor man! To lose his wife and child in one dreadful blow—

"Bloody hell," Lord Hadley swore. "And here we've been absolutely callous bastards, celebrating my own Jane—" His voice broke.

"Oh, Kieran." Sir Rafe wiped his eyes. "Ye should have told us."

Master MacTavish shook his head. "What did it matter, once she was gone—"

"We could have grieved with ye!" Lord Hadley bellowed. "We could have been more sensitive tae yer pain!"

"If ye want to help me with ma grief, stop keeping things from me!" Master MacTavish roared. "Youse found something in Aberdeen, and ye willnae tell me! Did ye find out something about her? Is that it? How can I even sleep when—"

"There was an *explosion*, Kieran," Sir Rafe interrupted. "The ship exploded."

Master MacTavish froze, eyes bouncing between Ewan and Lord Hadley.

"What?" he whispered.

"The ship exploded."

"But . . . how could ye know that—"

"Massey survived, too. He and Cuthie were tossed clear of the blast," Ewan said. "That's what we discovered in Aberdeen."

"Did ye bloody Massey?!"

"No, we only spoke with his wife. She didnae know where he'd got hisself off to. But he described the events tae her, how the ship exploded and how they survived."

Master MacTavish stared at each of his friends in turn, eyes sightless and full of such anguish.

"I'm so sorry, Kieran," Ewan whispered. "But if the ship did indeed explode . . . Jamie . . . and your child . . . they *have* tae be gone."

20

So . . . Jamie is a woman," Violet said.

"Aye," Ewan replied, swallowing back the emotion of the past hour.

"I feel terrible that my attempts to diffuse the situation resulted in so much pain for Master MacTavish."

"Och, the conversation was long overdue. The others needed to know the true extent of Kieran and Jamie's relationship."

He and Violet were walking the moonlit path to Kilmeny Hall. Ewan had left Andrew and Rafe to console Kieran and coax him to sleep.

Violet had said a maid could walk with her back to the house, but Ewan insisted on accompanying her. He couldn't bear the thought of leaving her to manage the way alone.

The truth of Kieran's words had struck him hard—

Your loves live and breathe! Ye will go home to them in a day or two and hold them in your arms and thank the heavens that your lot is not mine.

Not that Ewan had a lady *love*, per se—

He liked Violet.

He admired her and thought of her constantly.

He adored her throaty laugh. The quick turn of her mind. Her care and desire to help others. Her general optimism and cheery spirits.

But did all these things amount to *love*?

As Andrew loved his Jane? Or Rafe loved his Sophie?

Or as Kieran loved his Jamie?

Ewan pondered the thought.

His heart hammered in agony at the thought of never seeing Violet again. Or at the idea of her being hurt and him far away and unable to help. The sheer devastation of such a pain . . .

So . . . perhaps Ewan was closer to true love than he had supposed.

Ewan could not fault Kieran for his grief and despair.

"Jamie was . . . a force of nature," Ewan said, darting a glance at Violet, walking at his side. Her skirts rustled the grasses which grew along the path's edge.

Night had finally fallen. Fortunately, a full moon hung in the sky, light glinting off the ocean. The bright moonlight turned the path through the gorse into a milky stream, easily traversed without a lamp.

"I imagine she would have had to be," Violet agreed. "How did she come to be aboard the ship? I thought Jamie was the carpenter's mate."

"She was. Jamie's father, Charles Fyffe, was Kieran's mentor. On his deathbed, Mr. Fyffe wrote a letter requesting Kieran to hire his son, James. Kieran felt an obligation to his mentor and wrote back, agreeing to hire the lad, sight unseen. But it was Mr. Fyffe's *daughter* who came aboard in place of her brother, James. Her true name was Eilidh." Ewan leaned into the syllables—AY-lee. "But she was only ever Jamie to us all."

Ewan stepped over a larger stone on the path. He half-turned, ensuring that Violet saw the hazard.

"I have read of such things," she said, jumping lightly over the stone. "Stories of women donning trousers and joining the Royal Navy. Wasn't there a book some years ago? *The Female Shipwright* or some such?"

"Yes, there are many tales of women taking to the sea, though Kieran claims it is rare. He was the first to discover Jamie's true gender. As the journey progressed and we all became better friends, Kieran and Jamie took us into their confidence, enlisting our aid in protecting Jamie's secret from the rest of the crew. We formed a brotherhood. A misnomer, of course, as Jamie was not a man, but it felt fraternal, nonetheless. Only Kieran ever saw Jamie as anything other than a sibling. Their love was a slow growing thing, but by the end, it felt almost unbreakable."

"And you witnessed their marriage? But . . . why did Kieran not invite the others to join in witnessing it? And once Jamie died, why not tell the rest of the Brotherhood?"

Violet stopped on the path, causing Ewan to pause. The moon rose behind her, casting her face into purple shadows. *Violet* shadows, he supposed.

"Jamie wished to keep the marriage a secret. Kieran respected her wish. It is as simple as that," Ewan replied. This was an old argument between Kieran and himself. "Once Jamie died, Kieran continued to honor her request. I think he saw it as an act of devotion, to carry on as she had intended. I've been trying to convince him for over four years to tell the others."

"That poor man. To carry such pain alone." Violet wrapped her arms around her waist.

"Aye. Kieran was finally starting to truly heal from the grief of Jamie's loss last summer. We all hoped that he would finally be able to move on. Then Rafe discovered Cuthie alive in Aberdeen." He paused, shaking his head. "The results are as you saw tonight. Knowing that others survived the wreck rekindled hope, ripping open the wound of his grief. I fear Kieran will tear the world apart trying to find answers, eventually killing himself in the process."

"I am sorry you lost a dear friend in Jamie," Violet whispered. "It is as you said about Dahlia, such a death . . . it *stings*. A thousand tiny cuts reminding us of what we have lost."

"Aye," his voice rough with emotion.

She lifted her hand at that, stretching out as if to touch him. The motion almost involuntary. As if his pain were something she simply *had* to soothe.

Just that wee act lent him such . . . *strength*.

He extended his arm, encouraging her to thread her outstretched hand through his elbow. She readily did so, the press of her fingers a burning weight through his sleeve.

Seizing a deep breath, he turned and motioned for them to continue.

"I admire how you harnessed that pain into visual form," she said, squeezing the hand wrapped around his elbow, sending shocks up his arm. "Your painting captures a woman of spirit and life. *Both* paintings, in fact, are a beautiful echo of the person Jamie was."

"Thank ye," Ewan's reply was reflexive but then he frowned. "Both paintings?"

"Well, yes, the one I caught you painting that day atop the cliffs. The one with the blackhouse. That painting had Jamie in it, too, did it not?"

Ewan's breathing abruptly tightened, a vise gripping his chest.

Agree with her.

Just say it, 'Why, yes, of course that was Jamie, too.'

But . . .

Did he wish to lie?

Or rather . . . did he have the courage to tell Violet the truth?

He could sense that sinking, cold feeling creeping in, its salmon-tinged edges grasping at him.

They walked on for a moment, the ocean waves a distant murmur against the stark silence of the evening.

He had never realized how quiet a Scottish night could be until he had ventured to other parts of the world. As it turned out, in most places, nighttime teemed with sounds: crickets, frogs, birds, alligators in the tropics, and an almost endless rustling of nocturnal animals.

But even in the height of summer, Scotland was silent. A deathly hush that was nearly a hum unto itself it was so still.

Now the silence rang with a damning condemnation.

Ewan swallowed back the panicky taste in his throat.

How could he ever muster the courage to paint his demons if he couldn't even *speak* them aloud to Violet?

"Ewan?" Violet tugged on his elbow, a silent plea for him to stop.

He cleared his throat before turning to face her.

"The woman in the painting isnae Jamie."

"Pardon?"

"The woman in the painting . . . she isnae Jamie," Ewan repeated.

"But . . . who is she then?"

Ewan looked past Violet, staring out over the midnight-blue ocean.

"I should like to know, if you will tell me." Violet canted her head. "She means something to you, that woman. You even said as much."

"Aye." Why was there this catch in his voice? "She does."

Violet waited. The moonlight still rendered her face in shadowy shapes, painted in deepest violet and inky blue-black. But her lovely eyes caught the moon, reflecting flecks of silver.

This brave woman. She had shared the pain of her past with him.

Ewan had to match her courage.

He took in a long breath. Released it.

"Mhairi," he breathed, voicing her name. "The woman is my younger sister, Mhairi."

"Mhairi," she repeated, giving the name the same Gaelic intonation that he had done—VAH-ree, trilling the *r*.

Ewan could feel the questions crowding Violet's tongue.

Why do you paint Mhairi?

Why that house? That scene?

"Why do I feel that Mhairi is lost to you?" she asked instead.

Ewan flinched.

"Will you tell me?" she continued, stepping closer to him. "I would like to know you, Ewan."

Her words cut.

I would like to know you.

He swallowed.

He would like that, too. He would like to be known.

He held out his hand to Violet, palm up, a supplication. She looked at it and then slid her own hand down his forearm to thread her fingers through his.

Her bare palm pressed into his.

The touch burned, sending skittering sparks up his arm.

Hand in hand, they began once again up the path.

Ewan had told the story of Mhairi only once before . . . to Alex. It had spilled out of him that awful night.

After rescuing Rafe and Andrew from *The Minerva*, Ewan had carried Andrew's heavy, unconscious body from the torched village to the safety of the hill above it. Rafe had staggered beside him, bleeding from several wounds. The sheer brutality of the physical effort required and the fear for his friends' health had kept Ewan's mind off the village burning behind them.

But after gently setting Andrew down on a makeshift pallet Alex had formed, Ewan turned to view the village aflame.

Everything had caught up with him then.

Terror. Anguish.

Memory.

It had been like a club to the head, taking him to his knees, shaking uncontrollably.

And then Kieran had appeared, running up the hill, screaming at them, begging someone to help him go after Jamie.

Ewan had grabbed Kieran, holding him back before he could jostle Alex in his work of stitching up Andrew and Rafe.

Kieran thrashed in agony, sobbing. Jamie was at Cuthie's mercy aboard the ship, and there was *nothing* they could do about it.

All while the village burned.

Ewan rocked Kieran, holding him tightly, arms trembling, tears falling.

The chain of events had hurtled Ewan even farther back in time, forcing him to relive the horror of another night, huddled on a different beach, cradling Mhairi as she screamed and sobbed.

Eventually, Alex finished stitching up Rafe and stabilized Andrew, and then persuaded Kieran into taking some laudanum, anything to prevent the man from harming himself.

Alex had then sat himself beside Ewan, extending the flask of whisky he usually kept in his physician's bag.

They had stared over the glowing embers of the village, Ewan drinking a few swallows of the precious whisky. Alex had been a steady oasis of calm at his elbow, patiently coaxing the story out of him.

And now, with Violet's hand tucked in his—walking up another hill, overlooking another ocean—Ewan found himself telling the story again into the dark of night.

"I was born in a blackhouse along Loch Carron, a sea loch on the mainland just north of the Isle of Skye," he said, eyes trained on the path before them. "My parents were crofters, trying to eke a living out of the land and sea. My da was a braw man with broad, muckle shoulders like myself. My ma was tender-hearted with a shock of red hair. They had plenty of bairns together, but only myself and my younger sister, Mhairi, survived childhood. We were poor, but we limped along, year after year."

Ewan paused, remembering running down the path toward the blackhouse, Mhairi squealing behind him, trying to catch him. She had been three years his junior. His shadow, he called her, both in fondness and exasperation.

Violet said nothing at his side as they walked.

"Then what happened?" she asked.

"Then . . . came the fire."

"Oh, Ewan—" Her voice caught at the end.

He sucked in a deep breath, forcing the words out. "I dinnae ken tae this day how the blaze started. It doesnae matter, I suppose. It was late in the evening, and I was out tending tae one of the sheep who had just lambed. I saw the flames against the sky and raced toward the house. My da met me at the stone fence, carrying Mhairi who had burned her legs." *Care for Mhairi. Keep her safe.* "He ran back inside the burning building tae save Ma. The roof collapsed before they could get out."

Ewan felt Violet's gasp in the spasm of her fingers.

That wee bit of empathy stung his eyes. He clutched her hand tighter.

How could this *still* be so raw? The events of that night were over twelve years past.

But he could still feel the sting of smoke in his eyes.

Still taste the ash in the back of his throat.

Still hear the horrific crash of the roof collapsing, silencing his mother's screams.

Still feel the shaking in his own body as he held Mhairi against his chest, realizing that they would only have one another going forward.

"How old were you?" Violet whispered.

"Fifteen."

She inhaled sharply. "Too young."

"Aye, far too young tae be thrust out into the world. But there was no other family to help us. We buried our parents the next day. From there, I did what I could tae provide for Mhairi and myself. We fashioned a lean-to out of the remains of the blackhouse. I sold some of the sheep, and Mhairi helped the fishwives with their catches, despite being only twelve years old. We managed tae survive that first winter, but it wasnae easy. I grew too much. A man in the village said that if I went to Kyle of Localsh, I could earn half a crown for fighting. Or, rather, for allowing myself tae be beaten. They promised I wouldnae be killed."

"Half a crown? For allowing yourself to beaten?!" She leaned her weight into their joined palms and clutched his arm with her free hand, her fingers wrapping around his elbow. "That's horrific!"

Ewan shrugged, pulling her a wee bit closer as they walked. "I had nothing tae lose at that point. And so I went, fully expecting tae come home bloodied but with enough money tae fill our bellies for a month—"

"You won, didn't you?"

"Aye. I did." He snorted. "And from there, I shifted my focus. Prize-fighting suddenly appeared a way to provide for myself and Mhairi. An older prizefighter agreed tae train me, tae show me all the tricks and tips tae fighting. Initially, he even arranged bouts for me. But soon, I'd grown beyond his knowledge. I fought every chance I got, traveling as far as Fort William or even Inverness once for matches. I used the money I won tae move Mhairi out of the ruined blackhouse and into a small white-washed cottage. It even had a wood floor and glass in the windows. Can you imagine the luxury?"

He said the words flippantly, but he supposed there was a part of him that wanted Violet to understand the massive chasm between them. That her life of privilege was a world away from the hard-scrabble existence of his past.

"Then what happened?" Violet asked.

Her voice was steady, no hesitation. As if she were saying, *I see what you are doing here, but I am made of sterner stuff. You will not frighten me off.*

They approached the high, stone wall surrounding the kitchen garden. The door through the wall was just ahead. He would leave Violet here, as she would be safe once through the garden door. Not that he *wanted* to part with her, but he could not be seen with her at this late hour.

"And then?" Ewan took on a long breath before uttering the words that hurt the most. "Mhairi betrayed my trust."

"She betrayed you?!" Violet came to an abrupt halt, tugging on his hand and forcing him to stop. "What did she do?"

Ewan could hear the outrage in Violet's voice. He wanted to feel angry, too. To feel that burst of stinging betrayal.

But after so many years, he recognized that his anger had been replaced with a profound, bone-deep hurt.

He sighed and leaned his shoulders back against the garden wall, looking into the shadows of Violet's face, her hand still clutched in his. "I am sure if ye were to ask Mhairi, she would say she *saved* me. But it's always felt like a betrayal." He scrubbed his free hand over his face, knowing he had to finish the story. "By the time I was nineteen, I was fighting more and more. Mhairi was sixteen, and I worried for her future. I was determined tae earn enough money to provide her with a small dowry that would allow her tae marry well. A shopkeeper or blacksmith, perhaps. Mhairi wanted me to stop fighting altogether and focus on my painting."

"Ye have too much talent, Ewan, tae be throwing it away on boxing. If ye're going to be a painter, then be a painter. I tire of this game. Go make a name for yourself," Mhairi would say. *"Cease this milling. Ye hate fighting, and I hate tae see ye doing it."*

"Just one more match," he would reply. *"Just one more, and I'll have enough for your dowry."*

"I dinnae want a dowry, Ewan! I want ye alive and painting somewheres far away from here."

"I was adamant. She was stubborn. I returned from a fight in Oban tae find she had married."

Violet gasped. "She what?!"

"She eloped with another crofter from up the coast, Michael McDoughal. The man had been introduced to her through his cousin who was a neighbor of ours. McDoughal was nearly three times her age, but that didnae stop him from pursuing Mhairi. His wife had died the previous year, and he wanted someone tae be a drudge—part-wife, part-servant. I knew the man had his eye on her, and I had heard stories of him, of how he had driven his first wife tae her grave. But I thought Mhairi had more sense. She *knew* what he was like. She *knew* what her life would be with him. Of course, a sixteen-year-old girl doesnae need permission tae marry in Scotland. Bans dinnae need tae be read over the pulpit for three consecutive Sundays. No one needs to wait. Mhairi recited her marriage vows with his brother and the local tacksman as witnesses."

Ewan hung his head, gritting his teeth against the pain of that moment. Of arriving home and learning what she had done. The realization that Mhairi had viewed his love as a burden. That allowing him to care and provide for her had been a gift she was unwilling to receive.

He clenched his jaw and continued. "I marched over tae McDoughal's house and demanded to see Mhairi. McDoughal blustered and said she was his now. That my guardianship of her ended with her marriage. I threatened him. Finally, Mhairi came tae the door, angry and stubborn. She told me—" His voice broke. He shook his head, refusing to allow the tears that clogged his throat. After a moment, he managed to continue, though his voice was tellingly hoarse. "She told me that she didnae want tae see me. That she had chosen McDoughal, and I was tae leave her be. She said I was only tae return once I had made a name for myself as an artist."

"Oh!" Violet pressed her free hand to her chest, her entire body swaying toward Ewan. "She sacrificed her future for yours."

"Aye." Ewan dragged his sleeve over his eyes. "She slammed the door in my face, but I couldnae accept it. I left and journeyed tae Fort William, convinced that I could earn enough from fighting to steal her away from McDoughal." He hiccupped, the memory a vicious weight. "I returned months later, begging her tae leave with me. She adamantly refused. Said she was happy in her life with McDoughal, though I could scarcely believe it. She seemed pale tae me, as if life was slowly draining all the color out of her. But she could be so . . . *stubborn*."

Mhairi's final words echoed still, their cruelty an endless loop.

I've already cast ye out once. Ye need tae stay gone, Ewan. I dinnae ever want tae see ye again.

"McDoughal made it clear that he would have me tossed in gaol for interfering with his wife. And so . . ." Ewan's voice trailed off.

"And so . . ."

"And so . . . I left." A terrible deadness echoed in his words, a finality. "I havenae heard from her since. After a few years, I decided tae try to make amends. But it's been in vain. I've written over and over, even reaching out tae the vicar in a nearby village, but tae no avail. I dinnae even know if she yet lives."

Why had he not done more over the years? Why had he not tried harder to reach her?

He had long blamed Mhairi for abandoning him—for giving up on *him*—but somewhere that dynamic had shifted.

Now . . . was he now guilty of abandoning her?

21

Violet's heart thrummed in her chest, a struck bell.

It was as if a thread were tied to Ewan and each pang of his own heart reverberated in hers, echoing with the grief of remembered pain and loss.

They both had sisters who had made disastrous marriages. At least Dahlia had written after she eloped. Violet had never felt cut off from her sister; she had never felt a lack of love.

How devastating for Ewan. To fight for Mhairi's future, only to have it cast back into his face.

But . . . how equally devastating for Mhairi. To deliberately consign herself to a life of hardship and drudgery in order to force her brother to chase his talent as a painter.

Ewan was frozen, watching her, his eyes glittering in the dim light. He leaned against the wall surrounding the kitchen garden. The moonlight raked him, casting him into a hodgepodge of shapes—triangles, rectangles, circles. He towered over her, a sentinel guarding her path.

And yet, he clasped her palm with attentive reverence, his thumb drawing soft swirls on the back of her hand. That simple point of contact hummed.

"Where did you go?" she asked him. "After Mhairi . . . cast you out that second time."

"I traveled south." He shifted his weight. "Or, put another way, I literally fought my way out of the Highlands."

"Oh, Ewan."

"I allowed hurt and anger to fuel my fists. I had always had a talent for prizefighting. But I forced myself tae become lethal. I took on bout after bout. I changed the spelling of my name from Eòghann Caimbeul to Ewan Campbell and shed my Gaelic roots more and more with every mile I traveled south. I even acquired a moniker—the Red Renegade. I *felt* red . . . blood and choler and madness. For a while, I lost sight of my goal."

"That is understandable. What changed?"

He snorted, shaking his head, a shadowy motion. "One afternoon, at a particularly low point, . . . I met a kind, refined lady who took pity on me."

Violet gasped. "Me?"

"Aye, lass." He used his free hand to tuck a loose lock of hair behind her ear, the touch sending gooseflesh skittering. "When ye rescued me that day . . . when ye allowed this brute of a Highlander tae stay in your carriage . . . I finally accepted that I couldnae continue on like I had. There were good people like yourself in the world. I needed tae realign my life, to begin again to pursue my hope of becoming a serious painter. I needed tae ensure Mhairi's sacrifice mattered."

He dragged his coat sleeve over his eyes again. The brutal efficiency of the motion tugging again on the string connecting them.

"Mhairi was not wrong, you know?" she said, squeezing his hand.

"How is that, lass?"

"You *are* destined for greatness."

He absorbed her compliment with a mere nod.

"Have you truly not seen Mhairi since?" she asked.

A beat.

"No," he whispered. "I have heard nothing at all of her. All my letters have gone unanswered. But . . ." His Adam's apple bobbed as he swallowed, a rolling shadow. ". . . I have not done all that I could to contact her. I have tae face the truth: I'm a coward."

"How so?"

He paused and then, "I worry that Mhairi will reject me again. I worry that she no longer lives. I worry that I will find her worn and haggard before her time and, like before, I'll be helpless tae assist her in any meaningful way. I fear my own impotence in the face of her pain."

A quiet hush waited between them.

Life needs more of this, Violet realized. This truth-telling . . . spilling words into the muted silence of night. It was communing, soul to soul, in its purest form.

And perhaps it was this sense of stillness that loosened her tongue.

"You are anything but a coward, Ewan Campbell. From that first moment in my carriage, I knew that you were one of the strongest men I had ever met. Literally, of course." That earned her a weak chuckle. "But also in ways of the heart."

Her words appeared to hit him like a blow. He sucked in a quick breath, the rise and fall of his chest a shape-shifting shadow.

"You paint me a wee bit of a saint, lass. But ye must know that isnae the case. I've spent many a year angry at Mhairi. And yet, time has helped me see the situation from her point of view. 'Tis a heavy burden tae be beholden to another, tae watch them sacrifice their life for ye. Mhairi couldnae do it any longer, and so she flipped the table on me, forced me to accept the weight of *her* sacrifice for my freedom. But . . ." He drifted off.

"But?" she prompted.

"But . . . when the dust settled from her decision, Mhairi had chosen a life of hardship." He swallowed again. "And she ensured there wasnae a bloody thing I could do about it. For my sister, I fear that duty has been a cold comfort in the end."

The words struck Violet with almost preternatural force.

Duty is a cold comfort

She knew that, of course.

Was that what Dahlia had been left with, too, when the excitement of her elopement wore off? Duty and regret?

Or had Dahlia truly been happy in her marriage?

And would Violet ever know the effects of her own encouraging words?

She supposed this was the perilous bit of midnight conversations. That when traveling in the dark, one risked knocking loose stones, uncovering buried pain and unseen truths.

Ewan had offered her so much of his soul tonight. His bravery encouraged her own.

She stepped closer to him and lifted her free hand.

It hung in the air between them for a spare moment, the moon wrapping her skin in silvery light.

And then she placed her palm onto his chest.

This time, when he gasped, she *felt* it. The sharp rise of his ribs, the hard plane of muscle.

He instantly raised his free hand, covering hers and pressing it against his sternum. She stepped even closer, her skirts tangling with his kilt.

"Perhaps . . . ," she began, voice soft, eyes staring at his larger hand wrapped around her palm, ". . . perhaps that is why my decision-making abilities have been so taxed. As I've told you, I had started out thinking that I simply could not decide which path to take. There are too many variables and unknowns to know which way to go. But you helped me understand that I struggled to decide what to do because I did not know what I wanted my future to be. That I needed to research the options, so to speak. And that is true."

She rubbed her hand up his chest, still staring at her fingers peeking out from underneath his. His lungs expanded sharply. She dared to look up at him. His eyes glittered in the moonlight, refracted pools of gold.

"But now I see the paths before me clearly . . ." she continued. "One path is a colorless duty. The other is a flamboyant mayhem. So though I find the flamboyant mayhem much more alluring, I struggle to know which path truly will be the best in the end. It's like . . . facing the ocean cliffs." She darted a glance over her shoulder, calling attention to the distant murmur of waves against the rocks. "I know what it's like at the top of the cliff. I walk there frequently. It's sometimes temperamental and often windy, but it's also secure. I know that if I don't get too close to the edge, I will be safe. And safe can be good. But it can also be . . . monotonous. A colorless duty, like my known path. And so, I sometimes wonder—what would it be like to jump? To take off running and leap from the cliff's edge? I imagine that the first few seconds of falling would be incredible. The flamboyant mayhem of flying, soaring through the air.

"But what happens after those first few seconds? Am I dashed against the rocks and crippled? Or do I splash into the ocean and find it cleansing? A new world with fascinating wonders to explore? And so I stand here, facing the ocean, desperate to jump . . . but so terrified of the landing that I cannot do it."

"Ah . . . ye have the heart of a poet, lass," he whispered, pressing her fingertips to him. "'Tis an apt analogy. Mhairi *pushed* me off the cliff, and I didnae like the decision being made for me."

He paused, as if assessing his hand at cards, and then deciding to lay them all out at once. "What would ye want if ye could guarantee a safe landing? A safe but exciting way down the cliffs?"

You.

I want you.

She didn't hesitate.

But even the silken quiet could not quite coax the admission out of her.

Such words felt a little too much like jumping in earnest.

He answered the question anyway. "I ken there is a third way down the cliffs. What if someone chose to remain at your side. A true friend with a rope, helping ye down. Letting ye fall for only a short way before pulling the rope taut, breaking your flight before ye can be hurt. I think *that* is what ye search for."

His words were too much. Too close to her innermost truth.

Violet closed the remaining tiny distance between them and did the one thing she had ached to do for weeks.

She extricated her palm from his chest and pressed it to his cheek.

He hissed at the contact and snaked his hand around her waist, his fingers reflexively curling into the small of her back.

He lifted their other hands, still joined, and pressed a kiss into her knuckles, causing *her* to hiss at the soft feel of his lips.

Violet caressed his face. His cheeks were rough with evening whiskers, shooting tingles up her arms. He made a sound—half moan, half sigh—and leaned into her touch, nuzzling into her palm.

"Ah, lass," he whispered, pulling her flush against him.

She gasped at the solid feel of his body, her eyes closing, breathing in the scent of him. In her world, men smelled of sandalwood and bergamot, expensive spices from far-flung places.

But Ewan . . . ah, Ewan . . . he smelled of *home*.

Heather and gorse.

Wool and ocean spray.

"Ah lass, I want tae be the one at your side. The one with a rope. But I cannae see how." His words were a rejection, but he nipped at her fingers as he spoke.

"I know." Silence and then on a whisper again, "I know."

"We come from worlds so far apart."

"I know," she repeated, leaning farther into him, stretching on her tiptoes to drag her nose along his neck, following the exact path she had traced earlier, only this time daring to fully touch him.

"I'm no' going to stop painting." His voice was ragged shards, his head arching into her hands.

"I would not ask it of you," she whispered against his skin, running her lips along his jaw. "You cannot stop painting any more than I can cease being a countess."

"I dinnae belong in your world, lass." He ran a hand up her spine, cupping the back of her head. "I'm not one to attend balls and manage estates. And ye cannae abandon your responsibilities and live the life of a bohemian artist."

"No, definitely not," she breathed against his mouth.

"And yet, I wish to be by your side, lass. Tae guide ye down the cliff."

"Yes. We shall simply find a length of strong rope and tether ourselves together."

And then she kissed him.

It felt an inevitability. As if from the moment he stepped into her study all those weeks before, they had been hurtling toward this.

Her, in his arms.

His lips on hers.

Her arms twined around his neck, standing on tiptoe, pulling his mouth down to hers. His arms tightened around her back, half lifting her up to him.

Ewan's kiss was emblematic of the man himself—impossibly gentle and forcefully devastating. The soft hunger of his lips. The steel strength of his shoulders.

The heady exhilaration.

Falling.

Falling.

Falling.

And as she had suspected . . .

It. Was. Glorious.

. . . the tumbling lift in her belly . . .

. . . the weightlessness of her body against his . . .

She almost didn't care if she dashed upon the rocks after all.

22

Violet expected to regret kissing Ewan.

    She truly did.

But she awoke the next morning full of cheer and a surprising lack of *whathaveIdone!* running through her head.

Hmmmm.

It was an unanticipated development.

Perhaps she was less of a proper lady than she thought. Which was not entirely a revelation, truth be told.

Or perhaps it was her heart telling her that she had *finally* discovered what she truly wanted.

Or, most likely, Violet was still delighting in the thrill of falling, the exhilarating plunge from the cliff.

The only question on her mind—

When would she have the opportunity to kiss Ewan again?

They had parted the night before with a few more lingering kisses and promises to talk the next day. That they would find the binding rope they envisioned—a way to forward, together.

Violet awoke determined to see Ewan as soon as possible. But before she could slip away for a walk to the castle, Lord Hadley and Sir Rafe stopped by to pay their respects as they were departing with Master MacTavish.

Sir Rafe recommended several excellent texts on agriculture and then left her with some advice:

"Ye can only truly understand farming if you've lived it, spent time in the fields, and talked with your stewards and tenants and such. Try it, I say. Getting out and doing will inform you more than anything."

"Aye, Rafe has the right of it. Also, know that I am here to offer advice or lend a hand, if ye need it . . . earl to earl, of course," Lord Hadley said before fixing her with a steely look. "And have a care with our Ewan."

Violet barely suppressed a laugh as she waved the gentlemen off in their carriage.

Oh, she would care for their Ewan. Probably too much, truth be told.

Because the problem, as Violet saw it, wasn't that she didn't know her own mind as it pertained to Ewan.

She did. The decision to like him—to caress him, to kiss him—had been easy to make.

No, the true problem was what followed next:

What was to come of her caring?

Ewan's points the night before *were* true.

She would never ask him to leave off painting.

And she could not quit being a countess.

Moreover, she knew firsthand how vicious gossips could be. She had endured rejection and derision over Dahlia's behavior.

Imagine the toll should Violet *herself* make a similar choice. The Lady Grahams of the world would trumpet their displeasure. She would become an outcast; many would not receive her. Ewan would be scorned and vilified for reaching so high above his station, perhaps even jeopardizing his career.

And even if Violet and Ewan were willing to face such things in order to be together, Aster and Rose *would* pay a hefty price, as her father had repeatedly warned her.

A woman's marriage prospects were only as high as her respectability. Violet's actions could doom her sisters to marrying men of lesser stature—i.e. financial resources. Yes, both her sisters had dowries, but the sums were not large, certainly not enough to live on. The men her sisters married needed to bring their own financial reserves to the table if they were to have a life together.

Heavens, even Violet's *own* children would likely struggle.

How could she tally all the consequences of such a choice? It felt as if they would roll on and on into the future.

And what about Dahlia, who *had* made such a decision?

Violet vividly recalled Dahlia's letters those months after her marriage. Her sister had said all the right words to appear happy enough on paper, but Violet still wondered. The clues were in the smaller details. Dahlia requesting money to pay for additional coal to ensure the baby did not grow cold. Dahlia's passing comment that her husband was working long hours and rarely at home. Had these simply been the minor irritations of life? Or more stark cries of distress?

But even if her sister had bitterly lamented the path of her life, she would have been too stubborn to admit it.

And Violet's situation was not quite the same as Dahlia's. Ewan had prospects and friends in high places. Violet had means and income to see them through. Certainly that counted for something.

She liked Ewan.

A lot.

She wanted to be with him.

A lot.

For once, Violet found herself almost helplessly making a decision.

As if the choice had a voice of its own.

She could not turn away from him. She could *not*.

Perhaps they could forge a path forward together, as he had said. Find a length of rope and glide down the cliff in a controlled descent.

In the end, she simply couldn't seem to care about the consequences for herself.

The thrill of the fall was too intoxicating.

If she dashed on rocks in the end . . . well . . . the happiness of *now* was worth the pain.

She would simply have to find a way to protect her sisters from true harm.

EWAN STARED AT the blank page in his sketchbook.

He was again in his greenhouse studio. The glazier had come and gone, repairing leaks in the skylights, allowing Ewan to move his work back into the glass house. He had left most of his canvases in the great hall—no need to risk getting them wet or damaged—but he had brought the painting of Mhairi and the blackhouse out with him.

It now sat on his easel, half daring him to address it.

Ewan stared at his sketchbook, wondering if he had the courage to face his past in line and color.

Andrew, Rafe, and Kieran had departed earlier.

Before leaving, Andrew and Rafe had subjected Ewan to good-natured banter over Violet.

"Do ye require any instruction in the finer art of kissing?" Rafe had asked, voice casual, clearly wishing to set Ewan to blushing.

His words had their intended effect.

"Aye. We'd be happy tae walk ye through the process," Andrew agreed, grinning unabashedly at Ewan's scalding cheeks.

"Off wit youse both." Ewan pushed them both out the door. "I dinnae need your bamming ways."

Kieran had managed a thin smile as he shook Ewan's hand and followed their friends out. Kieran had recovered somewhat, but his spirits were still depressed. That morning, he had gently wrapped the canvas with Jamie's likeness and tucked it under his arm. He had not asked if he could take it, but Ewan understood. He had never really considered the painting to be his own.

Ewan was beginning to better comprehend the grief that drove Kieran.

Ewan loved Violet.

Somewhere along that ribbon path last night, he had fully accepted the fact.

He loved her. He adored her.

He was determined for them to scale down the cliff together, tethered to one another for safety.

He pressed the palms of his hands to his eyes, images and sensations of their kiss the night before rushing in.

The rise of her body to meet his lips.

The lush press of her against his chest.

The unspoken words of her actions.

You are worth risk.

You are worth the chance at love.

Ewan savored the sensation for several minutes, memorizing the hum in his blood, visualizing the colors and lines it painted.

When he opened his eyes, blinking against the sunlight flooding his studio, he saw the scene clearly in his mind's eye.

The exact moment that *had* to be committed to paint and canvas.

He swallowed. That same feeling rose, panicky and pink-tinged.

Part of him understood it better now.

Despite how much he disliked prizefighting as a sport, he was a fighter inside, a man used to protecting himself and others.

Because of this, he had given every last ounce of his heart to protecting Mhairi. And she had thrown it away.

The feelings that clenched his chest when he thought of his past were tied to that failure. To the instinctual need to retreat and protect his heart.

But . . . no more.

Today, he met that salmon-colored emotion head-on.

Today, he summoned the courage to face his demons.

He picked up his charcoal with shaking fingers and began to draw.

VIOLET'S DAY HAD been a busy one.

After Ewan's friends had left, Mr. Shambles arrived with a proposal for using elms to protect the fields along the north river.

And soon after Mr. Shambles left, her father and sisters returned home from their house party.

While assisting Mr. Kerr out of his great coat, Irvine blithely told of the illustrious guests who had departed that morning, how the gentlemen had dined with Lady Kildrum but spent the night with Sir Joshua and Mr. Campbell.

Her father's gray eyebrows had drawn down as Irvine waxed on.

"A word, daughter." Mr. Kerr fixed Violet with a hard stare, nearly dragging her into the drawing room with his blue eyes alone.

The door had scarcely clacked behind Violet when her father whirled on her.

"How many gentlemen were here? Have you *no* thought for your reputation, girl?!"

"Father, all was proper. Uncle was with me the entire time."

Well, except for that glorious walk back up to Kilmeny Hall. But that was her secret to treasure.

"Moreover," she continued, "I would have presumed you to be thrilled to discover that Mr. Campbell has well-connected friends."

"What do *Mr. Campbell's* connections matter? He is merely a temporary fixture in these parts, utterly irrelevant to your future—"

"Pardon?" Violet flinched back at her father's words.

"I am concerned about Lord Graham." Her father waved a hand. "If he were to hear of such behavior, he might withdraw his suit and then where would we be?"

Her jaw nearly hung open. "Father, I have not accepted Lord Graham. Besides, the more I have pondered the match, the more I am convinced that he and I will *not* suit."

"Pardon? Will not suit?" It was her father's turn to look aghast. "What is there not to *suit* about the man? He is handsome and kind and wealthy. He is the perfect image of an aristocratic gentleman."

"Precisely! He is the very picture of *noblesse oblige*. But I cannot find it in me to marry that!"

"Who else will you marry, Violet?" He leaned closer to her, pointing his finger. Dimly, she noted that his hair was grayer now, more salt than pepper. When had that happened? "No matter how much you prevaricate, it has been *seven years* since your come-out. Seven years to discover this mythical man who meets all your needs. You *must* marry someone like Lord Graham, and soon, so why not have it be Lord Graham himself? How will you manage the estate without a gentleman like Lord Graham at the helm? How will you pay off the Manna Loan without his financial assistance? Who will sponsor your sisters for their Season?"

He turned in a circle, waving an arm as he lectured her, his lean shoulder blades pressing against the fabric of his coat. When had her father become so thin? Was he eating enough? She disliked noting these tiny instances of his humanity.

She wanted to remain angry.

She wanted her father to be strong enough to bear the burden of her anger.

"I shall find a way, Father." Violet threw her hands in the air. "But hurling myself upon the altar of marriage as some sort of barbaric sacrifice to a man I do not love will not be the solution—"

"You must cease with this selfish thinking, Violet! As I have repeatedly said, true love is built upon a foundation of similar upbringing, breeding, and expectations. Burning passion is fleeting, quickly reducing itself to caustic ash. The earldom has already experienced the devastation of one profligate daughter. Do not think to add your name to the score. We cannot bear another scandal. Your behavior, more than anything, will set the stage for us all. You are being willfully blind to reality!"

The conversation had gone on in circles.

It ended with Mr. Kerr storming out of the room and Violet flushed and angry, bruised by the truths buried in his loud words.

She found herself pacing the empty drawing room, the paintings of the past scrolling by in a sequence of powdered wigs and gilt scepters. The cumulative judgmental eyes of her forebears weighted upon her.

She finally paused in front of the portrait of her mother with Violet and her sisters.

Violet's gaze lingered on Dahlia, staring at her sister's vibrant face.

Had Dahlia truly been happy in her marriage? And even if she hadn't been, it did not follow that Violet would regret her own path, did it?

Surely, Violet and Ewan could find a way. They *had* to.

She could not imagine life without him.

Regardless, the entire experience forced Violet to act. As she had said to her father, she could not marry Lord Graham. She simply could not.

She wanted more from a marriage than Lord Graham could offer her. She had merely been too afraid to reach for it.

As for Lady Graham and her sponsorship of Aster and Rose, Violet would simply have to find another solution.

And so before she did anything else, she penned Lord Graham a polite letter, kindly but firmly refusing his offer of marriage. She told him the truth—that she could not envision a future with him.

And then she slipped out of the house to sneak a kiss with her painter in his studio.

Life had never been so glorious.

FOR EWAN, THE weeks passed in a sort of hazy, dream-like wonder.

He spent his days as he always had: painting, drawing, modeling when needed. He laughed with Sir Joshua over lunch and trekked up to Kilmeny Hall most evenings for dinner. The meals were boisterous affairs, everyone blithely ignoring Mr. Kerr's stern glances. Ewan told tales of his travels, and Lady Aster and Lady Rose eventually dragged out a large atlas, insisting he show them everything on the map, from Loch Carron where he was born to the likely location of *The Minerva's* wreck.

Once a week, Ewan would arrive with his supplies at Kilmeny Hall and continue his portrait of Violet. He had finally decided how he wished to paint her, but he kept it secret, refusing to show her the painting in progress. As a bonus, the chaperoning maid often fell asleep in her corner, allowing Ewan to steal a kiss.

But it was the truly private moments with Violet he treasured most. Nearly every day, she would slip away from her duties and meet him— painting in his greenhouse studio, walking along the cliffs, kissing in the leeward side of the castle and hidden from view.

Every day he fell a wee bit further.

Violet told him that Lord Graham had proposed marriage, but she had refused him. For Ewan, knowing that his Violet was actively choosing him, just as he chose her, set him to smiling for days on end.

She regaled him with stories of her hours spent studying agriculture. He saw her tromping the fields from a distance, talking with Mr. Shambles and learning from him. She had hired another steward and was taking tentative steps toward managing her own lands.

And Violet finding her footing inspired Ewan to push himself harder and higher.

His painting for the Royal Academy Exhibition poured out of him, a frenzied burst of creativity sprawling across the canvas in vivid color. It was painful and anguished and brutally honest.

The only spot of darkness came in the form of a letter from Andrew about a month after his visit:

> *My Runner has confirmed that Cuthie accepted command of a ship and, along with Massey, has sailed for Jamaica. So until they return, answers will be difficult.*
>
> *Additionally, Kieran has utterly disappeared. We cannot find him, at the moment. I've sent my Runner after him, so hopefully he will*

resurface somewhere. There is nothing we can do until then. As you can imagine, we are all greatly concerned . . .

But even worry over Kieran could not dampen Ewan's spirits. Violet shone too brightly.

ONCE SHE KNEW the shape of her future, Violet found herself expressing opinions and giving instructions with surprising ease.

Miss Compton returned—as her mother's health had improved—soothing Violet's worries over her sisters. Their governess *cum* lady's companion was a positive influence on Aster and Rose.

Violet took up Sir Rafe's advice and began actively learning from Mr. Shambles and other farmers in the area. The hours were often long, but her mind whirred from the possibilities.

So when Mr. Lawyerly asked her, yet again, what she wished to do with the unsold tack, she had an answer—*I wish to manage it myself.*

She knew that such a decision meant she had to find another way to pay the upcoming Manna Loan. But the note was not due until autumn, and she still had time to arrive at a solution. Perhaps she could mortgage the London townhouse and simply economize further at Kilmeny Hall to make up the difference. She kept tallying the numbers, trying to find a way to make it all work.

In the meantime, with Mr. Shambles' help, she hired another steward and tasked him with employing a group of tradesmen—carpenters, glaziers, laborers—to assist in maintaining the hundreds of tenant properties and lands attached to the large tack.

Though Ewan did not help her with any of it, she could feel the steady presence of his support at her back. He listened patiently, offered sound advice where he could, and most importantly, expressed his belief in her abilities to conquer the problems she encountered.

This, Violet realized, was the truest essence of friendship and love. Providing words of encouragement, a kind shoulder to lean on, a strong arm to support her when she was bone tired. It was rather shocking, to be honest. She had been alone in her burdens for so long that having a sympathetic ear felt akin to a revolution. Having a true friend who cheered one on was life altering.

Of course, Ewan's support came with the added bonus of being snuggled against his mammoth chest and drowned in the heady delight of his kisses.

If Violet thought she was retaining at least some portion of her heart, that was quickly dashed one beautiful day in mid-June. The deadline for submission to the exhibition was rapidly approaching, and Sir Joshua was in a frenzy to finish his painting in time.

Violet had sneaked away from Kilmeny Hall, desperate for a few moments alone with Ewan. She had to be careful when she visited, as she did not wish to set tongues wagging (any more than they already were, to be sure). And so she usually would visit Sir Joshua first, knowing that there was no harm in paying a call upon one's uncle.

On this day, she slipped into the great hall quietly. Not that she secretly longed to observe Ewan in a state of undress.

Oh, gracious. Who was she fooling?

She absolutely wished a repeat performance, but she had yet to experience one. And given how far along Sir Joshua was on the painting, it was not likely to happen.

So Violet wasn't too disappointed to find the great hall deserted when she stepped through the door. But she was surprised to see Sir Joshua's enormous canvas leaning against the wall. Her uncle, after all, was notoriously secretive about his works.

But today, the canvas stood front and center.

And it was magnificent.

Figures writhed in the foreground—Greek men in armor, horses trampling soldiers . . .

. . . and Ewan's body *everywhere*.

A bare shoulder on a Persian captain. The chiseled pectoral of a

Greek's chest. The clenched thigh of an officer. It was like seeing Ewan in a room lined with mirrors. Every turn reflected another part of him back.

But her eye was drawn to the dying soldier in the foreground, the exact image she had witnessed Sir Joshua painting that day—Ewan sprawled across rocks, the red silk of a cloak wrapping his hips. Her uncle had captured the curves and sinuous shapes of him. Violet raised her hand and traced the round slope of Ewan's shoulder with her fingertip. A blush burned her cheeks as she imagined doing the same with the flesh and blood man.

She left Kilmeny Castle with one thought:

She did not want life to be a choice between dull duty and brilliant desire. As her knowledge of land management had grown, so had her interest in it.

Perhaps she should apply that same logic to her relationship with Ewan in earnest—

Find a way to meet her obligations and still enjoy the glory of love.

23

Ewan's work on his submission to the Royal Exhibition consumed him. It was as if once he let loose the floodgates on his memories, a tidal wave of pain poured out of him.

Sir Joshua had not been wrong.

We bleed every time we paint. Never forget it.

Every day Ewan dabbed his paint in the blood of his grief and spread it across the canvas. A vivid physical rendering of his pain.

Some days he could not see for the tears.

But the farther he progressed, the more the entire process became a catharsis. In facing his demons, he was also taming them, easing the horror of his memories.

The painting fought him, though. He struggled to get proportions right—the angle of the arm here, the twist of the fingers there.

So much so, that he finally asked Sir Joshua's advice.

The older man traipsed down to Ewan's studio to view the canvas. Sir Joshua stared at it for a solid five minutes in utter silence, his expression impassive.

"You are to be commended," he finally said. "This will be your first masterpiece."

Ewan basked in the compliment for a full two minutes and then buckled down to listen as Sir Joshua pointed out minute problems with his proportions on an outstretched arm and how to address them.

Ewan rushed to make adjustments to the canvas, completing the revisions Sir Joshua had suggested. He and Sir Joshua would leave in just four days to transport their respective paintings to London for submission.

Two days later, Violet arrived just as he finished pulling down the gauze blocking direct summer sunlight from the skylights overhead. He needed the light and heat of the greenhouse to help the painting dry before the trip to London.

Violet bustled into the studio in a windswept burst of skirts, hand clapped on her bonnet to keep it from sailing away.

"The wind never ceases," she laughed, tugging the battered hat off her head to survey the damage.

Ewan was at her side in a moment, bending to drop a kiss on her upturned lips.

How he adored this—the privilege of kissing her.

"How fares your painting today, Sir Ewan?" Her voice rang with playful teasing.

She had taken to calling him that—Sir Ewan. His Violet was convinced that it was only a matter of time before he was knighted for his 'artistic prowess.'

Realistically, Ewan recognized that such an accolade—were it to fall on him—was decades in the future.

But that did not stop his heart from lurching every time she mentioned it.

"If ye are angling tae see your own painting, lass, you're bound for disappointment." He steadfastly refused to let her see it. It rested in the great hall with his other canvases. He only brought paintings out to his studio as he worked on them.

"Very well. Then is today the day I get to finally see this one?" She pointed at the painting on his easel.

He raised his eyebrows.

Grinning, she darted to the right, attempting to get past him.

This was another game they played. Violet tried to see his Royal Academy painting, and he blocked her.

The game ended when he caught her about the waist and pulled her in for a lingering kiss.

Needless to say, the game usually ended very quickly. Ewan was quick on his feet, and Violet was not opposed to being caught.

Smiling, Ewan darted in front of her, preventing her from seeing the painting.

"What would ye do if I said yes?" he asked.

That got her attention, her expression instantly sobering. "Truly? Are you for certain? I know how deeply you have suffered for it."

"Aye. 'Tis time." He studied for a moment, her green-blue eyes wide, her lips turned up in excitement. "Close your eyes."

Obediently, she snapped them shut.

Grinning, Ewan turned the easel around and placed it in front of her.

"Very well. Ye may look."

Violet opened her eyes, staring at the painting.

Ewan wasn't sure what he expected from her. A gasp? A squeal of delight?

She did none of those things.

Instead, Violet stood intensely still, her body taut, as if bracing for a blow.

Only her eyes darted—back and forth, side to side—with an almost unholy frenzy.

Was this good? Or bad?

"You're terribly quiet, lass," he said. "Do ye not like it?"

VIOLET WONDERED IF this was how a prizefighter felt after receiving a blow to the head—the buzzing in her ears, the hum in her breathing.

The image before her . . .

Oh, Ewan, her heart sobbed in her chest. *What have you borne?*

She recognized the scene from his telling of the tale. But seeing it splashed across a canvas in such vivid color . . .

A blue sea.

A cliff.

A different sea and cliff than the ones she knew.

A house ablaze dominated the image. A blackhouse, its thatch consumed in flames of blood red and burnt orange that rose to tangle with the fiery sunset of the sky.

Shadowy shapes of villagers ran in the background, scrambling for buckets.

Two figures dominated the foreground—a tall boy and a slender girl. The girl pulled at his hand reaching toward the house, a dramatic diagonal slash, as if desperate to rush toward the building. But he held her tight, wet sooty streaks raining down his cheeks.

The pain of the moment was echoed in the dreamlike quality of the lines. This was no crisp drawing. The colors bled into one another, shapes blurring at the edges, everything having the suggestion of form but begging the viewer to supply the sharper details from imagination.

But no matter where Violet's eyes landed in the painting, they eventually worked their way back to one stark, ghastly detail—

A hand stretching out a window of the burning house.

A silent scream for help, for rescue, for mercy.

How had he done that? How had Ewan taken the cacophony of the moment—the color, the motion, the drama—and distilled it down to that solitary, horrific detail?

Something wet hit the back of her hand. She raised her fingers to her cheek, astonished to find tears there.

"Oh, lass, I've made ye greet," he murmured.

"Tears are . . . *necessary.*" Such an outpouring of emotion could only be met with more emotion.

"Are they?"

"Yes," she nodded, hiccupping. "The painting is b-brilliant. It will b-be selected, I have no d-doubt."

He reached for her, and Violet collapsed against his chest, burying her face in the plaid of his great kilt.

It felt too much—the sheer miracle of him.

That he had lived when others had died.

That he and wee Mhairi had been left alone, tossed out into the world like unwanted refuse.

That he had not crumpled, but had instead risen like a phoenix from the ashes of that fire, literally fighting his way free.

All to end up in her carriage that day, beaten and battered, but indomitable.

If he had deviated even the slightest—

"There, now," he murmured in her ear. "It isnae that bad, is it?"

Violet pulled back with a sniffle. "I cannot bear to think of you hurt. I simply cannot bear it. What if you had not survived? What if you had succumbed to starvation or deprivation or—"

"Ah, lass." He wiped her cheek with his thumb. "I'm here now, am I not? There were a thousand 'what ifs' between the painting and my standing in this place."

Violet hiccupped.

"But I *am* here," he continued, stroking her cheek.

She popped up on her tiptoes and wrapped her arms around his neck before even realizing what she was doing.

Her kiss said what words could not.

That she adored him.

That she could not bear being parted from him.

The answering hunger in his lips said he understood. That their souls breathed in synchronized time.

One of his large hands pressed against the small of her back, the other traced her jaw, his thumb continuing to brush her cheek—

A crash sounded.

Violet flinched.

"Unhand my daughter this instant!" A harsh voice cried behind her.

Violet lurched out of Ewan's hold, whirling around with a terrified squeak.

Her father stood in the doorway, eyes bulging, face turning red. The greenhouse door still quivered on its hinges.

"How dare you touch her!" Her father advanced on Ewan. "I shall have you arrested!"

"Father!" Violet jumped in front of Ewan.

"Go back to the house, Violet. I will deal with you later." Her father didn't even look at her, his blue eyes slicing over Ewan. "I wish to speak with this . . . *man*." He all but spat the last word.

"No." Violet folded her arms.

"Lass," Ewan's voice was soft behind her, "perhaps ye should—"

"No," she repeated. "If you have something to say to Ewan, Father, you can say it with me present. I will not be shoved aside. Whatever you say to him, clearly pertains to me as well."

Now her father turned his head to stare at her.

Resentment clogged Violet's throat. Her father was always like this. Quick with an opinion about how she should be behaving. Quick to judge her choices. Just as he had with Dahlia.

But never one to help. Never one to listen.

She hated that, to him, affection only moved in one direction—from a child to her parent, never the other way around.

Worse, she could feel age creeping up on him. That he would continue to rage, his mind forever stamped along one track, the volume of his threats eventually growing weaker and weaker.

Their relationship did not need to be like this. There could be understanding and love.

She reached behind her, a silent plea for Ewan to take her hand. The warm weight of his palm slid into hers, their fingers interlocking. A bond of support and love.

"You foolish, idiotic child," her father began, blue eyes snapping.

"I would be careful how ye speak to Violet," Ewan rumbled behind her.

Her father was a tall man, but he still had to raise his head to meet Ewan's gaze.

"That is Lady Kildrum to you!"

"Enough!" Violet said.

Her father continued on, as if she had said nothing. "You will be the ruin of us all, you foolish, selfish chit! The family barely survived Dahlia and the scandal she tossed on our doorstep. But two daughters behaving in such an unseemly matter? I am still guardian to the twins. It is my duty to ensure their future happiness." Her father made a slicing motion with his hand. "How many times must I say this? Society will *never* forgive it. Are you so lost to propriety that you would condemn your younger sisters to lives of penury?"

Violet rolled her eyes, squeezing Ewan's hand. "Father, you are being a bit melodramatic. They have dowries—"

"Money is not everything. You think me old-fashioned and controlling, but I am neither. If anything, I am an oracle, prophesying doom." Her father's gaze morphed into a weary anger. A nearly desperate pleading that tugged at Violet more than his rage ever would. "What respectable man will marry your sisters after you and Dahlia so thoroughly tarnish the family reputation by cavorting with men of such lowly status—"

"Father, I will not have you disparage Mr. Campbell."

"Mark my words, child. If you continue down this path—" He jabbed a finger over her shoulder at Ewan. "—you will doom your sisters to spinsterhood. Their dowries are not large enough to encourage a respectable gentleman to overlook the scandal. Moreover, you haven't the funds to increase their dowries."

Violet clutched Ewan's hand tighter. "My sisters are beautiful, charming girls who surely can commandeer a man's affections without having to pay excessive coin."

"Like Dahlia did?!" Her father snapped upright. His tone was belligerent, but Violet could see the pain lingering in his eyes. "And how did that end for her? Was she happy in the lowly squalor of her marriage?"

Violet gasped at the vitriol in her father's voice.

Mr. Kerr continued, "And what about your own financial obligations, daughter? Where is your promised solution to pay off the Manna Loan? Marriage to Lord Graham would have been the answer to all our prayers, but you are selfishly putting your own personal wishes above the larger collective needs of your family."

"This isn't helpful, Father. There are solutions. I simply need to decide which—"

"Violet, you are being willfully blind to reality. You believe that there are these mystical *decisions* just waiting for you to pluck them down. But you are wrong. *Reality* offers you no such choice."

"I beg to disagree—"

"Enough!" her father all but roared. "You think that you are strong enough to weather the storm that such a misalliance would bring." He looked again between Ewan and Violet, his chest heaving, but his eyes held a grim sadness. "But I tell you, daughter, you are not."

He took a step back, his eyes dropping to their hands, still clutched together.

"Father—"

"No." He gave his head a final, decisive shake, as if the pain were too great. "In the folly of youth, you think that love will be sufficient. That it will overcome. But I tell from the wisdom of my years, it is *not*. Sometimes, child, . . . love is not enough."

24

E wan woke the following morning in a truly foul mood.

Love is not enough.

Mr. Kerr's refrain rattled in his head, an irritating pebble of noise.

Love is not enough. Not enough. Not enough.

Ewan knew this. He had known it from the beginning, had he not?

Violet was a *countess*. Her life encompassed strata he could never lay claim to. Did he think to be Cinderella rising from his hearth to claim his princess?

He rolled his eyes at his naiveté.

A princess did not marry a peasant, no matter what fairy tales said. And if she did, the princess would be cast out of the palace . . . if not literally, then at least figuratively.

If they continued forward together, how dire would the consequences be for Violet? Not to mention himself, always looked upon as less than, as the man who *sullied* Lady Kildrum.

Worse, their relationship was driving a wedge between Violet and her family. Would her sisters truly suffer as her father had said? Ewan rather thought that they might.

And *why* had he not connected marriage to Lord Graham with the repayment of the Manna Loan? How could that obvious detail have escaped him? How was Violet to pay off the loan when it came due in the autumn?

The more he pondered it, the more the words would not let him be. *Love is not enough.*

Vividly, Ewan recalled a morning in Rio de Janeiro. They had stopped there to resupply, and Andrew had requested a fine suite of rooms and luncheon for them in a local inn. Maids had brought in platters of food and two pitchers of cheery orange juice.

The drink was deliciously sweet and impossibly *tragic.*

Because even as Ewan sipped it, he *knew.* He knew this would be the one and only time in his life that he would taste orange juice. The fruit was far too expensive to acquire in Scotland.

So he drank it, knowing the memory of its sweetness would linger. That years on, he would long to have the moment back, to experience it once more . . .

Would this be the fate of Violet, as well?

An impossibly sweet memory that haunted the edges of his future attempts at happiness?

Love is not enough.

The problem, of course, was that the painful thudding of his heart seemed to disagree with the idea. His heart felt like love *would* be enough. That if he and Violet faced the world together, side by side, they could overcome anything.

He knew such thoughts were insidious. Wishful thinking had never altered the nature of truth.

Yes, Ewan may have noble friends, but he would never be a member of the peerage. He would forever be an outsider.

He and Violet *had* been living in a dream world.

Now, he needed to view the situation through the harsh light of reality.

After his angry words, Mr. Kerr had insisted Violet return with him to Kilmeny Hall. Ewan had no idea when he might see her again.

And so, he did what he always did when upset: he painted.

He left his Royal Exhibition piece to dry in the greenhouse and joined Sir Joshua in the great hall. He worked feverishly on finishing Violet's portrait, mixing pigments and layering in colors until late in the evening. And then he began again the next morning after only a few hours' sleep.

He could feel Sir Joshua's eyes on him as he worked, the older man's gaze heavy and pensive. Finally, as the sun climbed to its zenith, Sir Joshua tossed down his palette and paint brush.

"Well, I have had about enough of this brooding. Care to talk about it?" The older man stretched, knuckles cracking.

"Not particularly," Ewan replied because he was . . . well . . . *brooding*.

"I don't know precisely what happened yesterday," Sir Joshua said, "but given how David all but dragged Violet back to Kilmeny Hall, I can imagine."

"Can ye?" Ewan winced at the sharpness of his tone. He tossed down his own palette, setting his brush beside it. "I'm sorry, Sir Joshua. I shouldnae take out my foul mood on yourself."

"Don't apologize, my boy." Sir Joshua waved a hand, that same pensive look hanging in his eyes. "I understand a little too well the pain of being separated from one's love."

Ewan managed a weak smile and stepped over to the basin and pitcher against one wall. He washed his hands, scrubbing with soap and a bit of turpentine to get the pigments off his fingers.

"David is a bit of a firebrand," Sir Joshua said behind him. Ewan glanced over his shoulder at the older painter. "He and I may be opposites by nearly every measurement, but we are similar in our dedication to our passions. Mine, obviously, is to create brilliance." He swept a hand over the masterpiece leaning against the wall. Ewan smiled despite himself. "My brother's passion is to moralize us all to death. Don't allow him to put you off."

"Put me off?" Ewan said, reaching for a towel and turning fully around. "You understand that Violet and I . . . that we . . ."

"Of course, lad. I have eyes in my head. I see how you look at my niece. How Violet dotes upon you in return."

Ewan hung the towel up to dry. "And ye don't . . . disapprove?"

"Bah! My niece needs someone who will always put her interests first, who sees her as Violet and not just Lady Kildrum. You discount yourself, my boy, but you are a rising star. Though you feel unequal to Violet's station in life, I predict that will change. Your work will be recognized and sought after. Give it a decade and instead of you being known as Lady Kildrum's husband, she will be known as Mr. Ewan Campbell's wife."

Ewan placed his hands on his hips, wanted desperately to believe the truth of Sir Joshua's words. He wanted Violet to be known for Violet, but oh!—how he wanted her to be his wife, too.

Sir Joshua continued, "My brother in his moralizing fails to understand this. Despite his gruff ways, David does love his daughters. The problem, of course, is that he equates security with happiness. I disagree."

"Ye do?"

"Indeed. Security can bring contentment, which is a close cousin to happiness, but not quite the same thing. True happiness results from giving love and being truly loved in return. Something I'm not sure David has ever experienced." Sir Joshua paused, a bleak blankness touching his eyes.

"But you have?" Ewan knew the question was probing, but it tumbled out nonetheless.

"Yes. That I have, lad." That same bleakness settled over Sir Joshua, his eyes turning inward to some painful memory. He shook his head and clapped his hands, as if banishing thoughts. "Well, I think we've both had enough maudlin talk today. We will have plenty of time to discuss this further on our trip to London. Right now, if I know you, that enormous stomach of yours is desperate for some food. Let's head into the village and find ourselves some lunch at the public house."

OUTSIDE THE CASTLE, the air hung motionless and stifling.

Scotland was perpetually cold. But one afternoon a year, the country decided to pretend to be a more tropical place. A clime with blinding sun, dripping humidity, and heat that bordered on sweltering.

So given that Ewan felt figuratively confined to purgatory, he considered it a rather poetic irony that the weather chose to echo the sentiment. Standing in solidarity with him, as it were.

Granted, the solidarity had Ewan mopping sweat off his brow long before they reached the village.

The cool interior of the inn was a welcome respite. A cold pint even more so. Given the crowd of men in the inn's dining room, Ewan and Sir Joshua were not alone in their thoughts.

But they eventually settled into a corner table with pints of ale, crusty bread, and a hearty smoked fish pie. Sir Joshua had been right, of course. Perhaps this whole mess would look better on a full stomach. To that end, Ewan ate with systematic intensity.

As Ewan mopped up the last of his pie with some bread, commotion at the entrance to the inn drew his attention. Men were gathered in a cluster, talking to someone.

Lord Graham appeared, pushing his way through the crowd, striding toward their table.

"Sir Joshua," Lord Graham said affably, motioning for them to remain seated. "I see your would-be artist is still in residence." Lord Graham nodded at Ewan, his smile not reaching his eyes. "Mr. Campbell."

"Lord Graham." Ewan kept his tone even, meeting the older man's gaze straight on.

"I admit to being rather surprised to find you still here, Mr. Campbell." Lord Graham snapped a pair of riding gloves against his thigh. "I thought perhaps you would take up my advice like the sensible person you seemed to be."

Lord Graham continued to stare.

Violet had refused this man, but how much did Lord Graham know about Ewan's involvement with Violet? Given the hostility Ewan could sense rolling off his lordship, Lord Graham suspected enough to wish Ewan gone. As if removing Ewan would somehow lead to Violet liking

Lord Graham more. Anyone with half a brain knew that love simply didn't work like that.

Was Lord Graham like Mr. Kerr then, broken in his understanding of what love was?

"Your advice, my lord?" Ewan kept his own tone light, as if he deliberately missed the implied threat in his lordship's words.

"Yes. I still insist that you should pursue a career as a prizefighter. Why, I would even put a tenner on you to win under certain circumstances."

Ewan gritted his teeth. The slight sneer in Lord Graham's tone indicated that he thought Ewan's life only *worth* a tenner.

This man represented everything he detested about prizefighting—the arrogant talk, the loud posturing. The attitude that some men were objects first, people second.

"I should think Ewan worth more than a ten-pound bet, my lord," Sir Joshua interjected with a coughing laugh, as if Lord Graham had told a joke. He kicked out the chair opposite with his foot. "You seem like a man who could use a drink. Allow me to buy you a pint."

Lord Graham ignored Sir Joshua's offer, his eyes still riveted on Ewan.

"I have a theory, you see," his lordship continued. "Mr. Smith! Come join me," Lord Graham called over his shoulder.

The group of men at the door broke apart, and a strapping fellow separated himself from them, joining Lord Graham.

"Gentlemen, allow me to introduce you to Mr. Thomas Smith." Lord Graham motioned toward the man. "Though you perhaps have heard tale of him through his moniker—the Menace of Cornwall."

Sir Joshua nodded a greeting. Ewan followed.

Ewan *had* heard of the man. The Menace was said to be a rising star, having won a recent high-profile bout in London.

What was Lord Graham about? Trying to set up a fight?

Ewan sized up Mr. Smith, looking at a man in a way he hadn't done in years—

Tall and broad, loose-limbed. The Menace would be quick on his feet. But did he have the muscle mass necessary to deliver a punishing blow?

The Menace appeared to be doing the same with Ewan. A faint, puzzled dent appeared between the man's brows.

"Mr. Smith has been kind enough to assist me in perfecting the finer points of pugilism," Lord Graham said. "I figured it was only sporting to offer his expertise for yourself, Mr. Campbell. Perhaps spar a bit together."

"Pardon?" Ewan's eyebrows shot upward.

"I believe you have potential, Mr. Campbell, and the best way to suss out that potential is in a trial match with Mr. Smith." Lord Graham said the words lightly, but the hardness in his eyes belied them.

Ewan took in a slow breath, his mind quickly piecing together the situation.

Lord Graham was out for blood, it seemed. He had paid a well-known fighter to travel the length of Britain with him, all for a chance to humiliate and perhaps seriously hurt Ewan in a rather public fight.

The entire dining room had gone quiet, heads swiveling, men leaning forward in their chairs.

"Come along, Mr. Campbell," Lord Graham continued, turning to note the listening crowd. "Don't make me call you a coward for refusing this. I am trying to help, you see."

Cleverly done, your lordship, Ewan mentally congratulated him.

Challenge Ewan in a public place. Use a condescending sense of *noblesse oblige* to make it seem like a favor. Call Ewan's manhood into question.

But Ewan had never been one to be moved by manly posturing. He would not fight merely because Lord Graham decreed it.

This would be your life, a quiet voice in his head pointed out. *Were you to marry Violet, this would be your life. Endless wee abuses. Small set-downs intended to cut and harm. Worse, they wouldn't only be directed at you. They would be aimed at Violet, too.*

Ewan stared at Lord Graham and then transferred his gaze back to the Menace.

That puzzled dent between the man's eyes had deepened.

There was nothing to do but make the situation clear.

Slowly, Ewan stood, rising to his full height. The Menace was tall, but Ewan still had at least six inches on the man.

The Menace watched Ewan stand, his eyes going wider and wider.

"Do you not see, Mr. Smith?" Lord Graham motioned toward Ewan, as if showing off a prize bull at the village market. "He is a marvelously strapping specimen. Do you think you could make a fighter out of him?"

Ewan was looking at the Menace as Lord Graham spoke, so he saw the point recognition set in.

The moment that the Menace realized who stood before him.

"You!" the man pointed a finger at Ewan. An astonished, marveling sort of wonder bloomed on his face. "The Red Renegade! As I live and breathe!" The man nearly vibrated with excitement, his sentences coming in fragmented bursts. "I was there! I was there, you see! Outside Warwick. It was the most marvelous! There was the hit and— Oh! Then you vanished into thin air. Poof! Never heard nor seen again. They said that you were perhaps a phantom, but I said no! That couldn't be!" The Menace became more and more animated as he spoke, taking on the look of an eager puppy. In other words, utterly *un*-menacing. "Please allow me the honor of shaking your hand!"

A murmur ran through the gathered crowd.

Ewan managed a weak smile and shook the other man's outstretched palm.

Lord Graham had been brewing a small thundercloud of outrage as Mr. 'The Menace' Smith enthused.

"What is all this?" he said, tone clipped.

"He's the Red Renegade, my lord." Mr. Smith tossed his thumb toward Ewan, nearly bouncing on the balls of his feet. "I'm sure you read about it in *Boxiana*. The fight between the Red Renegade and the Hammer? 'Twas all they wrote about for months. The Hammer was supposed to win by a large margin. Said he would take the heavyweight title for all of Britain at Five Courts, they did. And then the Red Renegade showed up and flattened the Hammer in the seventh round. Boom! Out cold!" Mr. Smith mimed a powerful uppercut to the jaw. "I could scarcely believe my eyes. The Red Renegade was astonishing—lightning fast, powerful blows, weaving and darting." Mr. Smith was now dancing around Lord Graham, throwing pretend punches. "Incredible, I tell you! The Hammer went on to win the heavyweight title the next year. But they've always said that the Red Renegade should be the true title holder." He stopped and faced Ewan, his expression the very definition of *wonder*. "And here you are!"

"Is this true?" Sir Joshua asked, eyes wide.

Ewan felt the blush creeping up his cheeks.

"Aye," he nodded.

"Why . . . I am astonished!" Sir Joshua laughed, as if this were an absolute lark. "A brilliant painter *and* a celebrated prizefighter, to boot. Is there anything you can't do, lad?!"

Experience public scrutiny without blushing, was the first suggestion that winged through Ewan's head.

Marry the lass I adore more than any other, was the second.

Lord Graham's expression could best be described as thunderous.

"Well, if this *is* true," his lordship said, "then a bout with Mr. Smith here should perhaps be more interesting—"

"Whoa, now!" Mr. Smith interrupted, hands upright with a self-deprecating laugh. "I won't be fighting the Red Renegade. A man knows when he's well and licked."

Lord Graham turned his angry eyes on the prizefighter. "Mr. Smith, I specifically have asked you—"

"I know that you have, your lordship, but you haven't seen the Red Renegade here in a fight. The man is a legend for good reason. A prizefighter that wishes to have a long and healthy career needs to know when to bow out." He tapped his skull. "I prefer to keep my wits in my head, thank you very much."

Lord Graham continued with his taunting for a few more minutes, but Mr. Smith stood his ground.

"You can lead a horse to water and all that, Lord Graham," Mr. Smith finally said. "But I'm not foolish enough to step into the ring with Mr. Campbell."

It made Ewan respect the man even more.

Lord Graham turned back to Ewan, raking him up and down.

"Fine," he said, doffing his hat and beginning to shrug out of his coat. "I will fight Mr. Campbell myself to prove that you are a coward, Mr. Smith."

Several men hooted their approval, pushing tables back, eagerly clearing a space.

This was the best entertainment they had seen in months.

Mr. Smith's eyes bulged out. "I fear you're acting a bit mad, your lordship!"

"Yes," Sir Joshua joined in. "I don't know what good a fight will serve."

Their reservations only stiffened Lord Graham's resolve.

"Mr. Campbell claims to be this Red Renegade fellow." Lord Graham tugged at his cravat. "I am simply calling his bluff. 'Twill be easy to determine if he truly has the skills he claims—"

"I willnae fight ye," Ewan said, voice rumbling through the crowd.

The last thing he needed—that *Violet* needed—was for Ewan to end up pummeling Lord Graham in a tavern brawl.

Besides, fighting the man would be akin to whipping a dog.

Lord Graham strutted into the makeshift ring.

Ewan didn't move a muscle.

"Come along now, Mr. Campbell." Lord Graham taunted. "Afraid?"

"Not sure you're going to be able to get out of this one, my friend," Sir Joshua murmured in Ewan's ear. "Just try not to permanently damage his lordship, though I can appreciate the temptation."

Two day-laborers grabbed Ewan by an arm and pulled him into the space, facing Lord Graham.

Ewan still did nothing.

What good would fighting this *eejit* serve?

"Hands up!" Lord Graham danced in front of him, his fists in a typical milling stance. The man's form was not *entirely* appalling, but the slowness of his movements would be no match for Ewan's reflexes.

Ewan noted all this with a sort of casual interest. As ever, when he fought, his mind instantly transformed into line and shape. It was odd to think that there were similarities between fighting and painting, but they were linked.

Prizefighting was merely painting in a three-dimensional space. Lines created trajectories that intersected with others, all dancing around one another. His mind's eye laid it all out like a map, charting paths and projecting movements.

Case in point, Lord Graham shifted his weight backward. Ewan knew that the man would throw a punch high and right a full second before the fist landed.

Or rather, attempted to land.

Ewan blocked it with his forearm, swatting Lord Graham's arm away.

Lord Graham hissed.

The crowd of men hooted and hollered.

Out of the corner of his eye, Ewan could see bets being exchanged, money wagered on his body, his reflexes.

Old memories surfaced.

He hated this.

He hated the smell of dirt and blood and sweat.

He hated the cheers of gathered men, savoring the violence and brutality.

Lord Graham continued to throw punches. Ewan either darted away from his lordship's fists or blocked them with his arm. At one point, he simply grabbed Lord Graham's hand in his own and pushed the man back.

The more Ewan refused to engage, the more incensed Lord Graham became, taking wild swings.

"Fight me!" Lord Graham ran at him, throwing a flurry of fists. "Stop dancing away like a coward."

Ewan snatched the man's hands out of mid-air, clamping down on them, holding him tightly.

"Highland bastard! You were born vermin and you will die vermin." Lord Graham snarled, low enough that only Ewan could hear him. "But until then, learn your place and stop sullying that which you have no right to touch."

"Pardon?"

"You disgrace her with your affection. Did you think I would not hear? Her father and my mother have ensured I thoroughly understand the nature of your relationship with her ladyship. Lady Kildrum will forever bear the mark of your foul touch."

Ewan considered himself a man slow to anger.

But this . . .

Abruptly, he remembered *why* he had fought in the first place. The motivator that had driven him into the boxing ring.

To fight for a woman.

To give Mhairi choices.

And now . . . to defend Violet.

She would always be worth fighting for.

He shoved Lord Graham off him, finally engaging his full strength, sending the smaller man sprawling.

"Fine." Ewan arched his neck, cracking his joints. "Ye want a fight? Let's have a fight. But I want everyone here to acknowledge that ye've been warned. That I tried tae avoid this. Because now . . . I willnae show mercy."

The crowd hooted and laughed their approval.

Lord Graham snarled, scrambling to his feet. "I will not need mercy from an upstart like yourself."

It was not much of a fight, in the end, to the disappointment of onlookers.

Lord Graham came at Ewan, swinging wildly.

Ewan ducked, darted to the right, and threw one single punch.

His intent was only to rattle Lord Graham's brain cage, show the man what he was truly up against.

But even that mild hit was too much.

Lord Graham collapsed, out cold.

Mr. Smith was in high alt, all but dancing around Ewan and begging to buy him a pint.

Ewan declined, choosing instead to return to Old Kilmeny Castle with Sir Joshua.

He shook out his fist as he walked.

"That did not go as I planned," Sir Joshua sighed as they walked.

"Pardon?"

"I had hoped to lure you from your doldrums, not mire you further."

"Ye had no way of knowing Lord Graham would appear and make an arse of himself," Ewan muttered, still massaging his bruised knuckles. "I had forgotten how hard a man's head can be."

"Lord Graham's, in particular," Sir Joshua snorted. "You acquitted yourself well back there. No one will fault you. You were only defending yourself. Lord Graham had it coming to him."

"Aye."

But that knowledge did not loosen the knot in Ewan's chest.

The problem?

There had been a good deal of truth in Lord Graham's words:

Lady Kildrum will forever bear the mark of your foul touch.

Ewan had been so ready to use his fists to defend her honor, but what if standing beside her in life was the true offense?

Violet *would* be sullied by associating with him. That was how society functioned. And as Mr. Kerr had said, she would disgrace her sisters along with herself. They would suffer.

Besides, how would Violet pay off the loan? How many would endure hardship for that, too?

Sometimes . . . love simply wasn't enough.

Ewan became lost in morose thoughts.

How could he remain here with Violet, knowing the pain it would eventually cause her and her family?

But how could he leave? The thought of never seeing her again gripped his chest like a vise.

Both he and Sir Joshua were so distracted, they were cresting the final bluff to the castle before Ewan finally noticed it:

A plume of smoke and flame rising into the golden sun.

25

E wan sprinted toward the castle.

At first, he feared the entire structure was aflame.

But coming closer, he realized the truth.

It was not the castle.

His greenhouse studio was on fire, flames licking toward the sky.

No!

His painting!

As he stared at the blaze reaching skyward, a slashing streak of burnt orange and sienna smoke, all he could think was:

It is over.

That is my future burning.

Again.

The bitter, bitter irony.

What was to become of Violet and himself now?

Later . . . *later* he would come to grips with the reality that his painting for the Royal Academy Exhibition had been destroyed.

But for now, he pushed his leaden limbs to stumble down the hill.

Just like that night so long ago, witnessing the family house burn, he forced himself to keep going. To keep moving forward, despite watching his future vanish in a billow of smoke.

He joined the army of servants and laborers racing from the fields round about to form a bucket brigade. They tossed pail after pail of water on the fire, dowsing it before the flames spread to the castle.

Only then did they piece together the tragedy—how could a building of stone and glass burn?

Ewan briefly wondered if Mr. Kerr or Lord Graham had set the blaze intentionally, determined to undermine his bid for Violet's hand.

But it was Sir Joshua who pointed out the pile of ashy rags in one corner and quickly deduced that refracted light through the windows had set the oily, highly-flammable rags afire.

As for the painting . . .

It was a charred husk.

The painting of the fire that had destroyed his past, the masterpiece that was to have secured his future . . .

. . . crumbling into a plume of smoke and flame just as inexplicably cruel as that first fire so long ago.

As Sir Joshua thanked the gathered crowd for their help, all Ewan could do was stare at the smoking embers in shock.

The past rolled over him in disorienting waves.

The scent of smoke searing his lungs.

Care for Mhairi. Keep her safe.

The clamor of people calling and yelling.

His mother's tortured screams.

Mhairi tugging on his hand, sobbing, "Mama, Mama!"

The past surged up and over, a consuming tidal wave of grief and horror and never-ending anguish. A slashing blow, tearing the wound anew.

Was this to be his life? The past never truly reclaimed or redeemed? Was he doomed to relive it, again and again?

The first fire had sent him on the path of duty, to care for Mhairi. And she had then figuratively burned down his sense of duty when she married McDoughal and forcibly cast Ewan out.

Since then, Ewan had been racing away from that past, desperate to extinguish the pain of Mhairi's actions. But somewhere along the way, he had become so lost in his desires to become a famous artist, that he had neglected the duty he still owed his sister. The occasional half-hearted letter to the vicar was all but giving up the fight.

The flames of that first fire still licked at his heels.

He realized that now.

How could he have allowed his anger to drive such distance between Mhairi and himself? How could he continue to wallow like a petulant child in the cesspool of his hurt at her betrayal?

Just because Mhairi had declined to choose him, he had not needed to return the sentiment—to reject her just as cruelly as she had rejected him.

Staring at the smoldering ashes of his greenhouse studio, his hand opened and closed, as if searching for Mhairi's wee fingers pressed into his palm.

How could he have left his sister so alone?

VIOLET FOUND EWAN hours later, sitting alone atop the cliffs, facing the sea with sightless eyes.

She had panicked when she first saw the pillar of black smoke extended toward the sky. Was the castle on fire? Were Ewan and Sir Joshua inside?

The inhabitants had emptied out of Kilmeny Hall at a run.

Violet had ascertained soon enough the truth of what had happened.

She offered a prayer of thanks that Ewan was physically unharmed.

As for the emotional consequences—

She scanned Ewan's face as she approached. He was tucked against that same rock where she had nearly tripped all those months ago.

His face was a blank, as if he sketched the pain of his memories on a canvas only he could see.

He had yet to change his clothing. She did not know where his coat had gone. His kilt was streaked with soot, his shirt torn on one arm.

The agonizing ache that had taken root behind her heart surged upward, as if desperate to reach him, to offer comfort.

He did not move as she sat beside him, tucking her skirts around her ankles and reaching for his hand. ·

He was silent, but he did lace his fingers with hers.

"I am so sorry, Ewan," she murmured.

He didn't pretend to not understand.

"I will repaint it," he replied. "Eventually, that is."

He could repaint. And he likely would.

But not before submissions to the Royal Academy's Exhibition. The deadline was too close.

She did not add that bit.

"I have known loss," he continued. "Fires that consume one's future. I will find a way onward. I always do."

The unspoken anguish in his voice set her eyes to stinging.

She had heard what happened at the inn in the village. Lord Graham's relentless taunting. Ewan's gentlemanly conduct in return. Ewan's eventual capitulation and the subsequent pummeling of his lordship. The petty part of Violet hoped Lord Graham nursed a black eye for weeks to come.

Her father had made his opinion crystal clear.

Cast him off, Violet, he had warned. *Cast Mr. Campbell off before the damage is too great, before everyone sees how derelict you are in your duty to family and title. You threaten all our futures with this willfully selfish behavior.*

Part of her still considered her father's anger an overreaction.

But the incident with Lord Graham was telling of the opinions of those of her social class.

Was it a portent of things to come?

Would this be their life together? Ewan, fighting noblemen who took exception to his audacity to marry one of their own? Violet, enduring endless snubs and the thousand little cuts that other women inflicted with biting words?

For herself, she would tolerate it all. A life with Ewan was worth it.

But could she make that choice for him?

"It was meant for us," he finally said. "The painting was our future, ye see. A way for me tae perhaps . . . bridge . . . the social chasm between us. But now . . ."

Oh, Ewan. "You know I do not care about that—"

"Aye, lass, I ken that ye dinnae care." He paused and sucked in a slow breath, drawing their clasped hands to his chest. "But *I* care." He turned to her then, defeat nearly visibly draped across his shoulders. "I care that I cannae meet ye as an equal in at least *some* capacity—"

"You *are* my equal, Ewan!" She shook their joined hands. "You are my soul's other half. How can I make you see that?"

"How can I be enough when I cannae offer ye anything other than my hard-working hands and my tattered heart?"

Violet nearly laughed at the frustration in his voice. "That is all I want, Ewan! I only want your heart. Your clever mind. Your capable hands. I don't require anything else."

"I love ye, lass." He cradled her face with his free palm. "You're the very heart beating in my chest. I cannae think that I will ever love anything so well as you."

"Then why do I hear doubt in your voice?"

"Because all the reasons your father stated are *true*, lass." She sensed that he laid the words carefully, a painter gently dabbing in color. "We *are* living a wee fairy tale."

"Ewan—"

"Nae, *mo chridhe*. Let me finish. For ourselves, we dinnae care what Society thinks of us. 'Tis likely better for my career as an artist tae be seen as a wee bit of a rebel . . . a dash of Lord Byron or Mr. Coleridge. And ye have been kind enough tae say ye dinnae care what the consequences are—"

"I don't," she whispered. "I truly don't. Any snubbing I might receive is a small price to pay for having you at my side."

He stroked a thumb down her cheek. "But there is a rub, lass. Our decision doesnae affect only ourselves. Ye have obligations that weigh on ye. How will ye pay off the Manna Loan? How will ye provide for your tenants and your family?"

"We'll find a way, Ewan. We will!"

"Perhaps. But at what cost? I live with the pain of having bought my future on the back of a sister's misery. I thought I had set that grief behind me—that I'd put that fire out—and accepted Mhairi's sacrifice—" He gasped, biting hard on his lower lip to stop it quivering.

He swallowed. Hard.

The actions of a man desperate to hold back an emotional storm.

It was too much.

His pain was her own, and she could not sit helplessly by. That had always been their dynamic, had it not? From that first meeting in the carriage so long ago when she had found him, a tormented creature half-feral with anguish over Mhairi's actions.

Violet leaned forward and kissed him.

She pressed her mouth to his, threaded her fingers into his hair, and let her body speak her truths.

You are worthy of love.

I will happily bear the consequences of our decisions.

I stand with you.

Ewan returned her affection ten-fold.

The hunger in his mouth, the near desperation in his taste. The trembling of his hands cupping her cheeks.

He pulled back, pressing his forehead to hers before reluctantly removing his hands and sitting back.

"I've sat here—" He waved a hand toward the ocean. "—and all I can see is my own self-portrait, over and over in my head."

"A self-portrait?"

"Aye. But 'tis not a straight-forward image. It's a cacophonous jumble. Shards of glass and my insides turned out, all reflected in shattered bits. A guttural scream of line and color titled *Grief: Man Broken.*"

"Ewan, my heart—" She licked a tear from her upper lip.

"Your da is right." He met her eyes then. "Sometimes the price of *love* is too high. Sometimes the price of *success* is too high. My father gave me a sacred duty tae care for my sister. And yet I left Mhairi—" His voice broke. "—I left her in squalor and despair. I purchased success on the back of her pain and disregarded the love between us. How could I do that tae her? How could I think that nursing my hurt pride was more important than her life and well-being?"

"She cast you out! You had no choice!"

"Didn't I?" He sank his head into his hands. "We always have choice. And in the case of Mhairi, I moved on. I embraced my desires for my own future and, over time, I thought I had accepted Mhairi's decision—" he gasped. "That the wound of her betrayal did not require *action* on my part. That in rejecting me, I had to do the same to her. I had to *un-choose* her. Today . . . today has shown me that I still have an obligation to her."

He dragged his knuckles across his eyes, the joints bruised and red from his altercation with Lord Graham.

Violet was quite sure her heart looked similarly battered.

"I have paid a steep price for my current life, and it's destroying me, bit by bit. I ken that now." He let out a long, shuddering breath. The sound of a giant breaking. "I have tae embrace my duty again. To make things right with Mhairi before I move forward again. I chose the shape of our lives for Mhairi and myself as children. But then she turned the tables, choosing the shape of our future. It is time for Mhairi and I to choose each other. To cease this back and forth."

"But . . . but what of . . . *us*?" Violet all but cried the words.

"Ah, my love. That is the problem, is it not? Choosing me means *un-*choosing others. Like me, you have obligations to your own. You—my beautiful, precious lass—need tae look at those lovely sisters of yours and decide if ye can choose an uncertain future for them. Can you purchase your happiness at the expense of theirs? Because, I can tell ye from my own experience, it is a terrible cross to bear."

The anguish in his voice nearly broke her.

Her heart pounded a frantic panic in her chest.

"I cannot lose you," she gasped. "I cannot! I will not!"

"Ye say that now. But what will ye do when your sisters are poor and cast off because of whom they marry, like Dahlia? Or when they are forced tae marry men who use them ill, like Mhairi? How will ye feel then, when it's their hardship on your head? How will ye feel when your own children suffer the same?"

Violet hiccupped and pressed a fist to her mouth.

She could not answer.

Dahlia had *chosen* that life deliberately, and had it given her happiness in the end?

"I cannae bear the thought that ye will suffer the same pain over your sisters' future as I have borne for Mhairi," he continued. "For myself, I cannae accept that I, once again, will choose happiness on the back of others' misery. I cannae do it."

He paused, gazing out over the sea, swiping those red knuckles under his eyes, pressing the wetness of his tears back into his skin, as if absorbing their grief.

"I love ye, *mo chridhe*." He turned to her, his hazel eyes glossy "But I will be leaving in the morning to find Mhairi. The journey to Loch Carron is not a short or easy one, so I cannae say when I will return."

"Ewan, p-please. P-promise you will return to m-me?"

"Violet." Her name left his lips in an anguished rush. "I know we had hoped tae find a third way down the cliff, to secure ourselves with ropes or some such. But in that vision, we failed tae understand that we were both already tethered to others. That our fall topples them with us. I fear there is no rope strong enough to hold us all together. That no matter what we do, we will *all* be dashed upon the rocks."

He trailed a finger down her cheek.

"I choose *you*. I will *always* choose you. But . . . I choose all of ye. Even the parts of ye that must adhere tae duty and protect those in your care . . . the part that includes *not* choosing me. Sometimes, *mo chridhe*, love is truly not enough. And knowing that," he hiccupped, his parting words nearly a sob, ". . . I cannae see a happy ending for you and me."

26

Violet woke the next morning with a pounding headache and an aching heart.

Ewan said he would be leaving at first light, determined to track down Mhairi on the banks of Loch Carron.

Her lungs constricted at the thought of him leaving, of the real possibility that she might never see him again.

Why had she not pressed him harder?

Violet dressed quickly. Perhaps he had not left yet. Perhaps there was time still.

An hour later, she ran up the main stairs of Old Kilmeny Castle.

"Violet, I wondered if I would see you today." Uncle Joshua turned from packing his masterpiece for the journey to London, a rueful grimace on his face. Though his waistcoat was as colorful as ever—a vibrant green shot with silver thread. "I could pretend that I don't know why you are here, but that would be futile." He sighed, wiping his hands on a nearby rag. "Ewan is gone."

"Truly?" She made no attempt to hide her devastation.

"Yes. He left before the sun rose. I am sorry, child."

Violet lifted her head to stare at the ceiling, willing the tears back.

But it was no use. They tumbled and spilled free.

"Here." Uncle Joshua pressed a handkerchief into her palm and led her to a chair before the hearth. The air was warm again today, so no fire was lit.

She dabbed at her cheeks, sniffling.

"Did Ewan tell you?" she asked.

"Some." A pause. "Enough."

Violet hiccupped. What was she to do? Ewan's words would not let her be.

"He wouldn't stay." A hitch in her voice. "He left."

"I understand that he felt there were matters that needed to be resolved."

"Yes, but he refused to say when or *if* he will return. He fears he will make me unhappy. Do you disapprove of a match between Ewan and myself?" She had to ask it.

"Heavens, no! If anything, I have been encouraging it."

"You have?" Violet's head snapped upright. "Despite our difference in station?"

"Of course." Sir Joshua smiled fondly at her. "Ewan is a remarkable man. I can think of no one who would be better suited for you. I've been trying to convince him of that fact. He can be a bit stubborn at times, if you hadn't noticed."

"But . . . why? Why would you encourage us?"

"You know my past, Violet." Her uncle shook his head, a tired sadness there. A glimmer of an ache that had never healed. "I find it distasteful to separate two kindred souls over something as paltry as parentage or social station. I know your parents both wished you to marry Lord Graham. But I do not like him . . . well, not for you at least. He would always see you as an object to be protected, not a woman to be loved. There is a meanness in his lordship that will only grow over time. More to the point, I wish you to have greater freedom than I was given."

Oh! Her uncle's kind words sent her tears tumbling again.

Violet wiped her cheeks. "Ewan fears we will claim our happiness on the backs of my sisters' misery. That in choosing him, I will also choose an uncertain future for Aster and Rose."

"Ah." Sir Joshua's chin went up. "That is a valid concern. I hadn't thought of it in precisely those terms, but . . ."

"But?"

"But Ewan is not wrong to be worried about it."

"Dahlia's choices nearly destroyed us as a family," Violet whispered. "I encouraged her, you know. She was so in love with Mr. Martinelli, and I hated seeing her turmoil. I wanted her happiness—"

"And she was happy, Violet. She *was*."

"But was she truly? In hindsight, I have often wondered. Did I encourage Dahlia because it was the best decision for her? Or was I caught up in the romance of her forbidden love, too? Was I so stifled in my role as heir that I pushed her to rebel and elope because *I* could not? So in the end, her choice was more mine than hers."

"I hadn't realized that you still suffered so from Dahlia's decisions. You cannot lay her choices at your feet, Violet."

Violet sat back in the chair, gaze drifting upward to rest on the plasterwork ceiling. "I regret that she suffered. I regret that *she* may have regretted her decision—"

"Dahlia *never* regretted her decision, Violet."

His tone caused Violet to snap her head upright. Uncle Joshua's expression was deadly earnest.

"You were not the only one who encouraged her decision. I did so, too."

"You did?"

"Yes. I wished to give Dahlia and her husband the support and understanding that had never been shown to me. And so I wrote to her often and sent money when I could. I can say, unequivocally, that your sister was luminously happy in her life. She *never* regretted her choices. I visited her, you see, about a month before she died. They were living in a row house on the edge of New Town in Edinburgh."

"Why have you not told me this?"

"I did not think it mattered, child. You grieved Dahlia, as we all did. I feared describing my visit would only serve to remind you of all you had lost, and I did not wish to add to your pain." He sighed. "I can see now that I erred."

"Tell me. Tell me everything."

"Dahlia was well when I visited. Mr. Martinelli had acquired several new patrons, and they had been able to hire a second maid. Dahlia was . . . radiant." Uncle Joshua spread his hands, as if trying to capture the emotion. "She laughed and chattered gaily. I dangled her son on my knee and stayed long enough to ask her more serious questions, to truly gauge how much of her attitude was mere playacting and how much was genuine." He fixed her with an intent stare. "Violet, you must believe me in this: Dahlia was *sincerely* happy. She loved her husband wholly. She was excited about his prospects. Money had been tight here and there, but she wasn't troubled by it. Her wants were simple, and she had all she needed in her husband and son."

Violet buried her face in her hands, her body shaking with sobs.

Why had she needed to hear this so badly? Why did this feel strangely like . . . absolution?

Uncle Joshua waited for her weeping to quiet.

Finally, she felt equal to raising her head and meeting his gaze.

"Listen, Violet." He sat forward. "Early on, I suffered the pain of having the love of my life torn from me. From there, I spent my life as a painter. And being an artist for me meant living my life with a foot in two worlds: the world of Society and privilege, and the world of bohemian creativity that resides outside of that. As you well know, those who live in Society judge those who willfully choose to leave. They prefer to dispense cruelty to the rule-breaker, as the only alternative is to feel discontent for their own safe—and often regretted—choices."

"But that cruelty has acutely real repercussions, Uncle."

"It does. Had I been permitted to marry my love, I know I would have spent more of my life on the fringes of Society. But . . . I would have had the other half of my soul every hour of every day. Ewan and yourself face a difficult decision: do you willing to bear the consequences for choosing to have a foot in both worlds?"

He paused, sitting back and tapping his fingers on the arm of his chair, as if lost in memory. Finally, he shook his head and met her gaze, his own eyes shining and intent.

"If you hear nothing else, child, believe this from an older man who has seen much of sorrow and regret." He sucked in a tight breath. "Life is long. Hardship is guaranteed. Suffering is certain. The only gift we've been granted is the ability to choose who will be at our side."

Violet sniffed, taking in a stuttering breath. "For myself, I would choose Ewan in a flash—he is my heart's desire!—but duty demands that I—"

"Ah, child, I do not like to hear you frame this choice as a difference between duty and desire. They are not opposing viewpoints. They are two sides of the same coin. Desire fuels duty and duty fuels desire. They must go hand-in-hand."

"Perhaps, Uncle, but my sisters will suffer—"

"Ugh! Enough about us!" Aster's voice came from the doorway of the great hall.

Violet swiveled around to see Aster and Rose stomp into the room.

"We saw you sneak out," Aster began. "Miss Compton has a headache, so we were at loose ends."

"And we're so tired of being left out of all the delicious goings-on," Rose continued.

"So we followed you."

"And lucky we did! Miss Compton never tells us anything."

Violet frowned. She had perhaps overestimated Miss Compton's control over the twins.

Her sisters sat down in the remaining chairs before the fire.

"You need to go after Mr. Campbell, Violet." Aster's face was deadly earnest.

"Yes," Rose agreed. "It's imperative."

"We won't tolerate any other solution," Aster continued. "You and Mr. Campbell are perfect for one another. And you will be miserably unhappy without him."

Violet sniffled back more tears.

Ah, her sweet sisters.

"Aster, Rose, you do realize that me marrying Mr. Campbell isn't wise, correct?" She rested her head against the back of her chair, a tiredness settling into her bones. "You and Rose will face genuine problems if I choose to marry him. I've already destroyed the chances of Lady Graham sponsoring your Season in London—"

"Thank goodness!" Rose exclaimed.

"Amen," Aster shuddered. "That woman is an utter harridan. We're both most glad that you refused Lord Graham. It shows your good sense."

Violet resisted the urge to massage her pounding temples. Her sisters were appallingly feather-headed at times.

"Violet," Rose said, "I know that you think Aster and I are terribly feather-brained at times—"

Violet snorted. They had no idea.

"—but we have truly thought about this, you know. We *do* understand that there might be consequences to ourselves based on your choice of husband."

"Yes," Aster continued. "But the reality is this. First, we like Mr. Campbell."

"He is good *for* you." Rose leaned forward. "And he is good *to* you. And you deserve that. You need happiness in your life."

"But you will suffer." Violet tried to help them understand. "I will be *choosing* that hardship for you."

"So?" Aster shrugged. "You suffered after Dahlia' elopement, did you not?"

Violet sat back, not sure she liked where this was heading.

"Did you hate Dahlia for that?" Aster pressed her point. "Did you hold a grudge against her for making a choice that added difficulty to your life?"

"Of course not," Violet all but sighed. "Dahlia was *happy*."

Tears welled again at the words.

Dahlia *was* happy.

Her sister's choices, though unconventional, had won her that happiness.

"Exactly." Aster's gaze had turned soft.

"Aster's right," Rose chimed in. "You were willing to endure the snubs and disdain of our neighbors because you knew that the alternative was Dahlia's *unhappiness*. And we all loved Dahlia enough to want her to be happy, even at personal cost to ourselves. Please allow us to choose the same for you."

The sincerity in her sisters' voices set Violet to crying again.

"Violet," Aster said, eyes frightfully serious. "We've already lost one sister to a marriage that Father deemed unacceptable. We will not lose a second sister to grief over a marriage that was abandoned for duty's sake."

"And you need to stop worrying about us," Rose said. "Aster and I will manage. We are nothing if not resourceful."

Violet swiped at her cheeks. "You darling dears, you are too good to me. But I cannot allow you to sacrifice—"

"Bah!" Rose waved a careless hand. "It's hardly a sacrifice! I will not be forced to marry an elderly, respectable man. It's more of a relief, I tell you."

"Yes!" Aster agreed. "And if you will not take our word for it, I am fully prepared to ruin myself."

"Aster Meredith Kerr!" Violet gasped.

"I am." Aster's face was resolute. "Have you *seen* the new blacksmith in the village?!"

"Oh, he is delicious!" Rose enthused.

"No! Neither of you are allowed to ruin your reputations!" Violet all but shouted.

"Well, then, you will simply have to marry your Mr. Campbell to ensure it." Aster pretended to inspect her fingernails. "I cannot be held accountable for my actions otherwise. It's my *choice*, after all."

"Besides, I think you are perhaps being a smidgen melodramatic, Violet," Rose said. "There is every reason to believe that marrying Mr. Campbell will not harm us. Well, at least, not in the long run. Mr. Campbell has wealthy, powerful friends. He is talented and his star is rising. There are those who will see your marrying him as wildly unorthodox—"

Aster coughed, though it sounded suspiciously like, "Lady Graham."

"—but none of us wish to associate with those people anyway," Rose continued.

"True!" Aster agreed. "Can you imagine if Lord and Lady Hadley decided to take us into their circle?"

"Wouldn't that be delightful?" Rose clasped her hands.

"But what about Father?" Violet said. "He will be so angry and cold, just like he was with Dahlia—"

"Let me deal with my brother," Uncle Joshua returned. "I think I can help him understand what's at stake here. I often think my brother's negative reaction to Dahlia's choices and death had little to do with anger and more to do with mismanaged grief. Some people allow grief to soften and grow their heart. But for others, grief calcifies it into bedrock. David alone must be the one to chip away at the stone around his heart. But we are here to help him. He loves you all. I know he does. And I think, in time, he will come around. In the meantime, my mind is already pondering solutions to help Violet and Ewan on their way."

"Uncle, Aster, Rose, I . . ." Violet's voice faded off. "I don't know what to say."

"Say you'll go after Mr. Campbell."

"Go after him?" Violet frowned.

"Yes! He needs that," Rose said, voice very matter-of-fact.

"Pardon? He left *me*. Why should I go haring after *him*?"

"I have to agree with Rose on this, child," Sir Joshua said. "I have often sensed that Ewan is used to doing and giving for everyone else but is rarely on the receiving end himself. He has, quite literally at times, spent his life fighting for others. But has anyone ever truly chosen, and fought, for him?"

Ewan's parting words rolled over Violet:

I will always choose you. Even the parts of ye that must adhere tae duty . . . the part that includes not choosing me.

Was this her answer? That she needed to choose Ewan? Publicly and thoroughly?

Her uncle paused, gaze pensive.

Then, he pushed out of his chair and wandered toward the left side of the great hall.

"Ewan will likely be upset with me for doing this, but I think you need to see this, child."

Violet followed her uncle.

Sir Joshua tugged at a cloth draped atop a frame in the corner. The cloth covered what was likely an enormous canvas, at least eight feet high.

The cloth fell.

Violet gasped.

She stared at herself, draped in the shimmery aqua-blue gown she had chosen for her official portrait.

She stood in the middle of the canvas. A desk rested against a flowing drape on one side. A vast landscape opened on the other.

The sunlight peeked through clouds behind, rimming her head in a halo of light and casting a shadow of glowing armor around her. Scales sat on her desk, resting beside an orb of justice.

Ewan had painted her like Joan of Arc, the champion of her people.

Moreover, he had littered the painting with all the things she could do and be. Ledgers were stacked on the floor. Farmers worked the field behind her. But there were also children's toys in one corner and a basket of unfinished embroidery.

Most importantly, however, she held a sword in her hand. An honest-to-goodness claymore, the tip resting on the ground by her feet, its blade unsheathed and gleaming silver.

The message to her was achingly clear—

You can be anything you wish. The power is in your own hands.

How could she still have any tears left to shed?

And yet, her eyes pricked and stung, the paint blurring into a hazy mass of color.

How profound . . . to understand how he perceived her.

Everyone else saw her as a *thing* to defend. A land to be won and conquered. Lord Graham had wanted to wield a sword on her behalf.

But not Ewan.

No . . .

He had no desire to mold her into his own making. He felt no need to fight her battles for her.

He did not see her as someone requiring protection.

Instead, he was the friend who pointed out the sword in her own hand—

A champion in her own right. A crusading knight.

Any part of Violet that did not already love Ewan Campbell crumbled.

She adored this man.

And she knew what decision she would make with blinding clarity.

She would pursue and marry him.

Everything else was so much dross.

Uncle Joshua was right, after all. Life was long. Hardship was guaranteed. But she had been granted the gift to choose who would be at her side.

And she chose Ewan.

She was going to go after him. She was going to fight for him.

Ewan Campbell would know how treasured and adored he was.

But first, she had two things she had to do.

27

It seemed fitting to arrive on a dreich day.

Ewan looked for the poetic in things, and this one was impossible to ignore.

The clouds hung low over Loch Carron, sending the rain dribbling down in a fine mist. He had left the small inn hours earlier, choosing to walk the last few miles. He pulled the top section of his great kilt over his head, wrapping the whole around him like a hooded cloak, wearing the kilt as his ancestors had on this very road for generations before him.

How odd. He left this place nearly nine years ago, but it might as well have been yesterday.

The journey had been long. He had known that it would be, which was why it had taken so many years to reach this point again. It wasn't simply the literal distance—which had taken nearly eight days on horseback to traverse the mountainous terrain—but the emotional backtracking in time.

Every mile farther from Violet had exponentially amplified the gap between them. How could he think that a poor lad from this backwater corner of the world could ever aspire to a life as the consort of someone like Lady Kildrum?

In the harsh light of reality, it appeared laughable.

Once west of Inverness, English was heard less and less. He had easily sunk back into speaking Scots Gaelic, his first language.

And now, as he rounded the final bend before reaching his family's original blackhouse, it was almost as if he had never left.

The whole of Loch Carron extended before him, the endless peaks of Wester Ross dotting the horizon. The water echoed the stormy gray of the sky.

And there sat the blackhouse, on its small rise, overlooking the whole.

The building had not been repaired. The burned roof timbers were long gone, leaving just the foundation stones. Blackhouses were dismal places, and the ongoing Highland Clearances ensured that the population was diminishing. Who would want to inhabit it?

Time had begun to cover the blackened stones with moss and creeping vines, but the walls still stood about five feet tall.

He stooped under the small door lintel, bending nearly in half to enter. The central hearth was no longer visible. But if he half-closed his eyes, he could envision his parents' box bed in one corner and the built-in stone shelves along one wall. He could hear the pigs and sheep snuffling through the single wall that divided the living quarters from the stable. He could remember the sense of comfort and belonging.

How much had that one fire destroyed?

Ewan sank back, resting against the damp moss that dotted the walls. He would begin his search for Mhairi in earnest tomorrow.

But today, he had needed to come here. To weep his grief, to mourn that which had been lost.

He worried if he didn't *greit* today that he would act rashly if and when he discovered Mhairi. That his choler would run too high, and all his pain would spew from him in a flurry of fists directed at those around her. He had already altered his sister's life enough, as it was. He did not wish to cause her further harm.

But if her life were as miserable as he suspected it to be, he would have to extricate her somehow. Spirit her to Aberdeen and away from her cruel husband.

What would Violet think of that? Of Ewan turning his sister fugitive?

He ran a hand over his face, wiping away the damp there. Tears or rain? Did it matter?

He swallowed back the ache in his throat when thinking about Violet.

The golden sound of her laugh.

The fiery hunger in her kiss.

The kindness of her heart.

The clever turn of her mind.

He would never relinquish the memory of her. She had thoroughly ruined him for any other woman.

Ewan wasn't sure what caught his attention.

Some vague sound?

A sense of awareness?

A tingling prickle down his spine?

He pushed upright and pivoted around, looking over the foundation stones.

All the air whooshed from his lungs.

He blinked.

But no, she was still there.

Violet.

His Violet.

Standing in front of the house in a rain-soaked red cloak, wet tendrils of hair clinging to her cheeks, the blue-green of her eyes vibrant.

All of her a brilliant slash of color against the gray sky.

VIOLET DRANK IN the sight of him.

At last! She and Uncle Joshua had caught up with Ewan.

His broad shoulders were tucked into a long length of Jamie's tartan, the end wrapped over his head, red hair peeking out.

She recognized the house from his destroyed painting.

It felt dramatic somehow, to meet him here. That the aftermath of a second life-altering fire would lead them both to ruins of the first.

"Lass," he whispered. His eyes darted past her, likely seeing Uncle Joshua who had held back to give them some privacy. "Why . . . I mean, how . . ."

Ewan was already ducking through the low doorway, coming toward her as he spoke.

Violet rushed to meet him, shamelessly wrapping her arms around his waist and burying her face in his broad chest. He enveloped her, the warmth of him utterly surrounding her.

"You're here," he murmured against her hair. "How are ye here?"

Violet hiccupped and swallowed, trying to stem her tears, but it was no use. She pressed her face into the wool of his kilt, releasing a tidal wave of amassed emotion.

He said nothing, merely pressed his face into the top of her head and kissed her hair, holding her steady through the storm.

When she finally felt equal to talking once more, she pulled back and looked up at him through blurry eyes.

He brushed her wet hair from her face, smoothing it back over her ears.

"I made a d-decision," she hiccupped. "I finally made a very crucial d-decision."

"Ah, *mo chriodhe*." He pressed a kiss to her forehead. "That is wonderful."

Violet swallowed and took in a deep breath, attempting to steady her voice. Her next words were so vitally important.

"I have spent years trying to choose a set of actions or a goal or something that would guide me." She looked up into his eyes. "But I've realized that sometimes that isn't what a future is. Sometimes the future is simply a person."

"Violet—" His voice broke.

"*You* are my future—my best and last and *only* decision. I choose you."

A sort of pained wonder flashed across his face.

"But, lass—"

"Hush." She pressed a kiss to his mouth. "My sisters are supportive. I shall have to tell you of our plans there. But I have come all this way to tell you this."

She paused, waiting until he opened his eyes to meet hers.

"You are enough," she whispered. "I love you. I love you exactly as you are. You are worth love. No—" She hiccupped. "—you are worth traveling for days on end through hostile country on horseback. You are worth stinging remarks and callous comments. You are worth my father's disappointment and my neighbors' misguided scorn. A life with you is worth *everything*. B-because without you, my dearest heart—" She licked a tear from her lip. "Without you, life simply is not worth living."

With a choking sob, he kissed her. A ravenous thing that pulled her tight against him, enveloping her in the strength of his arms.

"You wonderful, incredible lass," he gasped against her mouth. "I dinnae deserve such regard—"

"You worry that love isn't enough, but I disagree." She framed his face with her hands. "Life is so uncertain. It could go all pear-shaped, like it did with Dahlia. But it could just as likely be brilliant. Dahlia understood this. And now I do, too. I am absolutely willing to chance it because a life with you is worth any risk. Because with you at my side, I will be home."

28

E wan passed the next twenty-four hours as if in a daze.
Violet had come.

She had braved the elements, crossed the entire country through hostile terrain, to reach him. Sir Joshua, as well. The older painter had sent his completed *Battle of Granicus* to London in the care of several trusted footmen and chosen instead to accompany Violet here.

But if the smile and murmured, "Well done," Sir Joshua had given him were any indication, the older painter had no regrets.

"'Tis rather bizarre to think that we are still on the Isle of Great Britain," Violet said over dinner after listening to Ewan laugh with the innkeep in Gaelic.

They were tucked into the tiny inn in New Kelso on the shores of Loch Carron, eating in the equally small dining room. The inn did not see many travelers and only had two rooms to accommodate them, but Ewan and Sir Joshua readily shared one of the bedchambers.

She continued, "I haven't heard a word of English that was not spoken directly to me. It all feels quite foreign."

"Aye, lass. Most here speak Gaelic natively." Ewan nodded. "I ken it is partially why the English have always vilified the Highlands. We dinnae speak their language, and as such, we must be foreigners. Never mind that Scots were living here long before the Anglos and Saxons arrived down south. They invaded *our* lands, not the other way around." He paused and dared a glance at Sir Joshua, "No offense tae present company."

"None taken, my boy. I feel honored to see where you began life. I hope we can spare a week or two to sketch the landscape. Once we find Mhairi, of course."

Ewan nodded, his throat tight.

After leaving the old blackhouse, they had walked an extra mile to a wee cluster of houses where McDoughal's cousin lived. Ewan figured it was the best place to start.

Unfortunately, McDoughal's cousin was not at home. The house sat dark and silent. Ewan peered through the windows, trying to ascertain if the cousin even lived there any longer.

An elderly neighbor strolled over to the fence, curious—or, more likely, suspicious—as to why three fancy Sassenach, as he called them, would be on the banks of Loch Carron.

One good look at Ewan had changed all that.

"Well, I'll be damned." Old Mr. Logan doffed his cap, rounding the stone wall with a wide grin. "If it isnae wee Eòghann Caimbeul."

Before long, Ewan was surrounded by old friends, everyone eager to shake his hand or hug him tight.

"We thought ye dead," Mr. Vass said.

"Or conscripted into the army." Mrs. Bruce shook her head.

"Or forced tae work for some dreadful lord." Mr. Gillies rolled his eyes.

Ewan quickly set them to rights, sketching his life since leaving the area.

"Have ye heard word of Mhairi?" he asked, throat tight.

"Aye." Mrs. Bruce pursed her lips. "McDoughal died some six or seven years ago."

"Och, it was only five years ago," Mr. Vass countered.

"Nae, I recall well. It were at least six." Mrs. Bruce and Mr. Vass continued to go back and forth, arguing with one another in a way that Ewan remembered well.

All the while, Ewan's brain hummed with emotion, a tangled knot of colorful threads he struggled to untie. Relief that Mhairi had escaped her marriage with McDoughal's death. But terror that she had been cast out into the world five (or six or seven) years ago with Ewan none the wiser.

"Regardless," Ewan interrupted after a moment, "do either of youse know where my sister is now?"

Mrs. Bruce blinked and then let loose a merry laugh. "Oh aye, lad, ye dinnae care how long it's been, I reckon. Your Mhairi is there." She pointed at a village barely visible on the opposite side of the wide loch. "She re-married the innkeep across the way in Plockton."

That is how, the next morning, Ewan found himself on a boat being ferried across Loch Carron to Plockton. He held Violet's hand as the boat rocked.

How this exquisite creature could love him was almost beyond his ken. That she was with him now, at this moment, when he confronted his past—

Ewan swallowed back the tightness in his throat.

His heart hammered the closer they drew to Plockton.

Was Mhairi here? Would she welcome him? Or would she slam the door on him as she had eight years ago?

They disembarked on a wee pier. Violet tucked her hand into his elbow, giving his arm a comforting squeeze. Undoubtedly, she could feel the jittery tension of his muscles.

They climbed their way up a small rise toward a cluster of buildings.

A woman stood beside one of the houses, emptying a bucket. She shaded her eyes, looking toward them. Surely visitors, particularly well-dressed ones, were an anomaly.

Abruptly, the woman dropped her bucket, hiked up her skirts, and sprinted toward them. The motion dislodged her matron's cap, sending a spill of bright red hair down her back.

Finally, recognition sunk in.

With a hoarse cry, Ewan dropped Violet's hand and met the woman half-way, scooping her hysterical body into his arms.

"You're alive!" she sobbed in Gaelic, her face buried in his shoulder. "You're alive! You're alive! Ah, my darling Eòghann, you're alive!"

Ewan wanted to speak, but only a muffled cry emerged.

He held her fast, not knowing where his trembling ended and hers began.

"Mhairi," he gasped. "Sweet Mhairi. I am so glad I've finally found ye."

He marveled at the slight weight of her. But that had always been Mhairi; her personality larger than her actual person.

"You're here! You're here, at last," she wept into his shoulder.

Her body shook from the violence of her sobbing, great gusting cries.

"Hush, Mhairi," he crooned, just as he had when she was a wee bairn.

"I'm so s-sorry," she hiccupped. "I d-dinnae m-mean what I said."

"I should have come tae ye sooner. The fault in my own—"

"I d-dinnae mean tae f-force ye away so thoroughly."

"All is forgiven, sister mine."

"Nae." She shook her head, the motion rocking against his chest. "I'll never forgive myself for it. I was young and foolish and so incredibly s-stupid—"

She broke off with another soft cry.

Ewan clutched her to him as they both released their grief and relief.

Finally, he set her down, pushing her away enough that he could see all of her

"Enough," he said, still speaking in Gaelic. "Let us both admit tae being wrong and try to forge a better future."

She sniffed, "Very well."

"Let me look at ye properly." He stepped back.

"I'm a mess!" She pushed her hair out of her face, stopping to wipe her wet cheeks with the apron tied around her waist. "Can ye not see?"

"I dinnae care," he laughed. "Mhairi, my heart fair sings tae see ye."

"Ewan, ye must have come so very far—" She paused, finally noting his traveling companions.

Ewan turned to see Violet wiping her own cheeks with a handkerchief. Even Sir Joshua appeared emotional.

"Oh!" Mhairi blushed bright red. "Ye have fine guests, and here I am, a shambles. I cannae—"

"Nae, Mhairi. They are as glad to see ye, as I am. I have tae know, are ye happy, sister? How I have worried about ye—"

"Me?! Och, it all came aright with me. McDoughal died about two years into our marriage, may God rot his soul—"

"Mhairi!"

"'Tis the truth. He was a beast of a person, that man. But I found my Callum after that. Though Mr. Callum MacAlpin would say he found me," Mhairi blushed again in earnest, her entire demeanor softening. "However it happened, I couldnae want for a better husband or father."

"Father?!"

"Aye," Mhairi laughed, a joyful peal of sound. "Ye're an uncle, dinnae ye know it! I've a wee lass, Catriona, and a rowdy lad, Ian, and they both run me a merry dance."

"I cannae wait tae meet them."

"And ye shall. But what about you? Ye seem tae have landed on your feet. Are ye a famous painter yet?" She darted a shy glance at Violet and Sir Joshua behind him. "I would hope so, seeing these fine folk with ye."

Ewan laughed. "I do paint. I attended the Royal Academy and have been painting for several years now." He turned to Violet and Sir Joshua, switching to English. "As ye have probably deduced, this is my sister. Lady Kildrum, may I present Mrs. Mhairi MacAlpin."

"*Lady* Kildrum." Mhairi's eyes nearly popped out of her head. She muttered to him in Gaelic. "Och, brother, I told ye tae make something of yourself, but I didnae expect ye tae reach so high. But then, ye've always been a wee bit of a show-off."

He pulled Mhairi close, pressing a kiss to her forehead.

"I'm just glad it all led me back tae you."

MUCH LATER THAT evening, Ewan relaxed before the fire in the dining room of Mhairi's wee inn, Violet curled into his side.

Sir Joshua sat at the only table, regaling Mhairi and Callum with the story of his and Violet's journey to Loch Carron. Callum was a stocky fellow with a quick smile. Ewan's niece, Catriona, was curled into her father's shoulder, sound asleep, red curls plastered to her cheeks. Ian was playing with dogs at his mother's feet.

Ewan could practically see the bands of gold and silver weaving between them all, casting the scene in a warm, burnished light that spoke of deep-seated love and comfort.

This. *This* very moment.

All the hardships, all the grief . . . would this brief point in time be so extraordinarily sweet without the pain that had come before it?

"You seem to be thinking quite hard there, Mr. Campbell," Violet murmured against his chest.

He smiled.

Yes, it was scandalous to be holding her like this. But the tolerant eyes of Sir Joshua and his sister said they did not begrudge him this wee indulgence.

Mhairi was happy. She was loved and cared for. Callum was indeed a good man. His eyes sang with devotion every time he looked at his lovely wife. Ewan could not have wanted better for his sister than this.

And Violet was here.

"Part of me still cannae believe that you're here, *mo chridhe.*" He pressed a kiss to her head. "That even after seeing with your own eyes the abject poverty of my upbringing, the enormous differences between our stations—"

"Ewan Campbell, I will chant this litany for years until you believe it. I adore seeing the land and people that formed you. I love seeing how much you were missed and treasured."

He held her close for a moment, struggling to help his Violet understand. He wanted a life with her, but he did not lie to himself that it would always be easy.

"I love ye for it, lass," he said, "but I suspect part of me will always wrestle with the unequal footing of our relationship. Of course, I will bear it. I love ye enough tae endure any hardship. But I worry that the weight of it will slowly erode the foundation of our love. That we are perhaps naive to think we can overcome it."

"Ah, my love, I think that you are not quite viewing the situation through the proper lens." She nuzzled in closer. "Critics might see us as unequal in this moment, but you and I feel no true unevenness when we are together. And I would argue that this outside perception of inequality is a fleeting thing. You are just embarking on what promises to be a spectacular artistic career—"

"Which one bad injury could end tomorrow."

"Of course, it could. But it might not. Someday—and someday soon, I predict—I will be known as the wife of the famous artist, Ewan Campbell."

Ewan frowned. Hadn't Sir Joshua said something similar just a few weeks ago? Perhaps it was time he more fully believed it.

Violet continued, "Either of us could suffer some irreparable harm tomorrow, but it would not change the fundamental structure of my love for you. Do you not see? Our fortunes will surely ebb and flo. Our duties will change over the years. But our commitment to one another—our desire to forge a life together—will not. We must simply cling to the bedrock of our love."

"I ken that, but it feels like too much—"

"Would it help if you were somewhat perturbed at me?"

Ewan pulled back to look down at her.

"Pardon?"

"I may have done two things before I left Kilmeny Hall . . . well, myself and Uncle Joshua." She bit her lip, her eyes darting away. "You may not like them. No. Scratch that. You likely will *not* like them."

Ewan's smile grew. Her concern was adorable.

"What did you do?" He jostled her with his shoulder.

Violet sighed and pushed upright. "Well, as you surely know, Lord Hadley when he visited was very stern in his admonishments to me—"

"Was Andrew rude to ye?" Ewan's brows drew down.

"No, no, nothing like that." She placed a hand on his arm. "But he did tell me that I could ask for help from him, if needed. Earl-to-earl, to be exact."

Ewan grinned. That sounded like Andrew.

"What did ye ask for?"

Violet laced her fingers together. "I wrote him a letter and requested Lady Hadley's help in sponsoring my sisters for a London Season next year—"

"That is a brilliant suggestion!"

"Do you truly think so?" She looked at him shyly.

"Aye. Jane will happily take it on. I'm sure that Rafe's wife, Lady Sophie, will help, too. Between the two of them, they are acquainted with half the *ton* and related to the other half, so it will go well for your sisters, I am sure. Ye were right clever tae think of it, Lady Kildrum."

"Thank you."

"Why did ye believe that would upset me?"

"Well, I am taking liberties with your friends."

"As you know, any true friend of mine will be a true friend of yours, lass."

"I'm coming to understand that."

He leaned down and, darting a quick glance to verify that no one else was looking, pecked her lips.

"What was the second thing?" he asked.

Violet heaved a long sigh, pursing her mouth.

"Violet?" He nudged her again. "What did ye do?"

"Uncle showed me your painting, the one you did of me."

Ewan froze. Was that good?

She smiled at him, a watery, trembling smile. "I adore it. It is luminous and perfect and so . . . me! I couldn't allow it to languish, and so perhaps . . . uhm . . ."

"Perhaps?"

She closed her eyes and said the next words on a rush, "Uncle Joshua and I talked it over. In short, he sent the painting to London with his own to be submitted to the Royal Academy Exhibit."

Ewan barely stopped his gasp.

"Ye did . . . what?"

"We sent it to London." She turned to him, eyes pleading. "It was too brilliant *not* to be sent. And Uncle Joshua made a compelling argument. He said that instead of being circumspect, we should be bold in declaring our love. The painting is a vivid advertisement, if you will, of how much you and I love one another. Uncle thinks it will sway popular opinion. I have no intention of hiding in the shadows, Ewan Campbell. I want the world to know."

"How much I love ye, lass?"

"Yes," she nodded, wiping a tear off her cheek. "I want *everyone* to know that we have *chosen* this happiness."

"Love *is* enough."

"Precisely," she said. "And we shall live happily ever after to prove it."

And she emphasized her point with a very public, very loud kiss.

EPILOGUE

Y ou look exquisite tonight, wife," Ewan murmured behind Violet, pressing a slow kiss into the juncture of her neck and shoulder.

She shivered from the contact and then met his gaze in the looking glass before her.

"As do you, husband," she smiled.

Ewan did appear equally striking, tall and imposing in his tight-fitting coat. He had foregone his usual kilt tonight in favor of more traditional evening clothes. But the slash of Jamie's tartan across his chest loudly proclaimed his heritage.

They stood in their assigned bed chamber at Hadley House. Violet's maid had just put the finishing touches on her ladyship's hair before curtsying and slipping out as Ewan stepped in, his eyes gleaming in appreciation when he saw her dress.

She smoothed her hands down the layers of gauze and blue silk . . . the very dress he had painted.

He wrapped his arms around her waist, and Violet turned in his embrace, arching up on tiptoe to place a lingering kiss on his lips.

"Are ye sure we have to attend the ball this evening?" he asked.

"Quite sure," she replied on a sigh. "We are rather the entire *point* of the ball. It is a celebration of our wedding, after all."

Violet often laughed at the sheer wonder of her life. Every day, she gave thanks that she had not given up, that she and Ewan had found the courage to carve a life together.

After discovering Mhairi and her family happy and whole on Loch Carron, Ewan had been reluctant to immediately leave. He wished to spend time with this sister and get to know his niece and nephew. Sir Joshua had been excited to linger, as he wished to paint the local scenery.

And so Ewan and Violet had passed an absolutely idyllic pair of weeks with Ewan's family. It had been everything she imagined leaping off a cliff would be—exhilarating, flying, freeing.

She had fallen deeply in love with the place of Ewan's birth. The shocking beauty of Loch Carron on a cloudless day. The dramatic rise of the Cuillin mountains on the Isle of Skye looming across the Inner Sound.

She and Ewan took long walks, him showing her every nook and cranny of the land that had formed him. She would sit reading for hours—treatises on agriculture, as was now her bent—as he sketched and painted. It was on one those afternoons that Ewan sank to one knee and officially proposed marriage. She had joyously accepted.

In the days before their departure, Ewan and Violet made an important decision. Knowing that Mhairi and Callum could not leave their wee inn to travel to Kilmeny Hall for the wedding—the distance was simply too great and the time required too long—they had asked Ewan's family to join them for a handfasting ceremony.

Violet would forever remember walking down the path to the beach,

Uncle Joshua escorting her, a crown of heather on her head and a bouquet of wildflowers in her hand. A small crowd had awaited them. Mhairi and Callum, with wee Catriona and Ian. A few other villagers.

And then Ewan, magnificent in his great kilt of russet and blue plaid, a matching sprig of heather tacked to the lapel of his coat. He had smiled to see her, the expression so achingly in love, Violet feared her heart would break from sheer happiness.

The waves had lapped the rocks as she and Ewan plighted their troth to one another, declaring their love and life-long devotion. Mhairi acted as a witness, binding their hands with a length of silk cord, tying Ewan and Violet together both literally and symbolically.

Violet cried. Ewan scrubbed his cheek with his knuckles. Even Sir Joshua had reached for his handkerchief.

The tears and emotions of the moment had been echoed six weeks later, when she and Ewan exchanged vows again, this time before God in the parish kirk near Kilmeny Hall. Her father and sisters were in attendance, and her father even mustered a wan smile and handshake for Ewan afterwards.

Uncle Joshua had been able to help his brother see reason. Her uncle contended that reputation depended upon public opinion, and if family and close friends supported Violet's marriage, many others would follow suit. By withholding his support, her father was ultimately doing more harm than good.

Miraculously, her father had agreed, giving Violet and Ewan his blessing.

And now, weeks later, they were in London, about to attend a wedding ball in their honor hosted by Lord and Lady Hadley. Parliament was still in session this year—there was much to do with a new king on the throne—and most of Polite Society remained in London. Lady Hadley said this would be the last engagement before her confinement.

"Will we be snubbed tonight, do ye ken?" Ewan murmured.

"Unlikely. Lady Hadley is well-liked, and it would be odd for members of the *ton* to accept her invitation just to publicly snub us. If anything, the ball tonight will be a crush. Everyone is eager to meet you."

"Me? Nae, lass, we've already been over this—"

"I will hear no more dissembling, husband." Violet leaned back in his arms, fixing him with an amused smile. "You are the talk of the Town, the latest sensation. Your painting—"

"*Your* painting," he clarified.

"Very well. Your painting of me has become the highlight of the Royal Academy Exhibition, which to be honest, surprises me not at all."

That was the truth.

The Academy had accepted the painting into the Exhibition and, yes, it had been hung 'on the line' in great prominence at Somerset House. And, as Uncle Joshua had predicted, the power of the work had sparked public sympathy for the more intimate relationship Violet shared with its creator, now her husband.

One of the broadsheets had run a long, favorable article about it, describing in glowing terms how the painting was an allegory of marital adoration. The sentiment had caught the public imagination and had turned the young couple from outcasts to societal darlings almost overnight. Lord Hadley and Uncle Joshua had jointly hinted that they may have had a hand in the timing and placement of the newspaper article.

"Consider it a wedding gift," Hadley said. "I would not see one of my closest friends vilified, particularly if there is anything I can do about it."

Of course, the highest sticklers—Lady Hadley's high-handed brother, the Duke of Montacute, for example—would forever shun Violet for her choice of husband.

But as Jane dryly put it, "I do believe we can all lead happy and productive lives without the Duke of Montacute's approval. In fact, I daresay a fulfilled life is easier to obtain *without* such people in it."

Jane had, indeed, agreed to sponsor Aster and Rose. She was ecstatic to help and considered the timing fortunate, as she would have recovered from her confinement in time to prepare the twins for presentation at Court. Jane's assistance had greatly eased Violet's fears for her sisters' future.

Though Violet felt it only fair to warn Jane. "My sisters can be some-what . . . high-spirited."

"If by high-spirited, you mean forthright and plucky," Jane had laughed, "then I think we will get along quite well indeed. I appreciate young women who are not afraid to speak their minds."

As for the Manna Loan, Violet had compromised. Instead of selling the London townhouse, she mortgaged it. And then immediately let the house to a wealthy banker. The rents collected would pay the mortgage in five-years' time, after which they could retake possession of the townhouse. It was a small sacrifice, in the end. A way to hold on to a place that held so many happy memories but still meet the earldom's financial needs.

For herself, Violet had found immense satisfaction in managing her own lands. Helping tenants and discussing problems and solutions with her stewards had given her day-to-day interactions deeper meaning.

Violet knew that Ewan was cognizant of his own future. He had already repainted his lost fire canvas, and in Violet's estimation, this second version was even more powerful than the first. It was as if the first had abruptly become a practice sketch for the true masterpiece.

Ewan had no intention of showing the painting before next year's Royal Exhibition, but Sir Joshua had already arranged for a few elite members of the Royal Academy to see it. Her uncle had disclosed that he intended to put forth Ewan's name for acceptance into the Academy as an official member. Sir Joshua had every confidence Ewan would be admitted.

The only cloud of gloom to mar their happiness were concerns over Kieran. They had been unable to locate him. But Lord Hadley was confident his Runner would turn up leads.

For now, they could do nothing but wait.

And celebrate the happiness life had granted them.

"Ready tae face your admirers, Lady Kildrum?" Ewan asked, extending his arm.

Violet smiled with a shake of her head. "You know I prefer it when you call me Mrs. Campbell. I like the possessive sound of it. That you and I are united together."

"Ah, *mo chriodhe*." He bent to kiss her, as she threaded her hand through his elbow. "We are forever united. Ye've chosen me, lass. Ye cannae take it back now."

She laughed in earnest, giving him another lingering kiss. "I love you, Ewan Campbell."

"And I you, Violet Campbell." He straightened upright. "Now, shall we go set the world afire?"

She tightened her hold on his arm and waved her free hand. "Lead the way."

AUTHOR'S NOTE

As usual, writing a Regency-era romance is an endless mix of historical fact and imaginative adaptation. I will attempt to separate the two for you here, though be warned, there are major spoilers ahead if you have not yet finished reading *Loving a Lady*. Consider yourself forewarned.

Yes, women could inherit an aristocratic title in their own right. Though rare, there are a number of peerages in the United Kingdom that can pass through the female line if there are no male heirs. Whether or not this occurs is entirely dependent on the language which initially created the title.

But even if a woman could inherit her father's (or mother's) title, the rules varied. In England, all female heirs were considered equal (regardless of birth order). As a title cannot be divided between sisters, if there was more than one female heir, the title would go into abeyance (i.e. become dormant) until a clear heir surfaced in subsequent generations.

The Peerage of Scotland had no such rules. If allowed, a Scottish title could pass to the eldest daughter in the absence of a male heir.

Consequently, women inherited Scottish titles with some frequency. The situation in *Loving a Lady* is based on historical fact. The Earls of Orkney went three generations without a single male heir being born, the title passing from mother to daughter over and over.

Tacks and tacksmen were another unique Scottish feature. The practice of tacks and tacksmen was very much on the wane in 1820, but parts of the Highlands still retained the social structure, particularly in the area north of Aberdeen (where this book is set).

The whole system was medieval in its origin. Historically, a tacksman functioned like an English knight to his lord. The knight raised men for the earl or duke, and in return, the lord granted the knight lands to manage. Similarly, the tacksmen would raise soldiers for a laird when called upon.

In Scotland, lairds leased *tacks* of their lands to tacksmen (usually younger sons or other relatives) who then, in turn, managed the tenants and their farms directly. The tacksman was a middleman between the laird and his people, the administrator who collected rents and saw to repairs. And, when called upon, raised soldiers for his laird.

By the time of the final Jacobite uprising in the 1740s, tacksmen were on the wane. This made it difficult for some nobles (the Duke of Argyll comes to mind) to muster the soldiers necessary for the war with the English. Some contend that this contributed to the downfall of the Scottish army. Regardless, after the Battle of Culloden, tacksmen continued to disappear from the Highlands.

I find the whole system of tacks fascinating and yet difficult to explain.

Tacks worked much like leasing a car today. A tacksman would pay a fee (a grassum) to assume the lease of the land for a specified period of time (usually 19 years, which is bizarrely specific). The tacksman would then manage the land as if it were his own, collecting the tenant rents, seeing to repairs, etc. Each year, he would pay a tack-duty or basically an on-going payment to maintain his lease. (Again, just like we do today when leasing a car.) At the end of the term of the lease, the tack reverted to the original landowner, who could then lease the tack anew.

In society, tacksmen were considered gentlemen and belonged to the gentry class, one of the few groups to bridge the gap between the lower classes and the aristocracy in Scotland.

The year 1816 is generally referred to as the Year without a Summer. The entire northern hemisphere experienced cold temperatures, frosts, and even snow throughout the summer months. The gloomy weather inspired Mary Shelley to write *Frankenstein*. But these same factors led to devastating food shortages. Modernly, we know this drop in temperature was the result of the massive eruption of Mt. Tambora in April 1815. The ash from the volcano spread around the globe, cooling temperatures and interrupting weather patterns.

Prizefighting was every whit as popular as described. In fact, many claim the era from 1800 to 1820 was the Golden Age of bare-knuckle boxing. The sport with its ardent followers (often called the Fancy) was certainly at its zenith. *Boxiana*, a journal during the era written and published by Pierce Egan, celebrated all things related to prizefighting and the Fancy. Prizefighting in and of itself was not illegal (apparently the government didn't care if two people decided to beat themselves bloody), but the gathering of large crowds to *watch* such fights was deemed dangerous and an act of unlawful assembly. Consequently, most fights were held in rural locations outside the ready oversight of a magistrate. That said, there were indoor locations in London (like Five Courts) that regularly held prizefighting matches.

Boxing champions and renowned artists, along with famous actors and opera singers, were the sports heroes and celebrities of their day. They would dine with kings even though they were of lower birth. It was a way someone could (sort of) climb the social ladder.

As for the Royal Academy and its annual Exhibition, they are as described. That said, I did adjust the timeline of the annual exhibition to fit my own needs. In the book, I have the deadline set as sometime in late June with the actual exhibition beginning in August (or so). In reality, entries to the Exhibition would normally be submitted in March for display beginning in May and running through August. Also, John Constable's *The Haywain* was selected for the 1821 exhibition, not 1819 (as I state in the book). When considering which art works to reference in the book, I wished to choose pieces that readers might recognize, hence why I fudged the date of *The Haywain*.

Even in 1820, the living conditions among the lower classes west of Inverness and the Great Glen were appalling and had not changed much in thousands of years. Blackhouses (which were not, in fact, black but simply bare stone) were a single-story relic of a much earlier time. Generally, they were two room dwellings—one room for people and the other for animals. They featured an open fire in the center of the "people" room, the smoke filtering up through the thatched roof overhead. Beds were built into large wooden boxes in the room, enclosing the inhabitants while they slept. Blackhouses are still easily seen today along the north-west coast of Scotland and particularly in the Western Isles.

White-houses, which took their name from the white lime coating their exterior, were a more "modern" adaptation of the early 1800s. They were usually two-stories and featured a fireplace and chimney at each end of the house. Today, white-houses are everywhere in Scotland and are seen as a typical form of traditional architecture.

Traveling in 1820, particularly into the Highlands, was a fraught endeavor. Roads north of Edinburgh and Glasgow, in particular, were not well-maintained. In fact, the government hadn't even built any roads west of the Great Glen in 1820. (The Great Glen is a series of valleys that runs in a straight line from Inverness in the north to Fort William in the south. You can see it clearly on any map.) At that time, most travel in the Highlands was by horseback on rough tracks or via boat. There are still areas of Scotland today that can only be reached via boat. Even now, roads in the Highlands are narrow single-tracks which render travel there slow.

Handfasting is an ancient practice, likely Celtic pagan in origin. In England, handfasting historically referred to a period of engagement before the actual church ceremony. In Scotland, however, handfasting when properly witnessed was viewed as a legal marriage (recognized civilly, though not religiously). It was a prevalent form of marriage in the Highlands and Western Isles for hundreds (if not thousands) of years.

The ceremony was simple. The couple would plight their troth and a witness would tie their hands together with a knot (hence *handfasting*), symbolizing the couple's commitment to bind their lives together.

Lastly, the revelations concerning Jamie are based on very real historical fact. In particular, Mary Lacy and her autobiography, *The Female Shipwright*, was widely circulated at the end of the 18th century. There are numerous tales of women taking to the sea disguised as boys.

I know I've mentioned this before, but for those reading one of my Scottish books for the first time, allow me to also comment on Scottish language and pronunciation. It's always a struggle to know how to write an accent, particularly in a historical novel. Scotland today recognizes three distinct languages: Scottish Gaelic, Scots, and English. Historically, Scottish Gaelic has been spoken in the Highlands. Most Lowland Scots in the early 1800s (i.e. those from Glasgow and Edinburgh) would have spoken a mix of Scots and English. (Sidenote: If you want to read some Scots, Wikipedia actually has an entire dictionary written in Scots—sco. wikipedia.org.)

Of course, I realized fairly quickly that a modern, primarily American, audience would struggle to understand Scots.

So, what to do?

After much consideration, I decided to go with a slightly more modern Scottish accent and syntax, simply to aid readability. I write novels, after all, not history texts. I've used modern spellings of Scottish pronunciations and, even then, restricted myself to a few key words to give a Scottish flavor to the text. So at times, the accent as written is not perfectly consistent; this was done to help readability. That said, I have continued to use more common Scots words wherever possible—e.g. *ken/kens/kent* (think, know), *eejit* (idiot), *glaikit* (foolish), *muckle* (enormous), *youse* (you all), *greit/greet* (to weep), etc.

I have created an extensive pinboard on Pinterest with images of things I talk about in the book. So if you want a visual of anything—including the paintings described, prizefighting in the era, blackhouses, etc.—pop over there and explore. Just search for NicholeVan.

As with all books, this one couldn't have been written without the help and support from those around me. I know I am going to leave someone out with all these thanks. So to that person, know that I totally love you and am so deeply grateful for your help!

To my beta readers—you know who you are—thank you for your editing suggestions, helpful ideas, and support. And, again, an extra-large thank you to Rebecca Spencer, Annette Evans, and Norma Melzer for their fantastic editing skills. And a shout-out to Julie Frederick for her keen observations, as usual.

With this book, I am particularly indebted to Shannon Castleton. Thank you, my dear friend, for coming back into my life at this crazy time of plague and unrest. You pulled me through this novel more than you will ever realize.

Erin Rodabough also deserves another round of applause for her endless help. Thank you for being my writing *and* travel buddy.

Finally, thank you to Andrew, Austenne, Kian, and Dave for your endless patience and support.

And to all my readers, thank you for continuing to read and recommend my work!

READING GROUP QUESTIONS

Yes, there are reading group questions. I suggest discussing them over lots of excellent chocolate (solid, liquid, frozen, cake . . . I'm not picky about the precise state of matter of said chocolate; chocolate in any form is good chocolate).

Also—fair warning—there are definite spoilers inherent in these questions if you have not finished reading the book as of yet.

1. The plot of *Loving a Lady* takes the typical high-born lord and low-born woman trope (which started with *Pride and Prejudice* and continues to this day) and turns it on its head with a countess falling for a lowly Highlander. How did the gender swap change your perception of the principles involved? Did you like the change? Why or why not?

2. Violet finds it difficult to make decisions. Have you ever felt this way yourself? What has helped you to make difficult decisions?

3. Throughout the book, both Ewan and Violet struggle to balance the demands of duty with the more personal desires of their hearts. Where is the line between duty and desire? Do you feel the characters walked that line well, in the end? Why or why not?

4. Along the same line as the previous question, do you feel that duty and desire are opposites? Or do you think that they are two sides of the same coin; that in a balanced life, they must walk hand-in-hand? Why or why not?

5. How did you feel about Ewan's dealings with sister, Mhairi? Ewan left her in a terrible situation when she married. Did he make a moral decision in doing that? Why or why not?

6. Did you see the plot twist with Jamie coming? Did you like it? How did it change your perception of not just this book, but the entire series? (And before you go looking, none of the Brotherhood use a gender-specific pronoun when referring to Jamie before the reveal in this book or previous ones.)

7. Clearly, this book contains a lot of information about Scotland and Scottish culture. Did you learn something new or unexpected? If so, what was it?

8. How did you feel Ewan and Violet were suited for one another? Did you truly feel like Ewan and Violet had come to genuinely love each other? If so, what makes you believe that their marriage will be a lasting one?

9. Violet has a somewhat difficult relationship with her father. She loves him and he loves her, but they struggle to relate to one another's point of view. She wants her father to be more accepting of her choices, and he wishes she would be more obedient to his wishes. How did you feel about this dynamic? Did you like how the author balanced it in the book? Why or why not?

Other Books by Nichole Van

BROTHERHOOD OF THE BLACK TARTAN

Suffering the Scot
Romancing the Rake
Loving a Lady
Vying for the Viscount (Spring 2021)
Remembering Jamie (Autumn 2021)

OTHER REGENCY ROMANCES

Seeing Miss Heartstone
Vingt-et-Un | Twenty-one (a novella included in *Falling for a Duke*.)
A Ring of Gold (a novella included in *A Note of Change*.)

BROTHERS *MALEDETTI* SERIES

Lovers and Madmen
Gladly Beyond
Love's Shadow
Lightning Struck
A Madness Most Discreet

THE HOUSE OF OAK SERIES

Intertwine
Divine
Clandestine
Refine
Outshine

If you haven't yet read *Seeing Miss Heartstone*,
please turn the page for a preview of this
Whitney Award Winner for Best Historical Romance 2018.

SEEING MISS HEARTSTONE

. . . My lord, news of your current financial pressures has reached many ears. I know of an interested party who would be honored to discuss a proposed joint venture. They have asked to meet you along the Long Water in Hyde Park tomorrow morning, where they shall endeavor to lay out the particulars of their proposal . . .

—excerpt from an unsigned letter posted to Lord Blake

In retrospect, Miss Arabella Heartstone had three regrets about 'The Incident.'

She should not have worn her green, wool cloak with the fox fur collar, as Hyde Park was warmer than expected that morning.

She should not have instructed her chaperone, Miss Anne Rutger, to remain politely out of earshot.

And she probably should *not* have proposed marriage to the Marquess of Blake.

"P-pardon?" Lord Blake lifted a quizzical eyebrow, standing straight and tall, rimmed in the morning sunlight bouncing off the Long Water behind him. A gentle breeze wound through the surrounding trees, rustling newly-grown, green leaves. "Would . . . would you mind repeating that last phrase? I fear I did not hear you correctly."

Belle straightened her shoulders, clasped her trembling hands together, and sternly ordered her thumping heart to *Cease this racket.*

Swallowing, she restated her request. "After much consideration, my lord, I feel a marriage between you and myself would be prudent."

Lord Blake stared at her, blinking over and over. Belle was unsure if his reaction denoted surprise or was simply the result of the dazzling sunlight off the water behind her.

Silence.

Birds twittered. Branches creaked. Leaves rustled.

Eternities passed. Millennia ended and were reborn.

Belle gritted her teeth, desperate to bolster her flagging confidence. *You are strong and courageous. You can do this.*

In the past, her passivity over the Marriage Matter had nearly ended in disaster. So, Belle had set her sights on a more forthright course— propose marriage herself. Yes, she struggled to talk with people and preferred anonymity to attention, but her current situation was critical.

She needed a husband. Decidedly. Desperately. Immediately. As in . . . yesterday would not have been soon enough.

At the moment, however, her mental encouragement barely managed to convince the swarming butterflies in her stomach to not free her breakfast along with themselves. Casting up her accounts all over his lordship's dusty Hessian boots would hardly nurture his romantic interest.

At last, Lord Blake stirred, pulling a folded letter from his overcoat. He stared at it, eyebrows drawing down, a sharp "V" appearing above his nose.

"You sent me this message, asking to meet me here?" He flapped the letter in her direction.

"Yes." Belle bit down on her lip and darted a glance behind at her companion. Miss Rutger stood a solid thirty yards off, studiously facing the Long Water. "Well . . . uhm . . . in all truthfulness, Miss Rutger wrote the letter."

Lord Blake raised his eyebrows, clearly uncaring of the minutiae involved. "So you are *not* a gentleman interested in my business venture in the East Indies?" He unfolded the letter, reading from it. "'*I know of an interested party who would be honored to discuss a proposed joint venture. They have asked to meet you along the Long Water,*' et cetera. This 'interested party' is yourself?" He returned the letter to his pocket.

"Yes, my lord." Belle commanded her feet to hold still and not bounce up and down—the bouncing being yet another effect of those dratted nervous butterflies.

Lord Blake's brows rose further. "And you are offering . . . marriage?"

"Yes, my lord," Belle repeated, but she had to clarify the point. Apparently, she had no issue with being thought forward and brazen, but heaven forbid Lord Blake imagine her a liar, too. "Though . . . I *am* proposing a joint endeavor."

"Indeed," he paused. "Marriage usually implies as much."

Lord Blake shuffled a Hessian-booted foot and clasped his hands behind his back. A corner of his mouth twitched.

Was the man . . . amused? If so, was that good? Or bad?

And at this point, did it matter?

Belle soldiered on. "There would be significant advantages to both of us with such a match."

More silence. An errant draft of wind tugged at his coat.

"You have me at a disadvantage, Miss . . ." His voice trailed off.

"Heartstone. Miss Arabella Heartstone."

"I see." He removed his hat and slapped it against his thigh. "And why have we not met in more . . . uh . . . typical circumstances? A ball, perhaps? A dinner party where we could be properly introduced and engage in conversation about the weather and the latest bonnet fashions before leaping straight to marriage?"

"Oh." It was Belle's turn to blink, absorbing his words. *Oh dear.* "We *have* met, my lord. We were introduced at Lord Pemberley's musicale last month. We did discuss the weather, but not bonnets or . . . uhm . . . marriage."

She hadn't expected him to recall everything, but to not even *recognize* her? To not remember their brief conversation—

"How do you do, Miss Heartstone? It's a pleasure to make your acquaintance." Lord Blake bowed.

"The pleasure is all mine, my lord." Belle curtsied. *"Lovely weather we're having."*

"Indeed, we are."

It did not bode well.

The butterflies rushed upward, eager for escape.

"Right." Blake let out a gusting breath and shook his head, sending his hair tumbling across his forehead. The morning sun turned it into molten shades of deep amber, curling softly over his ears.

Lean and several inches taller than her own average height, Lord Blake was not classically handsome, she supposed. His straight nose, square jaw, and high forehead were all too exaggerated for classical handsomeness.

And yet, something about him tugged at her. Perhaps it was the breadth of his shoulders filling out his coat. Or maybe it was the ease of his stance, as if he would face the jaws of Hell itself with a sardonic smile and casual *sang-froid*. Or maybe it was the way he ran a gloved hand through his hair, taking it from fashionably tousled to deliciously rumpled.

Mmmmm.

Belle was going to side with the hair. Though sardonic smiles were a close second.

Regardless, her decision to offer marriage to him had not been based on his physical appearance. She was many things, but *flighty* and *shallow* were two words that had never been attached to her.

Replacing his hat, Lord Blake studied her, blue eyes twinkling.

Yes. Definitely amused.

That was . . . encouraging? Having never proposed marriage to a man before, Belle was unsure.

"Enlighten me, if you would be so kind, as to the particular reasons why you think this . . . joint endeavor . . . would be profitable." He gestured toward her.

Oh! Excellent.

That she had come prepared to do.

With a curt nod, she pulled a paper from her reticule.

"A list?" His lips twitched again.

"I am nothing if not thorough in my planning, my lord." She opened the paper with shaking fingers, her hands clammy inside her gloves.

"Of course. I should have expected as much. You arranged this meeting, after all." He tapped the letter in his pocket.

Belle chose to ignore the wry humor in his tone and merely nodded her head in agreement. "Allow me to proceed with my list. Though please forgive me if my reasons appear forward."

"You have just proposed marriage to a peer of the realm, madam. I cannot imagine anything you say from this point onward will trump that."

"True."

A beat.

Lord Blake pinned her with his gaze—calm and guileless. The forthright look of a man who knew himself and would never be less-than-true to his own values.

His gaze upset her breathing, causing something to catch in her throat.

Belle broke eye-contact, swallowing too loudly.

"Allow me to begin." She snapped the paper in her hand. The words swam in her vision, but she knew them by heart. The paper was more for show than anything else. She had done her calculations most carefully.

Taking a fortifying breath, Belle began, "Firstly, you have newly inherited the Marquisate of Blake from a cousin. Your cousin was somewhat imprudent in his spending habits—"

"I would declare the man to be an utter scapegrace and wastrel, but continue."

"Regardless of the cause, your lands and estates are in dire need of resuscitation." Belle glanced at him over the top of her paper. "You are basically without funds, my lord."

"As my solicitor repeatedly reminds me." He shot her an arch look. "It is why I am trying to fund a business venture in connection with the East India Company, as you are also undoubtedly aware."

"Yes, my lord. That is why I am proposing an enterprise of a slightly different sort. Allow me to continue." Belle cleared her throat, looking down to her paper. "My own family is genteel with connections to the upper aristocracy—my great-great grandfather was the Earl of Stratton—though we have no proper title of our own, leaving my father to make his own way in the world. I, as you might already know, am a considerable heiress. My father was a prominent banker and left the entirety of his estate to me upon his death three years past."

Belle clenched her jaw against the familiar sting in her throat.

Blink, blink, blink.

Now was *not* the time to dwell upon her father.

"Are you indeed?" he asked. "Though I do not wish to sound crass, I feel we left polite discussion in the dust several minutes ago, so I must enquire: How much of an heiress are you, precisely?"

Did she hear keen interest in his tone? Or was Lord Blake simply exceedingly polite?

"I believe the current amount stands somewhere in the region of eighty thousand pounds, my lord," she replied.

Lord Blake froze at that staggering number, just as Belle had predicted he would.

"Eighty thousand pounds, you say? That is a dowry of marquess-saving proportions."

"My thoughts precisely, my lord."

Her father had originally left her a healthy sixty thousand pounds, but she was nothing if not her father's daughter. Numbers and statistics flowed through her brain, a constant rushing river. She had used these skills to grow her fortune.

It was what her father would have wanted. Refusing to see her gender as a barrier, her father had taught his only child everything he knew—financial systems, probabilities, market shares—even soliciting her opinions during that last year before his death.

By the age of sixteen, Belle understood more about supply-and-demand and the mathematics of economics than most noblemen. Knowing this, the conditions in her father's will allowed her to continue to oversee her own interests with the help of his solicitor, Mr. Sloan. At only nineteen years of age, she currently managed a thriving financial empire.

She could hear her father's gruff voice, his hand gently lifting her chin. *I would give you choices, my Little Heart Full. A lady should always have options. I would see you happy.*

Belle swallowed back the painful tightness in her throat.

Now, if she could only land a husband and free herself from the guardianship of her uncle and mother.

Family, it turned out, were not quite as simple to manage as corn shares.

Her mother, hungry for a title for her daughter, was becoming increasingly bold in her attempts to get Belle married. She had all but forced Belle to betroth herself to a cold, aloof viscount the previous Season. Fortunately, the viscount—Lord Linwood—had asked to be released from their betrothal.

But the entire situation had left Belle feeling helpless.

She *detested* feeling helpless, she realized. And so she used that unwelcome sensation to suppress her inherent shyness and overcome her retiring personality.

Belle would solve the husband problem herself. She simply needed to reduce the entire situation to a statistical probability and face it as she would any other business transaction.

"Eighty-thousand pounds," Lord Blake repeated. "Are husbands—particularly the marquess variety—generally so costly?" He clasped his hands behind his back, studying her. "I had not thought to price them before this."

"I cannot say. This is my first venture into, uhmm . . ."

"Purchasing a husband?" he supplied, eyes wide.

Heavens. Was that a hint of displeasure creeping into his voice?

"I am not entirely sure I agree with the word *purchase*, my lord—"

"True. It does smack of trade and all polite society knows we cannot have *that.*"

A pause.

"Shall we use the word *negotiate* instead?" she asked.

He cocked his head, considering. "I daresay that would be better. So I receive a sultan's ransom and your lovely self, and you receive . . ." His words drifted off.

"A husband. And in the process, I become Lady Blake, a peeress of the realm."

"Are you truly so hungry to be a marchioness? Surely eighty thousand pounds could purchase—forgive me, *negotiate*—the title of duchess." His words so very, very dry.

"I am sure my mother would agree with you, my lord, but I am more interested in finding a balance between title and the proper gentleman." She cleared her throat. "You come highly recommended."

"Do I?" Again, his tone darkly sardonic.

Oh, dear.

But as she was already in for more than a penny, why not aim for the whole pound?

"I did not arrive at the decision to propose marriage lightly. I had my solicitor hire a Runner to investigate you. I have armed myself with information, my lord."

Belle wisely did not add that, after crunching all the statistical probabilities, Lord Blake had been by far and away her preferred candidate. She was quite sure that, like most people, he would not appreciate being reduced to a number.

"Information? About me?" he asked.

"Yes. For example, I know you recently cashed out of the army, selling the officer's commission you inherited from your father. All those who served with you report you to be an honest and worthy commander—"

"As well they should."

"Additionally, you are a kind son to your mother. You send her and your stepfather funds when you are able. You visit regularly. Your four older sisters dote upon you, and you are godfather to at least one of each of their children. You are a tremendous favorite with all of your nieces and nephews. All of this speaks highly to the kind of husband and father you would be."

After her disastrous betrothal to Lord Linwood last year, Belle was determined to not make the same error twice. She learned from her mistakes. Her mother and uncle would not browbeat her into accepting one of their suitors again.

If nothing else, eighty thousand pounds should purchase—*negotiate*—her a *kindhearted* husband of her own choice.

Lord Blake shuffled his feet. "I-I really am at a loss for words, Miss Heartstone. I am trying to decide if I should be flattered or utterly appalled."

Belle sucked in a deep breath, her mouth as dry as the Sahara.

Stay strong. Argue your case.

She pasted a strained smile on her face. "Might I suggest siding with flattery, my lord?"

Visit www.NicholeVan.com to buy your copy of
Seeing Miss Heartstone today and continue the story.

ABOUT THE AUTHOR

THE SHORT VERSION:

NICHOLE VAN IS a writer, photographer, designer and generally disorganized crazy person. Though originally from Utah, she currently lives on the coast of Scotland with three similarly crazy children and one sane, very patient husband who puts up with all of them. In her free time, she enjoys long walks along the Scottish lochs and braes. She does not, however, enjoy haggis.

THE LONG OVERACHIEVER VERSION:

AN INTERNATIONAL BESTSELLING author, Nichole Van is an artist who feels life is too short to only have one obsession. In former lives, she has been a contemporary dancer, pianist, art historian, choreographer, culinary artist and English professor.

Most notably, however, Nichole is an acclaimed photographer, winning over thirty international accolades for her work, including Portrait of the Year from WPPI in 2007. (Think Oscars for wedding and portrait photographers.) Her unique photography style has been featured in many magazines, including Rangefinder and Professional Photographer. She is also the creative mind behind the popular website Flourish Emporium which provides resources for photographers.

All that said, Nichole has always been a writer at heart. With an MA in English, she taught technical writing at Brigham Young University for ten years and has written more technical manuals than she can quickly count. She decided in late 2013 to start writing fiction and has since become an Amazon #1 bestselling author. Additionally, she has won a RONE award, as well as been a Whitney Award Finalist several years running. Her late 2018 release, *Seeing Miss Heartstone*, won the Whitney Award Winner for Best Historical Romance.

In February 2017, Nichole, her husband and three crazy children moved from the Rocky Mountains in the USA to Scotland. They currently live near the coast of eastern Scotland in an eighteenth century country house. Nichole loves her pastoral country views while writing and enjoys long walks through fields and along beaches. She does not, however, have a fondness for haggis.

She is known as NicholeVan all over the web: Facebook, Instagram, Pinterest, etc. Visit http://www.NicholeVan.com to sign up for her author newsletter and be notified of new book releases. Additionally, you can see her photographic work at http://photography.nicholeV.com and http://www.nicholeV.com

If you enjoyed this book, please leave a short review on Amazon. com. Wonderful reviews are the elixir of life for authors. Even better than dark chocolate.

Made in the USA
Monee, IL
17 October 2024

67395295R00204